sandman

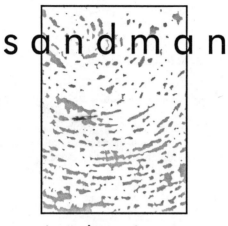

s a n d m a n

j. robert janes

First published in Great Britain by Constable & Company Ltd.

Published by
Soho Press Inc.
853 Broadway
New York NY 10003

Library of Congress Cataloging-in-Publication Data

Janes, J. Robert (Joseph Robert), 1935-
     Sandman / J. Robert Janes. — 1st U.S. ed.
          p.   cm.
     ISBN 1-56947-106-1 (alk. paper)
     I. Title.
PR9199.3.J3777S26   1998
813'.54—dc21   97-20991
                                                          CIP

First U.S. Edition 1997

10 9 8 7 6 5 4 3 2 1

Only in sleep is truth hidden until the nightmare comes.

author's note

Sandman is a work of fiction in which actual places and times are used but altered as appropriate. Occasionally the name of a real person appears for historical authenticity, though all are deceased and the story makes of them what it demands. I do not condone what happened during these times; I abhor it. But during the Occupation of France the everyday crimes of murder and arson continued to be committed, and I merely ask, by whom and how were they solved?

acknowledgement

All the novels in the St-Cyr-Kohler series incorporate a few words and brief passages of French or German. Dr Dennis Essar of Brock University very kindly assisted with the French, as did the artist Pierrette Laroche, while Ms Bodil Little of the German Department at Brock helped with the German. Should there be any errors, they are my own, and for these I apologize but hope there are none.

This is for Susan and Jan Carr

When the snow landed on the girl's face it did not melt even under lights so strong they made her eyes glisten—lights that disturbed the doves which cooed and fluttered until one wanted to shriek, Shut up! Stay still. As still as she.

It lay on the backs of her hands and dusted the dark navy blue of an open overcoat. It touched the rumpled white woollen kneesocks, the white knickers, dark blue pleated woollen skirt, pushed-up sweater and still-buttoned white shirt-blouse, the chin sharp and jutting up, the head back, lips compressed. Blood oozed and congealed at a corner.

Silently, St-Cyr crossed himself. Hermann, who had just lost his two sons at Stalingrad, blurted, 'Ah *Gott im Himmel*, Louis, she isn't more than eleven years old. Her boots are brand-new. Where ... where the hell did her parents get rubber and felt like that?'

On the black market, of course, for this was Neuilly and the Bois de Boulogne and money, but it would be best to save all that for later, best to shrug and say, 'I don't know. She's hardly worn them.'

Hermann liked children even more than he did. 'Look, why not . . .' hazarded St-Cyr.

'Leave? No, I'll stay.'

'Then please do not be sick. You will only embarrass us in front of the préfet's men.'

That gawking ring of *flics* stood in their capes and *képis* just outside the dove cage, some manning the lights. Barred shadows fell on her bony, bare knees and auburn pigtails but, through some accident of kindness, did not touch her face.

She was of average height and skinny, like most girls who are just beginning to shoot up. The face was pinched, the nose sharp. The eyes were of a deep, dark brown and large under long dark lashes and softly curving brows. The ears were large, and St-Cyr knew beyond doubt that she would have hated them and would have prayed to God and the Blessed Virgin for compensating breasts.

'Louis, there's a giraffe.'

'Pardon?'

'A toy. Over there, under one of the boxes. The poor kid must have had it in her hand when he caught up with her.'

So there was.

The killer had all but smothered her with the weight of his body. He had had her by the throat, had not had time to do more than tear open her coat and push up her sweater and skirt. He had then forced her head back and had driven a steel knitting needle straight up under the chin and deep into her brain. A concierge's needle. One of those sturdy grey things the sweater-women who ride the trains use to annoy others.

Mercifully, she had died instantly. The blunt head of the needle still protruded a good four centimetres, but the thing had been bent by the force used until its end touched her chin.

'Her toque, her beret perhaps, is missing,' said St-Cyr grimly. 'The schools will still be closed for the holiday, yet she wears the uniform.'

'A convent, then. A boarder who was left to languish with the nuns over Christmas and the New Year.'

'Yet she has apparently come to the Bois without any of the

sisters to watch over her. All alone, Hermann, but for a toy giraffe she is too old to play with and would have been ashamed to be seen carting around. She has, it appears, put up little if any resistance.'

'Too terrified, poor thing. Petrified.'

Between the ring of *flics* and the lights, the cage, one of gilded wire with scrolls and fleurs-de-lis in the style of the Sun King's hunt marquee, held perhaps two hundred white doves that at nesting times were kept in little boxes beneath its green-and-gilded leafy branches, which were richly carved and provided roosting places. Doves of royalty, then, in a time of war and privation, of hunger so great, one had to ask, Where the hell was the custodian while this was going on?

The branches extended everywhere above the nesting boxes, behind which, in a narrow corridor lined with bins for the droppings, the child had been all but hidden from view.

'Yet surely, Hermann, someone should have seen what was going on or heard her cry out?'

'To them he'd have been standing here with his hands on something they couldn't see. She'd have choked, Louis. She'd have . . .'

Kohler turned and rushed from the cage into darkness. Everyone could hear him throwing up. It had happened again. For one so accustomed to seeing death, he could no longer stand the sight of it. A detective! A former bomb-disposal expert and artillery officer. A Hauptmann of the last war.

The murders of children were especially difficult, always grim.

Hermann was a Gestapo who had been called up against his will and was hated by his confrères because he did not believe their Nazi doctrine, nor would he do the horrible things they did. A Bavarian. A Fritz-haired, greying giant of fifty-five with the ragged, glistening scar of a rawhide whip down the left cheek from eye to chin. The SS had done that, a little matter near Vouvray they hadn't liked, ah yes. There were shrapnel scars also but from that last war, and drooping bags under often empty and faded blue eyes, the graze of a bullet wound, too, across the brow, a more recent affair but now healed.

'He's not himself,' confessed St-Cyr to that silent ring of men. 'We've only just got in from Quiberon and the submarine pens at Lorient. A dollmaker, a U-boat captain . . . a girl of about the same age.'

They said nothing, those men. With the bovine insensibility of Parisians the city over, they sought details of the corpse. Had she been violated? Were her lips torn, her tongue perhaps bitten through during the forcing open of the jaws, her hymen ruptured?

Ah Paris . . . Paris, he said sadly to himself, you are both the heart's rejoicing and the soul's lament.

It was the night of Sunday the tenth of January 1943, yet, in spite of the black-out regulations, lights burned here in a city that, with its suburbs, had a population of nearly three million. A city so darkened by its bilious wash of laundry blueing and black-out curtains, no lights but those infrequent pinpricks were allowed. Most people travelled on foot in blindness, the city silent after the curfew but for the tramp of Wehrmacht patrols, the screech of Gestapo tyres and sometimes a piercing scream from the cellars of Number 11 rue des Saussaies or some other such place, or the rain of rifle butts on a door to shouts of '*Raus, raus!*'—Get out, get out!

Hands up. Backs to the wall—*you*, *you* and *you*! Crash! and it was all over. For every German killed by an act of 'terrorism', one, two, five—ten—hostages must die. Most were taken from the jails because it freed up much-needed space. Some, though, were plucked from the streets. To date, these acts of 'terrorism' were few and far between, but the defeat at Stalingrad would feed their flames, and if not that, then the hated, indentured labour in the Reich or some other such injustice.

France was on her knees and bleeding in the grip of a winter that could only promise to be far harsher than the last one.

Looking like death, not like a member of the Occupation's dreaded Gestapo, Kohler staggered back into the cage to prop himself against the nesting boxes. 'Louis, I think I must have the flu. It's like it was last winter. I'm sweating when I should be freezing.'

The flu . . . ah *merde*, must God do this to them? Last

winter's had been terrible. 'You didn't give it to me, did you?' hissed the Sûreté vehemently. 'If you did, I . . .' He gazed up and said, 'You didn't look well on the train. Ah no, no, my fine inspector from the Kripo, you were sleeping fitfully. You awoke several times. I know! You were having nightmares.'

Kohler pulled his coat collar close and lamely gave that indisputable signal of absolute truth in the matter. 'I don't want a cigarette. You could offer me ten and I wouldn't touch a one.'

Ah *nom de Jésus-Christ!* the lousy air on that lousy train, the wretched food—what food? No sleep for days, none now either, and von Schaumburg on their backs. 'Von Schaumburg, Hermann. Forget about having the flu. Don't be an idiot! Old Shatter Hand simply won't believe you.'

He wouldn't either. The Kommandant von Gross-Paris was a Prussian of the old school, a real Junker's bastard when it came to former N.C.O.s who had had the great good fortune to find themselves in a French prisoner-of-war camp in 1916.

'Hey, my French is pretty good, eh, Chief?' quipped the giant, trying to grin. 'You take the left side, I'll do the right and try not to breathe on you. Then we'll compare notes.'

'You sure?' They hadn't been able to do this in nearly a year.

'Positive. We've got to find the son of a bitch. We've got to put a stop to him. I've already promised her we'll use the bread-slicer.'

Ah yes, the guillotine, but first . . .

The cable that had reached them on the homeward train had been brief:

SANDMAN STRIKES AGAIN. BODY OF HEIRESS FOUND IN BIRD-CAGE AMONG DOVES NEAR CLAY-PIGEON SHOOT BOIS DE BOULOGNE. REQUEST IMMEDIATE ACTION. REPEAT ACTION. IMPERATIVE VILLAIN BE APPREHENDED. REPORT 0700 HOURS DAILY. STURMBANNFÜHRER BOEMELBURG CONCURS AND PLACES YOU BOTH DIRECTLY UNDER MY ORDERS.

HEIL HITLER.

Boemelburg was Hermann's Chief and Head of Section IV, the Gestapo in France. Under him, the Kripo, that smallest and most insignificant of subsections, fought common crime, and every one of the *flics* standing around knew this, knew also that this particular flying squad was constantly held in doubt and challenged as to their loyalties. Two detectives of long standing but from opposite sides of the war, thrown together by circumstance and fate to become partners first and then friends. Ah yes, God did things like that. God also had not answered the silent cries of such as this one, which only served to emphasize He could not have stopped it from happening.

But never mind those who would claim He needed another eleven-year-old angel. Never mind all that sort of thing. Four other girls, each randomly chosen, each caught alone and of about this one's age, had been sexually violated and murdered in Paris within the past five weeks. Four over the Christmas–New Year holiday—what holiday? One to the east of the Bois, in the industrial suburb of Suresnes, near the Terrot bicycle factory; another to the north, in Aubervilliers, in a crowded tenement near an overworked soup kitchen; then one in les Halles among the barren stalls of what had formerly been the belly of Paris but was now but a forlorn reminder of it.

And the last? asked St-Cyr of himself.

'Up in one of the bell towers of the Notre-Dame, right in the préfet's backyard,' sighed Kohler without being asked. 'Only pigeons were witness to it. Pigeons then and doves now, and why us, Louis? Why? How much more does that God of yours think we can take?'

He always asked those questions; they were nothing new. God often figured in their troubles, especially at times like this. 'Let us remove the bins of droppings but do so one by one. She might have tucked something among them. It's just a thought.'

'Don't forget the giraffe, eh? Don't let some *flic* decide to steal it for his kids.'

St-Cyr lifted the first of the bins away and, squeezing his broad shoulders into the space, just managed to kneel beside the victim without disturbing her. Reaching well under the nesting boxes, he retrieved the giraffe. Faded red blotches marked its pale yellow hide. 'It has lost an ear. The left one,' came the droll comment to allay the distress they both felt. 'As with myself, injury is apparently attracted only to the left side. That eye has lost its black paint.'

'Made of real rubber?' asked Kohler, intent on something he had found.

'Real rubber . . . ? Ah, a stiff, rubberized composite, I think. Lots of clay to give it firmness yet keep its plasticity. Pre-war and not recent. Fabricated by injection moulding in an unlicenced shop, probably in Saint-Denis or Belleville during the early thirties. No date or manufacturer's name, but the number 979.12 has been written on the inner right hind thigh, with pen and ink.'

'From a crèche?' asked the Bavarian, still not looking up but now using a pencil to explore the bracelet that encircled her wrist.

'Perhaps but then . . . ah *mais alors, alors, mon vieux,* why number it?'

'*So as to prevent theft, idiot!*'

'Then why do so with ink that will wash off?'

It was but one of many questions.

'Was she left-handed, Louis? Is that why her charm bracelet is on the right wrist?'

Hermann needed to talk when working so close to a corpse. To heave an impatient sigh would do no good. One must be kind. 'Why not wait until I've had a closer look?'

'You'll take all night! Hey, I'm nearly done and you've hardly started.'

Hermann hated doing this. He really did. 'Her coat pocket has been torn a little. Did the one who found her do this, or did the killer, and if the latter, did he . . .' said St-Cyr.

Suspiciously the Bavarian's head shot up. 'Did he have to *check* who she was?'

'Ah, perhaps. But it may have been the *flics.*'

Had it given the Sandman a thrill to know who his victim was, wondered Kohler, sickened by the thought. It took all types. 'And who was she, Chief?' His stomach was just not right.

Those deep brown ox-eyes he knew so well looked out from

under a broad, bland forehead and bushy brows. Louis's battered, stain-encrusted fedora was judiciously removed and
perched atop the nesting boxes to signal work in progress and
not shade the corpse. 'Nénette Micheline Vernet, of *the* Vernets and money that would make even our friends in the SS
over on the avenue Foch sweat with envy. Age eleven years,
three months and seven days. The photo is good but the eyes
... ah, what can one say but that they are most definitely not
dark blue, as is written here on her *carte d'identité*, nor is her
hair black. Our *flics* have checked but have only taken time for
the photograph, the name and then perhaps the address, yes,
but not, I repeat not, for the descriptive details below them.
They panicked, Hermann. They accepted that it was the
heiress.'

'Then it's not her?' bleated Kohler.

'If it is, her parents, they have much to explain.'

The bushy brown moustache was plucked at in thought, the
robust, swarthy nose pinched, the rounded cheeks with their
depths of evening shadow favoured. At the age of fifty-two, and a
Chief Inspector of the Sûreté Nationale, Louis was not easily
ruffled.

'Only the photographs have been switched, Hermann. It's
not a competent job of forgery—ah no, nothing like that. These
are simply the identity papers of Mademoiselle Nénette Vernet,
over whose photo this one has pasted her own so as to hide the
other. Fortunately, the stamp of the Commissariat de Police has
not intruded, and doubtless the heiress has this one's papers,
though bearing her own photograph. But has the killer, having
ripped off the victim's hat and having perhaps torn the pocket to
see who she was, now gone after the other one?'

Verdammt! Another killing and so soon? Girls ... ah, just
what the hell had they been up to? Von Schaumburg would hit
the roof. False identity papers, et cetera, et cetera. 'Let's empty
her pockets, then. Let's see what else she can tell us.'

A dustbin of things came out of the left pocket. A tin pencil
case—a Faber *Castell*; a toy, hand-held, push-lever roulette

wheel with a tiny steel ball bearing to roll around; frosted and unfrosted marbles; four of the gritty vitaminic 'biscuits' all children were given at school in lieu of fresh fruit, vegetables, milk, cheese and meat, et cetera, at home. 'A crystal of clear quartz,' said St-Cyr, gazing raptly down at the loot. 'A small pebble of poorly polished amethyst. A homemade ring of braided gold wire—scrap most probably and once saved for the jeweller's, perhaps. A tiny, zinc-cast Lone Ranger on his Silver, a pre-war thing from an American cereal box, perhaps, the horse rearing up so as to give chase to bank robbers. I've seen it myself in an American film serial, or was it in a Tom Mix film? There was also a wireless serial. She may have listened to it on the short-wave late at night. Not now, of course. Now she'd be arrested and shot, but we won't mention it, will we?'

Louis hesitated at something else. Kohler could hear him gritting his teeth in dismay. 'A death's-head cap badge, Hermann. Two of the gold wound badges, the Polish Campaign medal and a silver tank battle badge.'

'*Shit!*' They both knew the mere presence of such things would implicate the SS in von Schaumburg's mind—Old Shatter Hand *hated* the SS with a vengeance. 'Let's keep it quiet,' said Kohler and, snapping his fingers, demanded the badges. 'I'll take charge of them. That's an order. I'll toss them in the Seine if I have to.'

The look in Louis's sad brown eyes never left him—they'd been all through this sort of thing with the SS before and knew the consequences only too well, but still . . . 'Then perhaps you might like to keep this also, Herr Hauptmann *Detektiv Aufsichtsbeamter*, since so many of your number are attracted to our fair city to play at being artists?'

'Ah, don't get so pissed off about being one of the conquered and having to take orders from your partner who can't measure up to you in rank. Just tell me what it is.'

'A crumpled, empty tube of oil paint. *Mummy Brown* and, yes, made well before this war from ground Egyptian mummies. There is a use for everything in this life, and the Egyptians, they had so many dried corpses some enterprising soul decided to export the dust to Paris to satisfy Renoir and Degas and the others, all of whom had insatiable appetites.'

'*Mummy Brown*,' breathed Kohler, filing it away.

'Yes. It's not overly dark, I think, but a deep, sandy brown, perhaps not unlike the desert at dusk.'

'Since when did you ever see the desert?'

'Never. Only in my imagination, on the silver screen, and in the adventure novels of Saint-Exupéry, the airmail pioneer and aviator.'

'Ancient history. Then keep the tube and stick to the present, eh, Chief? Six Tarot cards,' he snorted, wanting to get it all over with and gazing at a naked Brünnhilde emptying two stone jugs at a pond. ' "The Star", it says.' He looked at the others. ' "The Lovers; the Nine of Swords; the Devil".' Puzzled, he raised his eyebrows. ' "The Eight of Swords", and finally "the Ace" of the same suit.'

'Will you be able to remember the order in which you found them?'

'Hey, are you forgetting I was a Munich detective before Berlin and then Paris?'

'Never. Absolutely not for one minute!'

'*Touché*, eh? There's also this. Lost, I guess, and found, or the other one is missing.'

'Just let me see it.'

The storm-trooper's stumpy middle left finger was wetted to stab the object and thrust it at him. 'Gold. The fob of an ear-ring.'

'The Virgin with welcoming arms at her sides. On the reverse, the cross and the twelve equally spaced stars denoting the Apostles or the twelve tribes of Israel. A first-communion present, perhaps, or one for confirmation, but not our victim's. Her ears, they are not pierced.'

Merde, it never bothered Louis to work so close to a corpse! Never! He enjoyed it. 'Her charm bracelet is of dogs, in silver. A dachshund, a spaniel, a border terrier, but one is missing. It's been purposely removed, I think. The loop that held it is still here but has been squeezed to death with the pliers.'

'Is there anything else?'

'Lots. A handkerchief bearing the heiress's initials. A small, gold-capped Lalique vial of perfume. Good stuff, too. And one turquoise-on-silver tiepin that's been stepped on and has its shaft bent. No clutchback to it, though. That's missing. And some chewing gum, the ersatz stuff. Pink and horrible and chewed to blazes before being wrapped in a scrap of newspaper.'

'To be saved for a rainy day.'

'Five forgotten raisins among the lint. No coins. Two elastic bands—extras for her braids, probably.' And then, anticipating Louis's question, *'Ja, ja, mein brillant Detektiv Französisch,* there are some tangled black hairs. Long ones.'

St-Cyr nodded grimly. 'Then our victim wears the coat not of herself but of her friend, the heiress, who may, perhaps, wear this one's.'

'And that, *mon fin,* can only mean they planned to switch coats again and must have thought they could get away with whatever they were up to, only the Sandman stepped in.'

'If it really was him. *If,* Hermann. This we really do not know.'

Were things not right? Kohler hesitated. He thought of the death's-head cap badge, the medal and the wound badges ... They'd have to go carefully. They couldn't jump to conclusions. 'Then let's keep the identity switch to ourselves for the moment, eh? Let's talk to the parents first and get a feel for what's been going on?'

This was heresy, but had the identity switch been done so as to throw the killer off? Just why had he had to rip off her hat and check her identity papers?

Had a mistake been made and, if so, did he not now realize it? And where, please, was her hat? Now thrown away or hidden, never to be found?

'First leave me alone with her. Go and talk to the sous-préfet.

Find out where the custodian of this cage is and ask him why he was not around to prevent such a tragedy.'

'At about three o'clock this afternoon, the new time. Berlin Time.'

And in winter an hour ahead, so four o'clock the old time and with the shadows quickly gathering. 'He'll have been flogging doves on the black market, Hermann. Pluck his feathers for us.'

Hermann needed little jobs like that. They brought out the best in him. Reaching over the corpse, St-Cyr said a whispered, 'Forgive me, my child, but we have to talk a little, you and I, and I cannot stand to look at your eyes any longer.'

Closing them, he knelt a moment seemingly in quiet contemplation while the cameras of the mind filmed the body from every possible angle, noting near the end that horse manure had been smeared among the droppings on the floor beneath the snow—the boots of the police perhaps, the killer, the custodian or themselves, the child also. The stables and riding trails were near.

Only then did he find between the last of the bins of droppings beside her left shoulder a small and folded scrap of white notepaper. It had been hidden by the snow.

Opening it, he read, *Je t'aime.* I love you. It was signed *Nénette.*

Outside the ring of lights Kohler found no comfort.

'Monsieur l'Inspecteur, the family . . . Please, someone must speak to them, yes? The aunt . . . Madame Vernet, is distraught. The uncle, Monsieur Vernet, he . . . he is a man of consequence. For us to . . .' The sous-préfet in charge of Neuilly gave a helpless shrug. 'For us to keep them from the body of their little niece is just not right and can only lead to trouble.'

An understanding nod would be best. 'All the same, Sous-préfet, we have to stick to protocol and to orders. The Kommandant von Gross-Paris has specifically stated the relatives are not to see her yet.' This was not true, but what the hell. 'Who told them it was her?'

The lead-grey rheumy eyes that had sought him out ducked away to the lantern. 'I did. Please, I have kept the news from them for as long as I could. Madame Vernet, she . . . she has torn her cheeks with her fingernails and is . . . is blaming herself.'

Kohler swept his eyes over the dodgy little pseudo-Führer with the tiny grey moustache. 'Self-immolation, eh? Hey, that means remorse, my fine one. Who reported the killing to you?'

'Remorse . . . ? Ah, Fournier, one of my best men. He . . . he was discreet. Please believe me, we held off for as long as possible.'

'Who invited the press?'

'No one. All will soon be charged with breaking the curfew and will spend the rest of the night in the cells. If we smash a few cameras that is just too bad, since it is all but impossible to replace them.'

Curfew was at midnight now unless otherwise reduced as a citywide punishment and reprisal in addition to the taking of hostages for some act of terrorism or disobedience. Kohler glanced beyond the sous-préfet to the darkened shapes of the members of the news media. *Paris-Soir, Le Matin,* et cetera, et cetera. All collaborationist and controlled, as were Radio-Paris and Radio-Vichy. 'Did your man tear her coat pocket when he took a look at her identity papers?'

Indignantly the sous-préfet leapt to the defence. 'Her pocket . . . ? Ah, but . . . but I myself have asked him this and he has denied it. Please, we are not so careless.'

'Then why the subservience, Sous-préfet? Why the hangdog look? I'm not about to eat you.'

'Nor I you, particularly as there are others who are hungry for the hearts and livers of a certain two detectives.'

'Where's Talbotte?' asked Kohler suspiciously.

It would be best to fry the goose in axle grease and not to smile as the flames consumed it, even though, when seen in the lantern light, the Bavarian, he was especially formidable. 'The préfet of Paris and the Île-de-France is keeping his distance, since the Kommandant von Gross-Paris is completely in charge of the investigation.'

'And your boss hates my partner with a passion. Hey, I think I've got the message.' Insidiously jealous of his turf, Préfet Talbotte had been flattened by Louis on a recent case. Unfortunately, the Sûreté's gumshoe had told the préfet in no uncertain terms that he had been gathering evidence against him. Evidence of corruption, outright collaboration and worse. Ah *nom de Dieu, de Dieu,* things were never easy and could only get more difficult. 'Let me talk to the one who found her. Tell the relatives we don't want to see them anywhere near here and will call on them shortly. Oh, by the way, where are her mother and father?'

The préfet had warned him of these two detectives. He was to 'cooperate' but to do so while keeping one hand behind his back, fingers crossed. 'Dead also, but some time ago.'

'Dead?'

'Yes. The aunt and uncle are raising her as their own. Monsieur Vernet makes things for the submarines of Herr Dönitz. Other little items also. Tank parts, gun parts, munitions and explosives. Classified things. He is very important, very well connected and not inclined to take no for an answer, but I, ah! I am sure he will find the will to understand your request, though he will most certainly bring the matter up when he confers with the General von Schaumburg at their weekly briefing. It is tomorrow, I believe. Yes . . . yes, now that I have thought the matter over, I am absolutely certain it is always on a Monday unless something interferes.'

Ah damn . . .

When the man joined him, Kohler drew him aside into deeper darkness but still, though he wanted to, could not find the stomach to offer a cigarette. It would be too much like bribery in any case, particularly as tobacco was almost always in such short supply.

'Begin at the beginning. Leave nothing out.'

'Of course. Part of my beat includes the Jardin d'Acclimatation, particularly the children's zoo, and amusement park. Sunday afternoons are busy, even in winter. At fifteen-fifty-seven hours I was patrolling near the Norman farm. Monsieur Amirault, the custodian of the doves, he has hurried to summon me. A murder, a child, the Sandman. Together we have run from there to the riding stables, then to the clay-pigeon shoot, and from there to the cage. He . . . he is also in charge of the clay pigeons. Sometimes one of the Boches, the Germans . . . Ah, excuse me, Inspector. Sometimes they . . . they command him to release a few doves so as to . . . to perfect their target practice.'

Hence the custodian's absence during the murder, was that it, and all carefully thought out so as to have an answer ready? 'We'll see. We'll have to ask him ourselves.'

'As you wish, Inspector. We are here to assist you.'

I'll bet, thought Kohler, snorting inwardly and cursing Talbotte for the bastard he was. Police couriers must have been hurtling back and forth. 'Was anything other than her identity card touched?'

'Anything else . . . ? But . . . but . . . Ah no, of course not. I have simply leaned over her to tease the ID out, then have put it back just as I found it with . . . with the pocket torn a little.'

'But to get at it you would have had to dig into each pocket?'

'I was lucky. The left pocket. I had no need to try the other one.'

'Good. Then tell me who lifted her change purse?'

Ah *merde*, had it been stolen? 'But . . . but there was no purse, Inspector. I swear it.'

'Yet she comes to the Bois without a sou? An heiress to what?'
'Billions.'

'Sweat a little, *mon fin*. Think about it, eh? To say there was no purse is to imply you had a thorough look. Let honesty touch your heart lest we haul you in, and haul we will if we have to. As sure as that God of my partner's made heiresses, He gave them the wits to take along a little change for the pony rides.'

'I . . . I will have to ask the others.'

'You do that. Now lead me to the custodian. Maybe it's his tongue that needs loosening.'

*   *   *

'Two girls,' said St-Cyr softly to the victim as the doves watched him with such sorrowful eyes he knew they were freezing. 'School friends who tried to switch identities. Both of you would have worn your school uniforms under your coats, since the hems of the skirts, the lower parts of the socks, the boots and gloves would have been seen. Yes, yes, am I right? The braids perhaps tucked underneath your hats and your coat collars turned up to further hide the difference in your hair—ah! yours is indeed turned up. Everything would have matched, but then what would be the sense of switching coats? A mistake, you say? A restaurant? A cup of that ersatz hot chocolate which tastes like clay and is not made with milk but with saccharine added? Ah no, my little friend.' He sadly shook his head. 'These days no one—I repeat no one—hangs their coat up in a public place for fear of theft. It's usually far too cold inside anyway. No, you see the switch was deliberate. We have the note you dropped. *Je t'aime*. Presumably, since it was in your hand when attacked, you treasured it and perhaps had received it only moments before. Therefore, unless I am very mistaken, your friend the heiress wore her school coat and uniform on this outing while you wore perhaps a brightly coloured coat and beret or toque—not your school ones. All else was the same so that at a distance, especially from behind, one could not tell the two of you apart except for the coats, the scarves and the hats—yes, yes, that's it, isn't it, but why was the switch made?'

He paused. He looked at her. He silently pleaded for answers, then breathed, 'You must have known you would be followed, but by whom? You had both planned it all well beforehand, hadn't you, but had not thought either of you would be killed once the mistake was discovered.

'Then was it the Sandman?' he asked and had to answer sadly, 'How could it have been?'

It was not good, ah no, it most certainly wasn't. The city was up in arms and demanding they put a stop to the killer. In this, Parisians were united with the Occupier, and God help His two detectives if the assailant turned out to be anything but French. Ah yes. There were perhaps one hundred and fifty or even two hundred thousand of the Occupier in Paris and its environs. Who really knew how many of them there were? The Germans coveted the city and used it for rest and recuperation, so the traffic in and out was constant. *Soldatenheime*—hotels and guesthouses—were scattered throughout to billet the common soldiers. The Ritz was for generals and very special people; the Claridge, at 74 Champs-Élysées, was for still more generals and holders of the Knight's Cross. Of the one hundred and twenty licenced brothels, forty were for the troops, four for their immediate officers, one for their generals, two for the SS and no less than *five* for the Gestapo, to say nothing of the countless 'trade' commissioners and buyers, et cetera.

Even some of the cinemas were reserved for their soldiers, while all the clubs, bars, restaurants and cafés were wide open and could not shut them out, though, by some tacit, unwritten rule, they did not go to certain places.

Even the lead cars of each train in the *métro* and on the railroads were reserved for them, even the first six rows of seats on the city's much reduced fleet of buses.

They had everything, including many of the women, and the trouble was, most of the Occupier believed it their just due.

They also had their garrisoned troops, and those that patrolled the streets, especially after curfew, or manned the checkpoints at each and every entry.

'So,' he said to her, 'I silently give a little prayer that we will solve this matter soon but that your killer will indeed be French. Otherwise General von Schaumburg, who despises us far more than he does Bavarian N.C.O.s from that other war, will give his two detectives a very hard time, and so will the SS over on the avenue Foch, the Gestapo of the rue des Saussaies, the French Gestapo of the rue Lauriston and others too many to list but including Talbotte, the préfet of Paris, and his men. Ah yes, my dear child, the life of a detective in these troubled times is not easy. Please be at peace. We will do everything we can.'

Gently he took a dove from its perch to warm and stroke it. Suddenly he had to make contact with things he knew and loved in this world of continual crisis. 'She did a brave but very foolish thing, this child,' he said, indicating the victim. 'They were being followed, and she deliberately drew the follower away from her friend. The switch in coats must have been made soon after leaving the Villa Vernet, but why switch identity photographs? Why not simply keep their own papers?

'Perhaps they did not think there would be time to hand them over to each other. Perhaps, then, too, they might have feared being caught up in a *rafle*, a round-up—yes, yes, but they would have known the Occupier seldom does more than glance at the ID photos of children. Still, why not simply keep their own papers, unless, of course, there was a deeper reason.'

He thought a bit. He stroked the dove, his eyes never leaving the girl. 'Did you know the killer?' he asked her. 'Did you wish to taunt him with the mistake he had made? Did you intend to show him your new ID as proof positive perhaps, or did you think he would demand it from you, only to realize then what had happened? Would that have been sufficient to have stopped him? Is this not what you, in your schoolgirl wisdom, thought?'

One had to put oneself into the mind of a child to understand the reasoning, flawed though it sometimes was and frightening.

Again he waited but asked at last and more firmly, 'How is it, please, that you knew you would be followed, and why, please, were you here without supervision if you were spending the holiday with the sisters?'

Questions . . . there were always so many of them. 'The time was midafternoon. Did the two of you lead the one who was following you into the Jardin d'Acclimatation? The Villa Vernet, it is not far. The heiress came out of her house with her own papers but with your ID photo on them. You had left the convent school and had done likewise with your own papers. You both knew you would have to exchange coats and hats quickly and continue on so as to allow for no break in being followed.

'Was the switch made among some fir trees or behind one of the puppet theatres or near the miniature railway where children of all ages congregate? Or was it in the zoo or at the little

Norman farm where uncomplaining goats and chickens endure the constant attentions of children? A place was needed where you would be shielded only for a moment. The coats and hats first, and then the note pressed into your hand.'

Setting the dove back on its perch, he shifted the contents of his overcoat pockets and patiently gathered the loot, carefully noting each item as he tucked it away.

Everything in him said to cover her, to ease the knitting needle out, to say, Forgive us for letting such a thing happen to you or to anyone else. We will see that it does not happen again. On this matter, you have my solemn promise.

Four other girls, he reminded himself. All killed in essentially the same manner, though this they would have to check. But for now there was at least a definite difference. Now it was two girls together, both of whom must have thought they knew what they were doing. 'You poor thing,' he said. 'We don't even know your name, do we, or where your parents are. Nor do we know where your little friend is.'

The heiress . . .

Carved among its oak flowers, the signboard said: THE GAME-KEEPER'S COTTAGE. Kohler hit the door with the flat of his shoe. The shock tore the feathers from the dove in the custodian's hands, causing them to flutter before a miserable fire of ill-gotten twigs.

The bird was dropped to join the row of others, all naked of their feathers and lying on the hearth. The hands crept up to throw their shadows on the tiled floor and timbered ceiling.

Stepping into the otherwise darkened room, Kohler used a heel to close the door behind him. Now only the sound of the fire and the gentle hiss of chimney droplets came to him as tears coursed from very worried, wounded eyes behind rimless glasses.

'So, a few questions, *mon fin*. *Don't* even think of lowering your hands. Hey, it makes me nervous, eh? Grab warmer air. Stretch for it.'

Gilbert Amirault was half-Italian by the look of him and

rounded about the middle from knees to neck. The tattered black leather jerkin was buttoned up so tightly two of the buttons had been lost forever. The plum-dark corduroy trousers had birdshit so ground into the knees they were irretrievably bleached.

'Getting ready for a banquet, are you?' asked the Gestapo's only honest detective. 'Tasty, are they?'

More tears were shed. The flabby lips quivered. Sweat—was it really sweat?—was gathering on his forehead beneath the thatch of untidy black hair.

'I . . . They . . .' The man swallowed and, farting harshly, grimaced at the accidental outburst and waited for a rebuke that never came.

Instead, Kohler spoke the sad truth. 'No potatoes, eh? And those lousy rutabagas again. Cattle feed while the spuds of France go to the Reich and the hospitals here are so overcrowded with bowel complaints and cases of appendicitis they are even parking them in the corridors. Look, tell me who shot the doves and when. This afternoon, eh? At about three o'clock—was it three o'clock and right when that poor kid was being murdered?'

Amirault's left hand dropped so fast Kohler yanked out a pistol and made the bastard wince as he waited for the *coup de grâce*.

It never came. Hurriedly the custodian made the sign of the cross over his barrel chest, then his hand crept upwards. 'Monsieur . . .' hazarded Amirault. His neck was so short his chin rested in the slot of his open collar.

'It's Inspector. Show some respect, and while you're at it, hand over the change purse you stole.'

Ah *merde* . . .'The . . . the purse, it is on the table for safekeeping, yes? I . . . I was just plucking the pigeons . . .'

'Doves . . . they're doves.'

The change purse was swept up and stuffed into the giant's coat pocket. 'The doves, Inspector, they are for . . . for the one who has shot them this . . . this afternoon.'

'Ah! Now we're getting somewhere. And who might that have been?'

'The . . . the General von Schaumburg.'

Ah *nom de Jésus-Christ*! what the hell was this?

'I am to see that they are delivered to the head chef at the Ritz tomorrow morning. They . . . they are for a little dinner party General von Schaumburg is throwing in honour of General Halder's visit.'

How cosy, and no wonder Old Shatter Hand wanted a certain two detectives right under his big Prussian thumb and no questions asked. Shit!

'All right, you can lower your hands, but put the last of the sticks on the fire and break up one of the chairs. I have to see you better.'

'The chairs . . . but . . . but they are from the reign of the Sun King?'

'Hey, he won't mind. Oh, all right, just the sticks. Turn sideways to the light. I want to see if you're not just a petty thief but a liar also.'

A liar . . . Ah *merde*, he had meant it, too. 'Please, I did not steal the purse. It had fallen from her pocket—the left one—and was lying there when I found her. I was afraid the cows—the police . . . ah! forgive me—would steal it.'

'*Mort aux vaches*, eh? [Death to cops.] The left pocket. You're sure of this?' In searching for her ID, the killer must have dragged the purse out.

There was a nod. When approached, the custodian stank of sour wine, no bathing whatsoever, lots of garlic to ward off hunger, and those damned rutabagas. Bad teeth showed nicotine stains, but glimpses of gold gave a hint of better times. 'Was von Schaumburg alone at the clay-pigeon shoot or were there others with him?'

Things would not go well, thought the custodian. The greatcoat was huge, the fedora fierce, the face . . . Ah, gentle Jesus, help this sinner . . . 'Alone. Just the Kommandant von Gross-Paris and myself. The time, it had been reserved, you understand.

Fifty of the clay pigeons and then . . . then the doves. I . . . I visited the cage twice, Inspector. Taking eight birds first because the General, he has thought they would be enough, then another four after he had explored the breasts of the others and had decided more meat was needed.'

A connoisseur. 'Did you see the child? Was she anywhere near the cage? At exactly what time?'

'From two-thirty until three-thirty, the shooting. "An hour of sport to tame the eye and calm the blood," the General has said. But at the last, the doves to fill the casserole, since one cannot eat clay pigeons, can one? It's impossible. I . . . I would have been at the cage from three-ten until three-fifteen—one does not keep a general waiting, so I ran from here to there and back, and the doves they are very tame and unsuspecting usually.'

'Hey, that's interesting. And then?'

'Again at three-twenty perhaps, or three-twenty-five, the . . . the new time. Berlin Time.'

The birds looked in excellent shape, not torn to pieces by birdshot that would only break the teeth if left. 'A four-ten shotgun?' asked Kohler curiously.

'The sixteen gauge, the full sweep so as to lead them on the wing and spread the pattern, letting only a few of the pellets caress the necks and kiss the heads.'

'And the child?' The fire was dying. The hearth was littered with white feathers . . .

'Well?' shot the detective suddenly.

It would do no good to lie to him. The slash down his face, the graze across his brow . . . 'I . . . I did not lock the cage as was my custom, Inspector. The child, she . . . she would have run in there to hide at . . . at about three-thirty. Or perhaps it was after I had first gone there, so at three-fifteen.'

The custodian shrugged as if to say, How is one to know exactly when one is occupied with other matters and does not even suspect such a thing of happening?

Kohler hauled out a packet of U-boat cigarettes and tossed it among the feathers. 'Okay, I think you're telling me the truth, but I'm still going to need your help or it's no deal with the change purse. Try to remember who else was about. The riding stables are just over there on the other side of this cottage, the route de Madrid passes behind the fireplace. There are woods in front of the clay-pigeon shoot. The allée de Longchamp is to my right and not two hundred metres away. Were there other children?'

Such an eye for detail demanded answer. 'Yes. Walking in the woods.'

'With the nuns?'

'Nuns? I saw no sisters of the cloth, Inspector. They do not like to come near here when . . . when the doves of peace are being slaughtered.'

'The doves of peace? There's no signboard proclaiming that.'

'Ah no. No, Inspector. It is only that since we are a . . . a defeated nation that . . .' Ah, why had he said it? wondered Amirault desperately. 'It is only since the war in Russia has turned against you . . . you people that . . . that some have taken to calling them such.'

Was it yet another sign of the growing discontent? wondered Kohler. People were beginning to think the end of the Occupation might come. Their only question was when. 'Okay, so a man . . . the Sandman. The child is running. She sees the cage and that the lock is off. She darts in there, but . . .'

'But he finds her, this *sadique*. He opens her clothing, pushes it up but . . . but there is no time. He kills her. Black . . . Ah now, a moment, please, Inspector. I did see something black out of the corner of my eye, but the General, he has told me to gather in the doves he has shot and I . . . I have done so.'

'The first or the last batch?'

'The first. Yes, Inspector, I am positive, because there were eight of them and one had flown into the forest and I had trouble finding it. The General, he has insisted he had taken it on the wing and has cursed me for doubting him. He was correct, of course.' The custodian ducked his head in deference.

'Then the time was between three-ten and three-twenty and

you saw someone in black. Black like your jerkin, eh? Black as in a Gestapo uniform? Black as in a woollen overcoat, or maybe it was dark blue like the one she's wearing?'

'I . . .' Ah *nom de Dieu* . . . 'I cannot be certain. Black, I think, but dark blue, I don't know. Perhaps.'

'And the cage?'

'Please, I . . . I should have locked it. I will lose my job. It isn't much, but . . .'

'But others depend on your salary,' came the sigh. Two hundred francs a day, would he be paid even that when a loaf of bread, if he could find it, would cost him at least a hundred? 'What does the General pay you for the doves?'

'Twenty francs each.'

'*Mein Gott*, the price of bloody crows on the black market is ten and they taste like hell even after hours of boiling!'

'You must use the mustard sauce.'

'Never mind the fucking sauce!'

Kohler pulled out the thin remains of a wad of notes that once would have choked a horse had it not been for the cook of U-297 on their last investigation. 'Here, I'll pay you one hundred each. You keep them here and I'll personally deliver them to the General at oh-seven-hundred hours tomorrow, or is it already tomorrow?'

It was. The countdown had begun for their first report. They had about six and a half hours left. No time to telephone Giselle and Oona at the flat to tell them he was home, no time to drop in and surprise them. No time even for Louis to go home to an empty house and a wife and son who were no longer there.

'The Resistance.' He let a breath escape in midthought, didn't really care if the custodian understood. 'They did it. Thinking my partner was a collaborator, they set a bomb for him. His wife and son came home from the arms of her German lover to an unexpected surprise.'

A month ago—had it been that long? he wondered. A little longer, he thought, and said, 'We try not to talk about it, and sure someone new has come along—war does that. It speeds up death and love, makes friendships instant but then destroys them. He's still on the Resistance's hit lists. Well, some of them, but he's no collabo. Now forget I said any of that and have the doves ready for me at oh-six-five-five hours. Leave them unwrapped. Just tie a string around each of their necks so that I can dangle them from my fist.'

Without another word he was gone from the cottage, gone out into the night to stand alone under the stars, looking up at them. The custodian could not know the detective had lost his two sons at Stalingrad not quite a week ago, nor that his wife back home on her father's farm near Wasserburg had just gained her divorce and was going to marry an indentured farm labourer. A French peasant!

They met outside the ring of lights as the police photographers went to work and the members of the press, with angry shouts and curses, were fighting off the truncheons and lead-weighted hems of the *gendarmes'* capes and their steel-cleated boots as well.

'Louis, I need a drink.'

'Me also. How's the flu?'

'Fine. I never felt better.'

Oh-oh.

'Lend me a fag, will you? I'm fresh out. I left mine with the custodian.'

The first of two *paniers à salade* was arriving. Clang, clang, and into the iron salad baskets with the press for transport to the overnight cells. 'Your heart's too big,' snorted St-Cyr. 'As a punishment, I ought to force you to try to roll one from the contents of my little tin.'

Everyone collected cigarette butts, but they had 800 of the best, well, 720 now perhaps. Kohler had lost count. 'Here, let me have a few of them. Hey, didn't I find you three tins of Dutch pipe tobacco in that U-boat warehouse?'

A press camera was being smashed and ground to pieces, a nose had been broken. 'You did, and I am forever in your debt. Please take the packet. I was only saving it for Gabrielle.'

His new and yet to be consummated love affair. A *chanteuse.*
'Ah, don't sound so wounded. I'll give you another. We'll make
it two. One from me and one from yourself.'

'*Merci.* Now, please, reveal to me what you are hiding.'

'Hiding? Hey, it's to be a surprise. I'll tell you all about it
when we meet Old Shatter Hand.'

'The clay pigeons . . . ?' bleated the Sûreté, leagues ahead
of him.

'Fifty in less than forty minutes and a dozen doves in a little
more than ten. The child was killed between about three-ten
and three-twenty. The custodian saw nothing out of the ordi-
nary in the cage, though he entered it twice before finding her.
Either the killer smothered her cries and is a cool one, or he
did it in one hell of a hurry and was just damned lucky not to
have caught a blast from von Schaumburg's double-barrelled
wonder.'

Kohler paused to take a drag. 'His coat was either dark blue
or black, or it was the child the custodian saw but briefly. A
blur.'

They could compare notes later, but he had to say it. 'Something is not right with this one, Hermann. I've asked for Belligueux to be brought in for the autopsy. He's by far the most
difficult but can't be bought or silenced. She's to go straight to
the place Mazas and on to ice. No one is to uncover her until
we have either spoken to him or done it ourselves. He will make
himself aware of the other victims so that we can discuss them
with him.'

'Good. Now we need some transport. Let's borrow the sous-
préfet's car until we can pick up the Citroën.'

'The sous-préfet's car? Is that wise?'

'Wise or not, that little runt is far too shifty and needs a
damned good kick in the balls.'

Ah *merde,* sometimes Herman didn't think of the consequences, but it would be useless to argue. Where once there
had been more than 350,000 private automobiles in Paris, to
say nothing of the lorries, there were now fewer than 4,500, and
most of those belonged to doctors, high-ranking civil servants,

bankers and industrialists or to the police, the Germans and the gangsters.

It was a city without wheels in a nation without gasoline. Well, almost. One could not forget the bicycles.

When the engine coughed to life under crossed ignition wires, the Sûreté threw his eyes up to God in despair and said, 'You would have made an excellent car-thief, Hermann. It's a pity there's a war on.'

'What war? The Führer, in his wisdom, thought it necessary to occupy the rest of France on the eleventh of November of last year, my fine Frog friend, or had you forgotten? Now stop grumbling and let me floor this thing while the sous-préfet sucks lemons. Hey! the tyres are bald. There's ice. Hang on.'

And pray.

2 BEYOND THE TALL IRON FENCE, AND IN DARKNESS, the softly falling snow gave to the Villa Vernet the caress of a moth. Beech, oak and plane trees graced an open parkland which, with formal gardens, over-looked the Bois and were but a kilometre and a half from the cage of doves, and right in the northwestern corner of the city, quite close to the Seine.

'It is perhaps the most prestigious address in Paris,' said St-Cyr, his voice hushed and uneasy, for they were not going to reveal the mistake in the identity of the victim right away and could not know where such a lack of forthrightness would lead. 'There will be no communal soup kitchens here, Hermann. The route du Champs d'Entraînement is home to but a chosen few.'

The powerful and the useful. Those who'd been allowed to keep their wealth and position. Those the Occupier hadn't kicked out so as to requisition their villas. It was money, one hell of a lot of money, that kid had inherited. The house, built in the style of Louis XVI, of Chantilly limestone blocks that softly glowed and sharpened shadows, was of two storeys. A

narrow balcony, recessed around the upper storey, made access
to the roof and chimneys easy. Here, too, the ceilings were
much lower than on the ground and first floor. 'The servants'
quarters.' Kohler nodded uncomfortably. 'A couple probably, or
a cook, maid and housekeeper. A governess, too, perhaps, even
though the kid goes out to school. Louis, maybe we had better
tell Vernet the truth and get it over with. He'll have connections other than von Schaumburg.'

The SS perhaps.

'Let's take a little look around first. If we ask, we will not be
given the chance. Indeed, it may be our only opportunity.'

'And the other?'

'We keep silent for now, no matter what.'

'Then don't blame me if we get our asses in a sling!'

'*Hermann*, this killing *was* different. Don't be an idiot! Something must be very wrong. There were *two* girls, not one, and
the victim could not have been randomly chosen.'

Leaving the car some distance away, they headed up the circular drive and were soon standing behind the house. Footprints that would have been made less than fifteen minutes ago
were now all but buried.

'A dog,' breathed Kohler, puzzled. 'A poodle probably, and
the one who came out with it. A woman in her bare feet, I'm
afraid.' He indicated a far corner of the garden where Doric
columns stood beyond the dark grey granite edges of a snow-
covered pond. 'You or me?'

'Me, I think. Check the coach house. See if there are living
quarters above it—the groundskeeper perhaps.'

They parted without another word, and when he neared the
folly, St-Cyr realized that it was in the style of the Parthenon.
Steps led down to the pond where water lilies would bloom in
summer beneath the shimmering wings of dragonflies as they
hovered above the lurking shadows of the carp.

He could barely see the woman, so deep was she among the
shadows. 'Madame, I regret very much this sudden intrusion
into your solitude. My name is Jean-Louis St-Cyr of the Sûreté
Nationale.'

'Was she naked? Did she suffer a lot?'

'Naked . . . ? Ah no. No, madame,' he said, conscious of the tremor in her voice, its shrillness. 'She suffered, yes, but . . . but perhaps not too much, if one can say such a thing was possible.'

'I loved her as my own. We were very close. We confided things to each other. She . . . she trusted me absolutely. I blame myself for what has happened.'

He had not moved, this detective from the Sûreté. He stood at the foot of the steps looking up at her through the columns into darkness. Was he wondering why she had come out here to this place? Would he question why she was wearing only this?

She plucked at the flimsiness of her peignoir. She said, 'Pompon has run off again. I . . . I should not have let him off the lead, but . . . but it was her dog, not mine. Actually, I have no love of dogs. Even the best of them are dirty and do disgusting things, but . . . but for a child's sake one has to make sacrifices, isn't that so? Do you have children, Inspector? Girls perhaps? Girls who might someday be . . .'

She felt his hands take her firmly by the shoulders. Cursing the flimsiness of the peignoir under his breath, he pulled off his overcoat and wrapped it around her. 'The house,' he said determinedly. 'Indoors, I think.'

'*Not yet! Please!* I . . . I have to tell you how it was. He . . . he won't let me say a thing. He'll see that he does all the talking. He'll send me to bed.'

Ah *merde* . . . 'Then come and sit on that bench out there. Let me warm your feet.'

'Give me a cigarette first. Let me fill my lungs.'

Kohler eased himself through the side door of the coach house to stand in the light as he let his gaze sift over the place. There was room for six autos but it held only two. A maroon Citroën coupé was up on blocks for the Duration and hadn't been requisitioned by the Luftwaffe for a favoured squadron leader. The forest-green, four-door sedan with excellent tyres, including a spare, was big, powerful and handsome.

Both cars shone, but this last was getting yet another going-

over at about 1.15 a.m. The chauffeur, his back to him, was pol-
ishing the leather of the front seat. Sleeves rolled up and held
by grey elastic bands, jacket carefully set aside in spite of the
cold. Vest and tie to complete the attire, with gold pocket-watch
and chain probably. One of the old school. Floor swept and
washed—not even an oil stain was evident. The stiff black high
leather boots glowed; the grey herringbone breeches were
creased by the welding iron of determination and discipline.

One had to be impressed. The S.P. sticker was just visible
beyond the left shoulder and was exactly where it ought to be,
bang up front inside the left lower corner of the windscreen.
The *Service Publique*, that much-coveted mark of distinction
that allowed a private set of wheels in this gas-thirsty world, to
say nothing of a chauffeur.

Ten jerry cans were ranked in a corner, so there was no
problem in that department. If you made classified items for the
Führer's war machine, a little petrol was your reward, among
other things, ah yes.

Still with his back to Kohler, the chauffeur straightened. He
set the tin of saddle soap lightly on the roof, gave the seat a final
wipe, a thorough scrutiny, then softly closed the door and did
the chrome-plated handle. A man of sixty years of age perhaps
and of medium height. Iron-grey, well-trimmed hair, thick, big
ears, a swarthy neck and broad shoulders that now slumped as
he stood in silence with head bowed and forearms resting
against the car's rain-gutter.

'Captain, it cannot be true,' came the bitter lament, not to
Kohler, for he had yet to be noticed. 'Our little Nénette gone
from us? Our treasure? Our constant reminder of you and your
dear wife?'

The fists were clenched, tears splashed the car and in that
moment a shudder ran visibly through the chauffeur. 'I *warned*
you not to go to England. I *begged* you not to leave us like that,
and what did I receive but the lash of silence from the tongue of
a man who had always listened to his sergeant. Always, especially in times of strife when the battle, it did not go well.'

The eyes were wiped, the nose was blown. The tears were

removed and the car polished so as so leave no evidence of them. The tyre pressures had to be checked all round and only then did he notice he had a visitor. 'Monsieur . . .'

The rugged countenance was marked by four years of war—an idiot could have seen it at a glance. The eyes were grave and deeply set, dark brown and ever watchful. Sun blotches and shrapnel scars, one of which had nicked off the tip of his nose, served only to emphasize a quiet determination and intense loyalty.

'She's a beauty. A thirty-seven Delage, am I right?'

All thought of tears vanished. The shoulders were squared. 'Monsieur, please state your business. If you have none, I suggest you leave.'

A ball-peen hammer lay to hand on the workbench. 'Kohler, Paris-Central, and yours?'

'Honoré Deloitte, sergeant to the child's father. Chauffeur to the Vernet family for the past twenty-four years since my repatriation and, before that other war, for six of the finest years of my life.'

The look seemed to say, I have killed far better Boches than you in my time but will gladly oblige another. There was a scar across the back of Deloitte's left hand, the slash of a bayonet that had missed its mark as his had gone home.

'Can we talk?'

'Talk if you wish. For myself, I will, I assure you, listen.'

It would be best to tell him something. 'Look, we can delay the investigation until all the staff are assembled, but we think there may have been two eleven-year-old girls involved and we'd like to know what's happened to the other one before it's too late for her as well.'

'Too late . . . ? Two girls . . . ? But . . . but that is not possible. Mademoiselle Nénette, she was most distressed to find that her little friend had at last gone to join her parents in Chamonix. The mother had had a crisis of the nerves and had not been able to invite the child to be with them for the holiday.'

How nice. The poor kid. 'And the name of this friend?' he

asked, all business now, the black leather notebook flipped open, pencil ready.

A sigh of resignation was released. 'Andrée Noireau. She was staying at the convent school but . . . but had left for . . .'

'Chamonix.' Kohler gave a nod. 'So who accompanied Mademoiselle Vernet on her Sunday outing?'

'Why, the Mademoiselle Chambert. She is a student at the university, the daughter of one of Monsieur Vernet's accountants.'

'A nanny.'

'Ah no, no, monsieur,' countered Deloitte. 'A member of the family since now nearly two and a half years, since the parents of our little Nénette went to England to die by the bombs of your Führer. *Die*, monsieur, in Coventry on the night of the fourteenth to fifteenth of November 1940.' He paused. He realized he had been incautious. 'Mademoiselle Chambert always accompanied the girls so as to . . . to give a little supervision yet allow them to assess each new situation and . . . and decide how best to handle things. Is that not the wisest way for one to ensure that young girls learn how to take care of themselves?'

But they hadn't, had they? said Kohler sadly to himself, his gaze one of emptiness. Mademoiselle Chambert had not been with them and Deloitte had suddenly realized this. He'd have to be loyal to the aunt and uncle. He couldn't jeopardize his future, not in these troubled times, even though he might well want to.

'Just tell it to me plainly.'

What has happened to Liline? wondered Deloitte anxiously. Why was she not there with Nénette? 'I . . . I drove the two of them to Mass at the Notre-Dame this time, as they liked to experience other churches than our own when possible. Then I delivered them to the Jardin d'Acclimatation. Though they wished to take the *métro*, Monsieur Vernet had issued strict instructions they were not to do so because of . . . of this sadist.'

'Vernet had their safety in mind, so, okay, we'll try to remember that,' said Kohler bluntly. 'And where, exactly, did you drop them off?'

Had this one been a Hauptmann in the last war? wondered Deloitte uneasily. 'I dropped them off at the puppet theatres and the giant doll's house. They were to spend a little time there and then were to have tea in the children's restaurant. Nénette was fond of taking tea. Her mother was British. The child used to say it made her feel closer to her dead mother.'

The doll's house might have suited the switching of the coats, but as for the rest of the outing, it had probably never happened. 'At about what time did you drop them off?'

'At thirteen-ten hours—it's in my log, in the glove compartment. Monsieur Vernet requires that I keep an accurate record of all trips just in case the authorities might wish to question his using his own car.'

'Don't be blaming me for what's happened, eh? Just stick to the matter at hand.'

'I will.'

'The eleven o'clock Mass?'

'The ten o'clock.'

'Two hours, then. What the hell did they do, Sergeant? Pray for that long?'

Sergeant . . . 'Mademoiselle Nénette wished to visit the belfries of the Notre-Dame, and one of the good fathers was prevailed upon to allow her to do so, since it was not a regularly scheduled time for such a visit.'

'Okay, so why the interest?'

'Look, monsieur . . .'

'It's Inspector.'

A fist was clenched only to be relaxed in defeat. 'Inspector, the master did not want Mademoiselle Nénette doing such a thing but . . . ah, the child, she has pleaded with me and I . . . Please, I . . . I could seldom say no to her, especially not after the deaths of her dear father and mother. It is to my discredit and shame that I let her and Mademoiselle Chambert disobey her uncle's wishes and now . . . now . . . all those trips I let them take on the *métro*, all that freedom, it has come back to . . .'

'Easy. I know how you must feel. The ten o'clock Mass, the belfries, and then the doll's house? That's fine, were it not for one thing I'm certain you're as aware of as I am. The Sandman has killed four others, and one of those murders was up in the belfries of the Notre-Dame.'

The chauffeur's head was bowed in defeat. Had the man a rifle and helmet, they would have hung at his sides, and how many times had he himself seen such things? wondered Kohler, remembering past battlefields and war-weary men.

'The belfry?' he asked gently.

There was a nod. 'Nénette had read all the newspaper reports. She and her little friend were both much concerned and wishing they could do something to . . . to put a stop to . . . to the killings.'

Amateur sleuths, then. Ah *nom de Jésus-Christ*, what had the two of them stumbled upon? 'Look, I won't say anything of this side trip to the belfries unless I absolutely have to. Just tell me where I can find Mademoiselle Chambert. I presume she went off somewhere because I don't think she was with the girls when it happened. Did she go home? Is she now under sedation?'

His expression was grim. 'Ah no, Inspector. You see, she has . . . has not yet returned.'

'Not returned.'

'No, and that is most unlike her.'

The snow continued, and all about the garden was a hush, that of the city, too, and one could never quite adjust to the silence where once there had been traffic and commotion at nearly all hours.

'Madame . . .' said St-Cyr. 'You mentioned a companion?'

'Yes, Liline Chambert.' The women drew on the cigarette and snuggled her toes deeper into the warmth of his hands. 'Liline and Nénette were always very close. Like two sisters, though one is much older, of course. Eighteen, I think, or is it nineteen now? Antoine . . . my husband, he gave the girl a part-time job to help fill the void that was created by the tragic deaths of the child's parents.'

'The bombing,' he sighed, for she had told him of it. 'Escape to England only to find no escape at all.'

'Not escape, please. We . . . we do not say such things. My brother-in-law went to England on business and to try to calm the fears of those people, and since my sister-in-law was British, she went along to visit her family.'

The detective indicated that he understood the delicacy of using such words as 'escape,' but made no comment about calming 'the fears of those people'. His hands had long since lost timidity and now gently massaged her feet. Had he a wife? she wondered. A woman? Certainly he seemed to understand her need to be calmed, yet he sat so like a priest in his suit and fedora, with the snow dusting his shoulders and sleeves, she had to wonder about him. Her long legs were stretched out; her back rested against an arm of the bench. She was cosily wrapped in his overcoat, but was it that he was worried she might explore the pockets of his coat? Was that what was troubling him? If so, he need not have worried, no, not at all.

She heaved an inward sigh and said silently, It was my duty, to examine those things Nénette had in her pockets. I had to make myself aware of what the child had discovered.

'Antoine,' she said. '*Bien sûr*, he . . . hc has done everything possible to make things right for Nénette. He gave up his beautiful house near Rambouillet, the house his father had given us at our marriage, and moved us in here. He kept all the servants. He *wanted* the child to feel at home in the house she had always loved.'

'And had inherited.'

'Yes. Yes, that is so, of course. The factories, too, when she comes of age—everything, you understand. Just everything. But . . . but now . . .'

She gave a ragged sob and burst into tears—flung the cigarette away and cried, 'Ah *merde, merde*, why did I not force Antoine to listen to her?' She sucked in a breath. 'Forgive me, I . . . I had best go in. I might say things I shouldn't. He . . . he's not to be blamed for what happened, is he?'

Passing her the clean handkerchief he always kept for such occasions and others, St-Cyr gave her a moment. He took out his pipe and tobacco pouch and began that pleasant task of preparing to settle down.

A spare few, careless crumbs of tobacco fell on her bare feet, a waste, a sacrifice he would normally never have made had he not wished to unsettle her—yes, yes. And she felt them as if they were grains of silicon carbide or the hot turnings of metal from a lathe in one of the factories, even to catching in her imagination the pungent odour of burnt cutting oil. 'Inspector ... Antoine just doesn't understand children. He's far too busy now, since the death of his brother. He's been dragged in from semi-retirement and forced, yes forced, to work for a living. Children have their little games, isn't that so? It was just a game, wasn't it? But ... but,' she blurted in tears again, 'it *wasn't* a game! It *wasn't!*'

Her feet began to leave his lap. He clamped a hand down on them and said, 'No, we will stay. A child has been murdered, madame. *Murdered.*' He softened his voice. 'Now, please, what game?'

'She ... she had been following the killings. She was convinced the ... the Sandman would strike again and ... ah, may God forgive me, and in the Bois, in or near the Jardin d'Acclimatation.'

He gave her another moment and at last, when he made no comment, she said, 'Antoine, he ... he dominates everything. He issues directives as the Occupier does ordinances. He believes I talk nonsense when really I spoke the truth and warned him the child was on to something.'

Snow was brushed from the detective's sleeve. A match was struck and then another and another. At last his pipe was lit and savoured in that first moment, and she knew then that he was delighting in the pause, that he was relishing the time to reflect on what she had said.

'They ... they went to Mass, Inspector. Liline and Nénette. Liline, she was like Antoine in that she didn't believe the child either but would humour her all the same. They ... I know they visited the belfries of the Notre-Dame. Nénette, she confided this desire to me the other day. She . . . she has said she had to see where one of the schoolgirls had been murdered.'

Again he waited. Again she saw his priestlike silhouette against the ghostly light of darkness and snow, the sharp angularity and curvature of box and yew. 'Nénette was a pack rat, Inspector. A magpie. She was always picking things up—a button in the gutter or on the *métro*, a tooth-brush or pocket comb she would then sell on the black market, a pin, a badge, a medal, a toy . . . She had found something she said and was convinced the police, they were not looking hard enough.'

They always got it in the neck, the cops. The poor, the wealthy . . . all held the same antipathy, even children. But was it the fob of an ear-ring she had found? Had it belonged to the Notre-Dame victim, and had Madame Vernet yet to realize exactly where the rubbish in his pockets had come from?

She must have realized it by now, for both hands were deep in those pockets. 'Had she any other friends?' he asked cautiously.

'Friends?' she shrilled. 'Only Andrée from school. Inseparable, those two, and both picking their noses at the same time at the dinner table! *I* caught them. The . . . the poor child's mother is a disaster. Very wealthy, very pampered. The parents left her at the convent school for the holiday but . . . but at last reluctantly requested to see her. She took the train to Chamonix three days ago. Antoine had to help the child obtain a *laissez-passer*. Nénette was devastated when she discovered what he'd done, and cried for hours. *"Right when we were so close to trapping the Sandman!"* she said. She hated Antoine for doing it. *Hated* him who has done so much for her.'

The detective made no comment. He simply drew on that pipe of his, and when the bowl touched her left foot, she felt the warmth of it seep slowly into her.

'The *laissez-passer*, madame?' he asked quietly, and she knew then that she had best be careful with him, that too much said in a moment of grief could so easily be misunderstood.

'Antoine meets regularly with the Kommandant von Gross-

Paris, who is a frequent dinner guest. A call to General von Schaumburg was all that it took. Andrée got her pass and . . . and went off to see her parents.'

'So it was only Mademoiselle Chambert who accompanied your niece to the Notre-Dame?'

'Yes. Yes, of course. Why do you ask?'

Had there been alarm in her voice? he wondered. 'Ah, no reason but clarity, madame. Things are always hazy. One always has to brush the snow or the cobwebs away. I take it they went on from there to the Jardin d'Acclimatation?'

'Yes, to tea in the children's restaurant. *Tea!*'

He waited. She said, 'Forgive me. Nénette had forced herself into liking tea because it . . . it reminded her of her mother, not that the tea they serve in such places in any way resembles the real thing!'

The tears were interrupted. Having finished its nocturnal wanderings, the poodle, on seeing them, rejoiced. It tore across the fish-pond, slipped, went down hard, crashed into the edge, yelped, yapped and threw its dark shape at madame, who gathered it in and said *'Darling!'* only to drop the creature in horror and kick at it. *'Get away from me, you filthy little beast!'*

The dog's head was quizzically cocked to one side. The ears flopped. Pompon thought it a new game and dashed away, only to race back in and up again.

'We'd best go in,' she said, suffering the licking, the cold wet nose. 'You can see how lonely he is, how he is missing her. He'll have to be put down now. Maybe we can bury him with her—are such things possible?'

He really didn't know if under-the-coffin money would help, but reached far back into himself for a suitable answer, and said at last, 'Perhaps . . . but then . . . ah *mais alors, alors*, with murders, madame, the authorities can be so very difficult.'

One look at Antoine Vernet was enough to tell them they were dealing with fire. Tall and trim, he stood before them in the entrance hall with arms lightly folded across his chest, and the look he gave was not cold or angry at the flagrant intrusion upon his privacy but merely so calm he could just as well have been cutting throats at a board meeting.

The dark grey suit was immaculate. The black leather shoes, pale blue dress shirt and dark blue silk tie allowed nothing in excess. Even the gold signet ring on the little finger of the left hand and the wrist-watch dovetailed perfectly into the image of wealth and success.

The face was broad, the forehead high, the fine grey-white hair not parted but brushed straight back and perfectly trimmed. The burnish of a slight windburn suggested he had recently been outdoors on holiday—had he been skiing at Chamonix?

A banker, an industrialist—a man not just of money and power but one who, as with every new situation, had already assessed this one and leapt ahead to the successful conclusion he wanted.

The eyes were a North Sea blue, the lips compressed, the expression, though calm, the merest touch quizzical.

'Gentlemen, I see you have met my wife. Bernadette, *ma chère*, give the inspector his coat and go upstairs. You will be freezing.'

He was leaning slightly back against a magnificently gilded ebony Boulle commode, and the Savonnerie carpet of the marble staircase swept upwards behind him beneath a gorgeous Flemish tapestry that must date from the twelfth century.

Dutifully she set the dog down and handed the leash to Kohler, who took Louis's fedora as well, while the Sûreté politely removed the coat from her and shrugged himself back into it.

Her bare toes formed crimson islands in the tiny puddles the dog began voraciously to lick.

'Bernadette,' said Vernet, with a nod so slight she bowed her head and whispered, 'Yes, of course, Antoine. It's ... it's only that my heart is broken. I ... *Pompon, don't do that!* Ah, you naughty boy. My legs, my snuffie, my little forest—'

'My dear, we are waiting.'

'Madame, a moment,' cautioned the Sûreté, holding the flat

of a restraining hand up at the industrialist. 'Your face . . . the scratches.' Hermann had reined in the dog.

Hesitantly she touched the scratches. Inflamed, they ran from high on a prominent cheekbone right down the narrow face to the lower left jaw. There were four of them.

'I . . . I did it in anguish. I tore my hair, I slapped myself, too.' She turned her right cheek towards him. 'As I said, Inspector, I am so distressed. Nénette was . . . was very dear to me.'

If Vernet thought anything of it, he gave no indication. Was he content to let her hang herself? wondered St-Cyr. Things were certainly not quite right. She was tall, a brunette with a fine, high chin, nice lips, a sharp and very aquiline nose, but eyes . . . eyes that pleaded for understanding and said, from the depths of their moist brown irises, You warmed my feet. You listened to me. Please remember what I said.

A woman of thirty-five, a man of sixty-four.

A maid came to take the dog away. Vernet didn't even glance at her but the girl, pale and badly shaken by the death, instinctively felt the master was watching her and avoided looking up.

Bernadette Vernet took the stairs with dignity and only at the curve of the staircase let the peignoir fall to the carpet to expose bare arms and squared, fine shoulders, the nightdress of silk.

Hermann was impressed and St-Cyr could hear him giving her credit for a perfect exit. A handsome woman and proud of it, but not entirely a happy wife. Ah no.

'Gentlemen, please state your business.'

'Our business is murder, monsieur,' said St-Cyr, swiftly turning towards him. 'Perhaps you would be good enough to accompany me to the morgue. There is some question of identity. A simple glance from yourself should be enough.'

Not a flicker of unease registered. 'What do you mean, some question . . . ?'

Ah! was he a glacier? 'Please, that is best settled with the victim before us.'

'And your partner?' asked Vernet, still unruffled and giving the tiniest glance at Hermann.

One must be affable. 'Detective-Inspector Kohler will question the staff, with your permission. Nothing formal. There is the absence of Mademoiselle Chambert, you understand. We are concerned that . . .'

Still there was no sign of anything, not even the flash of a more quizzical smile as between men who know of such things as Vernet was now about to impart.

'The girl had taken a lover, Inspector. A fellow student. She often stayed out beyond the curfew, and for her sake as well as ours, I had advised her to remain where she was. It's normal, I understand, for people to do such things.'

Even the clubs and bars would close and lock their doors, keeping the patrons in until the curfew ended at 5.00 a.m. It was that or have them risk arrest with all its consequences.

'A lover,' said Kohler. The cap and wound badges in that kid's pockets, eh? 'Can you put a name to him?'

'Alas, I considered the matter private.'

'But she was the last to see the child alive, monsieur,' urged Louis. 'Surely you must realize how important it is for us to talk to her?'

General von Schaumburg had said nothing of these two detectives, nor had Gestapo Boemelburg. Had their silence been a warning in itself? wondered Vernet, and decided that it must have been. 'My chauffeur will have the address and perhaps the name. Deloitte occasionally dropped the girl off on the way.'

'I'll ask him, then, shall I?' shot Kohler.

'Yes, of course, Inspector. Now if you will excuse me a moment, I will get my hat and coat.'

'Ah, monsieur,' interjected Louis, 'could I ask that your driver take us to the morgue? Monsieur Deloitte can then fill me in on the way while Detective-Inspector Kohler talks to the rest of the staff.'

'Very well, if that is what you wish, but I must caution your assistant to limit his activities to the kitchens.'

'*Sein Assistent* . . . ?' blustered Kohler. 'Ah *Gott im Himmel, mein Herr, Gestapo Mueller ist mein Vetter!*' This was not true, of course.

'Herr Mueller's cousin or not,' said Vernet in unruffled French, 'you will confine yourself to the kitchens and leave the bedrooms of Mademoiselle Chambert and my niece alone until such time as the Kommandant von Gross-Paris decides a search warrant is necessary.'

Verdammt . . . !

'Inspectors, my only wish is for you to find the killer swiftly, but because of my position, I must insist all formalities be observed.'

Left to himself, Kohler pointed a stiffened forefinger at the housekeeper to rivet her into silence, and went up the stairs like a rocket to open the first door on his right and catch a breath. Ah *nom de Jésus-Christ*, what was this? A flea market? A sorcerer's enchantment?

Softly he closed the door behind him. The room was spacious but seemingly cluttered. It had been done in white, with white lace throws on the bed, but there was gold, too. Gold in gilt-framed mirrors and mirrored trumeaux that threw the winter's-night light from the windows back and forth, laying detail upon detail until the whole was repetition of shape and form and it took the breath away.

'Ah *merde*,' he said. 'This can't be the child's room. It must be Liline Chambert's.'

Not a thing was out of place. All had been set exactly where it should be to ensure the total effect. Tall, branching, Gothic wrought-iron standards held candles on either side of a fireplace whose mantelpiece had been removed, though the curved supports remained and now held matching bronze sculptures with single candles in them. Roosters perhaps—very modern in any case, and with their beaks turned back to peck at their tails and one leg lifted straight overhead like ballet dancers.

Ivory candelabra were draped with beads of clear crystal. A sculptress's three-legged stand held the curly-bearded, curly-headed grey plaster bust of an ancient seer who impassively looked on so that one saw his head from four or five angles and these views were superimposed on and mingled with those of a

Greek torso, beautifully hung, the waist, the hips, the genitals complete, the candles, too, and the white, white of old lace and of chair and bed.

There wasn't a sound. The staff downstairs would all be listening for him, yet he had not taken another step.

Draped across a beautifully carved walnut blanket box at the foot of the bed, there was a fine white woollen, short-sleeved dress, very Greek-looking, very stylish yet simple. Borders at the neck, hem and sleeves were of bands of grey-blue perhaps—the light wasn't very good. A mid-calf-length thing, he thought, making no noise at all crossing the floor. It was not the sort of dress to wear in the dead of winter, not when most places these days weren't heated.

Right below the neckline, caught in the light from the windows, there was a cheap brass curtain ring. Nothing else. Just that.

He paused. He picked the ring up and asked himself, Was she about to go off for a little tryst? Young couples did that sometimes, though there weren't too many young Frenchmen around these days. They took the curtain rings and wore them, fooling no one, least of all the *patron* of some hide-away *auberge* in the countryside.

A photograph showed a haunting image of her in a moment of reflection, holding a teacup in both hands. The dark hair was worn loose, down over the front of the right shoulder of the dress, the wide-brimmed hat made the look in her eyes so very tragic.

A kid of eighteen or so. Nice . . . really nice-looking. Had she lighted the candles before getting into bed to sit watching their reflections and those of the torso and the head? Did she play games in here, was that it, and was Nénette Vernet now with her? Just what the hell had the three of them been up to, the two girls and this one?

Try as he might, he could not help but feel uneasy.

As the chauffeur drove through the darkness and the softly falling snow, St-Cyr sat in silence. All down the Champs-Élysées, and then along the rue de Rivoli, there didn't appear to be another soul. The city's streets revealed only blue-washed pinpricks of light from isolated lamp standards that seemed to cry out, See what you have done to me, messieurs. Ended freedom, instilled deceit and fear, made cheats and liars out of honest citizens.

Those who did not have some petty fiddle were desperate. With ten degrees of frost there was no coal except in those places the Germans and their friends occupied. Having even one roomer from among the Occupier guaranteed an element of supply but engendered suspicion, jealousy and hatred from one's neighbours if they didn't have the same or better.

In a land of officially-sanctioned favouritism, denunciations were rife. But slowly an opposition was growing from within. Brother now hated brother, children now told tales on their parents, and not to the Occupier, to the Resistance. The bloodbath of retribution was gathering day by day. When it came, it would be terrible.

They had arrived at Place Mazas. 'The morgue is over there,' he said gruffly to the chauffeur. 'Near the river so that the drains can easily take the blood and things.'

'Inspector, are you attempting to unsettle me further?' asked Vernet who, having insisted upon it, had ridden alone in the back seat while he, a Chief Inspector of the Sûreté, had been told to sit up front.

'Monsieur, I am merely commenting on the practicality of our city fathers. The old morgue on the Île de la Cité was also close to the river. Corpses are always hosed down and often opened.'

'Surely my niece does not require an autopsy and an ice-cold douche?'

Ah, damn you, St-Cyr could hear him saying. 'That is for the coroner to decide, monsieur. I have asked for Belligueux. He's very reliable, exceedingly thorough, and always does exactly what he feels is needed, since he cannot possibly be bribed.'

Was it a warning? wondered Vernet and, giving an audible sigh, decided that it was but could not understand the reason for it. Not yet. Ah *merde* . . . 'I really do wish you would try to realize I am entirely on your side.'

A dismissive hand was tossed. 'Of course you are. You are her uncle, her guardian. You have taken over the business interests and fortune of her father.'

'My brother, Inspector.'

'Are you the older or the younger?'

'Meaning that the oldest nearly always inherits the estate? How cheap and utterly mediocre of you. Henri-Claude was a brilliant designer. Not that it is any of your business, my talents lie in finance and in bringing the interested parties together. It was decided he should inherit and lead the company and I graciously acquiesced to our father's wishes and agreed to remain its vice-chairman and chief adviser until my brother's unfortunate and untimely death. He was nearly fifteen years my junior.'

That little loss of promotion could not have gone down well, family rivalries being what they usually were, but . . . ah, but one would have to wait and see and hadn't the wife said he had been yanked out of semi-retirement and put to work on the death of his brother? 'Why didn't they take your niece with them to England? To leave without her at such a time of crisis seems most callous.'

Just *what* had Bernadette said to this one to make him so suspicious? wondered Vernet. Damn her for meddling. 'All civilian flights had long since been cancelled, so they had to have permission from the military. Children were, of course, not allowed. The danger was simply too great, things far too tense. My sister-in-law's mother was gravely ill and not expected to last, but, yes, compassion would never have swayed the minds of our military. My brother went over to try to calm the British. We were, alas, convinced the Führer would never attack. They flew over on the twentieth of April, 1940, planning only the briefest of visits, but one thing led to another and they soon found it impossible to return.'

Norway had fallen to the Germans, Denmark's army had been demobilized. The Blitzkrieg in the West had been about to begin . . . 'A designer of what, exactly?'

'You know I cannot tell you that. Why, then, do you ask if not to further upset me? Impatiently Vernet indicated the morgue where only one lonely goosenecked lamp produced a paltry wash of blue. 'This place is closed.'

'Death never stops. Invariably the small hours of the night are the busiest. Monsieur,' he said to the chauffeur, 'please inform the Feldwebel on patrol that he has only to check with me if he questions your being out after curfew. Or is it that your employer has clearance?'

'He has,' said Deloitte flatly.

'Good, then there is absolutely no problem.'

The floor was wet, the drainboard pallets shrouded except where an attendant was sewing up a full-length incision while another, a damp cigarette butt clinging to his lower lip, prepared a female for burial and was scrubbing her down before hosing her off a last time.

Talbotte, the préfet, must have warned everyone to cooperate. Without hassle they were taken straight through to the storage lockers at the back where the appropriate drawer was pulled out.

'Death also is the great leveller, Inspector,' said Vernet, exhibiting a humanity so hidden it surprised. 'Of late Nénette had become very fond of the *ancien* Cimetière de Neuilly. Liline ... Mademoiselle Chambert often found her there among the Jewish graves, of all places, consoling the spirits of the departed. The child used to say it was the quietest place on earth next to the Bibliothèque Nationale, but I wonder if she would say it now? *Mon Dieu*, I hate to think of what has happened. My brother and his wife ... Now the three of them gone, and who is to carry on when I join them? Everything will pass into other hands to be broken up and sold. An empire.'

Was there no thought of Vernet's producing an heir of his own? wondered St-Cyr. Were such things so out of the question with his wife? 'Monsieur, I could give you a moment alone before uncovering her, if you wish?'

'No. No, I'm quite all right. Let's get it over with. Then there will be absolutely no question of identity.'

Ah! it was so hard to gauge him. His expression was grave, but would Vernet really regret the loss of his niece, since he would then most probably inherit everything? Would the mistake in identity cause him to panic?

The attendant stood ready. 'Leave us,' said St-Cyr with a curt toss of his head. 'Wait in the outer office.'

'Inspector, what is this?' demanded Vernet.

'A moment,' came the hushed command, as they watched the attendant reluctantly depart. The préfet would be furious with the man for not having listened in. Too bad.

'Inspector, am I some sort of suspect?'

Vernet had removed the wide-brimmed, dark grey velour trilby some well-placed Berliner must have presented to him. He stood immaculate in his Hermès grey-blue scarf, overcoat and black kidskin gloves, and the years of dealing with such people at more than infrequent intervals came tumbling in on St-Cyr, telling him not to judge too harshly, that wealth and power were not always corrupt. 'If you have anything to hide, monsieur, might I suggest you tell me of it now. Things are not quite right with this one, and that is why I have asked for privacy.'

'Then remove the shroud at once, *idiot!*'

'Of course.'

A breath was sucked in. The voice was blunt. 'That's not her. That is her friend from school. Now do you mind telling me just how such a mistake could have been made? I'll make you sweat for this. I'll have your badge.'

'Perhaps, but then . . . ah then, monsieur, perhaps it is that you can offer some explanation for the change your niece and this one made in their identity papers.'

'Pardon?'

Was it such a surprise? 'The photograph . . .' St-Cyr handed the papers over. Vernet looked from them to the child several times and at last swore under his breath. 'The silly little bitches. What the hell did they think they were playing at? Trapping this Sandman? Was that it, Inspector? The knitting needle, the . . .'

He thrust the papers back and turned away to hide his discomposure. 'Not dead,' he murmured. '*Not dead!*' And then, loudly, '*Bâtards!* You *flics* . . .' He turned, a fist clenched. 'How *dare* you do this to me? To *me*?'

And now, monsieur, is that the moisture of perplexity and remorse in your eyes, wondered St-Cyr, or that of relief and concern for your niece?

Vernet tossed the hand with the fedora in defeat. 'I had to put a stop to Nénette's nonsense. That is why I obtained a *laissez-passer* for this one to go to Chamonix to join her parents. I could not have my niece making such preposterous claims and saying she knew who the Sandman was and that if I did not summon the préfet to speak to her alone and at once, she would take the matter into her own hands.'

A stubborn child. The préfet no less and at once, and in private. 'And do you still believe she spoke nonsense?'

'How dare you ask me that? Would you humiliate me further? She's dead. Look at her yourself. A child. Innocence left to languish with the sisters while her . . . her no-good parents partied at Chamonix. Ah, damn that stupid, stupid mother of hers. I shall have to see that the couple are notified. There will have to be a funeral. As few as possible—we can't have the press getting wind of this. Those vultures would only feast on the carrion.'

'A funeral—yes, yes, of course, but burial where? In the *ancien* Cimetière de Neuilly?'

Vernet threw him a startled, questioning look. 'Burial wherever her parents choose. It's customary.'

He was still visibly shaken by the mistake in identity, but even as they looked at each other, St-Cyr could see the mask begin to descend.

'And what about your niece, monsieur? Is there anything you can tell us?'

Caution entered. 'Only that you had best find her before it is too late. I need not remind you, Inspector, that police bungling cannot possibly sit well with the Kommandant von Gross-Paris.'

'Then let us pay Mademoiselle Chambert and her lover a little visit. Perhaps it is that she can clear the matter up.'

'Liline . . . ? Ah! yes. Yes, of course. I had forgotten. The flat is in Montparnasse, on the rue d'Assas. Number eighty-four. The fifth floor, apartment two, facing the street. We will have to awaken the concierge, but fortunately that one is a light sleeper.'

Good, nodded St-Cyr inwardly. Your response is just as I have suspected. It is not only your chauffeur who knows of the address. The death here has rattled you.

A cube of sponge, a tangled white thread, a hope, a prayer, a silk chemise no student with a part-time job could ever have purchased. Not at any time and certainly not on the black market.

Kohler let the dried cube of self-preservation dangle from its braided umbilical cord. He saw himself in the mirrors starkly juxtaposed with the plaster head of the seer and the torso, grey on white and white on gold, the single candle he had lighted in contravention of the black-out regulations fluttering in some sudden draught.

When he found the address, it was on a folded scrap of paper tucked into the toe of a brown leather pump—memorized, since people could not walk around with such things in their pockets for fear of arrest.

'Forty-seven quai du Président Paul Doumer, room thirteen, Sunday at two p.m.,' he breathed, and in that one breath was all of a detective's dismay, a hope, a prayer of its own.

'Inspector, what is the meaning of this? Surely my husband gave permission for no such thing?'

Madame Vernet stood framed in the doorway and he saw her in the girl's mirrors, tall and statuesque, her dark brown hair a thick mop of curls, the image of her impinging on and overlapping the others, his own included.

Spaghetti straps held the full-length nightdress up. Laces criss-crossed the chest, leaving gaps between and glimpses of lots of cleavage. The scratches had been treated with iodine. 'Madame, we have five murders and the disappearance of this one. Was Mademoiselle Chambert pregnant?'

'Pardon? Surely you're not . . .'

'Look, I'll put it to you straight. Did she go to see a maker of little angels?'

'An abortionist . . . ? But . . . but *why*? Liline gave us no cause to think such a thing. She was distressed. Yes, of course. She and Nénette were very close about things but we . . . we just thought it was this . . . this business of the Sandman and that she was worried about Nénette taking it far too seriously.'

'Then why an assignation in a room in a flea-bitten tenement across the river in Courbevoie? Why something within easy walking distance of the Jardin d'Acclimatation? She was supposed to be with your niece, having tea. Your chauffeur had dropped them off after their climb up into the belfries of the Notre-Dame.'

'Exercise . . . Ah *merde*, I . . . Ah no, no, you must be mistaken.'

'Exercise before an abortion, eh?'

Damn him! 'Liline is too pure. A virgin. A sculptress—these things are her own. She studies and perfects. But a man, a lover . . . Please don't be so foolish. The boy she has been seeing will not have slept with her. This I can assure you.'

'Good. Then what about your husband?'

'Antoine . . . ? With Liline . . . ? Oh *mon Dieu*, you're serious. He's like a father to her. No, it's impossible. He's far too astute. I would have got wind of it. The girl would have been out on her ear.'

'Then tell me why she laid out that dress and dropped a curtain ring on it.'

'What dress?' She arched, quivering.

Moving swiftly across the room, she came to the foot of the bed. She felt the wool. She dropped it and grated, 'Antoine, you bastard. I didn't know. I *didn't*!'

'He was fucking her, wasn't he?' said Kohler harshly. 'That husband of yours had made her pregnant. A houseguest, eh? A visitor and companion to your niece? A girl in his care.'

She tore her hair and slapped herself in anguish, could not turn to face him but held her mouth to stop herself from vomiting and said, 'Sweet Jesus, what am I to do?'

It was now nearly 4.30 a.m. and St-Cyr was anxious. Painstakingly the burly Feldwebel with the Schmeisser shone his torch over the permit, billowing fifteen degrees of frost while his men, armed with Mauser rifles, inspected the black-out tape on the headlamps or stood about and coughed.

A pug-nosed, wart-faced Pomeranian dockworker with sad, boozer's eyes that looked so lifeless in the fringe of the torch-light, the sergeant grunted dispassionately, 'You are out when you shouldn't be.'

Ah *merde*, he couldn't read French! 'Mein Herr . . .' began St-Cyr, only to feel the touch of Vernet's hand on his shoulder.

'Herr Hauptmann, I realize it is late and you and your men have had a long and miserable night. We are on a little business for the Kommandant von Gross-Paris, yes? The matter is discreet, you understand. My permit, you will see, is stamped and signed by the General von Schaumburg himself, a personal friend. We will only be a few minutes and then we will be gone, so you need not make a note of the visit.'

Vernet's *Deutsch* hadn't just been flawless, he had used Low German so as not to distance himself too much.

'It is highly irregular, *mein Herr*,' grunted the Feldwebel.

'Yes, yes, I know, but these things, they can be so delicate. Honoré, my good man, is there not a little something we could offer the captain for his trouble?'

As if on cue, Deloitte found a bottle of brandy in the map pocket of the door next to himself.

'Warm yourselves,' enthused Vernet. 'Yours is not an easy but a most essential task.' Perhaps five thousand francs were handed over. 'Coffee and croissants for the boys and a little something for yourself.'

Perhaps another ten thousand francs changed hands, the torch going out so swiftly the men on patrol knew they would get only a taste of the bottle. But that was something more than they usually got, and the night was indeed cold.

They moved off, the sound of their jackboots and hobnails squeaking painfully in the snow.

'There, that's done,' sighed Vernet. 'Now let us find the flat.'

Only then did St-Cyr realize Vernet and his driver had known exactly where to intercept the patrol at 4.30 a.m. At a snail's pace Deloitte followed the patrol until, at last, he was able to turn on to the rue d'Assas unencumbered.

Awakened, the concierge, a portly, pasty-faced man of sixty in shawl, blanket and nightshirt over his everyday clothes, deferentially ducked his head and sleepily mumbled, 'Monsieur,' before retreating to his cage. Again largesse was spread, Vernet taking another five thousand francs from his wallet to set them on the counter.

As if by magic, the bills vanished and the slot was silently closed to leave them alone in the corridor under a forty-watt electric light bulb that would soon be switched off out of frugality.

A frequent visitor, ah yes, and well known to the concierge.

'Inspector,' confided Vernet as they took the lift and the night was filled with the sounds of it. 'Inspector, these things . . .' he said of the girl. 'You do understand.'

'Of course.'

Letting himself into the flat, Vernet first closed the curtains before switching on a light. The sitting room was a tasteful jumble from the twenties, the bedroom hadn't been slept in and there was no sign of anyone.

'So?' said the Sûreté, giving him the open-handed gesture of It's-your-turn again.

'The boy is usually here,' said Vernet, not liking it. 'Liline . . .'

He went over to an armoire to search it. He opened another in the narrow hallway and went through to the kitchen to stand in its emptiness and say, 'They've left. They've cleared out. The boy is a homosexual she had befriended. He was afraid of the *Relève*, of what our friends are going to do in February. Turn it into the *Service de Travail Obligatoire*, the forced labour in the Reich. She must have told him his name was bound to come up, so he buggered off.'

'And the girl, monsieur?'

'Liline must have gone with him. His rucksack, it's missing. Look, he was too timid for his own good. Though she didn't live here, she was always having to put the muscle into him. They'll have gone south like so many these days. He'll try to join the maquis of the Auvergne perhaps. Liline has relatives in Clermont-Ferrand.'

Ah yes, the maquis was growing and its young and not so young men were living in the wilds as fugitives, supplied by some and hated by others. A Resistance without arms unless stolen from the Occupier. But what about suitable *laissez-passer*, eh, and was Vernet so desperate he would fabricate? 'Monsieur, if the boy was in danger of this . . . this new *Service*, surely with your contacts you could have found a way of keeping him in Paris?'

'Don't be silly. I was fucking Liline. Would you have had me broadcast that little piece of information by placing his name on one of my lists of those who are to remain in France?'

The SS and the Gestapo would have known of the affair in any case and perhaps that, really, was why he had done nothing.

'Now we had best find Nénette, Inspector, or is it that you still want more from me about this?'

'No. For the moment we have sufficient, but I must ask, is Madame Vernet aware Mademoiselle Chambert is your mistress?'

'Bernadette? Of course not.'

'And Mademoiselle Chambert, monsieur, what of her? Did she come to you willingly or did you—'

'How dare you?'

'I dare because I have at the moment two lives to concern me. That of your mistress and that of your niece.'

Kohler followed Madame Vernet into the child's room, which was in a far corner of the house next to the staircase to the servants' quarters and the kitchens. He noted the amber and gold dragonflies on the stained-glass shade of the lamp she had switched on, the porcelain frog below it with walking stick, orange waistcoat, silk scarf and cream knitted trousers and silver-buckled shoes.

Above the mantelpiece there was a Meissen clock in white and gilded porcelain with a turbaned potentate riding atop the clock face, which rested on the back of an elephant. The bed was superb, a Louis XV canopied affair whose gold brocade rose to ostrich plumes at all four corners.

'This was her room. Nénette loved it. She used to say having privacy was next to being with God.'

There were more tears, more tearing of the hair and tugging at the laces across the chest of her nightdress. It was bad enough her niece being murdered by the Sandman, but to have her husband fooling around right under her nose was too much. Ah yes.

She broke down completely and he let her weep in a chair, didn't give her another thought. Christ, what had the kid discovered? A map of the city gave the locations of every one of the killings. Press clippings had been pinned to it. The tenement in Aubervilliers, the one near the Terrot bicycle works in Suresnes, the murders in les Halles and in the Notre-Dame . . .

Even the Jardin d'Acclimatation had been noted. *This one is next. Sunday afternoon, 10 January. I am certain of it.*

Bang on. Ah *merde* . . .

A Louis-Philippe *secrétaire* held pigeonholes and drawers the kid had stuffed and locked, some of them. School exercise books—French composition, Latin, Greek, religious studies, the catechism, et cetera, et cetera, and then . . . then, as he flipped quickly through them, a scribbled note. *Sister Céline hates us. We are the cabbages she feeds to her pigs after first giving them the names of each of us. We are her droppings.*

Trash overflowed the child's waste-paper basket. Things picked up in the gutters and on the *métro* filled several drawers. Where . . . where the hell to begin?

Using her letter-opener, he jammed it into the gap near the lock of the pencil drawer and snapped the blade in haste.

The pocket-knife the Kaiser had given him and countless others in 1914 did the task and the drawer popped open. No pencils. A simple crucifix of black wrought iron with the Christ pinned up by nails stared back at him, looking so like the top of a coffin, nestled as it was in that long, thin drawer, he had to wonder at the careful placing of it. The thing was heavy and about eight centimetres in length by four in width at the arms.

Beside it there was a Number Four knitting needle of grey steel, flexible and yet stiff.

He sucked in a breath. He felt the tremors within himself, heard the sobbing of Madame Vernet behind him.

Louis, he said to himself of the knitting needle. Louis, I think I need you here.

'Madame,' he said.

Tears streaked her cheeks. Blood ran from reopened scratches he was certain the poodle had never inflicted. 'Madame, would your niece have sought refuge with the sisters?'

'Sought refuge . . . ? But she's *dead*? He killed her. He used one of those to . . .'

She threw up, coughed, bent double and vomited again before hurrying from the room to stagger in the hall and turn. 'Dead . . . She *is* dead, isn't she? It was her, wasn't it?'

Ah *merde* . . . Sadly he shook his head and watched as she crumpled to the floor. Out like a light.

3 Two hours before dawn they shared a cigarette in the darkness of the Bois de Boulogne while they waited to make their first report to von Schaumburg. The clay-pigeon shoot was just to their left, the riding stables were very near.

'Louis, this thing, it looks worse and worse. We're to believe this latest killing was the work of the Sandman, but was it? Those two girls *knew* Nénette would be followed. They *planned* what they did.'

Hermann was really worried. 'Andrée Noireau was to have left the city on Thursday ... Madame Vernet has said she believed the child had done so, but was that woman deliberately taken in by her niece?'

'She must have been. She fainted at the news Nénette hadn't been killed. She expected the child to have been alone.'

'And Vernet claims his wife didn't know of the affair he was having...'

Kohler took the cigarette from him. 'But she must have, since she told me the boy at the flat could not have been having sex with Mademoiselle Chambert.'

It would have to be asked. 'Has the student-sculptress really gone south to take that boy to the Auvergne?'

'Or did she leave, as I think she did, to have an abortion while the other two were in the Bois, and if so, where the hell is she now?'

Oh-oh. Ah, it was not good and there was so little time. They had to find the heiress and quickly, they had to find this other girl, this 'companion', but what, please, would they find? More corpses, the clothing not just . . .

'Louis, that kid even stated, "This one is next. Sunday afternoon." She wrote it on that bulletin board she keeps in her room. She's got all the locations of the Sandman's killings marked.'

'Yet the crucifix and the knitting needle, they are locked away?'

'From prying eyes. The aunt's, if you ask me.'

'A Sister Céline . . .'

'That nun can't possible be the Sandman. Hey, she doesn't have the necessary physical equipment, idiot! *Verdammt*, use your head. We're going to really need it this time!'

'Then why lock those things away? Why try to keep them from the aunt?'

Louis was always asking difficult questions. 'A schoolgirl's world is very small. The nuns would have figured prominently in it,' offered Kohler lamely.

'Could Madame Vernet have gained access to that pencil drawer?'

Ah damn. 'I don't know. I wish I did.'

Well up in his sixties and nearing retirement, General von Schaumburg took his daily ride on horseback in the Bois near which he lived. Perhaps it toned him up and got the blood circulating, thought Kohler, but ah *merde*, he was too like something out of the last war. Tall and mighty and armoured in greatcoat and cap, the General sat astride his favourite gelding and let the horse blow twenty degrees of frost. A giant needing only a spiked helmet.

The blue-shaded railway lantern that hung from the pommel gave but a paltry light. The frigid air brought panic thoughts of mustard gas. There was even a ground fog to help things along.

'Kohler, *what* are you doing with my pigeons?'

He had forgotten all about them. 'They're doves, General. White doves—at least, they were.'

'*Verdammt!* don't back-talk me, Corporal.'

'It was captain, General. A Hauptmann.'

Oh-oh . . . 'General, you were . . .' began St-Cyr, only to hear the riding crop cut the air as it was raised. He continued anyway. 'General, the child was not the Vernets' niece but another. A case of mistaken identity and overanxious police. Nénette Vernet may well be a hostage of the Sandman, or dead. This we really do not know, for she and another friend are missing. But we must know, General, if you saw anything at all that might assist our enquiries.'

'*Mistaken identity? Overanxious police? Gott im Himmel,* Kohler, what is this one saying?'

'That préfet Talbotte and the Paris police need a damned good housecleaning, General. The *flics* glanced at the victim's ID photograph and made a mistake that should never have been made.'

'*False papers?*'

This was only getting worse. 'A simple switch, General,' interjected St-Cyr, wishing immediately that he hadn't done so.

The riding crop cut the frost as it was lowered. Snorting, the horse fidgeted nervously. '*Explain yourself.*' The French, thought von Schaumburg. St-Cyr . . . A pretty wife with carnal urges and films clandestinely taken of her fornications with Hauptmann Steiner, a favoured nephew of his own and an embarrassment. The Gestapo's Watchers were apparently still enjoying the films in spite of orders to destroy them. The pigs.

Right in the middle of his thoughts, von Schaumburg muttered, 'I sent Steiner to Stalingrad, St-Cyr, and now must bear the grief of his young wife and mother, which in no way excuses the disgrace our Erich brought to his family. Kohler, you have lost your sons. My condolences. War is never easy and always strikes the heart. Gentlemen, I saw nothing of this matter. I heard nothing. I was shooting. Ask that imbecile gamekeeper. If he had moved himself faster, I would have been gone from the area before the murder happened.'

All thought of Marianne and Hauptmann Steiner must be set aside. 'But you weren't, General,' said St-Cyr, taking hold of the bridle. 'The gamekeeper claims to have seen someone in a black or dark blue overcoat just before you took the last of your pigeons.'

'*There*, you see, Kohler? *Pigeons, Dummkopf!* A dark overcoat—a nun perhaps? Is this what he saw?'

For now it would be wisest not to mention the wound badges, the Polish Campaign medal and the SS connection. 'Not a nun, General. Apparently the sport-shooting has frightened away the good sisters from this part of the Bois.'

'The Sandman?' Again the horse fidgeted.

'Perhaps. Please try to remember, General. The child was being followed and ran into the cage to hide. Her coat was dark blue, but—'

'But . . . but that is exactly what the gamekeeper saw! The child.'

It would do no good to argue. As it was, they had got him talking, not ordering them around. Here was the man who issued the decrees that were posted and also published in all newspapers: *For acts of terrorism on_____and_____, the following hostages have been shot.*

Here was the man under whose authority fell the receipt of five million francs a day, the recently reassessed cost of the Occupation, since the country was now too poor to pay more. It was bad enough having to put up with the Germans, but having to pay for the privilege was far too much to bear, though nothing could be said of such things. Not yet. Not until the war ended, as it surely must someday to throw the country into an anarchy of a different kind. A totally French kind.

'Kohler, what have you to report?'

The birds were handed over and hooked to the pommel. Quickly Kohler went through the briefest run-down, ending with, 'Our investigation must first concentrate on finding the two missing girls, General. Perhaps they are together. If not, then perhaps Mademoiselle Chambert can tell us where the heiress is.'

'And the Sandman?'

'We'll get him. We won't stop until we do.'

'Good. Anything you need is yours. The full backing of the Kommandantur. Extra men, supplies, communications and money, but not beyond reason and fully accounted for. Do not hesitate to ask. Indeed, I will see that a carte blanche is issued. Use it.'

A cup of coffee—the real thing—would do about now, a nice warm boiled egg with a knitted cap to keep it hot and cosy in the hands, a slice of ham . . . 'We'll remember that, General, but right now we need transport to our garage so that we can pick up our car.'

'My driver will assist you. How is Vernet taking it?'

'As well as can be expected. Relieved, of course, but . . . Doubtless he'll fill you in.' And so much for searching rooms without permission.

'And his wife?'

'Not well at all, General.'

That massive head was nodded sagely. The horse's mane was patted. 'Discretion, Kohler. Keep my name out of it.'

'*Jawohl, mein General. Heil Hitler.*'

'Don't be an imbecile. Just see that it's kept quiet. I'll try to recall the afternoon. If there is anything, I will let you know.'

At a brisk canter, the General departed and they watched as his lamp winked in the night until the trees of the nearby wood finally hid him from view. Again it was so like that other war. Hermann was visibly shaken and could not speak for some time until at last he said, 'Chez Rudi's, Louis. Even detectives can't keep running on empty stomachs and Messerschmitt Benzedrine. You did take yours, didn't you?' And then, 'He made me think of the trenches. I was right back in the mud and shit hearing your shells whistling overhead and praying some son of a bitch like that wouldn't come along to order us over the top.'

'Me, too. I understand.'

'I've got to call Giselle and Oona. I've got to tell them we're back in the city. I'll do it from the restaurant.'

And I? asked St-Cyr inwardly. With only an empty house and no wife or little son, the phone could ring all it wanted.

I must get those films of her from the Gestapo, he said to himself. I must destroy them so as to let her rest in peace.

'I'll do it for you, Louis. I swear it,' said Kohler, not even having to be told. 'Now, come on, Chief. Let's find that driver and get us our set of wheels. Hey, I might even let you drive your own car!'

Chez Rudi's, a legend in its time, was on the Champs-Élysées and right across from the Lido. Beer-hall big and spotless, it was all but empty at this ungodly hour but would soon fill to overflowing.

Kohler chose a table to one side where Louis could watch that great big, beautiful Citroën *traction avant* the Sûreté had assigned him in 1938 and the Gestapo had taken away—well, almost—in 1940. He dragged over another chair and peeled off overcoat, scarf and hat, no gloves.

Blowing on his hands, he waved and waited. Rudi Sturmbacher's youngest sister, Helga, was on duty but had just finished making a heavy night of it and took her time. One blonde braid refused to be tied. There was gravel under her puffy eyelids. The pale blue workdress was so incompletely buttoned large glimpses of her ample bosom, unhindered by any Bavarian or French *soutien-gorge* of starched cotton and elastic or otherwise, were offered as she ground herself into an upper corner of Hermann's chair. Ah *merde*, thought St-Cyr. Like so many of the Occupier who dreamed of living like God in France, she had also come to Paris to find a man, but at the age of twenty-eight had discovered that sex was one thing, love quite another, and that war gave traffic only to such affairs.

'Well, *mein Schatz* [my treasure],' she croaked sharply at Hermann, 'what can we do for you at this hour?'

Kohler wrapped a giant's arm about her chunky hips and grinned up at her. 'It's a little too early for that, eh, Helga? But ... two boiled eggs, a pail of black coffee, three fried slices of that ham of Rudi's to remind me of home, melted cheese on top, brown bread, butter and none of that lousy approximate jam our French friends are so fond of but Rudi would never let within a kilometre of his establishment.'

She squirmed a little under his arm. She wished Hermann would really notice her. Approximate jam ... the fake stuff the French had to eat if they could get it. 'And for him?' she asked, testily motioning with her pad and pencil.

'He'll have the usual. Two hot croissants, *café au lait* with real milk, and the plum jam with real sugar just to tell him we still make it the same old way back home and that all this talk of shortages in the Reich is merely lies, right?'

There was no thought of ration tickets here, an embarrassment that always caused Louis to edgily watch the street lest others be looking in. Others of the Resistance, ah yes.

'Fräulein Sturmbacher, I will have the same as Hermann, please,' he said in German that was really very good. 'The gooseberry conserve if possible, as it is even more Bavarian to me and more piquant than the plum. We may not eat again for twenty-four hours, and here the food, it is always cooked to perfection and superb.'

'*Flattery will get you nowhere, pig!*' she hissed, tearing herself away from Hermann's arm. 'I really wish you two would agree *before* you dare to come in here. Now look what you've made me do!'

She tore off the page and, crumpling it, threw it at Louis. 'French bastards!' she shrilled. 'You ought to shoot him, Hermann. How—how can you *dare* to work with the likes of him?'

Ah *merde*, what was this? wondered Kohler. Certainly more than a broken love affair, more than a last night before the latest boyfriend was shipped back to the front, leaving only promises.

In tears, she blurted, 'If we have to feed him, let him eat in the courtyard.'

Kohler caught her by the arm. A button burst and then another. 'Helga . . . Helga, *Liebchen*, what is it? The defeat at Stalingrad?'

She nodded, and when he pulled her on to his lap, she buried her face against his neck and wept uncontrollably. 'The . . . the Wehrmacht are turning the air-raid shelters into machine-gun posts, my Hermann. The ones on the avenue Kléber, the esplanade des Invalides, here, too, along the Champs-Élysées. They . . . they are even going to cancel the horse-races at Longchamp this year and move them outside the city to Le Tremblay. Rudi . . . Rudi is asking them to put snipers on the roof in . . . in case of . . .'

She couldn't say it, and when Hermann did manage, 'A French revolt,' she straightened up to fondly touch the slash down his left cheek and let a shudder pass through her.

'General von Schaumburg and the others fear an uprising. They are preparing for . . . for the worst.'

Verdammt!

Even when their breakfasts came, there was still no sign of Rudi Sturmbacher, the Nazi Brown Shirt from Munich and great lover of gossip who, at 166 kilos, smouldered in his kitchens. Rudi had carved swastikas into the melted Gruyère that lay atop Louis's Black Forest ham.

An uprising . . . a citizens' revolt . . . Poor Louis stared at that hated symbol as Helga expectantly waited and watched.

Reaching across the table, Kohler took the plate and said, 'Hey, you've got mine, Chief. I said I wanted the gooseberry, right, Helga? He wants the plum.'

They ate in silence as the SS regulars and others of the Occupier filtered in with their copies of *Pariser Zeitung* or the previous Saturday evening's *Der Angriff* straight from Berlin and hot off the first Ju 52 of the day. They watched as workmen unloaded a Telefunken wireless set, lifted from a Rothschild villa perhaps, and set it up against the wall.

It was not yet 0800 hours Berlin Time and the city was still gripped in darkness, frost and, yes, distrust and fear.

'Come on, Louis, we've got work to do.'

'Don't they care that we have murders to solve and that the Sandman is out there somewhere? Don't they give a damn that a child and a girl of eighteen need desperately to be found before it's too late?'

'Of course they care. It's only a matter of priorities.'

'Then put on these gloves before that SS major notices I have relieved him of them. I hope they fit!'

They did. 'Hey, you're learning.' Kohler grinned. '*Das ist gut, mein Herr.* Stick with me, and your fortune will be made.'

'*Sicherlich! Dummkopf. Sicherlich!*' (I'll bet!)

Soot, garbage and clanking donkey engines gave to the port alongside the quai du Président Paul-Doumer the air of a busy place, but in truth, most of the river barges had been taken in the fall of 1940 for an invasion of England that had never happened and few had returned. Life on the river had gone on, ah yes, of course, but would it ever be the same? Impossible.

A mattress floated by, grey and ugly in the midst of the ice floes and rafting its crew of three terrified rats. A wooden crate was next, then a jersey, a man's perhaps, but one so encumbered by encircling sewage it remained afloat only because of the gas bubbles and the condoms.

The house at Number 47 rose five storeys to shroud its broken-shuttered attic dormers and hide unfriendly slates and moth-eaten copper sheathing. Liline Chambert had had an assignation here at 2.00 p.m. yesterday. It was hardly the place for an innocent girl of eighteen from the provinces to venture alone. She must have been desperate.

'Hermann, talk to the concierge. Leave the room to me.'

Though officially illegal and subjecting those involved not just to prison but to the threat of the guillotine, abortions could be obtained if one had the right connections and knew of a doctor and his clinic or hospital, but this . . .

'The place bears every attribute of housing a clandestine abortionist, said St-Cyr bluntly.

'Then I'll kick the door in and scare the hell out of the concierge.'

It would do no good to argue. 'Please announce our presence.'

The glass shattered, the wood splintered. The door banged back and forth to screams and cries from within and then silence as they took the stairs.

'Kohler, Gestapo Paris-Central, to see the occupants of Room thirteen.'

Death would have a better voice, thought the woman. A giant . . .

Kohler swept his eyes about the cage. Her teeth were still in their foggy glass beside the armchair, leaking stuffing. Her cheeks were sucked in, the faded blue eyes watered instantly. 'Messieurs . . . ?' she began, still concentrating on him as he reached over her head to pluck the ring of keys from their hook and hand it to his friend.

'Sit down, madame. Just a few questions to start your day off. See that they're answered truthfully. Otherwise you'll spoil mine. *Right?*'

Yvette Grégoire crossed herself and wet her hairy lips in uncertainty. He was formidable, this one. Had she the courage to face up to him? 'The magistrate's order, monsieur.' She snapped her ringless fingers. '*Vite, vite.*' Hurry, hurry.

Hers had been a life of strife, penury and little joy, but he couldn't let sympathy interfere. 'You should have been a magistrate yourself, madame, but don't be silly.' He leaned a hand on a well-padded shoulder. 'Sit down. It may be the last time you ever do.'

Kohler found two U-boat cigarettes and lit up, then placed one between her lips. 'Now start talking. The girl in this photograph came here yesterday.'

Quickly her chest was crossed, her eyes refusing to avert themselves but staring up at him as if he had just come back from the dead.

'Look, my partner's difficult, madame. He has a thing about hatchet abortions. You may pray if you like, but if that girl is dead from shock or anything else, he'll be demanding the guillotine for you.'

'I did not see anything! I was taken to the public baths.'

This was a new one. 'Explain yourself.'

Gestapo . . . he's Gestapo, she cried inwardly and winced. 'Once a month, on a Sunday, it is my practice to wash and tidy myself.'

He grinned but it was not a nice grin. He reached for her register and began to peruse it.

'Monsieur . . .'

'It's Inspector. You stink too much to have just had a bath, and don't try to tell me it's the fault of a miserable cube of that gravelly ersatz "National Soap" they make out of ground horse chestnuts and lye.'

'Inspector, the . . . the regular tenant was away in the north on business, so I . . . I have rented the room briefly to . . . to a Madame Proulx. A very suitable tenant. No trouble. Very quiet. A sweet lady in her middle years, a professional woman. Her . . .'

He was still not listening. Did he always doubt? 'Her brother came to see her yesterday, and . . . and together they left the premises at . . .' She indicated the register. 'At four-thirty in the . . . the afternoon. Her . . . her son had been taken ill.'

'The brother came.'

'Yes. A priest. A man of the cloth.'

'His age?'

'About sixty perhaps. The sad blue eyes, the greying temples, the high forehead and . . .'

Kohler flicked ash from the cigarette he had given her. 'Tell me something, Madame . . . ? Grégoire, wasn't it? Yes, yes, that was it. I never forget a name and it's on your licence right up there.'

He ripped the licence down and stuffed it into a pocket, thus putting her right out of business until she could get another. 'Now look, I told you not to lie to me, so how is it that you know they left when you've just said you were at the public baths?'

'Because I had returned before then. It does not take an old woman hours to have a bath, only the half-hour, since one has to pay for it and one is not allowed to have company even though one might still desire such a thing now and then.'

A tough one. 'And the girl?' he asked.

Dear Jesus save her now. 'Still in . . . in the room. That . . . that one, she has not come out. "She's resting," the good father said. "Resting."'

A priest . . . a black over coat . . . and a maker of little angels.

Alone, St-Cyr clenched a fist. Noise from the docks filtered into the shabby room on whose plain iron bed and rumpled sheets Liline Chambert lay with fists tightly clenched on her upper chest. The woollen dress and cotton slip were hiked just above her middle, the underpants were nowhere to be seen. Her black lisle-stockinged legs were spread slackly, revealing a slash of dark brown pubic hair and a large stain. And damn Maréchal Pétain and his bigoted, hypocritical government in Vichy that allowed things like this to happen so that the youth of the country could be replaced no matter the cost.

A squeeze-bulb syringe and nozzle long enough to penetrate the cervix lay with dirty rubber tubing on the floor beside two chipped enamel bowls of soapy, filthy water.

The abortion had failed. Air had entered her bloodstream to block its circulation, causing instantaneous death. One moment the girl had been alive and apprehensively feeling that thing going inside her as she lay anxiously praying with her knees up and spread, her shoes still on; the next, her slender frame had jolted as she had been flung back to grip her fists and gasp and stare at the ceiling.

Lying on a cloth, and unused, were long, pliable steel needles and a catheter in case the syringe's douche hadn't worked and the foetal sac had needed to be punctured and drained. Sepsis and gangrene would have been assured, a terribly painful death.

When Hermann tapped on the door, he wasn't allowed to enter. 'Vernet should be forced to see this,' grunted St-Cyr grimly. 'Call the sous-préfet and tell him the fingerprint boys and a photographer are necessary, also the stretcher-bearers. We'll put her on ice with the other one and let Belligueux have a go at her.'

'And Nénette Vernet?'

Hermann was visibly shaken, but it would do no good to avoid the truth. 'Is now without friends or parents and all alone if still alive.'

'Then I'll put a first call in to the industrialist and we'll have the bastard over for a little chat.'

'He can refuse to come.'

'I'll let Old Shatter Hand do the telling.' Messy . . . why must things always be so messy? *Verdammt!*

Sitting with the dead was always troubling, only the more so if young. She'd been an attractive girl, Liline Chambert, not beautiful, but with that blush youth so often wears so as to successfully find a mate and reproduce the species in love and honour. A sculptress, a student . . . Was this why the child had had the Faber pencil case in her pocket and the tube of Mummy Brown?

With difficulty St-Cyr found the items. The tin pencil case had seen years of use, but the child and her little friend would both have admired the picture of jousting knights on horseback and in colour. The red knight's lance was true and strong and outlasting all battles, an A. W. Faber *Castell* HB from Bavaria, the firm established in 1761. The white knight's lance had snapped in half, a not uncommon thing with cheap pencils, and now he was about to fall from his mount, stabbed right in the chest. There was a distant castle on a hill in the background.

He uncrumpled the tube of paint—the girls would have been fascinated by it. Without breaking the rigor, he could not examine her fingernails but wondered if there would be traces of the paint.

Suddenly he said aloud, 'Where are your underpants? It is a puzzle, for a girl such as yourself would not have gone without them. Not to here, not to any place, and they would have been freshly laundered and ironed as well.'

Though he searched the room as best he could without disturbing things, he could not see them. They'd been taken—he was certain of it. An interrupted attempt at tidying up, he wondered, or simply to either reuse or sell on the black market? Underwear was constantly in demand—after every film performance the usherettes in the cinemas collected the forgotten or misplaced underpants of those females who could find no other suitable place in which to make love. Needless to say, the boyfriends kept theirs on. Women had all the hard luck. Illegitimate babies were an ever-increasing aspect of the Occupation the Germans patently ignored, yet syphilis they dreaded and it, too, was rampant.

Nothing else had been taken. Not her gloves, her beret, her scarf or overcoat, all of which were of good quality and would have fetched far better prices.

Impulsively he yanked the dusty drapes aside to let in the cold grey light of day and stare emptily down at the Seine and ask, 'Did Vernet force his attentions on you—is that why you didn't go to him for help—help that would have saved your life? And *what*, please, of Madame Vernet? Surely she must have known or suspected what was going on?'

The industrialist should have taken precautions. It was a logical assumption, but he knew beyond doubt Vernet would have done no such thing. Too arrogant, too wealthy—why spoil the fun when you've got a naked eighteen-year-old girl in your lap? So many of the wealthy played around, their affairs were legend.

There were no bruises on her inner thighs, no love bites, though he hated the necessity of looking and apologized. No scratches, no signs of resistance or passion. Had she simply let Vernet do it to her in that room at the head of the stairs or in the flat he had rented for her friend?

And where, really, was that boy, that fellow student? Probably vanished into thin air like so many these days.

Von Schaumburg would hit the roof. Criminal abortions, sex out of wedlock ... A boyfriend who was a homosexual—that, too, would cause trouble.

Liline Chambert's identity papers gave her age as nineteen years seven months, a home address in Orléans, where the Vernet interests manufactured farm machinery, tractors and gasoline engines. It was a good place for an accountant to reside, especially if one's trusted employer was to assist in a daughter's education.

She hadn't even cried out as she had died. She had just been hit by the shock; a waste, a crime, a shame, a tragedy. There was no law that would blame Vernet. All would blame the girl. It simply was not fair.

'Where is Nénette?' he asked her gently. 'Has this business here or these things in my pockets any connection with your visit to the belfries of the Notre-Dame and the Sandman, and if we should be so fortunate as to find her alive, will she then lead us to him before it is too late for her, even though he may not have killed her friend? Or will the killer of that friend also hunt her down and kill her to protect himself?'

Only then did he take out the toy giraffe to stand beside the girl, looking down at it. A crèche . . .

'Louis . . . ?'

'Ah! Hermann.'

'The kid still hasn't come home. Vernet's gone to Rouen. Bomb damage last night. One of his factories. A necessary trip perhaps, or simply stalling for time.'

'Stalling, I think.'

'I'll tell the boys in blue to come up, shall I?'

'Yes, yes, but none of their lewd remarks. The photographs first, then the fingerprints. The others can wait in the corridor until everything else has been done. We've got to find the heiress, Hermann. Everything depends on her now.'

A kid at large in a city where virtually everyone had to walk or ride their bicycles or take the *métro* or the *autobus au gazogène* to get from place to place and it was still far too easy to hide even with all the watching that was going on. 'We'll try the convent school first, and then the *ancien* Cimetière de Neuilly. She has to be somewhere.'

But where? 'The *salon de thé* in the children's restaurant but at between three-thirty and four,' said Louis, a hope, a prayer if all else failed.

Kohler hated to tell him. 'You're forgetting she hasn't any money.'

'And you're forgetting her little friend could well have brought along a change purse of her own. This the Mother Superior may be able to confirm.'

'Or Sister Céline, the one the kid said hated her students. "We are the cabbages she feeds to her pigs after first giving them the names of each of us. We are her droppings."'

'Optare, optari.'

The voices of twenty-two uniformed girls in dark-blue tunics and white middies, and ranging from nine to twelve years of age, rose in unison. 'To desire, to be desired.'

'Optavisse, optatus esse,' announced Sister Céline from behind the lectern, tall and straight and determined to drill the students even though most were in tears and ashen at the brutal loss of one or perhaps even *two* of their classmates.

'To have desired, to have been desired.'

'Optaturus esse, optatum iri.'

'To be going to desire, to be going to be desired.'

'Optat!' said the sister sharply, causing them all to lower their eyes and voices in modesty.

'He desires, he is desiring.'

'Optabit!'

'He ... he ... he *will* desire, Sister. He ... he will be desiring.'

There were more tears, more burying of the faces in the arms and gnashing of teeth. Ah *Gott im Himmel*, stormed Kohler inwardly, how could she do it to them? Were they all little sluts to her?

'Easy, *mon vieux*,' cautioned St-Cyr, and softly closing the door of the classroom, left them both with a lasting image of Sister Céline, one that was haunted by tragedy, gaunt and raw and full of anger, the woman not unhandsome but street-wise, they thought, and ever watchful. A woman in her mid-thirties whose every look and gesture reeked of punishment to be meted out for sins imagined and otherwise.

The firm round chin and not unsensuous lips had only added to the fierceness of a straight and defiant nose, high and prominent cheekbones and wide-set deep brown eyes under brows that in another would have been an asset.

Kohler could imagine her blowing cigarette smoke through both nostrils as she had read the signs while still going on with her class and had sized the two of them up as if they were sailors in place Pigalle: five francs in exchange for ten minutes, or a couple of cigarettes, such was the scarcity of tobacco.

Not a sound was heard from beyond the door that had opened to put them so close to the sister she could not have avoided looking sideways at them in stark assessment.

'Inspectors, *please*,' whispered the little nun who had met them at the gate and had let them into God's sanctuary, she too upset and unsettled to object when they had asked to be conducted here without permission.

'Now you may take us to the Mother Superior,' said St-Cyr. 'Please leave this matter for me to explain. There will be no problem and you need say nothing of it, since I doubt very much if Sister Céline will mention it.'

'Then you do not know her, Inspector!' blurted the nun, swiftly crossing herself and begging God's forgiveness under her breath as she hurried away and they were forced to follow.

But once outdoors, and under a colonnaded walkway, she paused and, with eyes downcast, confessed. 'Sister Céline has not had an easy life, Inspectors. Her younger sister, Violette, is a woman of the streets, *une fille de joie*—a *paillasse*, a mattress, in the brothel of the rue Chabanais. Sister Céline is wise in the ways of sin and is only trying to warn our girls to be wary of it.'

'And the Mother Superior, Sister, does she agree with the warnings being given?'

'No. The . . . the two of them do constant battle over it. Innocence against reality, ethereal love against life's harshest truths.'

From one stone gateway to another, the inner courtyard of the convent school and Church of Our Lady of Divine Humility and Obedience held a world within its walls, a formal garden and *potager* of utter peace and contemplation. Now that the snow had been swept, sparrows fed on thin crumbs at the feet of the statues of the Christ and the Blessed Virgin, and in the hush of the garden, whose every branch and line of stone was defined, their tiny voices were muted.

Alone and with her back to them, the Mother Superior stood out so sharply in black she was set in memory against the grey of sky and spiked-iron walls and the whiteness of the snow.

'Reverend Mother . . .' hazarded the sister. 'Forgive me for disturbing your meditations, but two detectives are here to see you.'

'Detectives?' she asked without turning.

'Yes, Mother. I've told them Nénette Vernet did not come to school this morning as she should have.'

'Then leave us, Sister. Please return to your duties. The brasses . is it their turn today?'

'Yes, Mother.'

The nun retreated swiftly with head demurely bowed, and they waited until the colonnades had swallowed her up. Only then did the Mother Superior turn. 'Messieurs, this is a terrible hour for us. Our little Andrée taken from us so brutally? Our Nénette . . . What has become of her? A *voyou*, the Sister Céline would call that one. A delinquent, a guttersnipe, a picker-up of refuse. Never have I seen a child so impulsively committed to collecting the incidental things of life's tiny misfortunes. A button, a badge, a bit of string . . . Dear blessed Jesus, what did that child *not* pick up?'

They gave her time. They knew she was greatly distressed and had been trying to come to grips with things, since *Paris-Soir* and all the other rags had somehow managed a photograph of the victim and had splashed the news and her true identity across the city to pay the *flics* back for beating them up and denying them access to the murder.

She was not young or old, thought St-Cyr, but of that vintage the last war had left with a lover buried or the self rejected in favour of another after too long an absence.

He had seen so many of them but told himself the vocation itself might well have called her. A former nurse perhaps. That, too, passed through his mind, for she had a very capable look about her. Determined and ready to face things at all costs but cautious, too. A narrow face, sharp nose, pale skin, blonde brows and sincere deep blue eyes that missed little, ah yes.

'You must forgive me,' she said. 'Tragedy is so commonplace these days you would think we would be ready for it but'—she shrugged and tried to smile—'you find us ill prepared. What can I do to help? Please, you have only to ask.'

'Then let us walk a little in your garden, Reverend Mother,' said St-Cyr. 'My partner, Herr Kohler, must make a few telephone calls. Would it be all right if he was to return indoors?'

To spy on us, she wondered, to seek answers where . . . where none could possibly be? 'Of course. In spite of the shortages, we are blessed or punished with two telephones but only one line out. The first is in my office next to the infirmary, the other in that of Father Jouvand, who seldom uses his but insists it be there so that he can complain about its ringing. Sister Dominique, who brought you to me, will take you to either.' Why had they simply not asked Dominique to allow them to use the telephone first? Was it to be a case of divide and conquer? It must be.

'Father Jouvand's, I think,' grunted Kohler, fiddling with his fedora and unable to raise his eyes from the crucifix that hung around her neck and was so like the one he had found in Nénette Vernet's desk.

They waited for him to leave and when, at last, he, too, had been swallowed up, they walked a little. To put her at ease, St-Cyr found delight in simply beauty, a branch, a holly berry capped with snow, a single rose hip that had somehow missed the harvest but was still delightfully piquant and beneficial for the health.

He would tell her as little as possible. She knew this now and said, 'We share a love of the natural world, Inspector, but would you do something for me?'

'Of course.'

'A cigarette—have you one? I . . . I haven't indulged in years but suddenly feel the need.'

'I'm not making you nervous, am I?' he asked, and knew at once she regretted his asking.

'A little, yes. It's not often detectives pay us a visit.'

As he lit the cigarette for her, he said, 'Andrée Noireau was to have taken the train to Chamonix on Thursday, Reverend Mother. Why did she not do so?'

She filled her lungs with smoke, felt the nicotine rushing to her brain and could not help but remember the last war and a moment so terrifying she had never had another cigarette until now. 'She was ill—well, too ill, I felt, to make the journey. I had her taken to the infirmary—last winter's flu was so terrible I wasn't taking any chances. Her temperature was normal. At first I felt the excitement of seeing her parents after such a long absence might have upset her, but then she began to complain of terrible headaches and pains in her stomach. Sister Edith heard her retching in the toilets. Warmth and rest were called for.'

'And the Vernets, Reverend Mother? Were they notified? I understand Monsieur Vernet had used his influence to obtain a *laissez-passer* for the child. They thought she had taken the train.'

'But . . . but they knew the child was here? I telephoned the house and spoke directly to Nénette. I asked her to tell her aunt and uncle the trip was out of the question.'

'And when did you telephone?'

'Why, on Thursday at . . . at noon. We had had the doctor in. He had thought it might be the child's appendix. The threat of an operation caused poor Andrée to weep—ah, such weeping! I also asked Nénette to have her uncle notify the parents, since it . . . it is impossible for most to telephone to the *zone interdite* [the forbidden zone along the Swiss and Spanish borders, and in the northern and western coastal areas]. Was Madame Vernet too busy to remember? Was she having her hair done or . . . Forgive me. I speak out of turn. That wasn't called for. It was wrong of me.'

Too busy running around, was that it? wondered the detective—she could see him thinking this as he took out his pipe and tobacco pouch, wanting to prolong the interview. He would not see her as she had seen herself in that last war, with hands bound behind her back and the rifles of a German firing squad pointed at her. He would not know that the smell of pipe tobacco would simply reinforce such a terrible memory.

Puffing away at that thing, he motioned affably with it and said, 'Gardens like these, they are the oases to which the soul must come to drink even as the Cross calls us to prayer.'

In times of strife—she knew this was what he meant and that he had noted her solitary presence in the garden and would seek his answers even in the house and school of God. A scraper of mould, then, from the bread of life, searching for the truth, horrible as it must so often be.

The Kaiser's men had not executed her on that day. Their captain had only wanted to frighten her into revealing where the latest French positions were, a thing she had adamantly refused to reveal. He had taken off his cap and had bowed in apology, the pipe of meerschaum then, the smell of the tobacco the same.

'Inspector, little Andrée secretly left us well before dawn yesterday while we were all at Matins and thought her sleeping peacefully. Sister Edith went to check on her at eight a.m. the new time. I telephoned the Vernets only to find Madame fast asleep and the monsieur not yet returned from the previous evening, an engagement of some sort. The housekeeper told me Nénette was walking the dog in the Bois, a task I knew only too well the child detested. Ah! many times I have cautioned patience and said it was but a small duty in return for all her dear aunt and uncle had done for her, but Nénette hated that dog with a passion. Could the two girls have met in the Bois? They must have, mustn't they?'

Had Vernet been dallying with Liline Chambert on Saturday night? he wondered, but asked, 'Did you send the sisters out to look for the child?'

'Two by two. Nearly all of us went.'

'Sister Céline?'

'With Sister Dominique.'

He considered this and she could see him carefully filing the information away. Again he motioned with the pipe. 'Andrée's overcoat, Reverend Mother. The child wore her school uniform, yes, but . . .'

'But not its overcoat. On Sundays, and at other special times, the girls may wear another if it pleases them and they possess one. Andrée's was dark red with a matching beret. The scarf will have been a soft grey mohair, the gloves of brown leather. Why, please, do you ask, since you must already have seen it?'

He did not answer, this detective. Her cigarette was all but done, and she realized sadly that he had noted how necessary it had been.

'The war,' she said, excusing herself and not really caring if he understood how terrified she had been back then. 'Why ask about the coat?' she demanded.

Irritably, cigarette ash was flicked aside and then the thing extinguished between her fingers as if old habits could never die.

They had reached a bench in the farthest corner of the garden. 'It's too cold to sit and I must go in,' she said. 'These shoes of mine, the soles are now so thin even God cannot stop their total destruction, nor has He yet answered my prayers to replace them.'

'Had Andrée a change purse with her, Reverend Mother?'

'You've not seen her coat, then, have you?' she said, dismayed that he would not take her fully into his confidence.

'The girls switched coats. Both wore their school uniforms. They were, we believe, being followed but knew of this well beforehand and had planned for it.'

'Being followed . . . ? But . . . but by whom? This Sandman?'

'Everything suggests it, Reverend Mother. Well, perhaps not everything.'

'Then the switch was made to save the one and not the other? Is that how it was? *Tell* me!'

She was quivering.

St-Cyr found the note and handed it to her. '*Je t'aime . . . ?*' she said with tears welling up.

'Both believed the switch would save Nénette, who must have been the target.'

'The target . . . ? Then the Sandman, he . . . he has killed the wrong child and those silly, foolish girls believed if the switch was made, he would realize his mistake and let Andrée go? Is that how it was? And if so, why, *please*, would he do such a thing when he chooses his victims at random?'

She had put her finger right on it. 'That is precisely what I am asking myself, Reverend Mother. The girl's beret is missing. Did he remove it to see the colour of her hair or to take it away with him as proof of why such a tragic mistake had been made, or both?'

Quickly she crossed herself and turned to clasp her hands in silent prayer. Calmed a little, she said, '*Je t'aime* . . . It's so like them, Inspector. Two very lonely girls who wished they had had the same mother and father—Nénette's. She had lost her parents, and Andrée, why, may God forgive me for saying so, the poor child might just as well have lost hers for all they cared about her.'

'And the change purse, Reverend Mother? Please, it will have been in Andrée's coat pocket. Nénette will now have it.'

'Five hundred francs in twenties and fifties. Two hundred more in coins and ration tickets sufficient for the week she was to be away. No lipstick—I had removed that ages ago. No chewing gum either, I think—oh, I cannot say. *I really can't!*'

'Reverend Mother, forgive me for distressing you so much.'

'It's all right. The matter needs to be settled. The . . . the miniature prayer book Andrée always carried. The print is really far too small for her to read even with her glasses—ah, her glasses? Did she have them with her when . . . when found? Andrée couldn't see very well without them.' She held her breath so as to get a grip on herself. 'The rosary they all must carry and the small vial of perfume Nénette presented to her on Christmas Eve. That I . . . I could not remove. It would not have been right of me. A gift the child treasured so much she slept with it under her pillow.'

'The glasses?' he asked gently.

'You miss nothing.'

'It's a habit one has had to acquire.'

'Sister Céline had confiscated them, but I made certain Andrée had them beside her bed in the infirmary. The illness by then was so obviously emotional, Inspector, I . . . I had to let Nénette visit her. The girl came twice. Late on Friday afternoon and then again on Saturday, staying each time for about a half-hour.'

Her shoulders slumped in defeat, for she knew now that the visits had been to plan ahead, yet the girls had given no hint of it.

'And why were the eyeglasses confiscated?' he asked.

Would he leave no stone unturned? 'As . . . as a punishment for Andrée's writing in her diary when she should have been asleep. Sister Céline discovered the misdemeanour and blamed the illness on the late-night practice.'

'And this diary?' he asked.

Must his voice remain so calm when all around them their world was falling apart? 'Cast into the stove to offer its flames up to God and heat the infirmary a moment.'

The detective refolded the note and carefully tucked it away in a wallet that had seen far better days and had been mended several times with fishing line. He didn't say Andrée had had her glasses with her, but she must have, otherwise how could she possibly have read the note or seen what . . . what was happening to her?

When he dug into his overcoat pockets, she realized the things he dragged out had come from Nénette's coat.

'Ah! I have it at last,' he breathed, but held on to the toy giraffe and would not let her take it from him.

There was no way of avoiding the matter. He would only pursue it until successful. 'That is from the crèche Sister Céline had in her classroom. She used the crèche to give spiritual guidance, to help teach the girls Latin, and to lend a little interest to geography lessons that are often too barren of anything but words that must be memorized.'

'Was it stolen?'

'Stolen?'

'Taken, Reverend Mother, so as to upset the good sister?'

'Or taken on a dare, Inspector? The girls do things like that from time to time. One day it is the paintings of Pompeii Sister Céline brought back from Rome—they will all be hanging crookedly. The next, there will be no chalk; the next, her little display of volcanic rocks will be disturbed but very slightly so that only she will notice. The girls don't mean to hurt her feelings, nor did Andrée and Nénette, but ... but children are so often insensitive to the feelings of others. How did you come by it?'

'Please just tell me when the Sister Céline noticed the giraffe was missing?'

Andrée must have had it with her. 'Why, weeks ago. Since well before Christmas. The lesson on God's wrath through vulcanism and catastrophe, I suppose. Pompeii and the sins of the flesh. The ... the girls, they drove our dear Céline to tears over its absence, but the whole class denied any knowledge of its where-abouts and now you have made me see that my judgement of Nénette's character has been sadly flawed, and you have made me feel quite cheated. We will, of course, pray for her well-being, but when, God willing, she is safely returned to us, she will con-fess before us all and do penance. The floors, I think, and the toi-lets, but with plenty of prayer between and at all times.'

'Exactly how many weeks ago, Reverend Mother?'

Did the detectives suspect Céline of something and, if so, how could that possibly be? 'Since the first week of November.'

'A good two months.'

Of hell? Was this what he was thinking of Céline? she won-dered. That poor, tragic soul who had been forced to bear so much, the whispers of her girls, the smothered laughs and hur-riedly passed notes behind one's back, the cruelest of gibes from young minds that were far from filthy and simply did not under-stand what they were writing or whispering to each other.

It was not until they had reached the colonnades that St-Cyr asked who had accompanied Nénette on her visits to the infirmary.

'Why, no one. She came alone.' Why had he asked?

'And were they left to talk in private?'

'Why, yes. Yes, of course.'

'Even though Sister Céline had confiscated the diary?'

'Even then. We're not ogres, Inspector. We do love our girls, each and every one of them.'

Though a man who would possess a black overcoat, Father Jouvand was far too old to be nimbly plucking a maker of little angels from a flea-bitten tenement after a botched abortion. And come to think of it, that wasn't right, was it? wondered Kohler. A priest, a man of the cloth, rescuing an abortionist? The Pope would have a thing or two to say about it. Besides, Jouvand had been on duty all day Sunday, well into the evening, and could probably prove it a thousand times over, though the death of Liline Chambert had not even been mentioned.

With a parcel of nuns and schoolgirls to watch over, and a parish flock as well and no help but boys at the altar because of the war, he was a busy man and seventy if a day. But he did like tobacco. Chain-smoking U-boat cigarettes, the windy old bugger lit up again to taste the air of victory and deny the Occupier yet another cigarette.

'You were asking about Sister Céline, Inspector,' he said. 'Ah! pay her no mind. The good sister believes each child has the devil in her body.' He waved the cigarette perhaps to study its contrail. 'Given the home she came from, it's only natural, but she's not unkind and has the best interests of our girls at heart. The Vernets have always supported us most handsomely. I'd pay particular attention to our need for funds if I were you. Yes. Yes, indeed I would. Go easy, for the sake of the Lord's work.'

Was the bastard Irish? Had he studied in Ireland perhaps? Kohler heaved a troubled sigh. They'd been all through the grieving and the times of the Masses that would be said for Andrée Noireau. They'd been through countless other things, few of which had been of any use. 'Father, just tell me where she was on Sunday at about two p.m.'

The grey and unruly thatches of his eyebrows lifted. 'Is it that you think I set my clock by those nuns?' A stray shred of tobacco was examined and carefully saved on the blotting paper for another day.

'No. I'm merely trying to build a framework around the killing.'

'Then let us ask God's help. Down on your knees, my son. It'll take but a moment.'

He heaved another sigh as Jouvand let his dark brown eyes sift over him in condemnation of all non-believers, the rugged countenance of the priest wise to the wages of sin and all too ready to pronounce against it even to a member of the Gestapo who was honest and decent, though Jouvand could not know of this and had assumed the exact opposite.

'Look, we do need help, and quickly, Father. As you heard yourself while I was on the telephone, Nénette Vernet has still not returned home. Is that child afraid to do so?'

'Afraid? Now why would she be afraid of her dear aunt and uncle?'

'I don't know, damn it.'

'Please don't blaspheme in the House of the Lord. The child could well be with the Sandman or already dead. My son, if I were you, I would seek your answers elsewhere.'

Ah *nom de Jésus-Christ*! they were getting nowhere. Kohler got up to tower over the bastard. He swept up the artillery-shell ashtray, a relic of the Troubles perhaps, and, plucking the cigarette butts from it, tucked them away in his own *mégot* tin for later use.

Dismayed, Father Jouvand acknowledged the atrocity with a curt nod and, 'Now, if that is all, Inspector, I will gladly guide you to our front door and close it behind you.'

'Just what the hell are you trying to hide? Soup kitchens in Suresnes and Aubervilliers? Sweaters knitted for prisoners of war—hey, *mon fin*, don't you know those parcels are intercepted and sent on to Russia?'

'No, I did not know.'

'Then perhaps you'd tell me what those charts on the wall behind that thick head of yours mean, and while you're at it, give me a detail of the soup-kitchen roster the good sisters help out at. That is it, on the wall, is it not?'

Ah *merde, merde*, had they not had enough trouble for one day? wondered Jouvand. 'The soup kitchens are run by the Sisters of Charity to whom we give assistance on occasion. The sweaters are knitted by the good ladies of our parish and by some of the sisters. Mittens and scarves, woollen socks . . . ah! they turn their considerable talents to so many things when given the materials, which are in such short supply God Himself is doubtful of the venture, but no matter. Are you positive our relief parcels never reach their intended destinations?'

'It's only rumoured the things are sent to Russia, but sometimes the Wehrmacht's censors do get lazy with the mail. A month before they were killed at Stalingrad, my two sons wrote to tell my wife—ah, my ex-wife—that they had received Red Cross parcels from France destined for French prisoners of war.'

Ever so slightly Jouvand gave the Gestapo a nod of understanding, indicating that from now on all courtesies such as being invited into the parish office had been cancelled for ever. 'On Mondays, Wednesdays and Fridays the sisters, two by two, assist with the soup kitchens but not only in Suresnes and Aubervilliers, in other suburbs as well. The matter is decided by the Sisters of Charity, not by ourselves. On Tuesdays, Thursdays and Saturdays six of them knit sweaters and other things in the parish hall, which is right below our feet and unheated, you understand, except for the closeness of the other parishioners, who are engaged in the same task out of charity. Two hours at a time, I believe. Now, if that will satisfy you, I will take you to the front door.'

So much for knitting needles and crucifixes. Kohler went to dump his *mégot* tin into the priest's ashtray but was stopped by the hand of God.

'Please don't deny yourself on my account, Inspector. I would only throw them into the fire when we have one.'

'And here I thought only Bavarians were stubborn? That

would be a stupid waste and you know it. So tell me, how is it teaching sisters have time off to do other things?'

Those deep brown eyes sought him out again and held him fast.

'Because not all of our nuns are teachers and some of those are spelled from time to time, and because God's work is never done. Necessity demands our every effort. Would you have the children in those tenements starve when Monsieur Vernet sees that we have sufficient food and a little of it can be spared? Though we do not tell him this, I am certain he is aware of it.'

'Then let's make peace, eh, Father? We're here to help, not to condemn, and we've got a very lonely, terrified little girl we have to find and yes, please God, let us find her.'

Two packets of U-boat cigarettes were dragged out and pressed into the priest's hand, a temptation God Himself could not have resisted in these times of such terrible shortages.

'Violette Belanger is *une belle gamine*, Inspector, a good-looking kid, but the ache in the Sister Céline's heart is so great, God is very troubled. The one tries only to service the Occupier and make her fortune which her *maquereau* promptly pockets, while the other seeks constantly to change a heart that is granite-hard and content if only for spite's sake. If it is someone in the guise of a nun that you are looking for, why not try the house on the rue Chabanais, since, much to our continued discomfort and dismay, Violette Belanger makes a mockery there of that same sister under whose very care she was raised.'

Ah *nom de Dieu, de Dieu*, a convent classroom in a whorehouse and if not a 'nun', then a 'priest', ah yes, a 'priest'.

Kohler nodded his thanks, inwardly heaving a huge sigh of relief at finally getting somewhere, though he knew all such sighs could so often be premature.

'Tread lightly, Inspector. That *bordel* is the largest of the houses that are reserved for your soldiers. It is large enough to cater to every indecent and shameful act. Its madam is a most formidable and impossible woman, a creature of the gutters herself who is sly and wilful and very wicked. If she gets wind of who you are, she may play along but only for a while.

She absolutely detests the police and operates with complete impunity, having paid off the préfet himself but also having the sanction of the Wehrmacht, including that of the Kommandant von Gross-Paris himself. I give you fair warning. It is yours to have.'

But first they had to find the heiress.

4

'Biegelmann,' said St-Cyr sadly, 'Aron Jacob. Kahn, Adèle. Rosenthal, Marcel. Radetski, Leah . . .'

Vernet had said Liline Chambert had often of late found his niece here in the Jewish section of the *ancien* Cimetière de Neuilly and, yes, Nénette had been absolutely right, thought Kohler grimly. It was indeed the quietest place on earth next to the Bibliothèque Nationale. It was not two blocks from the Jardin d'Acclimatation and well within easy walking distance of the villa, school and church. But there was a problem. The Jews of Paris had all been taken. The *Grande Rafle* of 16 July 1942 had just been the start of it—the sealing off of five *arrondissements* by over nine thousand French police, not a German among them. More than twelve thousand terrified men, women and children, taken in the dark of that night alone, had been crammed into the cycling arena of the Vélodrome d'Hiver without sufficient water or toilet facilities. Eight days. From there they, and still others, had been bused to Drancy, and then the mothers and fathers had been sent by rail in cattle trucks to unspoken destinations, the children held for a time and then sent on themselves to God knows where.

When Louis and he had returned to Paris, Louis had patiently started piecing it all together. Talbotte, the préfet, had made money on the deal. Along with the SS, the Gestapo and the French Gestapo of the rue Lauriston, he had robbed the safe-deposit boxes, et cetera, et cetera, of those taken. They had really cleaned up, but the trouble was Talbotte now knew Louis had the goods on him. Apart from open hatred and out-right threats to Louis's life, the préfet's cooperation would not be forthcoming. They were living on borrowed time.

'Well, do we ask von Schaumburg to call out the troops to do a sweep of Neuilly and the rest of the city, Louis, or do we wait and hope the kid goes home?'

St-Cyr gestured impatiently. There were so many questions, so few answers as yet. Hermann and he had not been in the city more than fifteen hours, had not stopped since they had got off the train.

'Is she out here freezing, Louis? Is she terrified and crying her eyes out—hiding from us, too? Is she in that synagogue down the street where the windows are all broken and the slogans scream from battered doors?'

Hermann was ashamed of what had happened to that syna-gogue and to so many. 'Is she too afraid to go home, *mon vieux*,' asked St-Cyr, 'and if so, why is she afraid?'

'Is she even alive?' breathed Kohler sadly.

They began to search. They looked everywhere among the standing stones. There were no footprints in the snow . . . ah! too much had fallen, yet if sanctuary was needed, had the child not chosen well?

The thought brought only a silence of its own. Across the street, swastikas fluttered from several of the houses.

Andrée Noireau had written in her diary and Sister Céline had destroyed the thing. A knitting needle had been used in each of the four other murders and the child had had one in her desk at home.

All of the victims had been of about the same age, all school-girls but *not* all from convent schools, or had they been?

They simply did not know. They had yet to see the files on the other murders. When boiled down to its essence, did not everything hang on the contents of that child's coat pockets? wondered St-Cyr. Could he *not* find the time to examine them thoroughly?

The girls had stolen a toy giraffe, but that had been during the first week of November, time enough for a crisis to build in anyone, let alone Sister Céline. None of the class had informed on the thief. But why had the child had it in her hand when attacked?

Nénette must have given it to her after they had switched coats, the class secret revealed at last, perhaps. But had they then used it to taunt the killer, and if so, was that person Sister Céline?

'It can't be her. It's not possible,' he said aloud to himself as he searched.

A 'priest' had called to take the abortionist away, and that could not have been possible either unless . . . unless perhaps he was someone connected to the brothel.

'The child isn't here, Louis. Shouldn't we check the synagogue?'

Some crows took wing and they watched them fly to better pastures beyond the stone wall that surrounded the cemetery and shut it off from all else.

Hermann was always so impatient. The child seemed nowhere near. Could they leave things here and come back again? 'I'll do it now. Go and check the house on the rue Chabanais. See if Violette Belanger can tell us anything, eh? Perhaps Giselle can be of assistance.'

Giselle . . . Why must Louis continually remind him the girl would return to her 'profession'? Always it was the same.

'I'll have to call home. Maybe she isn't there. Maybe Oona can tell me where she is. Shall we meet at Chez Rudi's later, or the Villa Vernet?'

'Ah, I've done it again, haven't I? Forgive me. Giselle is okay. Old habits and opinions simply die hard. Meet me at the morgue, I think. If I can, I will have Madame Vernet and that husband of hers on either side of Liline Chambert when I pull back the shroud. We will let the girl's nakedness get us to the bottom of things.'

The children's restaurant in the Jardin d'Acclimatation overlooked a frozen lake and pond, where adults took advantage of the cold weather to skate alone, since the children were in school. It was getting on to 4.00 p.m. and the light was fast fading.

'A tisane of rose hips, please,' said St-Cyr. 'No saccharin is necessary, but if you have a little honey . . . ?' Would it be possible?

'Impossible, monsieur. I'm sorry but . . . ' The girl shrugged. 'So many ask, it's become a way of objecting. It's like the croissant stickers the children secretly paste to the tables and chairs. A symbol of what we are missing.'

'Please be careful what you say, mademoiselle. Ah no, I'm not one of them, but . . . ' He indicated the scattered clientele, many of whom were in uniform.

Her smile was grateful, and when she brought his tea, a tiny sugar-spoon of dark honey was tucked to one side. 'It's buckwheat,' she said. 'A soldier from Normandy gave me a small jar this morning even though I refused to go to the cinema with him.'

A larger than usual tip would be in order, and he wondered if he would have sufficient. Hermann was their banker, a position he had automatically assumed in September 1940, a keeper of their guns as well, until needed. The driver of their car also, of course. By now he would have paid a brief visit to the two loves of his life, both of whom shared the same flat with him. Ah! it was one of the Occupation's little miracles that they got on so well. Giselle was a beauty of twenty-two, a fiercely independent and intelligent girl with a mind of her own, a girl Hermann had rescued from the profession, if only temporarily; Oona was a

Dutch alien of about forty, a sensible and far more suitable woman, a realist whose husband the French Gestapo had questioned and had then buried in the Vélodrome d'Hiver to teach them a lesson, herself included, since the marriage had been mixed.

When his tea came, he filled the cup only halfway so as to keep the heat in the pot for as long as possible. Then he took out his pipe and began to stoke the bowl, the 'furnace', and when that was done, didn't stop until he had laid out everything from the dustbin of that child's pockets.

Two further items were set in the midst of the rubbish. A toy baby elephant from that same crèche, no doubt, and a child's pair of glasses.

He shut his eyes, and back across the silk screen of memory ran the film of the inside of the synagogue, its altar and lamps smashed, the menorahs bent and twisted, the Torah unscrolled and defecated on and scorched, the stiff, leather-bound copy of the Talmud thrown into a corner to lie open amid the shower of prayer books, and the dark stained glass from the shattered windows above.

Some snow had crept in, and though one could look at it in any way one wanted, still there was a star-shaped pattern the child had drawn on the floor.

There were no footprints in its snow. None were easily definable elsewhere, but on a broken corner of the altar a battered lamp had been placed; on another, the glasses and the baby elephant.

Calling out, he had heard, and heard again in the temple of his mind, the echoing of 'Nénette . . . ? Nénette Vernet? Please don't hide from me.'

Trust . . . How were they to gain her trust if she was still alive and free but afraid to go home?

A baby elephant the Reverend Mother had failed to mention, a pair of glasses Sister Céline had confiscated only to have them returned by the Reverend Mother . . . Nénette Vernet must have been wearing them.

The Lalique vial of perfume contained an old and superb scent 'borrowed', no doubt, from the aunt's dressing table. The tiepin that had been stepped on was cheap and gaudy and *not* the sort of thing the industrialist would have worn. No, it wasn't.

The gold fob from a first-communion ear-ring had definitely not been Liline Chambert's, he felt, and could not help but see her in the cold hard light of memory, the girl lying on her back with her legs spread slackly and fists still clenched high up on her chest.

Five raisins, four of the gritty ersatz vitaminic biscuits, unfrosted and frosted marbles followed. Then the death's-head cap badge, the two gold wound medals, the Polish Campaign medal and the silver tank battle badge, none of which he had before him since Hermann had confiscated them but all of which could never be forgotten. Ah no, of course not.

A spent tube of Mummy Brown. A toy giraffe. A crystal of clear quartz. A toy roulette wheel—he tried it and watched as he heard its little steel ball bearing bounce round and round until it settled on the three. Ah! he had never had any luck at gambling. Never! Was it an omen of more trouble to come? Should he have consulted the Tarot cards first?

'I'm sadly deficient as a reader of them,' he muttered. 'Perhaps I ought really to consult an expert.'

The charm bracelet was missing one of its dogs. A poodle? he wondered. The poodle Pompon? Nénette Vernet must really hate that dog.

Back came the words of Madame Vernet in the freezing cold of the darkened garden. 'I loved her as my own. We confided things in each other. She trusted me absolutely. The dog was hers . . . Actually, I have no love of dogs.'

And then, of Vernet, 'I have to tell you how it was. He . . . he won't let me say a thing. He'll see that he does all the talking.'

In the change purse Hermann had recovered from the game-keeper there were a few francs in tightly crumpled bills, perhaps two hundred in all, and several coins, both French and others. Some stray marks the heiress had picked up, a few pfennigs, a few lire, six guilders, four kroner, seven drachmas, a dinar and eight roubles—coins from all over Occupied Europe, and dropped or thrown away by the Occupier's nomads, common soldiers and sailors mostly, on rest and recuperation. Some Austrian schillings as well . . .

A rubber condom . . . 'The *bordel*, the house on the rue Chabanais?' he breathed and, taking it out, saw it against the coins and the memory of the tank battle and cap badges.

The thing had been used some time ago and its contents had long since dried and become fast like glue. Regulation issue. Wehrmacht and a pale shade of flaccid and unbecoming grey but . . . but how had the child come by it? What meaning had it had for her? Was it something with which to taunt the good Sister Céline or to prove to classmates that the nun's young sister Violette had fallen by the wayside?

Was Nénette Vernet the ringleader of the troubles at the school? She must have been.

Feeling decidedly uncomfortable, he tucked the thing back into the purse with the coins and suddenly remembered his tea. Ah! it was stone-cold.

The waitress came instantly with a fresh pot, and he knew then that he had been under constant surveillance. Not resisting the temptation to stare at the change purse, she said, 'You're a detective, aren't you?'

'It's not hard to tell,' he confessed, and, dragging out the *carte d'identité*, asked of its photograph, 'Do you recall seeing this child?'

He had such large, moist brown eyes, this detective, and was so very worried. 'That is Andrée Noireau, the child who . . . who was killed yesterday. It's in all the papers. She often came here with her friend from school and . . . and sometimes with an older girl of about my age.'

The lights had come on but he hadn't even noticed this until now. The black-out curtains had been drawn. 'And the school friend?' he asked guardedly. 'Has that one been in today?'

Rapidly her head was shaken. An anxious glance was thrown at madame *la patronne*, who sat by her *caisse* leaving nothing to chance, including the talking to police officers who dangled used condoms above their teacups!

'Please, you must tell me. It's urgent.'

Again a worried glance was thrown at Madame. 'But I'm not sure. I'm not!' cried the girl.

Hastily she turned to leave, only to be stopped by the hand of the Sûreté. 'Sure or not, mademoiselle, you must tell me now.'

It was his turn to look at Madame and he did it so fiercely Madame acquiesced with a curt nod.

'I . . . I think I may have seen her up in the woods. She . . . she reminded me of a wolf that is afraid and half-starved, monsieur. One moment she was there, looking down towards the cage of doves, the next she was gone.'

'When?'

'Today at . . . at about two p.m. We're never very busy on Mondays. I took a half-hour without pay for my lunch. I had to see where it had . . . had happened.'

'What was she wearing?'

'A red overcoat and beret.'

'And was there anyone with her?' he hazarded.

'I . . . I think so. I do! But . . . but he was well behind her and . . . and I think she . . . she must have been running from him.'

'A man in a black overcoat?'

'Yes.'

Ah *nom de Jésus-Christ*, Hermann! he cried inwardly. Why are we not together when that is most needed?

From a block away, the bell of the Bibliothèque Nationale gloomily shattered the frost and brought the night down. It was 5.00 p.m. Berlin Time and the narrow pavement next to the house on the rue Chabanais was awash with a constant tide of battle-weary men fresh in for release. They did not joke or laugh or even grumble like soldiers and sailors on leave. Stolidly they smoked their cigarettes and waited, two by two in line, patrolled by tough Feldgendarmen with chains and miniature breast-plates clinking softly against coat buttons and batons beating into mailed leather gloves.

Nur für Deutsche—Only for Germans, read the Gothic letters on a white signboard under a pale blue electric bulb that was caged in wire above a door that was now absolutely dark.

Several coughed. One nervous boy panicked and left the line. Immediately his place was taken by another.

Kohler was impressed by the control the Military Police exerted, but were they stationed inside as well? Were they standing on the staircase that must rise six storeys up the central well to attic dormers, no bed unused for more than a few moments? The girls ate, slept and lived most of their tiny lives in there, often doubled up for comfort and consolation in their off hours, sharing their tears, their colds and coughs or dreams and only going out now and then to see their pimps for an hour or two of coaxing or a beating, depending on the need to produce.

'The day-shift is ending,' whispered Giselle le Roy, and he felt the trembling in her, felt how terrified she was of this place. 'Broken, my Hermann. Most of the girls who work here are finished after six months. Two I know of went mad after only a week. One killed herself in the bathtub with electricity. There were three German soldiers with her and it caused a terrible scandal. The General von Schaumburg had the house closed for five days and Madame Morelle carted off to prison, but the demand is so constant he was forced to back down and have her released. Now she reigns in triumph and they're the best of friends. Ah! those few days she spent between sheet metal were far better than any medal he could ever have pinned to her.'

They were jostled by pedestrians, all of whom were forced to use the opposite of the street. Giselle's cheeks were cold. As she clung to him, her lips quivered with each urgent kiss until she whispered at last, 'Please be careful. Don't ever force me to work in there.'

' "Force you to work"? Hey, how could I do a thing like that to you or to anyone? Just wait in the café around the corner, eh? See what you can pick up. I want Violette Belanger's pimp.'

This was not the first time Hermann had used her for such things, and none of those times had been very good. Ah no, they hadn't. But this . . . ? Her horoscope hadn't been right. Her skin still crept. A killer with a knitting needle—the Sandman—ah! there could be no connection to the mackerel, the pimp, but still her apprehension would not leave her. 'I will see, that is all

I can promise, but if you feel the need to release your little burden in there because duty demands it, me, I shall try to understand.'

'Hey, you're the only one for me.'

'And Oona, please? What of her? Is she not also the only one for you?'

They had been all over this too many times. 'Relax. Aren't I looking after both of you?'

'You're never home, and when you are, you are either too busy visiting *les maisons de tolérance* or sound asleep!'

Each time the door opened to let someone in or out, the black-out curtains hid everything but the impatient shuffling of cleated boots on uncarpeted stairs.

'Sixty-seven girls,' said Giselle tartly. 'Twenty to a shift with seven in reserve and each will have between fifteen and thirty, maybe even *forty* slashes in Madame Morelle's little book when her working day has ended. Even the graveyard shift here is busy, since at curfew the doors, they are locked and all must stay within, and that is when the fun really begins. Ticks also, yes, in lieu of slashes.' She clucked her tongue and sucked in the breath of practicality as she tallied the take.

'Ticks for what?' he hazarded.

'For the things a girl does when a man wants a little something different. Actually, those times, they are often much quicker and a lot easier.'

'Oh.'

'Oh yourself. You will not find everything in there, my Hermann. Most of it will be the straight in and out with quantities of Vaseline or olive oil. Please see that you are not tempted even if it is necessary!'

In tears, she stamped on his toes and left him in the cold with only the sweet scent of her, bathed regularly because Oona insisted on it, touched with Mirage, that delicate perfume Louis's *chanteuse* wore, and warm if only in memory, her violet eyes no doubt flashing daggers of warning.

Half-Greek, half-Midi French and with skin so soft against the straight jet black hair, and cheeks as rosy as her nipples. A perfect hourglass in black mesh stockings and nothing else at times. Sweet heaven with strongly decisive brows and a mind of her own. She'd make one hell of a shopkeeper or barkeep and absolutely right for that little place in Spain or Portugal when the time came to start another family. Ah yes, and ah damn. The Occupation couldn't last for ever and he knew it, but would they be allowed to leave and would she really want to run a shop? Of course not.

Crossing the road, he spoke in German to the nearest Feldgendarm. 'Kohler, Gestapo Paris-Central, here to ask Madame Morelle a few questions.'

A breath of sauerkraut, boiled leeks and sausage overwhelmed him. 'Then wait in line. Take your turn. Hey, my fine Gestapo dick, do you want us to have a riot on our hands?'

Ah *Gott im Himmel!* 'Five hundred francs. Will that stop the riot?'

'Five thousand.'

He could tell the bastard was grinning, and waited for the rest. '*Und* you pay for all who have to let you go ahead of them.'

'Now, look—'

'Then wait in line. Heinrich, Martin, Klaus,' he called out. 'Hey, it's early yet, but already we have a troublemaker on our hands.'

'I'll wait in line.'

'You do that. We lock the doors at midnight and it all begins again at five a.m. Seven days a week.'

The thought of Hermann in there was worrisome. Faint blue pinpricks of light fevered the frigid darkness of the rue Chabanais as fireflies would the other side of the moon. Breath billowed, shoulders touched—Giselle's wooden-soled shoes kept up a constant click-clack on the icy pavement. No one gave way. People collided. The sound of bicycles out on the street was their only warning, their bells too late.

Unfamiliar with the area—ah! it had always been far too high-class a district for her—she much preferred Montparnasse, the boulevard Saint-Germain and the house of Madame

Chabot on the rue Danton. There, in her own little world, she had been content and welcomed always as one of the regulars. But here? she asked, feeling suddenly lonely. Here I am nothing. The rue de Rivoli, the Palais-Royal, even the Bibliothèque Nationale were all very near and nice, of course, but had always exuded vibrations of 'Stay away. You don't belong'.

Reaching the corner at last, she found a lamppost against which to lean and get her bearings.

'How much?' asked a voice out of the darkness, too near.

'It's not for sale.'

She felt a hand explore her seat and hip, a shoulder, the breath of him on her cheek, and said softly, 'I have a straight razor in my hand, monsieur. Please don't make me use it.'

'*Putain!*' he hissed and drifted off into the ether. Two others made their tries—did she telegraph vibrations of her own even after nearly six months of near-chastity with Hermann?

When she found the café, it was down two sets of iron-railinged stone stairs into an even deeper darkness from which the stench of urine, sour wine and cheap perfume rushed at her. Girls and their pimps kissed and made love against the walls in spite of the cold or perhaps because of it. She could hear them whispering, sighing, moaning urgently even as the muted sounds of the traffic from above came to her. The Café of the Turning Hour—she could just make out its name when a match was struck and a burly, pockmarked little *maquereau* glared lewdly at her and grinned.

Entering after the swift little parasite in his tight-fitting overcoat and fedora, she saw at a glance that the place was nothing more than a hole in the wall, a slot down which the zinc counter ran endlessly to one side, and at this, elbows touched as bankrolls were flashed to impress each other and apéritifs were sipped. A cosy place, the smell of oily onion soup mingling with that of cigarette smoke, *vin ordinaire*, pastis and brandy. A place where one could not simply ask for the name of a girl's pimp, since too many questions would be asked in return.

Squeezing between the clientele and the wall to whose

flaking plaster clung the peeling posters of another age, she made her way until at last, all eyes watching, she was able to take a place at the zinc. '*Un café noir avec un pousse-café, s'il vous plaît,*' she said. A coffee with a liqueur on the side. Ah *merde*, they had all stopped talking in order to listen.

'You're not from here,' said the *patron*, bald-headed, cruel and swift, about fifty and no taller than herself but muscular. A displaced Savoyard with a full and bushy grey moustache he must spend hours preening. An accent that would break glass.

'Me? Ah! I'm looking for work but cannot seem to find the house. My feet are killing me. I'm more than half-frozen.'

'The house of Madame Morelle?' asked the *patron*, wiping his runny nose with the back of a hand. Everyone had colds these days. Everyone.

'Yes. I've two kids and a dead husband. Someone has to support them.'

They looked her over, these sharks and barracudas in their pin-striped suits with big lapels and loud ties with gold studs. They sniffed the air of her, measuring the number of tricks she could handle. They even stripped her naked with their eyes. They were not young, most of these men who controlled the girls of the rue Chabanais. Some were middle-aged, some even older, so their assessment was not kind but harsh, and several found her wanting.

Ignoring her, those types turned their greasy, slicked-back heads away and continued on with their arguments, their bragging and their schemes.

'Look, I have to see Madame Morelle, but she sees no one until she needs another. I just want to get my name on the list.'

'Have you a licence?' asked the *patron*.

The yellow card all prostitutes must carry. 'Of course.'

Impatiently he snapped his fingers and reluctantly she dragged it out, knowing he would see that it had lapsed. 'I . . . I had to stop for a while, but I'm clean now.' She'd been lucky and had never had a venereal disease, but . . .

'Then let's see your health card.'

'He screens them for her,' confided the pockmarked one. 'He's married to her, though you wouldn't know it for all she cares about him.'

'*Yvon, that is once too much!*' shrieked the *patron*, getting red in the face and lunging across the zinc. '*Bite your tongue or I will bite it off for you. SHOW me the blood this instant or I will banish you forever!*'

Ah *merde* . . . 'The . . . the health card is at home.'

'At home?' Snap! 'Then let's have the photos of your kids. Two, was it?'

Blood was smeared across the four fingers of the mackerel Yvon's left hand. The *patron* nodded curtly at him, the argument settled.

With a sinking feeling, Giselle wondered if they would ever let her go. 'I haven't got any snapshots of them.'

She's a good-looking kid,' said someone, blowing smoke rings at the ceiling.

'Hey, Henri, undo her coat and let's have a look in the cupboard. She might do for the schoolroom, eh?'

There was laughter. 'Does she know the Mass?' asked another.

'The Angelus, eh, Henri? Get her down on her knees and we'll examine the bakery. Let's hear how she says the Our Father in Latin.'

The *patron* slid her coffee and the *pousse-café* across the zinc and, when she dumped the liqueur into her cup, stopped her hand and said, 'You really didn't come looking for work. You'd have had your coat off long ago—ah! we've a stove that fills the place with so much heat you're sweating. You'd have asked for a light, my fine mademoiselle, and would have made yourself right at home on the nest. So, why are you here?'

She could throw the coffee in his face and try to make a run for it but would never reach the door. Hermann, she wanted to cry out. Hermann, why have you asked me to do this?

'I . . . I really do have to see your wife, Monsieur Morelle. I . . . I may be able to help her. A little *confidence*, you understand. A little something I heard the other day.'

'From her astrologer or her fortune-teller?'

'Is the fortune-teller the same one Violette Belanger uses?' she asked curiously.

His eyelids narrowed. 'Who says Violette uses a fortune-teller?'

'Most girls do. I just wondered, since Violette's was the name that came up—well, actually, the confidence referred to her *maquereau*. He'd do just as well, I suppose.'

The *patron* did not give her that name—another mistake for her. Instead, he said, 'Then maybe if you can find my wife's fortune-teller over in Saint-Germain, my little pigeon, she will tell you when my wife will pay her a visit and that way you'll be able to give Berthe your little *confidence*.'

He wasn't buying a thing. She went to take up her cup, only to realize that he had somehow signalled to the others, who now closed in behind and to the sides of her. As anger rushed into her cheeks and eyes, the buttons of her coat were undone, and when it was pulled down behind her back so that her arms were pinned behind her, the *patron* explored her breasts and, satisfied, ran a hand under her chin to feel the softness of her throat. 'Just what's your game?' he asked.

'LET ME GO! *COCHONS*—PIGS! HOW DARE YOU DO THIS TO ME?'

'Henri, please. Enough is enough.'

'Ah! Father, forgive me. I didn't see you come in. It's just a little game of our own. A new prospect for my wife to consider, but the engine of this one doesn't look as though it can take the hills. She doesn't even swear like a whore. Tender, yes, and succulent—a breeder perhaps or a schoolgirl but—'

'Henri, I thought I said enough?'

'Forgive me, Father. You're always welcome, but the tongue . . . '

Morelle shrugged and, seemingly gruff in embarrassment, turned away to serve the silent others.

'My child, please allow me,' said the priest.

She felt her coat being lifted back over her shoulders. She turned and in that instant felt relief flooding through her as she looked into sincere and compassionate blue eyes. Grave, yes, and watery from the cold outside. A man of nearly sixty, she thought. Somewhat taller than herself and not unhandsome, though grey and ravaged by time. A real priest of the *quartiers*, a no-nonsense man, humble and kind.

'Father Eugène Debauve at your service, Mademoiselle . . . ?'

'Le Roy. Giselle.'

'Giselle, I like that. Come and I'll get you something decent to drink. This place is not for girls like yourself, but you must find it in your heart to forgive them. We're all God's sinners, only some more so than others.'

The house on the rue Chabanais stank to high heaven.

'Monsieur, what is it you want? Be truthful.'

'Me?' snorted Kohler, indoors at last but just. 'Ah, I'm looking for something a little special.'

'Yes, but all who come here seek the same,' said Madame Berthe Morelle, throwing him a sideways glance from behind her cage.

'Something young—about twenty-three perhaps, but looking much younger.'

The black curls shook. The large and deep brown, heavily-kohled eyes widened. 'Ah! that's just not possible. Experience is always an asset. Increase the years to sip the wine of success.'

Bravo! madame, he wanted to cry out, but business was business, and behind all that lace-clad ample flesh lay a heart of utter ice. 'Then try Violette Belanger. She'll do.'

The apple cheeks tightened, the thick ruby lips were impatiently compressed. 'Violette?' she shrilled. 'But . . . but it's her little holiday, *mon pauvre garçon*. Ah, I know how disappointed you and many others are. You all ask for her and me, I am left to convey the sad truth.'

What a catastrophe, thought Kohler, pleased again. Both of her pudgy, capable hands had been tossing the words about.

'Violette is in Marseille visiting her sister,' she said briskly. 'A week, or was it ten days . . . ?' she asked herself, and began to search for the schedule if such existed. Perhaps it was among the freshly laundered stacks of hand towels, perhaps among the boxes of condoms . . .

Kohler reached through the gilded bars to pluck her little black notebook from the counter, but she struck so swiftly with her fan his fingers stung. 'Now, please, monsieur,' she hissed, sizing him up yet again. 'Before I call the boys to throw you out, what is it you want of my Violette?'

He'd hate to meet her in a darkened alley. 'A word, that's all. My partner and I are working on the Sandman thing. Violette may be able to help us.'

'The Sandman . . . ?' The woman clucked her tongue and, deep under the thick, jet-black curls and waves of a hairdo that did little to stay the years—fifty, was it? he wondered—her mind began to weigh the matter. Caution would be called for, of course—to help the police with such a matter, ah! could it bring credit or trouble?

Suspiciously she asked, 'How could Violette provide you with information? In winter she never leaves the house except to visit with her *maquereau* or her parents. Her sister comes once in a while and causes much trouble.'

He struck, 'The name of her *maquereau*, please?'

Ah, what was this? 'Such things, they are difficult.'

'*Difficult?* We have information that leads us to believe the most recent victim knew her killer. That information has directed me here.'

He could know nothing. *Nothing!* 'What information, please?' she asked slyly.

It would only go round and round and all the while Giselle was out there on the street or in that café. The line-up outside had stalled and the unoccupied whores, so undressed they lounged in virtually nothing but boredom, waited in the ante-room just off the hall. Smoking, exploring their nether regions, a breast, a crotch, a rump, an armpit . . .

'We report directly to the General von Schaumburg, madame. If you like, I'll get him to inspect the house and condemn it.'

She tossed her curls. 'Ah! that's an empty threat. He already does. Once a month, and always on the first Monday, so we have just passed the Blitzkrieg with flying colours, and the kettledrums, they are still banging. The doctor attends as well. Both are old friends.'

Her pudgy fingers strayed to the push-button bell that was mounted on the counter. The black lace glove that all but encased them hesitated. Was she of Spanish descent, he wondered, or did she just like to do the flamenco or simply wear the dress and dream of faraway places? 'I wouldn't if I were you,' he said of the bell.

A *flic*, a detective, a Bavarian who spoke excellent French for such a one. A womanizer, a frequenter of brothels—ah yes, yes! Formidable also, a giant with a terrible slash down the left cheek. How had he got that thing? By duelling? she wondered. 'Violette is occupied. If you would care to wait, I will see that she comes to you in . . . ' She glanced at the gold pocket-watch that hung by a chain around her ample neck. 'In about ten minutes.'

'Just give me the floor and the room.'

'And two towels?' she shot back.

He shook his head. 'Not this time.'

'Then how long do you require?'

'Twenty minutes.'

'Fifty francs—no, two hundred. She's special, and ah! I have forgotten you can well afford it.'

'Then ring up Gestapo Boemelburg and tell him I require special dispensation of the funds. He'll send it right over, and I'll tell *them* to raid the place.'

'Your threats are hollow. I push the bell.'

'Now, wait . . . ' he managed.

Her eyes snapped vengeance. '*Scoundrel, bloodsucker, ruffian*,' she shrilled. 'I wait for no one. *Not* when I am insulted and the character of my house is called into disrepute!'

'Five thousand.'

'*Ten!*' she hissed, 'and Violette comes to you to be questioned in my presence!'

Ah *merde* . . . Two burly Feldgendarmen in their shirtsleeves had come thundering up from the cellars where they had been toasting their heels beside the furnace. 'All right, I'll wait.'

'Then sit with the girls,' she said. 'Find your place among them but please do not be tempted. *That* would cost you extra.'

Father Eugène Debauve placed his big, work-worn hands over Giselle's in friendship as his glasses winked in the pale light of oil lamps that had just been lighted. 'I'm the Bishop's emissary among the *lorettes* of the brothels that are reserved for the Germans, my dear. I hold Masses for them, hear their prayers and confessions, providing help whenever I can.'

A big, strong man, a good man who had unerringly known his way in the dark and had known his restaurants, too. The Brasserie de Tout Bonheur (of All Good Luck) was a turn-of-the-century place with dark, gleaming wood, etched glass panels, mirrors and a spiral staircase at the back that led to the private rooms and tables above. There were other customers, Germans, yes, and as it was early yet, not so many.

'If there is a word of advice I could give, my child,' he said, still warming her hands, 'it would be that you do not throw your life away. Ah! I know what you're going to say. A shopgirl's life is ten or twelve hours of absolute drudgery for very little, but it is honest and your children would always be able to worship their dear mother.'

She hated to have lied about the children, but that had been said in the other place and he must have picked it up. She could not remember when she had said it, or even if he had only just come in.

'My dear, women like Madame Morelle have only one goal and that is to accumulate as much money as possible no matter the cost to others. She takes the half of everything—I know. The girls, they have complained to me endlessly about it. It's all reinvested in real estate—Nice, Cannes, Bordeaux. That wretched woman even has property in Madrid and Barcelona and a fat bank account in each as well.'

Father Debauve waited while the waiter set the *soupe du jour* in front of them and placed a basket of bread and dish of butter near her—real butter and real bread, not the National stuff. Fresh and made with sifted white flour. No weevils, no rat shit, no ration tickets either, only a nod, and as good a black-market restaurant as she had been in. Better, perhaps, since the *patrons* wanted God on their side and treated the clergy with respect and kindness, for insurance purposes in the hereafter, of course.

'Enjoy,' said the priest. 'Warm your insides and think on what I've said. That husband of hers controls only the little *café-bar* she bought him. He's handy to have around, since he keeps track of the *maquereaux* her girls use. She's one who always has her ear to the ground, and he is often that ear.'

'He's a bad one,' she said, breaking bread and realizing suddenly how famished she was.

'A type,' acknowledged Father Debauve, not looking up.

'A number,' she added, casting the *patron* of the Turning Hour down a bit further but not yet relegating him to the rank of an 'individual'. The soup, a thick and fragrant purée of lentils, ham stock and onions, was magnificent.

'I come here often,' acknowledged the priest. 'They know me and do not question my not drinking alcohol of any kind like the others you see at this hour. Always the soup and a coffee perhaps; always a guest if suitably dressed. If not, why, I must use discretion and visit another of my places.'

Had he once been under the empire of alcohol? she wondered and decided that, yes perhaps the face so ravaged by time held memories of it. He was really very kind and again she felt guilty about the lie of two children, but such a thing had been necessary at the time and would be very difficult to retract. 'Do you visit all the brothels?' she asked.

'The forty or so, yes. I have a letter signed by the Kommandant von Gross-Paris, so have little trouble. He feels, as does the Bishop, that even the most depraved need to accept God into their hearts.'

And you, my dear? What of you? she could hear him asking and ducked her eyes away to her soup.

A bit of bread floated up, briefly resisting the clutch of the ground lentils until she had drowned it. 'I go to Mass every Sunday, Father, and twice on all the holy days. I do say the

Angelus in Latin—it's the only way, isn't that so?—and the Our
Father.'

'The Hail Mary?' he asked.

The Ave Maria. 'Of course,' she said demurely and wondered why he had not used that other name since he was so
concerned about the use of Latin. 'I was raised in a convent
school just . . . just as was that little girl who was murdered
yesterday.'

He kissed his ring and bit a knuckle to stop the pain of such
an anguish. Tears formed in his eyes. He said, 'That poor child.
Was she subjected to the indignities of a *lorette*? Did he do that
to her first? The female body is a chalice, my dear. A chalice.
Respect is its due. How could any man do such a thing to a . . . '

'Father . . . Look, I'll be honest, shall I?

She had such lovely eyes, a skin so clear, and lips that would
form each word of the Angelus with care and with but traces of
timidity. 'My dear,' he said, 'feel free to take me into your confidence. It's why I'm here.'

It's my job, my *raison d'être*. 'Hermann, my . . . my husband,
is a detective.'

'But . . . but you wear no ring, my child?'

'I do, Father, but I had to remove it when I went into that
café.' Another lie. Then why not put it on now—was he asking
this? she wondered and said, 'Hermann needs the name and
address of the *maquereau* of Violette Belanger.'

He spooned his soup. 'A mean one. A sponger, a depraver of
young girls and innocent women. A good-for-nothing that
wilful child dotes on.' He reached for more bread and tore it in
half. 'She has a sister in a convent, Sister Céline, much
admired by the Reverend Mother, loved by her students and
very devout. The good sister and I pray for Violette, but . . . ' His
eyes grew sad as he sought her out and shrugged at life. 'But
Violette will have none of it.'

'And the *maquereau*?' she asked earnestly.

Debauve clucked his tongue in distaste and tossed his head.
'Broken sugar is his weapon, the slash across the face that leaves

a welt far crueler than the knife. A monster. Morelle will have the address. Tell your husband to ask him.'

She swallowed hard at the mention of such cruelty, and he noted she understood only too well what the ruin of a pretty face could do to a girl of the streets.

'My dear, these things are harsh. You must forgive me. Please finish your soup. Here, put more bread in it. Break it up and let the soup soak into it. That's always best.'

And my Hermann, Father? she wondered. Why is it, please, that you do not ask where he is? Does your mind leap so far ahead of me you know he is at the house of Madame Morelle and have no need to ask?

Their coffee came, and it was the real thing and strong—ah! she wanted to drown herself in it and linger forever with the taste of it on her tongue. But gangsters used the chunks of sugar. These days, only in such places as the Café of the Turning Hour, for sugar was almost impossible to come by.

'My dear,' said Debauve earnestly, 'you must leave all thought of that house behind you. You're presentable—you've a fragile, very delicate beauty, if I may say so. Find some other type of work. Can you speak German?'

'A little,' she said softly.

He thought this excellent. 'They're always looking for people. Ah. I know of an escort service on the Champs-Élysées. Very classy, very aboveboard. Generals, lieutenants—they come to Paris and are lost without a little companionship. They simply do not know their way around and need guidance. The pay is, I believe, quite good. The Louvre, the Tuileries, the Tour Eiffel and such places.'

He searched his pockets and, finding pencil and scrap of paper, wrote the address down. 'This one's okay,' he said. 'The Germans won't bother you if you're stopped in the street and they find this slip of paper. Number 78. It's in the building next to the Lido. There's a Bavarian who has a restaurant across the street. Chez . . . Ah, what is it now?'

'Chez Rudi's,' she said and saw him nod.

'Ask for Mademoiselle Monique or Mademoiselle Claire. Tell either of them I sent you. They'll both understand and will look after you. Dresses and evening gowns they can supply. Their wardrobes are at your disposal, so you need have no worries about such expenses.'

Monique or Claire . . . It was like a dream. One never knew these days, and what was it her horoscope had said? The one in *Paris-Soir*, not the one in *Le Matin*—it was never any good. *You will meet someone new and exciting. Use caution at first—it's only natural—but when the time is right, give yourself to him entirely.*

A priest.

Kohler was intrigued and cried out inwardly, Louis, *mon vieux*, you should see this, but Louis wasn't here.

The dark brown hair was dishevelled and fell thickly to hide all but the centre of the girl's forehead, framing a soft oval whose deep brown eyes were shrewd and calculating.

Innocence sized him up and read him right to the core but did not smile or frown, though kept that hesitant stillness as if, knowing the worst, she waited only for it to happen.

'Monsieur, what is it you want of me if not the use of my body?'

Ah *merde*, she even had the voice to go with it. Violette Belanger's naturally red lips were lovely, her nose perfect, the set of the eyes neither too wide nor too narrow. And as for her age, he thought, she could be twenty-three all right but looked no more than seventeen.

'Just a few questions. Nothing difficult,' he said and heard his voice sounding uncomfortably strange above the general hubbub of the place, the constant comings and goings, the latest raft of whores lounging around in various states of undress but no longer boredom.

'Violette, you may sit,' said Madame Morelle.

The girl made no move to do so but stood demurely before them in her dark blue tunic with shoulder straps, white shirt-blouse and dark blue tie. Hands folded now in front of her as if waiting for the Mother Superior to begin, and why is it, he asked himself, that schoolgirls in uniform seem to drive most men crazy?

Grey smears and droplets of semen marred the pleated skirt and hem of the tunic. There were more of them on its upper part and some were still damp. 'Well?' she asked but not sharply.

He wished he could be alone with her. She was making him unsettled for even daring to look at her in a place like this, but the other girls were a damned nuisance. Some glared at the schoolgirl, pouting with jealousy. Others giggled and pointed hurriedly at her kneesocks or confided lewd whispers about him to each other. Then, too, there was the godawful heat of the place, the smell of soap and disinfectant, toilet water, cheap perfume, sweat, lye, semen, farts, talcum powder and hydrogen peroxide. Sloshed, watered wine, too, and cheap champagne, beer and cigarette and cigar smoke. Vomit also. The din was constant. So, too, the sound of boots on the bare planks of the staircase that did, indeed, go up and up.

'Madame, has this one paid for the time he is taking to undress me with those empty eyes of his or will he *not* pay until I remove my clothes?'

'Monsieur, please address your questions to our Violette.'

Kohler dragged out his notebook. 'Your sister, mademoiselle. Sister Céline. Did she come to see you yesterday?'

The day that child was killed—she knew this was why he had asked, but were his eyes always so empty? 'Céline did not come to see me, as was her custom. I waited—yes, of course. One cannot deny God's little messenger, but . . .' The girl shrugged.

'How often does she come to visit you?'

Had they found something? she asked herself. 'Not often. Twice a month. Sometimes three or four times if she's really upset, and not always on a Sunday. Usually on a Monday, a Wednesday or a Friday. It depends on her schedule.'

What was it Father Jouvand had said about the soup-kitchen days? Mondays, Wednesdays and Fridays. Ah *merde*. The same. 'Upset about what?' he asked.

Ah! The police, they were all alike. 'About myself, my profession. Her knees are always red and swollen. If she's really upset, I put ointment on them. She makes me do it as a penance.'

There, does that satisfy you? he could almost hear her asking.

One of the other girls came into the room to hand Madame Morelle the coffee can that sat on the floor beside every whore's bed or washstand to catch the rubber leavings, which were, of course, resold, especially in these hard times. 'Ten?' asked Madame Morelle, peering into the thing. 'What is this, Lilou?'

'I'm sore, madame. It itches.'

'Ah! such foolishness. Give it a wash. Go on. Get out and take this with you. Bring it back to me with thirty, you understand? *Thirty* or else! Now where were we?'

She wet her lips and took another sip of the advocaat and port that kept her going. One of the girls passed her a lighted cheroot, wine-cured and dark.

'Did your sister ever come with a priest?' he asked.

'A priest?' Violette swallowed, recovering quickly. 'No. No, she always . . . Ah now, a moment. Of course, you mean Father Jouvand. Yes, yes, they sometimes came together. The sisters, they must always be accompanied when they go out, isn't that so? They cannot walk alone.'

'Does a priest not call?'

'Those who wish to attend Mass go out.'

'That old priest is like a chancre,' seethed Madame Morelle. 'Always interfering, always telling us God condemns His daughters who fall by the wayside but never the men who use them. Never! Ah, celibacy is to the priesthood what marriage is to the *maisons de tolérance*. Both are to be sworn while making the lofty claims of sainthood when God knows the frock is up, the trousers down, and if not the anus of another, then the correct and God-demanded entrance of one of my girls.'

They roared, they hooted, and all the while a *sous-maîtresse* dispensed clean hand towels, marked the slashes in the little book, took the money and brought the girls out to meet their clients, since the room was occupied.

But Violette didn't alter the look she had first given him.

'I want another priest,' he said and watched as the faintest shudder of alarm passed through her. 'A man with a black overcoat.'

One by one the other whores looked at each other and for a moment an uncomfortable silence fell on the room.

'There is no other,' said Violette. 'When my sister does not come with Father Jouvand, she brings along one of the other sisters. It's most uncomfortable for me—ah yes, of course—but what can one do with such as them? We talk, we walk. I hear the same old admonitions, the same scolding, the same tiresome prayers. I wasn't a virgin when I first became a girl of the streets, Inspector. My father took that from me at the age of eight, but to Céline he is still a saint and blameless.'

'Blind ... Céline, she was blind to it,' acknowledged Madame Morelle, puffing on her cheroot and glad they had got over the impasse. A priest, a *maquereau* ...

'He broke my heart but taught me only one thing,' said Violette of her father, 'and that is that men want everything a girl has and they can take. Now, please, this is costing me money. May I return to my customers?'

'Does your sister hate young girls?'

'Ah! why do you ask? She's not a suspect, is she?'

He did not grin, this detective. He flipped his little notebook closed, stood up, got his overcoat and hat, and said, 'Go fill up your coffee can. I'll be back, and when I am, see that your tongue is loosened or I'll shut this place down so hard Madame's ears will flap for ever. Old Shatter Hand may be a friend of the house, but he's our boss on this and what we say goes.'

It wasn't Violette who made the sign of the cross, or even any of the other girls, but Madame Morelle herself, and the look she gave Violette told him he would have to come back.

'Your *maquereau*?' he asked, stopping the girl in the hall and seeing her wince with dismay. 'What's his name and where can I find him?'

She shrugged. She said, 'I haven't seen that one since he was knifed where he shouldn't have been and died in the street.

Since then I have kept my share of my little gifts for myself. At the end of the year I will have enough to leave this place. I'm going to Provence, to a farm I know of. I'm going to grow vegetables and raise birds. Peacocks and parrots to sell in the markets. Céline doesn't believe me, but you can if you wish.'

He felt her fingertips lightly trace the scar on his cheek and explore the bullet graze across his brow. 'Have you a woman?' she asked—he could hear the earthiness deliberately grating in her voice. She was lying, of course, about the *maquereau* and financing the dream. At the church and convent school Father Jouvand had said, 'Violette Belanger makes a mockery of that same sister . . . If it is someone in the guise of a nun you are looking for . . . '

A 'nun', a 'priest' and a 'schoolgirl'. Ah *merde*, Giselle . . .

'I don't like farming. I had enough of that as a boy, but I'll be sure to let my partner know. He's always going on about his retirement.'

'You do that, and if you see my sister, please tell her what our father did to me on my birthday.'

'You weren't to blame, were you?'

'No. No of course not. I was a child.'

 **F**ROM THE DEEPER DARKNESS OF THE FOLLY'S columns, St-Cyr looked down over the garden towards the Villa Vernet. He was so cold he was numb to it, but waited, and when a door softly closed behind the receding figure, he turned and disappeared inside the folly to strike a match over the stone table in its centre. He struck another and another, the wood so cheap and brittle, the nation's matches were all but useless, especially at times like this.

At last he had one lighted. Steam issued from the plate of soup that had been covered with a porcelain lid and wrapped in towels. The soup was a golden yellow and piping hot ... ah *nom de Jésus-Christ!* Why did God put such temptations in front of him?

The match went out and he stood in absolute darkness breathing in the last traces of sulphur and the first of an ambrosial aroma that made the juices run.

'A *potage purée de volaille à la reine*, the original,' he sighed. 'A soup whose recipe must date from the sixteenth century.'

Had the child arrived? he wondered. Was she now secretly watching him or a prisoner of the one who had been following her at 2.00 p.m., the one, most likely, who had killed her little friend? Dead . . . ? Was she now dead?

Exhausted from searching for her, and still arguing with himself whether to ask von Schaumburg to authorize an all-out search, he had not even been able to confirm she really had been seen. But to call out the troops would be to panic the killer if he had her, and that could not be risked for he would then simply kill her, too.

And if she is still free and hiding out, he asked, will she not simply freeze to death?

The soup was a purée of finely pounded breast of chicken that had first been roasted to a golden brown on a spit. The flour of a dozen sweet almonds and three or four bitter ones had been added, so, too, the yolks of six hard-boiled eggs.

A fortune in these hard times, or at any time. A treat the child must adore, and so the Vernet chef had prepared it.

'A consommé of chicken stock,' said St-Cyr aloud and into the surrounding darkness should the child be there to hear. 'Finely chopped leeks and celery stalks in season are added, the celery seed used now. Then cream or milk once the puréed ingredients have been given a final pass through the sieve. Saffron and honey, essence of roses, and a few pinches of thyme. Me, I admire your choice. Spooned over crumbled bread crusts to further thicken it, your soup, it is magnificent.'

Still she did not say a thing. He hated himself for depriving her of a most necessary meal. He wanted to cry out, I'm on your side. Why will you not please go in?

But she was not there and again, after much searching, he had to stand among the columns, though still asking, Are you with him? Has he now killed you? The one who murdered your little friend?

From the house a brief glimmer of light came, and then, among the ornamental box and yew, the darkened silhouette of a figure hurrying out with yet another plate of soup.

'*Nénette? Petite*, you must come in, isn't that so? We're waiting for you. Liline, Nénette. Liline, she has not returned. Has something happened to her? Is this why you won't come in?'

Soup plates were exchanged and only as this was done did the chef discover the first one had been drained and wiped clean with every last crumb of the bread.

'*Nénette*,' he said firmly. 'Your aunt has still not returned from the hairdresser's and another visit to that clairvoyant of hers. It's safe, little one. Your uncle, he stays in Rouen.'

The chef waited for her to answer. Perhaps he sensed he was not alone, perhaps the cold simply made him irritable. 'You always had a mind of your own,' he hissed. 'Ah! it's not good for girls to be like that. Can you not think of us? No, not you, eh? In spite of the mother who gave birth to you in my kitchen—I still hear her cries—you are *not* a Vernet like her or your father. You are more like the monsieur, I think. Now come down from there at once. Attend to me, Nénette. This is a craziness that must stop. I, Léon Kalfou, am your godfather. *Me, petite!* No one is going to murder you when we who love you are there to keep you safe.'

No one. Ah *merde* . . . 'Monsieur . . ."

The plate shattered. The chef shrilled, '*Sadique*, I am going to telephone the police!' He bolted from the folly only to slip on the steps and leave blood in the snow as he lay there not even moaning.

A scarf was sacrificed, the man propped up and gently brought to. 'A moment, monsieur,' said the Sûreté, 'and I will assist you to the house.'

More matches were struck and it was then that St-Cyr saw the error of his ways. Inside the folly, just under its roof, there was a gallery, and when he had climbed to it, he found a blue over-coat, a hand-me-down of Liline Chambert's perhaps, its lining ripped open and crudely restitched in several places after first having been thoroughly stuffed with dried oak leaves for insulation.

There were sealskin boots and mittens, a hat, too, and extra scarves, even blankets, and all he could think of now was had he driven that child out into the Bois on a night like this? Had she been up here at all since the murders of her friends, had she even returned? Or after the chase in the Bois today, had there been only a death similar to that of her little friend?

The coat would be very warm and snug. He must remember her invention. These days one never knew what one might need. But when had she done it? Well before the murder—last Thursday or Friday perhaps, or even before that, in the late fall when dry leaves were possible and best collected?

The late fall. All things must have been prepared then for a long stay in the cold, a plan that predated the Sandman's murders by at least several weeks.

But not, he thought, that of the placing of the crèche in Sister Céline's classroom and the stealing of the toy giraffe and then the baby elephant. Nénette had taken the one, Andrée the other, on a dare, to be later exchanged as a bond of solidarity.

When he found another old overcoat also stuffed with leaves and rolled up under a stone bench, he knew the truth. Both of the girls had planned to leave the convent school and the house and take to the wilds.

Voyous, street urchins—runaways in a land that had no use for them and was under an Occupier who fiercely demanded that all such types be cleansed from the streets and sent by rail to unspoken destinations.

The Brasserie de Tout Bonheur was full but there was no sign of Giselle. The Café of the Turning Hour held only watchful sharks bent on sucking their girls in to rip them off and keep them on their backs until their days as charladies came.

Kohler hounded the darkened streets and cursed the blackout that, if he used the unblinkered torch in his pocket, would see the *gendarmes* pounce and scream and pound him into oblivion. *Merde!* Where was Giselle?

Panic struck. He had let Violette Belanger's pimp get his talons into Giselle. One question of hers would lead to another until the bastard needed to know just why he was wanted by this detective.

So, he'd take her to a quiet place. He'd lead her on until she had no more to give . . .

A 'priest'.

Knowing that he had no other choice, he returned to the

Café of the Turning Hour to wipe the zinc with the fist of Madame Morelle's husband and let the others slip away or crowd round with knives drawn.

'Now I'll ask you one more time. Where did he take her?'

Two more girls came in looking for their pimps only to find the place draughty. Morelle didn't budge. The Savoyard must have come from a long line of hill climbers. The bulging dark brown eyes held the fierce hatred of a Corsican, and Kohler wondered if this, too, was not a part of his ancestry.

One of the girls, her back to the wall, sucked in a breath, and he knew then that trouble was about to break out.

Morelle's nose ran freely, dampening the bushy grey handlebars and webbing the hairs.

Ignoring it, the *patron* still waited. *Vache!* Cow! he shrilled silently. Cop!

'Giselle,' breathed Kohler and in that moment realized yet again that the kid really meant something to him, that life could never be the same without her and that Wasserburg and Gerda and the farm at home were now far behind him.

There'd be a butcher's knife under the zinc counter or a leather sock filled with lead, but they wouldn't want to cut him up or kill him here for fear of being accused of terrorism.

No, they'd knocked him out and drop him in the Seine. They'd have to.

He released the hand. He grinned and patted the shirt front, said, 'Why not be reasonable? She's just a kid. She doesn't know this part of town. Give her a break. It wasn't her fault.'

'And Violette?' hissed Morelle. 'Will she also get a break?'

A real crowd pleaser. 'Of course. Hey, I just asked her a few simple questions. My partner and me—he's the one out on the street with the boys in blue and the *panier à salade*—we're working on the Sandman thing. I thought Violette might have been able to help us.'

This one needed a shovel to finish digging his grave. 'Violette? But . . . but, monsieur, is the sadist her *maquereau*, do you think?' fluted Morelle, feeling firmly in charge, 'or is it a man of the cloth perhaps?'

It was now or never. 'Both pimp and priest.'

Death swiftly entered Morelle's eyes. Now it was there and now it was gone. As the zinc was wiped with the *patron*, glasses shattered, shrieks tore the air, the sharks tumbling back or lunging only to stop.

Kohler held the bastard's head bent back over the far end of the bar, strangling him until the Savoyard was plum-red in the face and choking.

Flat on his back with the neck of an upturned pastis bottle jammed into his mouth, Morelle could not talk but only swallow.

'I hate guys like you,' breathed Kohler, knowing they must have pawed Giselle and terrified her. Raising a cautioning finger to the others, he said, 'You move and I'll kill him and claim it was self-defence.'

Several teeth had been chipped, but the neck of the bottle hadn't been broken. Kohler set it aside. 'Now talk, my friend. Everything. Where she is and who he is. Don't stop until I tell you.'

'*BÂTARD*, I TELL YOU NOTHING!' shrieked Morelle, trying to get free.

'A loudmouth,' sighed Kohler. 'Hey, you—yes, you with the gold scarf around your pretty neck and the eyelashes that are about to fall off. Hand me a lump of sugar from the floor and we'll open his purse.'

The sugar . . . Morelle heard its cone being smashed on the zinc beside his head and then the pieces being picked over for the sharpest edge. 'His . . . his name is Father Eugène Debauve.'

There was a nod. 'Now his real name.'

Ah *nom de Jésus-Christ!* must this one gut him in front of the others? 'Father Eugène Debauville.'

A wise choice. 'Defrocked for what reason?'

The head was quickly shaken. Snot was flung until . . . 'All right. Please let me up.'

'Not until I hear it.'

Then die, *flic. Die!* 'No one knows. No one says, but . . .' The sugar pierced his skin. Blood began to trickle. 'But I . . .'

Morelle panicked as he realized his wife would have nothing

more to do with him if she found out he had ratted on his own, but the slash down the Bavarian's cheek mirrored what was about to happen to him. 'I . . . I think it must have had to do with children, with . . . *Yes, schoolgirls!* because he . . . he is so good with them. They cry every time.'

There wasn't a sound or a movement from the mourners at this little wake, only the endless flapping of the draught plate in the stove's chimney.

'Schoolgirls where?'

Ah, Christ! if Debauve ever found out—which he would— the priest would kill him. 'A convent school near Troyes. That . . . that is where his family has had property for centuries and that is where it . . . it must first have happened.'

Schoolgirls . . . Had the heiress been on to the Sandman after all? 'And does he like to knit?'

'*Knit?* He likes to *threaten*, and when they are on their knees, he . . . he has a special way with them.'

The sugar nicked the bridge of Morelle's prominent nose and he knew then that Kohler was about to split it in half and mark him for life. 'They . . . they will have gone to the Saint-Roch. He . . . he has the keys from the old days at the seminary, you understand. The keys to several churches. Since it is a Monday evening, that place will be closed and it is the closest.'

'What did you do to Giselle?'

Morelle told him. Kohler sighed and left the sugar balanced on the bastard's nose, saying, 'Hey, you touch her again and I'll find you.'

Louis . . . Where the hell was Louis?

'She loved that soup,' confessed Léon Kalfou, a towel with ice clamped to the back of his head. 'She always maintained she could die for it.'

A beautifully bright, golden soup that had once been the favourite of Queen Marguerite de Valois. 'The child has chosen wisely,' said St-Cyr, finishing yet another plate and wiping it clean with bread. They were sitting at a table in the kitchens.

The chef was so very near to tears his puffy eyelids bagged with moisture, making pools of the sad brown eyes. Large ears and still-reddened cheeks made him look like something flushed from the forest during the hunt, blinking still in dismay as the truth of being caught kept dawning on him.

The narrow cheeks and chin, a much-furrowed brow, ginger moustache and thinning sandy hair did nothing to dispel the image. A bachelor who would time the cooling of the soup and worry so much about its getting cold he would hurry out with another plate before needed. How long had he kept it up? Since darkness had fallen.

One must be gentle. 'Monsieur, the child was, I understand, quite prepared to run away?'

'Why must you ask it of me, Inspector? I am only the chef. I know nothing.'

'Now, please, we have to start somewhere. The soup is as good a place as any. You spent the better part of the day preparing it. You were worried. You felt she would not come inside. Out in the folly you said that it was safe for her to come in and that no one was going to murder her. Those are strong words to a detective.'

It would do no good to avoid the matter, but why was the monsieur not here to do his own answering, why not the madame, eh? demanded Kalfou angrily of himself. 'Mademoiselle Nénette, she . . . she missed her mother and father, that is all. She felt her place was no longer in this house. Ah! a romantic—her passion for the soup is evidence enough. A *voyou*, a brigand of the forest—they had crazy notions, those two girls. Both wanted to escape and take control of their lives. Absolute freedom from here and from school.'

'Yet she delays their escape. She waits and then begins to track the Sandman,' said St-Cyr, lost in thought. 'She feels the police, they are not doing their job. She is a pack rat, a magpie. She picks things up, and among the litter in her pockets there are things that may suggest she really does know who the Sandman is. It's a puzzle.'

'It's no puzzle at all, Inspector,' seethed the housekeeper, finding them alone and deep in conference. 'That child needs to be horsewhipped. Behaving like this? Lying? Stealing? Preparing to run away? *Claiming* she knows who that . . . that murderer of young girls is and yet . . . yet *refusing* to tell us until the préfet has been summoned? Of course the monsieur could not agree. It was a foolishness.'

Realizing she had said too much or had said it too forcefully, the housekeeper irritably folded her arms across her chest and stood there glowering at them. The smoke from a hastily lighted cigarette trailed up. '*Well*, what is it?' she demanded. 'Aren't you going to question me first?'

In-house protocol had been breached, but that wasn't the reason for her anger, and the cigarette she had lighted before entering the kitchen so as to calm herself was a failure. 'I would never have got past you, madame. In any case, circumstance'— he indicated the chef's cold compress—'dictated otherwise.'

Ah, damn him. 'I'll report this, monsieur le chef. I shall have to.' Irritably she took a puff on her cigarette before refolding her arms. The grey-blue woollen suit and soft mauve blouse suited the wavy, dark auburn hair and blue eyes, the pale cheeks and lipstick, but there was also that deliberate touch of not over-dressing for fear of offending. Had she been a widow when hired by the child's father, the widow of one of the men under his command in the last war? he wondered and thought it likely. Duties first, then, as a secretary perhaps, and later as housekeeper, a not unhappy fate but perhaps unwelcome.

'Inspector, where is she? Please tell us.'

'We do not yet know, Madame. . . ?'

'Therrien. Isabelle.'

'Madame, please take us back to yesterday morning. Nénette went out early to walk the dog.'

'It was something I told her she had to do since the Reverend Mother had recommended it, but the child was *not* to leave the garden. *That* was forbidden, not that she paid such orders any mind. Not any more.'

'But did she meet Andrée Noireau, and did Andrée then

spend the morning hiding in the garden folly waiting until the two of them could visit the Jardin d'Acclimatation alone?'

Alone and without Liline who was to have accompanied Nénette . . .

The woman glanced at the chef, for support, perhaps, and forgiveness. She wouldn't be reporting any insubordination, was really very worried and had spoken angrily out of concern.

'Nénette took the longest time, and when she came back, it was without the dog. I asked her where it was, and she said it had run off. "There are females in heat. You can't stop him when he gets a whiff of that. Don't you know anything?" she said and pouted. Ah! so much had been going on. The murders, the claims of knowing who had done them, I . . . I let the matter pass. I didn't give a damn about that silly dog. None of us did.'

'She had tied it to a tree in the Bois, hoping it would be stolen and eaten, Inspector,' confessed Léon Kalfou. 'I know—at least, I think I do—because she had often asked me for recipes. "How would one cook a dog, Kalfou?" she would say. "By roasting it on a spit? By boiling until tender or by braising?" I . . . I think even then, and it's a long time ago, she had planned to trap and eat dogs in the wild if necessary.'

But was it that she wanted to make sure the dog would not follow them and that if they did make their getaway, food would be at hand? A dog. The dog, Pompon.

He would have to go carefully. 'When, exactly, did these questions of sustenance begin?'

Again they exchanged glances, the housekeeper urging caution with a slight lift of her left hand.

The chef shrugged. 'Three weeks, a month ago perhaps. Yes, yes, now I remember. She asked if dogmeat would do for a Christmas feast. Roasted and basted with a sauce of apples, pears and ground chestnuts for sweetening. That child has a vivid imagination, Inspector. I would not, if I were you, place too much emphasis on whatever you have found in her coat pockets.'

'I won't. Now I want the precise time, monsieur. Was it not

early last November perhaps that the question of eating dog-meat began?'

Again a cautionary hand was raised slightly but he was ready for it and stood up abruptly. 'Now,' he said, 'your answer, madame.'

'In . . . in the first week of November. Liline . . . Liline had been ill. I . . .'

'The girl was pregnant, madame. Nénette must have realized it or at least have felt that something terrible had happened to Liline. She may have heard the girl crying in her room and gone in to her. It was then that the questions of dogmeat and other things began.'

Madame Therrien quickly crossed herself. 'How did you know?'

Was it time to tell them about the death of Liline? he wondered and decided that it would have to wait a little longer. 'I guessed, that is all. With crime one so often depends on intuition. Monsieur Vernet has been carrying on an affair with Mademoiselle Chambert and has confessed to this. For myself, I am surprised a man of his intelligence and position would not at least have taken precautions, but then . . .'

'Then *what*?' snapped the housekeeper irritably.

The chef swallowed his tears.

'Ah, it's nothing,' said the Sûreté, shrugging the matter off. 'I was only wondering why that child is afraid to come home.'

And there it is, thought Isabelle Therrien sadly. A child whose dear friend is made pregnant by her father's brother, and whose other dear friend had been all but totally rejected by parents who had preferred to ski alone, and is now dead.

'There was a tiepin,' she said. 'It was bent and had been scraped or damaged. Nénette was convinced it was important, but I don't know where she found it, nor do I think she really knew who had stepped on it or why. She was too secretive, Inspector. She really has told us very little.'

'Because she was afraid?' he asked, and saw them both exchange glances of alarm.

'Afraid?' managed the woman. 'But of what, please?'

'Of the Sandman. This I know,' confessed the chef, 'because last Friday before supper she told me he would strike again. "And very close," she said. "So close, Kalfou, you will feel the breath of him, but he will make a mistake and will have to let that one go." '

But he hadn't. He had killed her friend, though that killing had not been entirely like all the others.

Kohler floored the Citroën. He cried out, 'Giselle, I'm coming. Hang on, kid,' and shot across the avenue de l'Opéra, the beam of unblinkered headlamps piercing the darkness to dance illegally over the pavement, lighting up the startled faces of pedestrians. All gawking, all caught, trapped—*pinned* in the centre of the road—a *vélo-taxi* . . . another . . . an *autobus au gazogène*, a lorry . . . '*Ah shit!*' he cried, and slammed on the brakes.

The car slewed sideways. A gendarme blew his whistle and the beam from the headlamps made the man choke as the car slid towards him. Then the Citroën's *traction avant* grabbed paving blocks and tore down the rue des Pyramides to slew sideways again on the rue Saint-Honoré and come to a sliding stop.

'*Verdammt!*' he cursed and, leaving the headlamps on, bolted out and up the steps to the Church of Saint-Roch.

Its massive doors were unyielding. Though he pounded on them, it made no difference. 'Giselle,' he said, biting back her name and all the good things he had planned for her, the escape from Paris before it was too late and everything about this lousy Occupation came to an end. The false papers he still had to get for her and Oona and himself, the race still to plan, the crossing over into Spain.

And Louis? he asked, sucking in a breath as he ran up the passage Saint-Roch searching for another door . . . another door.

Louis would have to come with them. Louis wouldn't be allowed to stay in France, not with his name still wrongly embedded in the hit lists of certain Resistance cells. A mistake that Talbotte, the rotten son of a bitch, would be sure to use. 'Ah *merde*, Louis . . . Louis, I need you.'

He pounded on a door that must be near the altar. He heaved

on it and threw his shoulder against it, wiped tears from his face. 'Giselle . . .' He coughed. 'Ah, Christ, little one, what have I done to you?'

Things Louis had said about the Saint-Roch came rushing back, a tour nearly two and a half years ago, a lecture on the architecture of the world's 'finest city'. 'It is the paintings, the frescoes and the sculptures inside that are important, not the look of this place. It's a monolith of stone, a city block deep and, yes, not so pretty.'

The Assumption, the Nativity, the Purification of the Virgin and *Return of the Prodigal Son* . . .

He pounded on the door and kicked at it. He cried out, 'Debauville, I'll kill you if you harm her.'

Was she on her knees with that bastard saying prayers over her? Was she naked and freezing, a crucifix dangling between her splendid breasts, the black iron of it against the softness of her skin, her hands clasped, eyes closed, the dark lashes long and gently curving upwards a little? She was devout, had much to say about sin, her sins, was really not suited to the profession she had chosen. An innocent, though she did not like to think so. She had the nicest eyes, the clearest, most all-encompassing shade of violet. Jet-black hair and *Ave Maria, gratia plena; Dominus tecum* . . .

She could pray for hours when she felt the need to be absolved from her sins. Her knees would be red, the scourge giving her the innocence of a child until temptation again led her to stray.

When the torch beams of a Wehrmacht patrol, accompanied by several of Talbotte's men, caught up with him, his knuckles were bleeding and all he could manage was 'Kohler, Gestapo Paris-Central, the Sandman, I think he's . . . he's in there with . . .'

He couldn't say it. He saw her in the Red Room at Madame Chabot's over on the rue Danton that first time, she innocently looking up at this giant from Bavaria who had said, 'Kid, what the hell are you doing in a place like this?'

He had fallen for her and Louis hadn't liked the thought of
it at all—still felt the affair suspect, saying under his breath,
'You wait, you watch, *mon vieux*, and see if she doesn't return
to it.'

The rain of rifle butts on all doors resounded within and
when, at last, a terrified custodian reluctantly opened one of
them, they poured inside and lit the place up until the high
vault of the roof, the pillars, the paintings, sculptures and altar
glowed. The Cross, the Virgin—Jesus nailed up there and
Suffer the little children to come unto me . . .

'A glove. A leather glove,' said a *flic* from Talbotte's nest, a
viper. 'The brown leather glove of a child, Monsieur the
Inspector. Is it this for which you are searching while emptying
the oceans of your eyes?'

The glove was lying on the floor at the foot of the steps that
led up to the altar; next to it were a candle on its side and a
small pool of now-congealed wax.

Giselle? he begged, and, picking up the glove, stared emptily
at it.

'The child?' he asked at last. 'Ah *merde* . . . The "priest" must
really be the Sandman.'

In the darkness of the child's bedroom the amber and gold of
the dragonflies on the stained-glass lampshade finally glowed,
but still Madame Vernet did not see him. Unsettled, she
touched the waistcoat of the porcelain frog below the lamp and
turned sharply as the Meissen clock on the mantelpiece
chimed 9.00 p.m., Berlin Time.

'Inspector. . . ?' she said, but still St-Cyr wouldn't let himself
answer, nor had she seen him yet. He wanted only to study her
for a few moments, to watch as she searched the map of the city
the child had put up on the wall above her desk, the woman following the lines from press clippings to the site of each of the
Sandman's murders as if she could not stop herself until, at last,
she had read again perhaps, *This one is next.*

If anyone had wanted to kill her niece, there it was in black and white: *Sunday afternoon, 10 January, the Jardin d'Acclimatation. I am certain of it.* Her little friend would be away in Chamonix. Liline Chambert would be busy, a girl in great trouble, a tragedy.

Alone in the Jardin, while she waited for Liline to return, the heiress would be easy prey.

But Andrée Noireau had not gone to Chamonix and the girls had known Nénette would be followed.

As he watched her, Madame Vernet let her gaze drop to the things he had laid out and, seeing the crumpled, empty tube of oil paint, hesitated before picking it up. 'Liline, Inspector. She'll be able to tell you where Nénette got this.'

He did not answer and she silently cursed him for distrusting her, but where, please, was he? He had told them downstairs to send her up as soon as she had arrived home. Flustered and embarrassed, she had hardly had time to remove her coat and boots before climbing the stairs to pass by Liline's room, and reach Nénette's in this far corner of the house.

'The pencil tin is from the same source,' she said and heard her voice falter. 'It . . . it was just some man Liline met at one of her drawing classes at the Grande-Chaumière. He gave them to her. A German, a holder of the Iron Cross First-Class with Oak Leaves and other medals. "He . . . he's quite good," she once said, "but in bad shape. He wants only to paint children — schoolgirls." She . . . she took Nénette and Andrée to see his atelier in Saint-Germain and sat with them several times while they posed for him.'

A German . . . The wound and tank battle badges, the Polish Campaign medal, ah *merde* . . .

There, he could make what he liked of it, she thought, and perhaps the SS-Attack Leader Gerhardt Hasse had some answering of his own to do, since men, no matter how good as artists, should not just want to sketch schoolgirls.

Afraid of his scrutiny, embarrassed by it, she kept fingering the scratches on her left cheek while unconsciously her right hand touched that thigh as if for comfort. A forgotten woman, neglected by Vernet in favour of one so junior to her: Liline Chambert had been all but half her age.

The thick, wavy brunette hair was tossed in anger at his continued silence. She took a breath and, not turning, touched the base of her throat.

'Madame,' he said at last, 'where have you been?'

How cold his voice was. 'I won't stand for this, Inspector,' she said hotly. 'You've no right to ask in such a manner. I . . . I had an appointment at my hairdresser's, if you must know. Another power outage—they're always having to save electricity these days or cutting it off to punish people. The dryer went off while I was under it. I decided to wait.'

Perhaps, but then . . . ah then, he said to himself and, pushing in the plunger of the little roulette wheel, let the steel ball bounce round until it had found her number. A zero. The house would take all bets but those placed on that number.

'Where else did you go?' he asked.

Her eyes passed furtively over the objects before her. 'To my clairvoyant. Is that so wrong, please? Madame Rébé is president of the Society of Metaphysical Sciences. I . . . I went to consult her about my niece.'

'And?' he asked, joining her at last. She gave a shrug.

'I am to bring her a few items. Things that are the child's and typify her nature. Her tooth-brush, too, and the piece of soap she last touched.'

Uncertain of him, she tried to smile and read his mind in the light from those dragonflies. What could he see of me? she wondered. Are all my secrets so naked before him?

'Where, please, can we find this Madame Rébé?'

Ah, damn him! 'Look, she has nothing to do with any of this . . . this . . .' She gestured dismissively at the map and the rubbish on the desk. Her brown eyes glared at him fiercely. Every facial feature was sharpened by the light and the tension in her, the high cheekbones, the lips that were twisted up a little to the right, producing now a timorous and uncertain look.

'Please, we may need the clairvoyant's help, madame, isn't

that so?' he said, not taking his eyes from hers. 'Ah! I'm not averse to consulting them myself from time to time. My first wife was very committed to the practice and would not undertake any business venture without first the consultation.'

Had he deliberately made reference to that wife so as to make her wonder why the woman had left him? Might she then forget herself, if but for a moment? The bastard.

'She was a dress designer and had a little shop of her own, madame. My long hours and continued absences, these she simply could no longer take. Women need love. In marriage, it's expected. Now please, Madame Rébé?'

Cochon! she wanted to scream at him. She wished she could slap his face so hard they would hear it downstairs. '*Numéro* 10, rue de l'Eperon.'

It was in the Sixth, in Hermann's *quartier* and but a stone's throw from the house of Madame Chabot on the rue Danton and the flat he shared with Giselle and Oona on the rue Suger. A small world.

'And the atelier of this German artist?'

'This I . . . I do not know. Ask Liline. She'll tell you.'

'Ah! I wish it were possible, but you see, madame, the girl has left for the south. A hurried trip. Didn't your husband tell you?'

'*Bâtard,* he tells me nothing and you know it! Why distress me so? Are you all the same, you *flics?*'

'The same? Ah no, madame. No, there are differences.'

She turned away, she turned back. 'I don't know what you want with me. I've done nothing.'

'Then you have nothing to fear, have you?'

Her eyes darted down over the rubbish, and when they momentarily hesitated at the tiepin, he asked, 'What is it, please? Do you recognize something?'

'No. No, I . . . I just can't understand why that child had to pick up everything she came across. It's shameful. It's disgusting and unsanitary.'

But useful.

His mind made up, he took hold of her by the elbow, and when she heard his voice, his words, she shuddered inwardly and did not know what to do or say. 'Madame, please accompany me to the morgue. There is something I must show you.'

She could not bring herself to look at him. 'Honoré, the . . . the chauffeur, he . . . he will be having his supper. He . . .'

'I am sure he won't mind, but if you wish, I could telephone the Kommandantur for a car.'

Ah *merde, merde*, why must he do this to her? 'Antoine is the one you want, not me. *Bien sûr*, he's still in Rouen—he has an excuse, eh? Always he has an excuse.'

In the foyer, with the maid assisting, St-Cyr handed Madame her boots, first checking the soles until he had what he wanted and had inserted the bent pin of the turquoise-and-silver stud into the hole he'd discovered.

'Now we're getting somewhere,' he muttered to himself, not looking up at her. 'She stepped on this.'

The morgue was far from quiet. Scratchy strains of that pre-war classic, *J'ai deux amours*, 'Two Loves Have I', filled the entrance hall as the desk clerk logged in their names. Finches twittered in the distance of the autopsy room, singing along with Edith Piaf, as only she could render, before the war, that bittersweet longing for what had now become the France and Paris of other years.

'He's been in there since dawn,' seethed the man on the desk. 'One attends, one rewinds that cursed Victrola of his, and if I hear that goddamned song again I am going to personally put him on ice!'

St-Cyr gave the attendant a curt but understanding nod and, turning to lead Madame Vernet to a bench against the wall, said flatly, 'Please wait here until summoned.'

Quickly he left her, but saw her shiver suddenly and pull the mink coat more tightly about herself. A coat that was now worth nearly one million francs, such was the need for fur on the Russian Front. That same coat, in the fall of 1940, would have fetched no more than sixty-five thousand francs.

She'd keep on ice of her own. Ah yes and, cruel though that might seem, these things, they had to be done.

Hernand Belligueux was tidying up and took no immediate notice of him. Why should he? Weren't coroners indispensable? The Victrola-grinder was pale and painfully distressed—his feet must be freezing after thirteen hours in the cold room with barely time out to piss. Birdseed, harvested by the coroner in the wild throughout the fall, since none was available in the shops, was being doled out to the half-dozen finches in the ornate cage at his elbow.

Belligueux was nearly seventy years old and had been a bachelor all his life. That alone should make one wary of him. Slight, not tall, he was fastidiously dressed—waistcoat, shirt with sleeves carefully rolled up, and tie were all but covered by the tenth or twelfth white lab-coat he'd worn that day. From its pockets his notepads bulged. He would wash his hands and dry them as the need arose; sometimes he used gloves, most often not. The heart, lungs, livers, kidneys and stomachs would all have been opened and specimens taken for further examination. Nothing would be left to chance. Both corpses were shrouded under clean white sheets.

The thin red ribbon of the *Légion d'honneur* was pinned to the lapel of his lab-coat; below it, the yellow and green of the *Médaille militaire*. A patriot.

'Paris in winter is for the Boches, Jean-Louis,' he grumbled in acknowledgement at last. 'They deserve it. But, please . . . Ah! it's good of you to come, though in future I must ask that you wipe your shoes, eh? lest you track snow on my floor and cause unnecessary labour.'

He motioned to the attendant to clean things up, and quickly. He examined the palm of his left hand as if plotting exactly how best to say what had to be said, but did not, as was his custom on such occasions, remove the horn-rimmed glasses that only served to enhance the acid of his gaze and tongue.

'I thought detectives who ordered autopsies were to be present during them so as not to cause me to repeat myself?'

'Apologies, Coroner. The pressures of the investigation.'

'Pah! you people. At least have the courage to admit the matter was too delicate!'

The precisely trimmed goatee and hair had been dyed black. A nonsmoker, when virtually everyone else was dying for tobacco, he would not tolerate its use in his presence. But he was good, the best, and through the years had always looked where others had missed things.

'Well, I suppose I had better fill you in so that I can get to my supper—you have eaten, I take it? That is soup on your moustache? If it's not, then please *don't* come a millimetre closer. The flu this winter is terrible, our gift to the Boches from which one trusts they will all succumb.'

Only he could have said it unscathed. Even the hardest of Nazis were afraid of him because, in addition to all else, he was driven to gaze into their eyes before telling them exactly what diseases they suffered from and would, quite naturally, die of.

'First, the child,' he grumbled, not bothering with his notes. 'She suffered from tinea and if, as I have been given to understand by Préfet Talbotte, her little friend now wears the beret and scarf of this one, she, too, will come down with it. So much, eh? for the good sisters forcing the child to bathe under a sheet so that God would not see her naked, but one has to wonder why the evidence on her scalp was missed.'

Tinea, barber's itch and other such fungal infections of the skin were endemic, picked up in the public baths, schools and churches, the cinemas, too, and yes, the hairdresser's. Half of Paris had suffered at one time or another and had been in agony, what with no wholewheat or potato flour with which to dust the bedsheets so that one could at least roll around in it for relief.

'Her scalp,' he said, damning the nuns just in case they really were to blame. 'Two circular patches her comb has often worked on. Her underarms and seat. The child has had it for some time and has, no doubt, prayed constantly that the good sisters would not discover her affliction and force upon her a sulphurous shower bath. Or is it,' he asked suspiciously, 'that she was being punished and was required to bear the penance of such an affliction?'

The sisters would all have come down with it if that had been the case but ... but why had they not noticed it in the infirmary? Perhaps they had. They must have. 'And?' managed the Sûreté's mouse.

'*Speak up. I can't hear you.*'

Ah, damn Edith Piaf and the finches! '*AND?*'

'That's better. She was killed with a Number Four knitting needle. That is four millimetres in diameter, in case you didn't know, whereas the others were all killed with a Four Point Five.' He tossed a hand. 'Then, too, the weapon was not sharpened at the point as were the others. Also, the needle was not driven into the heart.'

'Not into the heart . . .'

'You should have read the reports.'

'We did not have time.'

'Hah! the Sûreté is as incompetent as always.'

'We have not slept. We have been working on this thing since we got in last night, Coroner. *Last night!*'

'Please don't shout. You will only disturb the finches, who are as innocent as the child.'

'Forgive me.'

'Certainly. How's your stomach?'

'Fine.'

'Good.' Belligueux removed his glasses and gravely polished them. 'Jean-Louis, there is something that even our nefarious press have only hinted at out of fear of reprisals from our illustrious government in Vichy, not out of any concern for decency or the parents of the deceased. With each of the first three victims, the Sandman attempted vaginal penetration and fellatio. Perhaps he was too anxious, too excited—who is to say what went through his mind—but premature ejaculation was common to all. Semen was smeared on their private parts and its stains were left on their clothes, but . . .' He paused to hold the glasses up to the light and look sadly through them. 'But with Andrée Noireau there is no such attempt beyond the hasty opening of her overcoat and pulling up of her skirt and sweater. Is it that he realized he simply did not have the time, or having failed before, did he fear he would do so again?'

'This killing was different, Coroner. What you are suggesting is that it was decidedly so.'

There was a curt nod of agreement. The recording came to an end. The needle scratched. 'The sleeve,' breathed Belligueux, tersely tossing the warning aside to the attendant. And then, 'With Andrée Noireau there are none of the bruises in those tenderest of places as with the others, all of whom had to suffer the harshness of the Sandman's fingers and bore several scratches inflicted by his nails.'

'Yet another difference,' said St-Cyr sadly. 'Is there more?' The look Belligueux gave him was grim.

'The attack in les Halles, Jean-Louis. In that one, sodomy failed, as did fellatio but not vaginal penetration. There it was complete and brutal with several tears. Please, I regret the unpleasantness, but you must have the truth. Semen was smeared on the face and buttocks and on the genitalia—a failed attempt at first and then completion but . . .' He paused before saying it again. '. . . but with your Andrée Noireau we have none of this. No attempt at rape beyond the dishevelling of her clothes. Soldiers,' he said of the les Halles attack and threw out his hands in despair. 'Was it a soldier? Is our Sandman one of the Germans here on leave?'

Had the threat of this brought tears to the Sûreté's eyes?

'The assailant's pubic hairs, Coroner? Can matches be made from victim to victim?'

Jean-Louis was desperate. 'Ah! this I cannot tell you, for there were no such hairs reported on any of the victims and I found none on this one either. Of course, they would be expected unless purposely removed afterwards by the "assailant" or "assailants".'

An unpleasant thought, for, if true, it implied an iron-hard calmness, an absolutely ruthless determination to hide his identity. A battle-hardened soldier perhaps. 'The semen stains?'

'Blood Group A with the Suresnes and the Aubervilliers victims. Indeterminable with the other two. For myself, I wonder if such tests were really done on those two.'

'Indeterminable. . . ? But . . . but that could mean Group O or a non-secretor? Surely if his blood grouping is A, the others should be the same?'

'This I cannot say, more than I already have.'

Ah damn. 'And the dates, the times of the murders, please?'

'All from one to three hours after the midday meal of soup. A Wednesday for the Suresnes killing, a Friday for that in Aubervilliers. The les Halles murder was done on a Saturday; that of the Notre-Dame on a Wednesday, after the crowds of "tourists" had left. And this latest on a Sunday.'

'Had she eaten?'

'Some bread, no butter. Two raw carrots and perhaps three of the vitaminic biscuits.'

'Wool . . . were there threads of black wool?'

'A few were caught under this one's fingernails.'

'But not in those of the others?'

'No, not with them, though I must emphasize I personally did not conduct those autopsies and all were quickly buried.'

'And with Liline Chambert, what have you for us?'

The finches sang, and for a moment Belligueux listened to them before sadly saying, 'At least three and a half months pregnant, a boy. Massive embolism. A disinfectant and soap but not the National one. No, this soap produced a copious froth. The filthy stuff was injected forcibly into the uterus. Air bubbles penetrated the mural veins. Death was instantaneous. One could ask, Was it deliberate? What better way to remove an unwanted lover? But this I could never prove and you know it. May God crucify the one responsible before she kills another.'

'My partner may have checked with Records. We may have fingerprints we can match with those of a known abortionist. He should have been here by now.'

'He's not. Ah! I'm forgetting myself. These things, they are never easy, are they?' Opening the birdcage, he released a finch to let it fly about the room. 'I find it helps. Their constant conviviality reminds me that life is what this world of ours is all about, not death. Mademoiselle Chambert was, I gather, the mistress of Antoine Vernet. This must be why Préfet Talbotte wishes me to dine with him tonight and why he is waiting for my telephone call and the confidences I shall not reveal to him if it will help your cause.'

Poised over the glacial crevasse of their times, the Sûreté was grateful to be pulled to safety.

'If you could, I would appreciate your not mentioning the differences in the killing of Andrée Noireau. Simply attribute all of them to the Sandman for now.'

'Of course.' Belligueux fed the finch a few seeds before returning it to the cage. 'Is it true you have the goods on our préfet? There are rumours.'

There were always those. 'It is. That dossier grows thicker and it is my sincere hope that when this Occupation is over, the Resistance will see I am no collaborator but was forced, as so many of us are, to work with the enemy.'

'Your partner is no enemy.'

'Hermann is special. A worry, yes, when it is all over and the Germans have to pull out but, for now, my friend.'

St-Cyr watched as the birdcage was covered with its hood and then a blanket. The gramophone was closed. Belligueux gave a nod. He would take himself off to find his suit jacket and overcoat, then would telephone the préfet to send a car round. 'I will give you ten minutes alone here if you wish,' he said, 'That way you will be gone before he arrives.'

'Please have Madame Vernet sent in. We won't be long.' Hermann must have been delayed. Hermann . . .

The house on the rue Chabanais felt draughty. The child's leather glove seemed to have a life of its own. As Herr Kohler gently smoothed it out on the counter of her little cage, Madame Morelle flicked a wary glance at the burly, grim-faced Feldgendarmen behind him and touched her heart.

The glove seemed to want to creep towards her, to rise up, its fingers spread to cry out, *Answers, madame. You must provide him with answers.*

'The child,' breathed Kohler. 'The Sandman, madame.'

'Ah! my heart.'

'Fuck your heart.'

He must have explained things to the Feldgendarmen. They were with him in this.

'Giselle le Roy, madame. Age twenty-two. Eugène Debauville, alias Father Debauve has her, and the child.'

'That one, he is not here!' she shrilled. Hurriedly she crossed herself, and the glossy black beads of jet she wore rattled. Again she looked to the Feldgendarmen for help, her big strong boys, her little boys, her *friends* to whom she had given so much. Free girls, free meals, free cigarettes, cognac and beer—much beer. Wireless sets, too, and lingerie, perfume and soap—good soap—to send home to their wives and mothers. Their grandmothers also.

Pah! men who would desire to ravish whores dressed as schoolgirls now all but wept openly at the loss of a real one and oh, *bien sûr,* they had every right, herself also, but *what* had Father Eugène been up to? Violating little girls again? Ah *non de Dieu, de Dieu,* was it possible?

She saw the pistol Herr Kohler fingered as he grinned. It was not a nice grin, and she knew he loved this Giselle le Roy and that Father Eugène, a friend, ah yes, of course—an associate also who had lent her money in the past to take this house; one must acknowledge the loan since it was not yet repaid with interest . . . Father Eugène would just have to take care of himself. Violette as well, but . . . but Violette was unique and haste was not wise in her regard.

'He's a strange one, Inspector. His needs, they . . . they are not those of a normal man.'

'Just tell me where he is or might be.'

May God forgive her. '*Numéro* 78, Champs-Élysées, the fourth floor. He . . . he runs an escort service from there.' She grabbed Kohler by the arm as he turned to leave. 'Has he really taken the child?' she demanded. 'Is he the . . .'

For one who had seen everything, did she still have a tender spot, or was it simply concern for her purse?

Kohler lifted her pudgy, beringed fingers from his arm and

dropped them. 'Is he the Sandman, eh, madame? A black overcoat, a man who gets his kicks out of little girls? You tell me,
and while you're at it, understand that being an accomplice to
the murders of six girls puts you in trouble so please don't
attempt to leave town.'

'*Six?*' she croaked. The whores, the customers were watchful.

'Five victims and Liline Chambert, eh? And now also Giselle
and Nénette Vernet. That's what we're dealing with until it's all
clear and those responsible await the blade and the basket.'

The morgue was not pleasant, and as she walked out across the
concrete floor in her mink coat and boots past drains that conducted fluids to the sewers, Madame Vernet felt the skin tense
up over her spine, causing her to shiver.

She clutched the coat more tightly about herself. 'Inspector,
what has happened? There are two shrouds. One is longer than
the other. Why is this, please?'

'Why are there not two of equal length? Is this what you are
wondering, madame?'

'*No!* I . . .'

'Please take a moment to steady yourself,' cautioned the
Sûreté, watching her so closely she cringed and could not
understand why he was looking at her in that way.

The smell of the place came to her, that of disinfectant,
formaldehyde, rubbing alcohol, old blood, death and dampness. The sewers . . . 'I have nothing to say. I *don't* know why
you have brought me here. I shall have to complain to the
Chief Magistrate.'

'Please do so, but before you do, madame, I would consult
your clairvoyant. Madame Rébé, was it?'

Ah, damn him. 'If . . . if that is . . . is Liline, you had better
talk to my husband, not to me.'

'I will, I assure you.'

'*Then remove the shroud, damn you!*'

Behind closed doors, between walls of stone and cold storage
lockers, there was nowhere for the sound of her voice to travel
but back to her.

'Please,' she begged, and he saw tears again and he asked, 'What have you done, madame?'

'*Nothing!* I . . . All right, I knew she was having an affair with my husband. *There*, is that sufficient for your appetite, Inspector?'

'It's Chief Inspector, and let us not just have the hors d'oeuvres but the main courses.'

'Pompon is mine. I . . . I don't know what made me lie about it. Fear perhaps. Nénette out there and dead, I thought. Antoine telling me to watch what I said, that I had no right to question him.'

'A tiepin, madame. Where, please, did you step on it?'

'I *don't* know. How could I? Ah, damn that child. Damn her for picking things up and thinking they were important. Perhaps it . . . it came from . . . from the *métro*. Yes . . . yes, *that's* where it happened. I felt a leak in my boot. I knew I would have to get the puncture mended.'

'Please remove the boot and let me see if it is wet inside.'

'How dare you doubt my word?'

'The hole I fitted that pin into did not go through the sole.'

'It *did!*'

He sighed. He let sadness register deeply in his eyes. 'Very well, let us uncover this one and you can confirm its identity so that the parents can be notified.'

He did it slowly, this Sûreté. There was about his every action a deep-felt sincerity and respect for the dead.

Uncovered, the pale and softly bluish face of Liline Chambert in slumber brought a shudder, a gasp, a sudden turning away to place her hands on the other pallet, only to lift them instantly and drop them to her sides. 'It's her. Please tell me how it happened. Was she trying to protect Nénette and . . . and Andrée? Is *that* how it was?'

She heard him take a step and then another. She thought that perhaps he was coming to comfort her after all, but no, he . . . he had drawn the shroud back a little more.

'It was a boy,' he said, and she saw that . . . that *thing* washed and dried and lying all curled up on a clean white towel upon its mother's breast.

Ashen, Madame Vernet tried to retreat by gazing at the concrete floor. At last she said, 'I . . . I didn't know she was pregnant. Please, you must believe me,' and when he gave no sign of this, her anger leapt. 'Where is Nénette, then, idiot?' she shouted. *'Nénette can tell you everything.'*

'Then let us hope she does.' Hermann . . . where the hell was Hermann?

Gold letters on a brass-framed, frosted glass panel met the eye, the soft image of a smiling, bright-eyed young woman with bouffant-styled dark auburn hair ghosting through from behind *Les Liaisons enchantées. Numéro* 78, Champs-Élysées, fourth floor, suite seven.

Kohler paused. An escort service, a *clandestin,* eh? He wanted to shout and pounce. An illegal brothel, but this logo of a member of the *petite noblesse* gazing at him said only, This is class. Let no others enter.

It was nearly 11.00 p.m. The place should be closed by now but wasn't.

'Monsieur, what can we do for you?'

There were two women in their mid-thirties behind the gilded Louis XVI desk, one sitting, the second standing with a hand on the other one's shoulder. They'd been going over the accounts . . .

'Giselle and the child. They're all I want.'

'Pardon?' said the blue-eyed blonde who was standing.

'Ah! Monique, the monsieur, he means Mademoiselle le Roy. Please,' said the raven-haired one, indicating that he was to enter another room. 'She is waiting for you, monsieur. She will explain everything, I think.'

'It's a pity he's not a general,' confided the blonde to the other one. 'He has the height and the duelling scar but not the clothes, the uniform, too, of course.'

'Mademoiselle Irène would be perfect for him, and there are still two tickets to the opera for tomorrow evening.'

Kohler stepped past them to enter a drawing room fit for kings. Shades of gold were nearly everywhere in the swirls and oak-leafed pattern of a black, Savonnerie carpet, in the herring-bone fabric that covered the settees and *fauteuils* and ran up the walls with darker gold bands between. Row on row of gold blending softly in with the painted ceiling and the portraits—all of men of distinction. The tall french doors were of white enamel with gilded mouldings.

Giselle was dressed as he had never seen her before, the soft crimson cashmere sheath worn off the left shoulder, with a diamond-studded clasp, black velvet choker, bracelet and ring to match. Red leather high heels, too.

'Kid, what the hell is going on?'

Are you jealous? she wondered. Red is my colour but this . . . this is something far, far different. Silk stockings, too, and silk elsewhere also. 'He's not what you think. He's good and kind—of course we prayed a little. He's a priest.'

'He isn't.'

'Oh yes he is. Did you think we would not hear you pounding on the doors of the Saint-Roch? He knew you would not understand why he had taken me there, so he brought me here. It's all very proper, Hermann. The girls are escorts. Nothing else.'

'What is the matter with you?'

'Has he hypnotized me? Is this what you are wondering?'

'Where's the child?'

'The glove . . . Ah! you thought she was here and he had taken us both prisoner.'

'Well?'

Hermann was jealous—she was certain of it, so maybe she would take the job and dine with a general or two just to see that he behaved himself in future. 'The child is not with him. He found the glove in the rue Chabanais this afternoon. She dropped it and ran and he could not catch up with her to return it. That is all.'

'She's alive?'

'Yes. And free.'

'At exactly what time did he see her?'

'In the last of the daylight and just before you left me to find the name of Violette Belanger's *maquereau* from those . . . those *salauds* in that Café of the Turning Hour where you should *never* have left me alone, Hermann. *Never!* If you valued me at all.'

Hesitantly he reached out to touch the softness of her cheek and press the backs of two fingers gently against her lips. 'I've been through hell,' he confessed. 'I feel as though I could sleep for a thousand years.'

'But there are no beds in this place, are there, my Hermann? Only *les liaisons enchantées* for those who do not wish to go with whores, even the very high-class ones.'

6 IN THE PRE-DAWN BITTER COLD AND DAMPNESS OF the Bois de Boulogne, the warmest place was next to the manure piles just outside the riding stables.

'Did you sleep at all?' grumbled Kohler, unable to light a cigarette. 'Christ, *why* does it always have to be us, Louis? Couldn't that God of yours smile on us just once?'

'He's too busy. He expects us to simply get on with the job.'

'Giselle is convinced Debauville is still a priest, but me, I have to tell you that little pigeon of mine is not the same. When we got home to the flat, she prayed on her knees for a good hour—Oona told me all about it. Tears and entreaties to the Blessed Virgin to savè her from a life of "consorting with the enemy and having unclean and lurid thoughts," begging Our Father to forgive her for "engaging in *wanton* sexual activities of a depraved nature with a member of the Gestapo, a *detective*. A man old enough to be her grandfather"! '

Hermann was in rare form and coughed.

'I fell asleep. I couldn't keep my eyes open. Her droning on and on beside the bed was hell. She's even taken to wearing the little gold cross she had as a child in the convent school. She says, "I am going to improve myself, *Herr* Kohler, *starting* with you." She's off later this morning to consult her clairvoyant. Her "future *must* be divined". '

'Madame Rébé?' hazarded the Sûreté, trying to light another match.

'That's the one. The rue de l'Eperon right next to the shop that sells crystal balls, bats, curses, rune stones and Tarot cards.'

'Madame Vernet's clairvoyant. President of the Society of Metaphysical Sciences.'

Kohler cleared his throat. 'Are you sure?'

'As positive as I can be at the moment, considering the lies and half-lies we have had to listen to.'

When an orderly came looking for them, they followed him to the gamekeeper's cottage. Having booted the custodian out, Old Shatter Hand was sitting in his shirtsleeves at the table before a roaring fire of, yes, chair legs and other furniture. The place was like a furnace and it was clear he had been here for some time. Clear, too, that the airwaves of Paris and the gossip lines had been vibrating into his ear. He wanted the truth and had been disturbed enough to have arrived early.

'Avail yourselves of the coffee and cognac, gentlemen. There are croissants in that newspaper. Eat while you talk.'

Ah, *nom de Dieu*, Talbotte must have told him something, thought St-Cyr, and that bit of news had upset him. The papers, too, no doubt.

Unyieldingly, those stern blue eyes settled on them. 'Everything. I'll have it from you, St-Cyr, and then from Kohler as needed. There are only the three of us, so please speak freely. Nothing you say will pass beyond these four walls.'

Berlin must have been after him, thought Kohler. Old Shatter Hand was close to retirement. Gestapo Mueller could easily have threatened to move the date up. An outraged citizenry, the threat of a revolt, et cetera, et cetera. A sadist to provide the spark. Ah, *merde*!

Louis cleared his throat. 'The Vernet child, if the report is true, General, is alive and was sighted in the rue Chabanais just before dusk yesterday. She dropped this glove.'

'Why wasn't she wearing it?'

'She was probably picking something up off the street and was frightened.'

'Of whom?'

It was coming now and had best be gotten over with. 'A defrocked priest, a pimp who uses the name Father Eugène Debauve.'

'Debauve . . . I met him at the house of that wretched woman in the rue Chabanais. Is he *not* the Bishop's emissary to the *lorettes*?'

'No, General. He is the pimp of Violette Belanger, whose sister is a nun and teacher in the convent school the girls attended.'

'He runs an escort service,' interjected Kohler quickly.

'He *what*?' stormed von Schaumburg.

They told him. Kohler dragged out his notebook. 'Records were not too forthcoming, General, but I did manage to pry the following out of them: Father Eugène, born 3 June 1883, the eldest son of the Debauvilles of Troyes. The family have extensive holdings and remain very wealthy. The son was drummed out of the Church and disowned by his mother twenty years ago for terrifying schoolgirls in the convent school where he was the Reverend Father. No sexual interference was proven, but apparently one of the girls hanged herself in the shower baths, using her sheet. Others then mentioned Debauville's questions to them during confession. Red faces all round, I gather, and tears. Since then he's managed to keep himself free of arrest.'

'But not of the girls, we gather.'

'The French!' seethed von Schaumburg, hitting the table with a fist and sloshing coffee all over the place. 'Bring the criminal in for questioning.'

'The escort service he runs caters to officers from your forces,' offered Louis blandly.

Oh-oh. 'It appears to be all above board,' shot Kohler, 'but I'd like to take another look.'

'Discretion, Kohler. Discretion. Why is it I am always in difficulty with you two?'

Gestapo Mueller had talked to him. Kohler was convinced of it and, digging deeply in a pocket, dragged out the badges the kid had collected. 'There's another matter, General. A death's-head. Two of the gold wound badges. The Polish Campaign medal . . .'

'Yes, yes, the SS-Attack Leader Gerhardt Hasse, a hero to Herr Himmler. An artist, a painter of children. Gestapo Paris's Watchers are aware Herr Hasse has sketched those two girls on a number of occasions. Pay him a visit. Ask what you will of him. He's not a well man.'

Discretion again, thought St-Cyr ruefully as he took the badges and the medal from Hermann, but why, please, did that child include the trappings of the SS-Attack Leader unless to say, These, too, they are important?

It was von Schaumburg who brought up the matter of the abortion and Liline Chambert's affair, having been informed of them by Talbotte, no doubt.

'Vernet,' he said levelly, 'is returning from Rouen this morning at my request. He'll answer everything truthfully. He assures me the affair was brief, that the girl, being away from home and missing her father, put temptation in front of him and that he is much saddened by its result. Indeed, I do believe he wept when I informed him of the girl's death.'

In love with her, then, was he? snorted Kohler, inwardly ridiculing foolish older men with young girls until he remembered Giselle and had to swallow on a lump of croissant.

It was Louis who said, 'General, neither of the Vernets has been truthful. Though each espouses a kind regard for their orphaned niece, the child had planned with her little friend to run away and now is afraid to return to the house.'

'Afraid?'

'Yes, General. Plans for running away began in the first week of November, well before the Sandman murders. Liline Chambert had been ill—morning sickness. It's my belief that it was this sickness which finally drove the child to make preparations to run away.'

'And the Sandman?' asked von Schaumburg.

'A toy giraffe and then a toy baby elephant were stolen from the crèche of Sister Céline, the sister of Violette Belanger, one of the prostitutes at the house on the rue Chabanais.'

'And Debauville's pigeon?'

'Yes, General. Sister Céline visits regularly, always pleading with her young sister to renounce the life. This the girl refuses to do and makes a mockery of the nun and the schoolgirls of the convent.'

'Those visits are usually on the days the nuns help out with the soup kitchens.'

'Two of the murders were near such kitchens.'

'There are threads and threads to this thing,' interjected Kohler apologetically.

'Then just see that you keep the shuttles going,' grunted von Schaumburg. Nuns, priests . . . 'Is the child safe for the time being?'

Louis reached for the coffee. 'This we really do not know, General, but if Debauville has her as a hostage, will an all-out search not cause her death?'

'Is he the Sandman?'

'This, too, we really do not know.'

'He wears a black overcoat, Louis. There were threads of coarse black wool caught under Andrée Noireau's fingernails.'

'But *not* under those of the other victims. General, though there are blood-group difficulties with those other murders, this last one was still quite different.'

'It was not a random killing, General. The child knew she would be followed. She and her little friend cooked up a plan to prove it. Nénette did not believe Andrée would be harmed.'

'She thought that once the assailant discovered his mistake, he would let Andrée alone.'

'What are you saying, St-Cyr?'

'Only that the killing may have been made to look like the work of the Sandman.'

'By whom?'

It would be best not to say too much until certain. 'General, we have a child, an heiress, who wished to run away from the home she loved and who then began to track and record the Sandman's killings. She insisted she knew who he was but would reveal this to no one but the préfet, in person and in private. This request was refused by her uncle. Either she does know who it was and the Sandman set out to silence her and made a mistake, or it was not him at all and she was being followed by someone else, but this person she must have known at least a little.'

'Two villains?'

'Yes.'

A brush with the truth or mere speculation? wondered von Schaumburg, turning to gaze raptly into the fire and add another chair leg. 'A black cloak,' he mused. 'I did see something. That is why I was here early. It was a nun. I'm certain of it and that, gentlemen, is why I did not connect the two events.'

'A nun?'

'The child was running towards the cage of doves—yes, they are doves, Kohler. I don't think she could see very well.'

'She didn't have her glasses,' prompted Louis. 'The other one was wearing them.'

'She went behind the cage and out of sight and that is when I saw the nun some distance behind her. The sisters of the cloth do not come to this place. Everyone knows of the "doves of peace" and their revulsion at the shooting of them for sport. Now that I think on it, she was striding angrily towards the cage and must then have entered it. I took no more notice and, indeed, let the matter pass from me.'

'The stables,' breathed Kohler. 'Could this "nun" have come from them?'

'How exactly did she "stride", General? Angrily, yes, but. . . ?'

The stables . . . a man wearing the cloak of a nun . . . Was it possible? wondered von Schaumburg, cursing age and what it did to the reflexes and the eyes. '*Stride?* Entirely like a man—quickly, determinedly and with no time to lose. Please see that he is apprehended before nightfall. I've an agitated citizenry on my hands, a press who are fomenting trouble by crying out for blood, and a préfet who is pestering my ears and demanding a thorough enquiry into your handling of this matter. If Berlin hears any more from him through the SS of the avenue Foch, you will be on your own and without the protection you now enjoy. I do hope I have made myself clear.'

Ah *merde*, the SS of the avenue Foch . . .

Kohler grabbed two croissants and stuffed them into his pockets. One never knew when they'd eat again.

The doves were everywhere and fluttering madly above them as Gilbert Amirault, the custodian, ruefully waited for the detectives to tell him what they were after. Both played their torches on the floor between the nesting boxes where Andrée Noireau had once lain.

'Manure,' said the one called Kohler at last, towering formidably above the cone of his torch beam, his ragged, scarred cheeks unshaven. 'There was horse manure on the floor, Louis. Boot-scrapings. I know there was.'

'Of course there was, but you've terrified him,' cautioned the Sûreté, and, taking the custodian aside, said, 'Monsieur, please try to remember. The assailant may have come from the direction of the stables. We really do not know yet exactly where the girls went before setting out this way. They may have thought the one who was following them had suddenly lost them. It is at least one and a half kilometres from the Jardin d'Acclimatation as the crow flies, but not a straight traverse for others. Those girls would have crossed the route de Neuilly and would most probably have taken one of the riding trails.'

A crumpled ten-franc note was straightened and pressed into the custodian's hand to help things along. 'They would have been seen by others. Once on the riding trail, their steps would eventually have brought them to the riding circle behind the stables. But did they lose the one who had been following them, and did he then come at them from the riding stables wearing the heavy black cloak of a nun or something so similar it gave that impression?'

'This I . . . I cannot say, Inspector. I saw only a dark blur, nothing else. My back was usually to the path that leads from here to the stables. Perhaps the General . . .'

'He has seen such a thing. I wanted only confirmation and now must ask for your silence in the matter.'

Later they sat in the car, sharing a cigarette and trying to get warm as they studied the map of the Bois. Two thoroughfares formed a broad X. To the north of its intersection, and in the V of its arms, lay the whole of the Jardin; directly to the south was the riding circle, which surrounded a horseshoe-shaped pond beside which were the dressage grounds and jumps onto which the stables backed. Three riding trails merged tangentially with the circle. To the south, cutting through the woods near the clay-pigeon shoot, a trail came out to cross the route de Madrid. This trail then left the circle half-way round and turned off to the north to pass through another woods and finally behind the Jardin before turning southwards to the circle to merge with its western side. It was all neat and tidy and splendidly laid out for maximum pleasure and variety, quiet rides through the woods alternating with the more open ones. Just to the west of the Jardin, the riding trail passed the buildings that housed the equestrian society of Paris.

'Is he a stablehand, Louis?'

'We'd best check.'

'Let me. I won't be long.'

Hermann strode off into the darkness. Frost from their breath had formed on the inside of the windshield and St-Cyr scraped at this to clear it and opened his side window a crack. The child would freeze to death in this weather without her overcoat of insulating leaves and sealskin boots and mittens. *What* had been going on in that house to drive her out? 'No one is going to murder you,' the chef had said in the folly last night, and just before this, 'Your aunt has still not returned from the hair-dresser's and another visit to that clairvoyant of hers. It's safe . . . Your uncle stays in Rouen.'

The child had confided to the chef that the Sandman would strike again. 'And very close,' she had said. 'So close you will feel the breath of him, but he will make a mistake and will have to let that one go.'

Had she been lying about its being the Sandman? he wondered. Had the murderer of Andrée been even closer?

She was the sole owner of the Vernet interests. Her uncle and guardian was having an affair with Liline, a student and dear friend, the daughter of an employee who would be dependent on Vernet—Mademoiselle Chambert would have worried terribly about this, ah yes.

The girl lived with them in that house. The child looked up to her.

'Madame Vernet knew of the flat in the rue d'Assas and of the boy, the homosexual Liline supposedly visited. She must have also known of Nénette's plans to run away, and certainly she knew of the map that child had put up in her room, the notation of where Nénette believed the next killing would take place and when.'

He thought to take out his pipe and tobacco pouch but had his hands deeply in his overcoat pockets, and did not want to relinquish touching the child's little mementos.

'Nénette was aware of the house on the rue Chabanais. There was a condom in her change purse. There were coins from right across Occupied Europe. Had she been inside that brothel to visit with Violette Belanger? Is that where the coins came from, and the condom?

'From one of the coffee cans,' he said and sighed. 'Debauve told Giselle he had found Nénette's glove in the street, but is he the Sandman? Does Violette know the child is on to him? Was the fob from that ear-ring a part of her schoolgirl costume?'

And then, fingering the giraffe, 'Nénette knew she would be followed on Sunday. The nuns went out two by two to search for Andrée, and this Nénette and her little friend would have anticipated. Sister Céline was accompanied by Sister Dominique, but were they in the Bois from three-ten to three-twenty and near the stables? Had those two nuns become separated?'

And then, heaving an impatient sigh, 'Hurt and angry Sister

Céline may well be with her students, but to follow Nénette Vernet so often the child becomes acutely aware of this does not make sense, and certainly that nun could not have sexually violated the other victims.'

Five murders, all of girls of about the same age, four done with a sharpened Number 4.5 knitting needle, the last with an unsharpened Number 4. Each of those needles would have been about thirty centimetres long. The nuns knitted sweaters and scarves, et cetera, for the prisoners of war, and Violette would have been aware of this.

When Hermann finally returned, St-Cyr said, 'Debauville must have realized Madame Morelle and her husband would betray him. He anticipated the husband's telling you he would take Giselle to the Saint-Roch and that Madame Morelle would give you the address of the escort service, but did he then betray them both, Hermann, by claiming he had found that child's glove in the street outside the brothel?'

'Tit for tat, eh?' Kohler switched on the ignition and let the car idle a moment. 'Madame Morelle uses a clairvoyant. Madame Vernet uses one, too—you told me this yourself, eh? Perhaps it's the same one, but guess whose son is a stablehand and was supposed to be here on Sunday afternoon but turned up late and hasn't shown up since?'

Louis waited. Kohler told him. 'Madame Rébé's son, Julien, age twenty-six and nigh on useless except for one thing, unless you count the hours he puts in playing mannequin to the life-drawing classes at the Grande-Chaumière over in Montparnasse and one hell of a lot closer to home. Hey, I'll leave all that to your imagination until we get him out of bed unless that mother of his has gazed into her crystal ball and told him to bugger off before it's too late.'

In the pitch darkness of the rue de l'Eperon, the rolling clang of opening steel shutters mingled with the sounds of shop doors coming unstuck as their owners coughed. Pedestrians, their heads shrouded by scarves, coat collars, toques and fedoras, hurried along, the sounds of their boots and wooden heels timidly sliding and clacking on ice that threatened to dump each squeaking-wheeled *vélo-taxi* or cyclist.

Faint pinpricks of blue light and of pre-dawn cigarettes appeared. The Seine was near, the dampness even more bone-chilling, the house at Number 10, a former mansion from the reign of Louis XVI now long since gutted, hollowed out and made over several times.

Like the rest of the *quartier* Saint-André-des-Arts, it was worn, not of the present, but the past and unwilling to relinquish its lingering passion for a more tranquil life.

'Hermann, go easy, eh?' cautioned St-Cyr. 'You live just around the corner. The neighbours will know you or know of you. Don't damage your reputation. It's not necessary. A few simple answers, that is all we require.'

'Piss off.'

The street resounded to his fist on that door, reacting with utter silence. Not a soul moved, not a foot stirred. For one split second fear gripped those nearest and instinctively it spread like wildfire to the rest.

Ah *merde*, it was as if God had struck them all numb, and both ends of the street had been sealed off for a *rafle*, a house-to-house round-up and arrest.

Again and again the door was bashed until, breathlessly, the terrified concierge managed, 'A moment . . . a moment,' and began to slide the bolts free and open the locks.

The Gestapo always favoured the small hours of the night or those just before dawn when sleep was at its deepest and one was too befuddled to escape.

'Messieurs . . .'

'Madame Rébé and son. *Vite, vite, imbécile*, we haven't all day,' said the giant.

The black-and-white-chequered tile and wrought-iron stair-well was huge and spiralled up and up, and right in the centre of it, the gilded iron birdcage of an elevator had been added perhaps in 1890.

'The stairs, Louis.'

'It's on the fourth floor.'

Hermann snatched the key from the concierge and began the climb. He wouldn't trust the lifts. Having been caught once and left hanging by a thread, he had sweated ever since at the thought of them.

'Please,' cautioned the Sûreté, a last attempt. 'Madame Rébé is well liked and respected. She'll sleep until noon.'

'Not today.'

A brass plate gave details. *Palms read, fortunes divined. Tea leaves, horoscopes, Tarot cards and crystal gazing are specialties. Dreams interpreted. Destiny foretold.*

The hours were given as from 2.00 until 7.00 p.m., six days a week with sittings also from 9.00 until 11.00 p.m., except when séances were held on Thursday evenings.

Enter only those who earnestly desire to learn the truth.

There were no refunds, and the fees ranged from ten francs for fifteen minutes, to fifty francs for more intense consultations. Those for the extended sessions were 'negotiable'.

'Shall I knock?' asked Kohler.

'Discreetly, I think.'

'He'll only bolt.'

'He might not even be here.'

'Then I'd best use the key, hadn't I?'

'We haven't a magistrate's warrant, or had you forgotten?'

'You don't need one. Not when I'm along.'

The flat smelled of scented candles, dust, dried flowers and a coal fire that had been awakened in the kitchen to add the aroma of real coffee to all the rest.

Kohler switched on a lamp. They were in the ante-room where clients waited their turn. Two flaking, gilded, straight-backed chairs with faded red velvet seats stood against a thread-bare tapestry which hung on the wall beneath an arbour of dried flowers. Roses, hydrangeas, carnations, sunflowers, corn-flowers and asters were bunched with sheaves and single stalks of ripened wheat and barley, oak leaves, too, and chest-nuts. A squirrel's feast of them. All covered by a fine coating of household dust, impossible to remove in these troubled times when business was so brisk.

A large and similarly coated bouquet, in a raffia-covered jardinière, sat on the floor between the chairs keeping lover from lover, husband from wife, friend from friend, or total stranger from stranger.

'Messieurs . . .'

'Ah!' began St-Cyr, touching Hermann's arm to silence him. 'Mademoiselle, please do not be alarmed. We are here to see the madame and her son.'

The girl was no more than seventeen, a maid of all work and receptionist also, the uniform changing with the passing of the hours. 'But . . . but Madame, she sleeps, and Monsieur Julien, he . . . he has not returned and has stayed elsewhere overnight because of the curfew.'

'Where?' demanded Hermann, flashing his badge.

Her large brown eyes began to moisten at the sight of that thing. 'I . . . I do not know, monsieur. He . . . he seldom tells me.'

She looked like death and why not? Gestapo . . . Gestapo . . . But there was no sense in stopping. 'Which one, eh?' he asked and snorted lustily.

She gave a quick, instinctive shrug and blurted tearfully, 'He has many. They . . . they all find him hard to resist. These days a young man like that, he can have any woman he wants, and Monsieur Julien, he . . . he has the appetite.' Dear Jesus save her now, she begged. Madame would be furious. 'He . . . he meets them at the . . . the life-drawing classes where he is a mannequin. There and . . . and at other places, of course. The Lutétia Pool as well.' Oh God.

Well-endowed, is he? snorted Kohler inwardly. 'Has he an overcoat?'

'A cape, made out of a horse blanket.'

'Is it black, as in *coal* black?'

'Yes . . . Yes, it is black and coarse.'

'Good. Switch on the lights and tell Madame we're here for an early-morning reading of her son's future.'

'*Hermann, must you?*' hissed St-Cyr when the girl had fled.

'A horse blanket—isn't that enough? Hey, I'll just find the woman's ledger, Chief, and scan it for names, visits and times.'

'You do that.'

'Then you look for other things, eh? Hey, that's an order.'

A tall and translucent trifold screen allowed those who waited to see those beyond it but only as blurred shadows, the viewer hearing every word of prophecy except for the whispered confidences and, at the completion of the session, seeing the results as the client then came back around it towards them.

St-Cyr was intrigued by the screen. Two young lovers, dressed in the finery of the late 1800s, embraced in secret on the middle panel before tumultous thunderclouds at dusk, while up in the sky the sun's last rays revealed among those same threatening clouds the shadowy face of the girl in multiple images. Now grave and wondering about her lover, now coy, now lecherous, the mask of old age removed and held away as the young girl laughed at life and fate and mischievously touched the back of her front teeth with her tongue.

Flowers embraced the central panel, cream-coloured roses climbing through gold to branch out and blossom next the cloud-faces that included the girl's skull.

It was magnificent, and he knew the work had been adapted from a painting by the Viennese artist Gustav Klimt.

Behind the screen, draped cream brocade with silk tassels formed a puffed and pleated backdrop to the bouquet of dried hydrangeas and roses that all but dwarfed the lace-covered table Madame Rébé used for the lesser readings. Zodiac signs were scattered throughout the lace, whose centrepiece was a deck of Tarot cards spread to reveal the Queen of Wands, the King of Pentacles and the Fool.

The straight-backed chairs were uncomfortable-looking, and he gave credit where due. Fifteen minutes in one would seem an hour to most, especially as they had already been kept waiting in a similar chair.

From here, more screens channelled the select client into

the inner sanctum of a small private sitting room where the more serious readings and the séances were held. Louis XVI settees in pistachio green and gilt, still with their original, now threadbare fabrics, mingled with armchairs covered in the same material. Silk orchids were everywhere—a tall pale, off-white and pink-fringed *cymbidium*, a deep pink *cattleya* and the butterfly gold-to-white and reddish amber of a *paphiope-dilum* were reflected in the crystal ball that sat on a three-pronged stand of bronze cobras that were poised to strike the unwary.

'Louis, take a look at this.' Kohler waved the appointments book. 'Madame Vernet has been coming at least three times a week for the past four and a half months. Usually at three p.m. and staying until four or later. Five sometimes, even six p.m.'

'But others have their fortunes told while she waits.'

'Or does she wait at all?'

'The tiepin,' breathed Louis. 'Did she step on it here?'

They moved into the corridor beyond and from there went quickly through to the bedrooms. Madame Rébé's door was closed, but when they found the son's cold unrumpled bed, they found the clutchback of the pin among the clutter of cheap cuff-links, assorted male jewellery and female ear-rings, garters, safety pins, and miscellany in the plain pine box on his commode.

It was enough.

Returning to the anteroom, they dutifully waited for the maid until Madame Rébé was at last ready to receive them in the *grand salon*, which was, of course, off limits to clients and reserved only for those most special, most private of guests.

'Messieurs, it's so good of you to be patient. One has to dress. One simply cannot snap the fingers or wave the wand.'

She was reclining nonchalantly in a gilded Louis XVI arm-chair whose slim arms and high, rounded back were covered with a flowered tapestry of soft faded gold that matched exactly the gown she wore. The fine silk crêpe de Chine was from the twenties, from the designer Fortuny, the sleeves pushed up a little to give the effect of a slight carelessness, the shoulders all but bare.

Her right arm lay along the arm of the chair so that her long slim fingers dangled over its end, while the fingertips of the left hand delicately touched a naked collarbone. Only two rings were worn and they were identical. One on the third finger of each hand, of diamonds.

The jet-black hair was piled up so that the carefully arranged wisps fell to fringes that all but touched her dark eyes and framed an animated, smiling face whose strong brows and long lashes had been further strengthened by pencil and mascara. The chin was determined, the nose was long. Diamond pendants dangled from half-hidden ears.

Ah! it was such a scrutiny they gave her, these two detectives from Paris-Central, but it was, yes, nothing to the scrutiny she returned and they knew it. The big one fiddled self-consciously with his fedora—had his lover ever come to her for consultations? Giselle . . . was the girl's name Giselle le Roy? Of course it was. Kohler the lover; Kohler the husband-to-be—was it possible? The stars, they had strongly advised against it, but the girl, she had not wanted to hear such a thing. 'He loves me,' she had said. 'Ah, I think he might. I must come back again for another reading—yes, yes, madame. Would this be possible?'

The other one, the Sûreté, was bemused perhaps but curious, and she did not like the look of either of them, but for different reasons. 'Inspectors, you flatter me with the urgency of your desire for a consultation, but, please, how may I help? So often I have prayed the police would come. I see things. I have powers.' She shrugged, but just the right amount . . . 'It's a gift one treasures, isn't that so? But one always worries that some day such a gift, it will vanish.'

The fringe over the brow was given just the lightest of touches. The head was turned but a little.

'Your son, madame,' said St-Cyr diffidently. 'We would like to know where he is.'

She sucked in a breath. Her bosom rose. 'My Julien? But at work, of course. He is the riding master in the Bois de Boulogne. Every day he starts so early, I . . . why, I hardly ever see him, the poor boy, although we're very close.'

A shit-shoveller elevated to riding master! snorted Kohler inwardly, but Louis's diffidence continued.

'Yes, yes, madame. Apparently he did not come home last night?'

'Nor has he been at his job today,' breathed Kohler. Giselle would hate him for this.

Madame Rébé tossed her head a little but did not frown. 'Not home? Not at work? But . . . but that is impossible, messieurs.'

'It's Inspectors,' grumbled Kohler, hauling out his badge only to hear her sing, '*Impossible*. Julien is very conscientious. We barely make enough to keep this place. Both of us need to earn our way.'

Ah *nom de Dieu*, her composure was magnificent, thought St-Cyr, and cleared his throat, excusing himself. 'A touch of the flu, I'm afraid—no, please, madame, do not concern yourself unduly. I will not sneeze. Your son?'

Consternation registered. 'But he teaches *les Allemands*? He must take them riding every morning before the sun rises and guide the new ones along the trails. He has eight men working under him. Oh! you are mistaken. Please telephone his office at once. Apologize for interrupting him.'

Dried hydrangeas now had mushrooms tucked in among them—such a waste. These flowers were everywhere and they, too, needed a careful dusting. Had Julien once had the job? 'There isn't a telephone at the riding stables,' grumbled Kohler, testily tossing his fedora on to a table.

'No telephone? But . . . but that is just not possible. Jeanette . . . Jeanette, *ma chère*, please bring me the address book at once. The Inspectors need Monsieur Julien's number at work.'

'Yes, madame.' The kid ducked her head and all but ran.

They waited for her to return. They stood there, these two from the Sûreté and the Kripo, saying nothing, not even sitting in the chairs that had been prepared for them, and it was on the tip of her tongue to ask, What has he done this time? But Madame Rébé knew she mustn't.

'He's a good boy, Inspectors,' she crooned.

'But there is no telephone,' sighed the one called St-Cyr.

'Which café or bar is he using, Louis?'

'The tearoom, I think.'

When the girl returned, Louis took the book from her but let her point out the number. 'The tearoom,' he said and sighed again. 'I recognize the middle two numbers, a double seven. They're sufficient for now.'

'So whom did he sleep with last night?' asked the one called Kohler, and he did have something about him, something very dangerous. The scar of a rawhide whip down the left cheek only proved it. The SS had done that, his Giselle had told her, because of a truth he would not ignore.

'I . . . I don't know,' Madame Rébé said and shrugged hotly. 'What is a mother to do, eh, my friends? I have only one son, one child. Shall I let *les Allemands* conscript him into forced labour in the Reich or . . .' Ah, *bon Dieu*, why had she said it? 'Or keep him gainfully employed in Paris?'

'And on the list of those who can't be taken,' breathed Kohler. 'Those whose jobs are far too important.'

They were making her very angry, but she would not give in, would not get up to pace about and demand a cigarette. Ah no—no, she would not let them see her like that. 'I tell you I do not know which of them he slept with.'

Louis let her have it. 'Then simply tell us about the *Relève*, madame. The "voluntary" labour service that is soon to become the *Service de Travail Obligatoire*, the forced labour. Antoine Vernet has influence. Madame Vernet is, it appears, a valued client. Or is it, Madame Rébé, that the industrialist's wife comes not to consult the future but to lie naked in the arms of your son?'

Vipère! Cobra! Ah damn him . . . 'I . . . I had nothing to do with their affair. If she wants to make love with my son, who am I to deny him the pleasure?'

'But you did have a lot to do with it, madame,' offered Louis. 'You ran, in effect, a *clandestin*. How much did she pay you for the use of your son?'

An unlicenced brothel . . . The matter was serious. 'Two hundred francs a visit. Three hundred if extended.'

No crystal ball was needed. 'And a guarantee of your silence,' grunted Kohler, 'so long as she made sure your Julien was not taken by the S.T.O. to find himself working eighteen hours a day in Essen tapping blast furnaces the R.A.F. had targeted.'

'Did Madame Vernet agree to see that your son's name went on the preferred list?' asked the Sûreté, hurling the words at her.

She wished they would leave but was a realist and knew they wouldn't. 'Yes! But he's done nothing wrong. Pah! So what if the woman craves a lover's arms when she is married to a cold fish? My Julien is good to her—ah yes, we have discussed her most intimate of needs. We're very close, as I've said. She's a Scorpio and very determined. She likes to have everything exactly right for her. The seat, the back, the mons, they are to be massaged both before *and* after the release of his little burden *and* hers, messieurs. *Hers.* The feet, the hands, the throat and forehead. If she is with child, it's her affair, not ours.'

Ah *merde* . . .

'Is that possible?' managed Kohler.

She had them now. '*Very!* since she *wanted* the feel of him in her. The ejaculation, yes? Ah! don't look so disconcerted, Inspectors. Some women do want to drink a man in and rob him of the life only he can give. She is one of them and insatiable. Always he has had to smother her cries of joy lest the clients be disturbed.'

They didn't say a thing. They simply left the flat in a hurry and didn't use the lift. She heard their car start up and, from the opened windows, watched in despair as they drove off towards the Seine.

'*Verdammt*, Louis, what better way for Madame Vernet to get back at that husband of hers for fooling around with Liline Chambert!'

'To be cuckolded by a stablehand and part-time mannequin . . . Ah *nom de Dieu, mon vieux,* our Madame Vernet must have acid in her veins!'

'A gigolo. The shame of it,' hooted Kohler. 'If word gets out, Vernet's associates will ridicule him into the grave!'

'And beyond it for at least the next two hundred years!'

'But is she pregnant by that stud, and if so, does she not *want* an heir of her own? Did she *arrange* to have her niece killed?'

Ah now, was it not time for the truth? 'And a marriage, *mon vieux*, that would have to continue not only because Liline Chambert had been taken care of but because Antoine Vernet could never—I repeat never—claim this other child was not his own, lest his wife tell everyone who the father really was.' He drew in a breath and sighed. 'It's perfect, Hermann. If true, she stands alone in infamy.'

A sobering thought.

Nénette Vernet had known she would be followed; Liline Chambert had gone to have her abortion.

Andrée Noireau had been killed, but that killing had been quite different from the others.

'Where is that kid, Louis? Is she still hiding out in that synagogue? Is she hungry and cold?'

And still afraid to go home. 'Or has Julian Rébé now dealt with her, if it was he who killed her little friend? A stableboy.'

A pack rat, a *voyou*, Sister Céline had called her. A petty thief of toy giraffes. An amateur sleuth who was convinced not only that she knew who the Sandman was but where and when he would strike next.

A victim. A target.

Dawn had broken, and from the flat Hermann had rented on the rue Suger there was a splendid view across place Saint-André-des-Arts towards the river and the Notre-Dame. Sunlight touched the belfries, warming both pigeon and gargoyle. Shadows gave a bluish cast to copper-green roofs whose faded orange chimney pots were so much a part of the Paris St-Cyr loved. But what had that child found up there? he asked himself. The fob of a gold ear-ring, was that it?

Liline Chambert had been with her, the older girl distracted, afraid of the abortion to come, the sin of it, the danger . . . ah, so many things would have been going through her mind. Perhaps she had snapped at Nénette and had told her such searchings were crazy, perhaps she had simply waited and had looked out across the river as he did himself. But had that child really discovered who the Sandman was?

Both of them had known things were not right at the Villa Vernet. Both had seen that things could not go on as they had been.

Everything in the child's coat pockets had had meaning for her, but what, really, had she been up to? Tracking the Sandman or trying to trap that aunt of hers or both?

'Jean-Louis, come and eat while it's hot.'

'Ah! Oona. Forgive me. The flat is pleasant and tastefully furnished. My compliments. I should have paid you a visit long ago but . . .' He shrugged. There'd been no time.

'The flea markets are helpful,' she said, knowing full well that things were not cheap there now and that Jean-Louis thought her the anchor that would keep Hermann from the storm when Giselle pulled out.

She was tall and blonde and blue-eyed, a pleasant—yes, *pleasant*-looking forty-year-old, she thought. Well, almost forty-one—but with a welcome bank account of common sense the Sûreté admired. And, yes, she could have had the pick of the Occupier—he knew this, too—but knew also she would settle for a *ménage à trois* that was not always easy. A patriot, an alien without proper papers. A woman who had fallen in love with his partner but was still too afraid to openly tell Hermann of it or give too many outward signs for fear of upsetting Giselle.

'Tarot cards,' he said. 'Let's have a reading.'

On the kitchen table she had placed the miserable loaf of grey bread that was their daily ration if they could get it. The bowl of muddied ersatz coffee had no sugar or milk. The flat was freezing, but it was home, and he saw her smile softly before raising her eyebrows in question and saying, 'Tarot cards?'

'Ah yes.' He fanned out the six of them and passed his fingers over them as a clairvoyant would. 'The Star can mean abandonment,' he said. 'We'll let it.'

'And the Lover?' she asked. 'It can mean just that if you wish.'

'I do. The Nine of Swords implies deception and despair, among other things.'

'Shame, in the reverse, and imprisonment—Giselle has been teaching me.'

'The Devil,' he said of yet another card. 'It can mean violence—blindness if reversed. Those and other things.'

She set her coffee down and urged him to drink his. 'And the Eight of Swords?' she said. 'It shows a young woman bound and blindfolded under swords that are ready to plunge into her. Is she the girl who . . .'

'That card is bad news, also sickness and other things, but in the reverse it can mean treachery, and that is what Nénette Vernet must have felt it meant for Liline Chambert and for herself.'

Treachery . . . They ate in silence, trying to savour each morsel while picking out the unmentionable and questionable sweepings that had found their way into the flour. 'And this one?' asked Oona of another card.

'The Ace of Swords. What would Madame Rébé have said of it?'

'That it is a very powerful card both in love and in hatred and that it can mean, among other things, triumph or triumph by force.'

'And in the reverse?' he asked.

Again he would seek only to have the card read as the child must have done. 'Conception, Jean-Louis. Childbirth and disaster.'

Swiftly he reached across the table to grip her by the hand. She had lost her children on the trek from Holland during the Blitzkrieg of 1940 and knew only too well the pain of their loss. They and her husband had gone to beg water at a farmer's well. The price had been far beyond their meager resources but they had been so thirsty they had hung around, begging. Then the Stukas had come, and then the Messerschmitts, and everyone had run for cover.

In the terror that had followed, she and her husband had

been unable to find their children and now he, too, was dead — a month ago. Was it as long as that? The French Gestapo of the rue Lauriston, a carousel and yet another murder. 'Forgive me,' he said. 'One is constantly reminding oneself to be careful what one says and does, but even so . . . Oona, your children may still be alive. You must always hope that someday they will be returned to you.'

'They're gone. I know they are. A mother feels such things. They're buried by the roadside in unmarked graves, and it's an emptiness within me that will never go away.'

With his usual boisterousness, Hermann returned from using the telephone in the café down the street and said, 'I held back on an all-points for Rébé simply because the SS-Attack Leader and artist Gerhardt Hasse is at home and expecting us, Louis, thanks to von Schaumburg. His friends over on the avenue Foch will try to shield him. They're worried about his interest in young girls. Apparently he can't get enough of them.'

Oh-oh.

Giselle wandered into the kitchen bundled in two overcoats, trousers, three pairs of Hermann's woollen socks, scarves, a toque and mittens. 'It's freezing in here,' she said and pouted, having just got out of bed. 'God is punishing me for cohabiting with the Occupier, especially one who is so patriotic towards the Conquered he will not ask for even a simple ration of coal!'

'Giselle . . .'

'Hermann, a moment,' cautioned Oona, and, taking the girl by the shoulders, sat her down at the table and began to warm coffee for her on the tiny hotplate that served for all cooking.

'What do those tell you?' asked the girl suspiciously of the Tarot cards.

'Trouble,' said the Sûreté, quickly gathering them up. 'Much trouble.'

THE IMPASSE MAUBERT WAS ONE OF THOSE narrow, dead-end streets that so delight the eye yet terrify the timid. Not far to the east of place Saint-André-des-Arts, and right near the quai de Montebello, it was not clean but was a half-hidden slot overtowered by ramshackle houses, some of which dated from the twelfth century. Walls were bowed out or in and all but naked of their covering plaster. Iron grilles defied entry, though not a shutter was in place. A street, then, of Balzac or Dumas, thought St-Cyr, with embrasures at eye level for the discharge of muskets.

But what struck the heart as they walked up the alley was the sight of a Daimler sedan facing them. Big, black, powerful and so obviously SS that Hermann hesitated.

A motorcycle courier had parked his bike just in front of the car and to the left. Narrow pavements on either side allowed only one person at a time to pass, and the house beyond that thing at the very end of the *impasse* rose up four storeys, windows two by two like an ancient god of warning.

'Vouvray . . .' said Hermann and, pulling off a glove, gingerly felt the scar on his left cheek. What had begun as a nothing murder in the Forest of Fontainebleau had ended with their being hated by the SS.

And now here, again, they were coming face to face with the bastards. Berlin wouldn't like it, the avenue Foch would be in a rage—'Hey, that's why the courier's here,' he said. 'Oberg's sent a love note to our friend ordering him to say nothing.'

Oberg was head of the SS in France, a former banana merchant, now with the power of life and death over everyone, themselves included.

They went on, each taking a side of the car, Hermann forgetting all about the glove he had removed. The car was ice-cold but utterly clean and so at odds with the street they threw a last look at it over a shoulder.

There was no lift. *Mon Dieu*, in a house like this, how could there be? But the staircase was steep and the sounds of their steps were many.

No concierge bothered them. That one had simply vanished.

The atelier was on the top floor. The door was open, their progress up the *impasse* had been observed, and at once the smell of turpentine, oil paints and canvas assaulted the nostrils.

Hasse had been busy. Stacks of canvases leant against whatever they could . . . a table leg, a wall, a chair. Others were hanging on the walls, masses of subdued colour, all greyish, all of smiling, laughing young girls of ten or twelve or fourteen years of age, no others.

He signed for whatever it was Oberg had sent over, and with the customary salute, the courier departed, contempt for them in the man's every look. Ah *merde* . . .

'Gentlemen, it's good of you to pay me a visit. Come . . . come, please, yes? There are chairs somewhere. Uncover them—just set things aside or put them on the floor. At this time of day I have to have the light. You won't mind, I'm sure.'

Like a stork that urgently searches for its chimney upon which to nest, Hasse went through to the front of the house to a room so cluttered with canvases, brushes, rags, spatulas, palettes and tubes of paint, trays on trays of them, he could not at first decide where the chairs must be.

Then he found them and, uncovered at last, they were usable.

The stand-up easel he had been working at—one of several—held a half-finished sketch whose faces they could not fail to recognize.

There, as in life but in those same subdued tones, were Andrée Noireau and Nénette Vernet, an arm about each other's shoulders, laughing, having just thought up the greatest of jokes. They were running a three-legged race against themselves. The windblown leaves of October were everywhere.

'What has happened is a tragedy,' he said. 'I find I cannot bring myself to finish this painting.'

The Sandman . . . was he the Sandman?

The stork was tall and thin, all bones and with gaunt grey eyes that looked beyond the painting into the past, to Poland and the Blitzkrieg in the East and children running in the streets through shellfire until dead.

'I have to work,' he said, pleading for understanding. 'Someone *has* to record their moment. Otherwise life is far too short.'

The black, receding hair was brushed straight back from the brow, the cheeks were thin, the lower lip much thicker than the upper. The nose was full and sharp; a once battle-hardened, very, very tough man. A killer now reduced to this.

He was from Salzburg and, without being asked, readily admitted there was a concentration camp there for Gypsies and that he had sent children to it, children he had sketched. 'It wasn't right of me, no matter what the Führer says.'

Louis found his voice. The SS things the child had found had not come from the house on the rue Chabanais but from here . . . 'Is that why you let Nénette Vernet have some of your badges and medals?'

Stung, Hasse turned on him. 'Why ask when I have just told you I could not possibly want those things anymore?'

The scars were there but no wounds were visible. Instead Hasse emanated shell shock. Like a tripwire tied taut across a lonely forest road, he waited for the bomb within himself to explode.

'What can I tell you?' he asked. His fingers trembled.

'Are you under doctor's orders?' asked Louis.

'*Yes!*'

'Morphine?' asked Kohler. 'Alcohol?'

'Don't be impertinent! All I need is to sketch. My work absorbs me.' He gave a wry laugh. 'What better escape than that of the artist? The world, but for the work at hand, has to be shut out, otherwise the piece simply does not get done and can never be satisfactory.'

'Tell us what you can about Liline Chambert,' offered Louis, trying to be diplomatic.

Already they were suspicious of him, thought Hasse. Both were ill at ease, as they should be with the SS! 'She was lonely and distressed about money and other things, and knew I was no threat to her. She did find it hard to reconcile my killing of children—yes, I admit it and did so to her. It was in conflict with my sketches but she understood I had suffered greatly. We met in a life-drawing class at the Grande-Chaumière. The mannequins on that day were children—three boys and a girl—but I had drawn only the girl. She said I had captured the child's apprehension, the worry in her eyes over her brothers who often strayed from their poses and fidgeted far too much for the drawing master. Their mother badly needed the pittance they would be paid, and the child was afraid it would not be forthcoming. Even at such a tender age, she had understood her duty.'

Again it was Louis who, lost in thought and wary, said, 'But you sketched only her.'

'Because I only want to paint young girls, Inspector.'

Ah *merde*, did Hasse feel it necessary to be so forthright? 'And Liline?' he asked, looking up at the unfinished canvas.

Hasse was conscious of Louis's every expression. He was really very alert—too alert, thought Kohler.

'We both taught a junior class at the Musée en Herbe—one has to do things like that. Children—yes, yes, I teach some of those who come to the Jardin d'Acclimatation. I did not *kill* any of them. I wouldn't. I've had enough of that. Look, I know it doesn't sound good, but . . .' He shrugged. 'I've always wanted nothing more than this.' He indicated the clutter, and when what must have been one of the *quartier*'s most torn-eared of strays leapt into his lap, welcomed it.

'I thought I could secure for Liline a commission for the Linz Museum. A wounded SS being assisted from the rubble of Stalingrad perhaps. I don't know. *Something* to get her a bit of money and the freedom she needed.'

'Freedom from whom?' asked Louis. Herr Hasse's French was very good.

'From Vernet, who else?' Did they not know of it? wondered Hasse. 'He wanted to divorce his wife and marry her. She hated living in that house. If it hadn't been for Nénette, she would have left long ago.'

To divorce his wife and marry her . . . Ah *merde*, thought St-Cyr. Madame Vernet must have known of it.

'Nénette needed Liline?' asked Kohler pleasantly enough.

'The child's parents were dead. The bombing of Coventry . . .' said Hasse.

'Yet the child could laugh as she posed for you, a member of the Occupying Forces?' asked St-Cyr.

Ah, damn this one, thought Hasse. 'I work from photographs. I have a camera with a telephoto lens. The girls did not know I was taking their picture.'

When the photograph was found, it wasn't the only one. Girls of from eight to fourteen had been caught in the Jardin d'Acclimatation, on the pony rides, at the puppet theatres, even on the steps of the restaurant and, yes, thought Kohler grimly, even near the cage of doves and the clay-pigeon shoot.

It was Louis who, holding several snapshots not of Nénette or Andrée but of others, said accusingly, 'That is the Lycée Fénelon in the background, Herr Hasse. The oldest girls' school in Paris is but a few blocks from here and just off the rue de l'Eperon.'

There was no need to tell them anything, thought Hasse. Oberg had stated this very clearly, but Oberg was not here to dictate what would or would not be said.

They were both looking at him. A photograph slipped and fell but the Hauptmann Kohler patently ignored it. Had he deliberately dropped the thing so as to unsettle him? Of course he had. 'I . . . I walk over to the lycée nearly every day—usually at noon, after the lunch break. There's a soup kitchen in the cellars run by some nuns. The girls come up and hang about for a few minutes if it's not too cold. Before, in the early fall, they would skip and play hopscotch. There are shots of their skirts flying up.' He stabbed at the photos. 'Look, if you must. I'm sure you'll see their bony knees. I know it must seem damning, but you have to understand the artist seeks only the absolute truth of each moment.'

There were schoolgirls and schoolgirls and then . . . 'That snapshot of Andrée and Nénette, Inspectors. It was taken in the early fall in the Jardin. Liline saw me take it, and it was then that I asked if she could bring the girls to pose for me.'

Kohler had no longing for a cigarette. Hasse electrified the air with unspoken accusations and denials: I KNOW YOU THINK I DID IT, BUT I DIDN'T!

It was Louis who tidied the photographs and searched among the faces. Were the Sandman's other victims there? he wondered. 'You must have made preliminary sketches of Nénette and Andrée, Herr Hasse,' he said. 'If it would not be too much trouble, we would like a look at them.'

Anger rose in his gullet. Hasse waited until it had abated. 'They're in the room I use for storage. Is this necessary?'

He could be cold when he wanted, still brutal, too, perhaps, but could he then calm himself, as the Sandman must have done, pausing long enough to remove all traces of pubic hair?

There was that little nod Kohler knew so well, a sadness to Louis's voice. 'As necessary as it is for you to tell us where you were last Sunday between two and four p.m. Several of these photographs are of children at soup kitchens, Herr Hasse. Poor children. Children bundled in rags. Several are also of the Notre-Dame and its belfries. Please, you do understand? We're only doing our job.'

Like police the world over, they were unwilling to give respite until satisfied.

'Well?' asked Louis of that Sunday.

Again that coldness came. 'I was not in Paris. I was in Saint-Germain-en-Laye staying with a friend.'

When Hasse came back with three sketches, Kohler asked if he would allow them to borrow the snapshots. 'Just for a little. They'll be returned. No problem.'

Ah, damn them. 'I could refuse, but I won't. You see, I *want* you to find the person responsible for the killings, especially those of Liline and Andrée.'

The sketches were good but showed two very subdued and uncertain girls who didn't really want to pose or be anywhere near the studio or the artist.

He would have to tell them. 'I paid Liline to bring the girls. Two hundred francs a sitting. They knew she needed the money and that it was a lot, so suffered through, but I couldn't change their opinions of me. They dreaded being near. That's why I have to use the camera.'

'Did they know she was pregnant?' asked the Sûreté.

'I think they must have, but we never discussed it. I thought, and said so each time, that the money would assist Liline in finding accommodations of her own.'

'But it was for the abortion?'

'Apparently so. A total of a thousand francs. Five visits. Even then the girls could not get used to being here. They thought it a prison, I suppose. Certainly a place of the dead, and they were afraid.'

Louis set one of the sketches aside and took up another. He preferred now to stand—so did Hasse.

The cat found its saucer of milk. In a city where there was virtually none to be had, here there was plenty.

'Herr Hasse, something is puzzling me,' said Louis, setting

the thing aside. 'A girl like Liline Chambert would not have readily known how to find an abortionist. Fellow students might have suggested a name, but . . .'

The stork tossed its head. 'I didn't, if that is what you are wondering. Indeed, had I but known, I would have seen she at least had proper medical care and . . .' Hasse paused to search him out. 'I would not have sent her to one of the Führer's baby farms in the Reich.'

'I'm sorry I asked, but one has to.'

'Then I'll tell you again, I am completely innocent.'

'That is what they all say. Please do not leave the city. We may need to question you further.'

Ah *merde*, Louis, go easy. He's SS, thought Kohler, but then caught a glimpse of the butt of a Mauser pistol jutting out from beneath a pile of rubbish. The cat scooted off, and he watched as it raced down the corridor to enter the room the Attack Leader used to store canvases. The room must be full of them. All of young girls, all of them with happy faces because that was the only way he could stand to see them.

'Saint-Germain-en-Laye,' mused Louis at the door. 'Please, the name of the party you were with.'

Verdammt, the insolence! 'A Mademoiselle Monique Reynard. She's from an escort service I use. A bit of company. Two single rooms, dinner and long walks. All very innocent, I assure you. A drive in the countryside she knows well. A short visit to the house of her parents. A failure, if an affair is what you are wondering about, Inspector. We never seemed to get to it. One tries to forget, but one can never do so.'

'And the name of this escort service?'

'Must you?'

'Please, it is necessary.'

'*Les Liaisons enchantées*. It's on the Champs-Élysées, at Number 78.'

'Did Liline Chambert know you used this escort service?'

Liline . . . Liline . . . why must they always come back to her? Why could they not concentrate on Andrée? 'Yes. Yes, we discussed it once or twice. I really can't remember. She had some notion she might be able to find work with them. On several occasions she offered to show me around Paris if I wished.'

How nice. 'And was this your first weekend in the country-side with this Mademoiselle Reynard?'

It was all one could do to resist giving the Sûreté the back of a hand. 'The fifth in the past four months. She's been assigned to me by the Generalmajor und Höherer-SS Oberg, Inspector. She's really very good. She's a qualified psychotherapist. One has to learn to live again, that's what they tell people like myself. Personally, I think it's a waste of time.'

'He'll kill himself, Louis, Let's hope to God the Butcher of Poland doesn't blame us!'

It hadn't been for nothing that Karl Albrecht Oberg had earned that nickname. '*Merde*, what are we to do?'

'Run for the Swiss border and try to get across it before night-fall, eh? One thing is certain. Our Father Debauve or Debau-ville must have SS clearance for his escort service and *that*, my fine Sûreté, means he's also under their protection and we can't touch him either, but what has he told the SS about our Attack Leader, eh? That the son of a bitch desires young girls and has to kill them, too? Ah *piss!*'

So many criminals had been released from prison to work with impunity for the SS and others. 'We have to find the child, and quickly, Hermann. Hasse didn't ask where Nénette was or express any concern for her well-being. He should have.'

'Maybe he has her. Maybe he knows she's already dead and can't tell us a thing.'

A search of the synagogue and cemetery was fruitless. At this hour, the Bois de Boulogne was all but deserted. Julien Rébé had still not shown up for work at the riding stables. The Jardin d'Acclimatation was shuttered, cold and empty, its signs for the puppet theatres, the miniature railway, Norman farm and zoo as bleak as the frozen breath of a solitary camel who peered out at the snow and ice from within the fake desert dune of its unheated stable.

Telephone calls to the convent school and the Villa Vernet

revealed only that the child had not returned. Was she riding the *métro* endlessly, as some did these days until the curfew stopped it, or was she wandering the streets in search of the glove she had dropped in the rue Chabanais—if she had really dropped it? Where . . . where the hell was she?

'The Bibliothèque Nationale,' muttered Louis. 'The number on the right hind leg of the giraffe. *That* is what it means. I knew I recognized it, but . . .'

The book was one of a collection of several hundred volumes that had been hastily stored in a corridor off the Reading Room and forgotten. Apparently, the American Embassy had donated the books just prior to 11 November 1942, the day the Reich had finally occupied the whole country and had forced the embassy, then in the South, to close its doors in a hurry and leave what had formerly been the Free Zone. The number was a Dewey decimal classification. 'A history of Arizona.'

One could not just walk in and take a book from the shelf. Tours were given; subterfuge had been necessary. A distraction perhaps.

When riffled through, the book yielded a note. It was dated Saturday, 9 January 1943.

Andrée, we will escape. I promise. We'll go to this place and never ever have to eat dog. Beefsteaks, Andrée. Real steaks grilled over an open fire of mesquite to whose perfume the coyotes will come at night so that we can shoot them.

It was signed, Nénette, your dearest friend in despair and now blood sister. We will each have a horse just like Silver but must be careful when shooting the coyotes not to stampede the herd. Otherwise, the owner of the ranch will have to dismiss us.

As promised, your extra reward for helping me in my time of deepest despair will be the crystal of clear quartz, the polished pebble of amethyst from Brazil, the braided ring of gold wire, the roulette wheel, the tiny Lone Ranger on his Silver and, yes, my charm bracelet of dogs. The perfume I have already presented to you, but as a Christmas gift.

How utterly French and practical of her even in the face of despair, thought Kohler sadly. The child had written the number of the book on the giraffe and had given the toy to Andrée on the following day, perhaps even as they had hurried from whoever had been following them.

Andrée Noireau had been the timid one but had given Nénette the little elephant she had stolen from that same crèche.

Records occupied the whole of the top and fifth floor of the Sûreté's former headquarters at 11 rue des Saussaies, now that of the Gestapo in France. None of the fingerprints from the tenement room on the quai du Président Paul Doumer had so far matched those of any known abortionist. No match could be made with those of Father Eugène Debauville either, but he had not stayed long in that room—if, indeed, it had been he— and would have kept his gloves on.

Julien Rébé had had several convictions for petty theft— bicycles, and the chairs from streetside cafés, which he had then sold back to their owners. Both were common enough rackets.

From among Liline Chambert's things, apparently only her underpants had been taken from that room. Nothing else.

'Madame Vernet, I think,' said Louis giving that curt little nod Kohler knew so well. 'Perhaps she'll be kind enough to answer a few more questions.'

The dog was dead. Whoever had slit its throat had held it down until the jerking had stopped. Blood was everywhere on the snow beneath an oak behind the Villa Vernet . . . Blood and urine. Frozen now, and disembowelled, the poodle was hanging from a branch, not turning at all in the wind because its entrails formed an icy column fast to the ground.

There were footprints everywhere, some bloodied, some not. Those of the one who had done it—oh, *bien sûr*, he hadn't cared. He'd been desperate. Those of the chef and the house-keeper. Neither of them had wanted to cut the dog down. Both had rebelled and refused. Both had felt the Sûreté and the Kripo had best see this, that things had long since gone too far.

It was the chef who pointed out the lesser footprints— toeprints mostly—and then the crushed remains of the silver poodle-charm Nénette Vernet had removed some time ago from her bracelet but had now chosen to leave.

Louis thanked him. Kohler told both of them to wait in the kitchens, that Madame might be needing sustenance.

'Julien Rébé,' he breathed as they watched the two leave. 'A warning to Madame to keep her mouth shut.'

'Yes, but is the child still free or has Rébé taken her? Is it that the child witnessed the killing of the dog in secret last night, having run from him for hours perhaps, or is it that she came upon it later, at dawn?'

The leaf-padded overcoat, sealskin mittens and boots were gone from the gallery of the folly, so, too, the hat. On the table below, as at a Last Supper, the soup plate held nothing, not even a stray crumb. It had been smashed.

There was a note among the shards. *I am alive and I will haunt you.* Nothing else but the wrought-iron crucifix from her bedroom desk and the knitting needle.

A housebreaker, too, then. An unlocked door and easy access to her room. The chef no doubt. 'Does she really know who the Sandman is, Louis?'

That was the question. 'Two killers. The one who follows her and intends to kill her but makes a mistake, and the other who strikes at random and pierces the heart but not the brain. Or is it simply the first of these and this whole business really has little to do with the Sandman except that she used those killings to try to trap the one who wanted to kill her?'

Madame Vernet did not look up or turn from the windows through which she continued to stare out at her dog. Ashen, unmade-up and still in her nightdress, gown, shawl and slippers, she waited for them to come closer. 'I know nothing, Inspectors. I did nothing.'

Her voice was so remote.

It was Louis who said, 'But you have an enemy out there,

madame. Perhaps you should tell us where you were last Sunday afternoon while your niece and her little friend were in the Bois.'

'Antoine is on his way. He telephoned from Mantes. He'll be here in another hour unless there are delays. Always there are delays. It's the bombing, the bombing. Honoré is at the Gare Saint-Lazare with the car, waiting to bring him home as soon as he arrives.'

'Sunday afternoon, madame?' reminded the Sûreté. 'Please, it is necessary.'

'I was restless. I went for a walk.'

'To where?' asked the one called Kohler, hauling out a note-book and swinging a chair round so that he could straddle it and rest his arms on its back. He was so close to her she felt the coldness of his overcoat and saw nothing but emptiness in his eyes.

She shrugged. 'Antoine wanted me to do something for him. A small errand. An envelope for the Reverend Mother. Don't ask me what was in it. Ten thousand francs probably. He's really very generous. Perhaps he feels it's his duty to help them assist in the feeding of the unfortunate.'

She glanced doubtfully at each of them and watched as Louis took out his pipe and tobacco pouch and began that ritual Kohler knew so well of silently sizing up a suspect. Not until he was done and had taken those first few puffs and waved out the match did the Sûreté say, 'But on Sunday, when you met with her, the Reverend Mother must have told you Andrée Noireau had not gone to Chamonix as you believed, madame, but had left the infirmary just before dawn. You did tell us you thought Andrée was in Chamonix.'

Ah why must he do this to her, *why*? 'I . . . I didn't see the Reverend Mother. I . . . I left the envelope with Sister Céline. Yes, she's the one. She'll tell you I did.'

'But that's just not possible. Please, I am sorry to be so upset-ting. Sister Céline and Sister Dominique were out searching for the child.'

'The little vixen should have gone to Chamonix! Why didn't she?'

They ignored her outburst. The one called St-Cyr was still standing but turned from her to gaze at Pompon as though he had all day. The one called Kohler scribbled something in his notebook and then waited for more. Did they always go at a person like this?

'Why didn't Andrée take that train to Chamonix, Inspectors?' she pleaded. 'That child was supposed to. Antoine had arranged everything.'

Those faded, empty blue eyes passed slowly over her. They took in her satin-covered thighs, her knees and slippers, then returned to the shawl she clutched.

'Don't mind him, madame,' quipped Kohler gently. 'Louis just gets huffy when he's being told lies and half-lies.'

'*I want the truth, madame*,' hissed the Sûreté, flinging himself from the windows to place both hands flat on the table beside her chair and rattle its cup and saucer. 'There's a child out there alive and waiting for that truth to be revealed so she can return. The Sandman may yet kill her, madame. *Kill her*, if we can't convince her it is safe for her to come in. You were carrying on an affair with Julien Rébé—oh, *bien sûr*, it was perfect. Exquisite!' He tossed a hand. 'A lout, a boy with a history of petty theft. A gigolo.'

'A shoveller of horseshit!' said Kohler.

'A part-time mannequin, madame. What more fitting and excruciating an embarrassment, since, if discovered, the affair would never allow your husband to hold his head up again. *Revenge. You wanted revenge!* You were going to lose everything.'

'He was going to divorce you, wasn't he?' shouted Kohler. 'He was going to marry Mademoiselle Chambert!'

Ah no, how had they learned of this?

'But,' breathed Kohler, seeing her trying to get a grip on herself, 'the boy had to be stupid and dependent, madame, so as to do your every bidding.'

Again the Sûreté gestured emphatically. 'This boy needs protection from the lists that are being prepared for the S.T.O., madame, the conscription into forced labour in the Reich. It's to begin in February, so there is some urgency.'

'You promised to see that Julien Rébé's name did not appear on any of those lists,' said Kohler. 'Instead, you must have agreed to place it among those your husband had designated as far too important to be taken.'

'Those lists would have been among your husband's papers—he would never notice. But what, please, did Rébé do for you in exchange?'

'His mother also, Louis. We mustn't forget the clairvoyant.'

'Nor what Madame Rébé says the stars and Tarot cards are telling her.'

'Two hundred francs a session,' breathed Kohler, letting his eyes settle on the base of her throat where the blade of the guillotine might pass. 'Sometimes three hundred if extended. You like your back massaged both before and afterwards, madame. Your seat, too, I gather. That son of hers had to smother your cries of joy lest the *grands frissons* you so enjoyed disturbed his mother's clients.'

The great shudders, the *orgasmes* . . . Moisture rushed into her dark brown eyes, anger, too, and she felt these, felt so desperate. *'How dare you speak to me like that? What affair, please? You've no proof of this. No proof at all!'*

The fists in her lap were doubled. 'Oh, but we have ample proof,' sighed the Sûreté sadly. 'If pressed for answers, that clairvoyant of yours will be only too willing to swear to it.'

Ah damn them! Damn Julien and that mother of his! 'What if I *am* pregnant? It's my body, my life, and since when do the Sûreté and the Kripo go around telling people whom they can have sex with—yes, sex, damn you—and whom they can't enjoy? He was a far, far better lover than my husband could ever have been and *yes!* he was good while it lasted, but it's over.'

Her chest quickly rose and fell as she waited for them to say something.

Very well, I will, breathed Kohler to himself, dragging out the page he had torn from Madame Rébé's register. 'Over perhaps, but not as of last Thursday, madame. *"The Vernet woman. Two hours. Two hundred francs. From two-thirty p.m. until four-thirty. A good session."* '

Ah no . . .

He tossed a look at Louis and saw him give a nod indicating, Let her have it. 'You knew Liline Chambert was pregnant and that your husband planned to divorce you and marry her, madame, and that you would lose everything—this house, all the money, the factories—but no one here knew you were also pregnant.'

'I have nothing more to say. I have done nothing illegal. I am totally innocent.'

'Then why, please,' asked Louis, 'is that dog of yours hanging out there?'

'I DON'T KNOW, DAMN YOU! I DON'T! I DON'T!'

What had begun in anger and rage had now turned into a disaster for Madame Vernet—St-Cyr was all but certain of this—but had that child really known who the Sandman was, and if so, why had she not left a name for them?

The bedroom felt so strongly of her it was as if he could hear her crying out, *I wanted to tell the préfet. I wanted to be alone with him just for a moment but was refused.*

She would have been afraid to tell anyone else but Andrée that she herself was in danger. She must have overheard something in the garden, in the folly perhaps at night, Madame Vernet out with the dog. 'Kill her,' he whispered, using words the woman might have said to Rébé. 'Make it look as though the Sandman did it. I'll take care of Liline. The girl will listen to me. She'll have to. She'll be no problem.'

A triangle. The mistake in the cage of doves, the abortion, and the child still alive and free.

Hermann was downstairs questioning the staff. For himself there was now that rare moment of reflection, a time too often denied.

The press were demanding answers. Vernet was not a name or man to be trifled with, but in so many ways he typified the industrialist.

Exactly four weeks after the armistice of July 1940 the Caudron-Renault Works had applied to the Ministry of Aviation to build hundreds of trainers for the Luftwaffe. To be fair, had they *not* stayed in business, their works would simply have been taken over and run by others.

In August of that same year, the nation's largest aero-engine plant, Gnome-et-Rhône, offered to supply engines and spare parts to the Luftwaffe. Orders for bomb components were filled by the Schneider-Creusot Works. The list was endless, and they, too—all of them—really could not have refused, but such eagerness. It was a tragedy and someday there would be a terrible reckoning.

But for now, where was that child and what, really, did she know?

He sat down at her desk and, taking the things from his pockets, carefully arranged them before the map of the city with its press clippings and locations of the murders.

'She knew of the house on the rue Chabanais,' he said, thinking of the coins from Occupied Europe and the used condom. 'She knew Violette Belanger was the sister of Céline, whom the girls of her class all hated with a passion. "Father" Eugène Debauve thus knows of the child. He has a history of interference with young girls and, through the escort service he runs, must also know of Herr Hasse and that one's problems, but is either of them the Sandman?'

They had so little to go on. 'The giraffe is stolen during the first week of November, well before the murders. None of the schoolgirls will own up to it, thus tormenting Sister Céline even more. Are her visits to Violette increased?' he wondered. 'Later, on a dare no doubt, Andrée exhibits her courage by stealing the baby elephant. It is proof that they are "blood sisters".

'A note is left in the Arizona book. They'll visit the library after they have proven beyond doubt that Nénette was the target. She knew it was a gamble. She knew of Madame Rébé and of her aunt's extended visits to the clairvoyant. The Tarot cards gave meaning, the tiepin its proof. The clear crystal of quartz, bought in the shop next door and perhaps with the cards, must have been her crystal ball.'

When he found the rest of the cards in a drawer, he found

the little booklet of instructions that went with them and saw where the child had marked those meanings he himself and Oona had used.

'We think alike in this matter,' he said and sighed, but then laid out the death's-head cap badge, the wound badges and medals, the tin pencil case and empty tube of paint.

The SS-Attack Leader Gerhardt Hasse was an enigma, and it made one decidedly uncomfortable to finger these objects while looking at the photographs Hasse had taken of soup kitchens and schoolgirls. But what, really, did all these things tell him? The fob from an ear-ring, a condom. Pseudo-schoolgirls being 'violated' by soldiers in a brothel, all in the name of pleasure.

That tiepin . . .

He shut his eyes and willed himself to find answers before it was too late. Madame Vernet must have sat here just as he was doing. She must have gone through the child's desk and her coat pockets, even to finding the key to the pencil drawer and opening it, but had Nénette been aware of this? Had that child trapped her aunt by deliberately placing things before her?

Beefsteaks over an open fire . . . a coat whose lining was stuffed with leaves, a crucifix and a knitting needle . . .

A note: *I am alive and I will haunt you.* Another: *Je t'aime.* She had found something. The tiepin. The Sandman would strike so close the chef would feel his breath.

But had she really known who the Sandman was, and if not, would she now seek refuge with him?

The housekeeper's wavy dark auburn hair had recently been brushed; her cheeks were still pale but made more so by the lack of lipstick.

'Nénette would not have wanted to see that dog killed, Inspector,' she said to Kohler, her blue eyes earnest. 'Oh, for sure she hated Pompon. We all did. The thing was always yapping, always peeing where it shouldn't. But for her to have had a dog of her own in the house with that creature was impossible. We gave her the charm bracelet to help. She loved animals, especially horses. That is why she and Andrée so often went to the riding stables to watch the dressage or simply to see them being groomed.'

Ah now, what was this? Was it too much to hope for? 'Did she ever mention a stablehand, Julien Rébé?'

The chef deferred to the housekeeper. Subdued and silent, the maid, a girl of eighteen, sat at the table opposite the housekeeper. The chauffeur had still not returned with Vernet.

Hesitantly Madame Therrien tapped cigarette ash into her saucer. She would have to tell him. 'Though it wasn't allowed, that one, he would sometimes let them help him. Nénette said, "I always present him with two five-franc pieces. One is for drink, the other for his amusement, since his mother refuses to give him a sou and he is not paid very much." She said he and the others used the manure piles in late summer and fall to cure the leaves for tobacco and tea. The heat from the decomposition does it.'

'The red beech . . .' said Kohler.

'Yes,' enthused the chef. 'It's really very good—there's absolutely no taste, so it remains neutral when mixed with tobacco. Nénette managed to get me a little. A small present.'

'The leaves of the currant bushes and mint also, Inspector. Leaves for the teas his mother would then serve to her clients as a "courtesy",' said Madame Therrien, causing him to wonder just how much she really knew of her mistress's affair.

'Then all three of you knew Julien Rébé's mother was Madame Vernet's clairvoyant?' he asked.

How polite of him, thought Kalfou, but said, 'Madame always spoke very highly of the woman, Inspector. Who were we to question so many extended visits?'

'Okay, so did those two girls consider Julien Rébé a friend?'

Madame Therrien had a very positive but attractive way of shaking her head. 'Not a friend, but friendly. A curiosity perhaps. Please don't forget they had been sheltered. They were both very privileged, yes, but coming into their own and desirous of experiencing the world.'

Amen, was that it, eh? he wondered.

'He let them watch a mare being bred, Inspector,' she confided. 'That was months and months ago. They peered through cracks in the walls and no one caught them. Nénette paid him fifty francs for the "privilege".'

Ah, *Gott im Himmel*, Louis should be here. 'And did the girls tell you this?' he hazarded.

'Oh, *mon Dieu*, are you serious?' she asked and flashed a rare smile that changed quickly to seriousness at memory. 'Liline told me. Nénette confided most things in her.'

'But not the identity of the Sandman?'

'No, not that. That she kept to herself.'

They fell silent. The fire in the stove hissed. The electric clock on the wall ground its way to 11.20 a.m. The maid had still not said a thing or looked up.

'Could Julien Rébé have been following Nénette?' he asked and saw Madame Therrien and the chef exchange hurried glances. Each began to tell him, only to stop for the other and then to clam up until pressed.

'I . . . I went to see him,' she confessed, reaching for the reassurance of her cigarette. 'It was on Monday morning. Nénette had not come back from walking the dog. I suspected she might have paid the riding stables a visit.'

'And had she?'

Herr Kohler would not always be so gentle, but it was appreciated. 'Julien Rébé was not there, nor was Nénette, Inspector. His employer was in a rage and said that of late the boy had been increasingly absent. "I give him a job," he shouted, "and this is how he repays me? Now he's here and I can count on him for the half-measure of sweat perhaps, but turn my back and *voilà!* he's gone. A magician, eh?" He thought the boy must be having an affair with one of the girls in the children's restaurant, in the . . . the tearoom.'

'But he was watching for Nénette and was following her, was that it?' he asked and saw all three of them duck their eyes away and swallow tightly.

'If he has killed Andrée, Inspector,' said Madame Therrien softly, 'I shall never forgive myself.'

'Nor I myself,' said the chef, all choked up. 'Nénette did say she was being followed—yes, yes, I admit it. But I did not discover who it was or think that it might have been that one.'

At last the maid found her voice, but barely. 'Madame is pregnant, I think, but . . . but it cannot have been the monsieur because I . . . I have overheard her saying on the telephone, "I have to get rid of it. You've got to help me." '

Again he wished Louis was with them. 'And to whom was she speaking?' he asked so gently the girl realized he would not tell the monsieur she had been listening in.

'To . . . to a woman named Violette. Madame Vernet has insisted on a meeting. This they . . . they have arranged for last Tuesday at noon. Apparently no other time was suitable.'

'In the Café of the Turning Hour?'

They would all hate her now, Kalfou and Madame Isabelle . . . all of them for not having spoken up earlier and given warning. 'The Brasserie de Tout Bonheur. It . . . it is on the rue Vivienne near the Bibliothèque Nationale. I made a point of going there, just to see it from the street, you understand.'

She saw him nod, saw him pass round more cigarettes, and when her fingers touched his, he telegraphed an urgency that frightened.

'Did Nénette ask you to do that for her?'

'Liline . . . Liline did so. She . . . she said she wanted to know for sure that . . . that things were being taken care of. She knew of the meeting but . . . but was afraid to go herself.'

Shit! 'What things?'

'She . . . she did not say, monsieur! *Please*, you must believe mé!'

'Élène, why did you not come to me with this?' demanded Madame Therrien only to be stilled by an upraised forefinger.

Kohler gave them a moment, then sighed as if the life had suddenly gone from him, and said quite simply, 'So Madame Vernet made arrangements not for herself but for Liline Chambert?'

The girl shut her eyes and hastily crossed herself, begging

God's forgiveness. 'Yes. That . . . that is how it must have been. The abortion for Liline, monsieur. *Liline!*'

She broke down and the others tried to comfort her as he left the room on the run to call up the main staircase for his partner and then to go into an urgent huddle with him that could not be heard in the kitchens.

'Louis, Madame Vernet went to see Violette to arrange the abortion. Debauve was probably present to lay down the rules. Fifty thousand francs . . .'

'Two hundred thousand at least, but why risk going to Violette and Debauve, who would be certain to ask for more whenever they felt like it?'

He had a point.

'Why, indeed, Hermann, unless Madame Vernet knew they would never come back at her.'

'No blackmail, then, because she could blackmail them. Ah *Gott im Himmel*, Louis, does that woman know who the Sandman is?'

Debauve.

A sickening thought. 'If she does and she has used it also in this matter, only God can answer for her.'

Had she made certain Liline Chambert would die, had she tried to have her niece killed?

'House arrest,' breathed Kohler sadly. 'Nothing official. I'll say it's for the family's protection from the press. I'll ring von Schaumburg and ask him to arrange it. She isn't to leave until we tell her to. I'll also ask for two of the grey mice to sit with her at all times. They're not to let her out of their sight.'

The grey mice, the Blitzmädel from the Reich. Stenographers and telegraphists. 'Vernet might object.'

'He won't, not if we tell him what we think is true.'

'He may have answers of his own to give.'

'Then we'll let him have his say and hold the rest in reserve. We'll keep the two of them apart for as long as possible.'

'He'll hate her.'

'She must hate him.'

*   *   *

The armchairs were big and deep and white and draped with white, crocheted throws. The floor was white, the walls were white, the ceiling, too, but there was gold in gilded frames and trumeaux whose mirrors tossed things back and forth, laying down detail upon detail. The plaster bust was of a seer who did not judge; the Grecian torso was of a naked young man who would remain headless, faceless and armless now forever.

St-Cyr sucked in a breath and released it slowly. 'In an instant Mademoiselle Chambert comes to us, Hermann. This room is not only filled with her but with the tragedy she had to face.'

When Vernet found them, the first thing he saw was that they were sitting in those chairs, the next, leaning against the ivory candelabrum among its draped strands of clear glass beads, a 20-by-20-centimetre black-and-white photographic print of Liline in that other room, the tenement on the quai du Président Paul Doumer.

'Inspectors, what is the meaning of this? Have you no sense of decency? How dare you force me to meet you here?'

Caught in the mirrors, the image of him—quite perfectly dressed in a blue serge business suit and tie, ah yes—bounced back and forth across the room, incensed.

'Please sit over there by the windows, monsieur,' said the Sûreté, indicating a chair. 'Light streams in, leaving few shadows. It will be better for us.'

'Where is Nénette? Why haven't you found her? Just *what* do you think you're playing at?'

They did not answer. They sat in those armchairs and all they did was wait for him to be seated where told.

He closed the door behind him. He was tall and not unhandsome. He was far more wealthy and powerful than anyone Liline Chambert could ever have aspired to had she been of that mind. But he was vulnerable and knew it.

Still, there was no harm in trying. 'I demand an all-out search for my niece. The Wehrmacht have tracking dogs. Let them use them.'

'But . . . but those are very vicious animals, monsieur,' said Louis, aghast.

Irritably Vernet passed smoothing fingers across his brow. 'They'll be kept on the leash. Don't be an idiot!'

Kohler had to tell him. 'All the same, monsieur, the child will be terrified.'

'And is she not already terrified enough? Is it that you want this . . . this Sandman to silence her? *Is it?*' he demanded.

His voice had not quite risen to a shout, but the agitation it implied would have to suffice for this simple suggestion to be made: 'Perhaps if we allow them to release the dogs, they will corner him for us, Hermann,' said St-Cyr.

Kohler tossed his head in doubt and shrugged. 'Perhaps but then there's Julien Rébé to think of, and we wouldn't want his throat torn out before he sings.'

Ah, damn them, damn them! Furiously Vernet tossed a hand. 'Look, I know nothing of this Rébé. Who is he?'

The truth at last, was it? 'A stableboy, monsieur,' said the Sûreté. 'Your wife's lover. The father of her unborn child.'

'Her *what?*'

'We told you to sit down,' offered Kohler. 'We were only trying to be kind.'

'The slut! I'll kill her.'

'Ah, no, monsieur,' cautioned the Sûreté. 'You will assist us in every possible way so that the scandals of her sordid affair and of your own here in this room, and with a girl under your care whose parents trusted you, can be hushed up as much as possible.'

Was it music to his ears? wondered Kohler.

No sigh escaped Vernet. He refused to sit down but forced himself to consider Liline's last moment and to softly swear, 'Things should never have come to this. What do you want of me?'

A touch of sadness, one of remorse perhaps—yes, yes, that would be welcome, but the industrialist had decided to fight back and would most definitely attempt to extricate himself. 'Everything, but only the truth,' said St-Cyr, not taking his eyes from Vernet. 'The time for lies and half-lies is over.'

They would push until they were satisfied but what, then, would they do? 'Very well, begin.'

Could bankruptcy have affected him more? wondered Kohler and thought it unlikely. The threat of a scandal and of ridicule still stood foremost in his mind. Or had Vernet been up to even more mischief?

Reluctantly the industrialist sat in the chair by the windows and right away realized why they had put him there. The rare sunshine of Paris in winter gave plenty of light. Though he couldn't see it, that damned dog of Bernadette's would still be hanging out there behind the house above a blood-spattered circle in the snow.

They had to break him, these two *flics* from opposite sides of this war. It would not be easy—they did not have much time and must find Nénette before it was too late. How deeply would they cut? he wondered. St-Cyr was still studying him; Kohler was debating whether to light a cigarette in a room where everything was pristine and there were no ashtrays but that of his own hand.

'Did you force your attentions on Liline Chambert?' asked the Sûreté swiftly.

'You raped her, didn't you, and in this room,' sighed Kohler. 'When . . . when did it first happen, eh, monsieur? Soon after she arrived to take up her studies—was it then?'

'Was it after that first attack that she had the room done over?' asked Louis.

'Look, we had an understanding, that is all.'

'She refused you,' breathed Kohler. 'She "tempted" you, eh? You're a man of position and power. You're used to having your way.'

'An understanding, is that what you called it?' asked Louis.

'All right, I had to have her. She was everything that wife of mine was not. Can you imagine what it's been like living with that woman? My father couldn't stand her. He warned me. He . . . Look, I didn't mean to . . .'

'To say that?' asked Kohler. 'Hey, he refused to leave the business to you and chose instead your brother who was much younger, "a brilliant designer", you said, and also well married.'

Bâtards! he wanted to shriek at them but said levelly, 'Father thought Bernadette corrupt. He felt that once I had passed on, she would sell everything and get out.'

End of family, end of name. 'So a flat was needed,' sighed Louis, drawing them right back to the matter at hand.

'Liline struck her own bargain. She would let me choose the location and arrange for the flat but would decide on the one to live in it. We would not come together here but only there. It was far too awkward, she said.'

'Too damned dangerous, you mean,' snorted Kohler. 'A wise girl, but not clever enough, since the boy she chose would never have slept with her, and that wife of yours found this out.'

'*What's Bernadette done?*' he hissed, his voice harsh and breaking at last.

Kohler let Louis handle things.

'Please, monsieur, a moment, yes? and I will tell you how it must have been so that we understand each other. You forced that girl into an affair she did not want but was afraid to refuse for fear of disgracing her family and losing her father his job with your firm. Don't pretend otherwise. This room of hers was designed to reflect it. Like all good art, it speaks from a soul in torment striving to reach out and touch the hearts and minds of others. She became pregnant, and you told her this was what you wished for more than anything. After the divorce, the mar- riage—with money, friends and power, even divorces can be arranged and quickly. But she was astute enough to realize Nénette, whom she adored and who trusted her implicitly, was the rightful heiress. So, what was to become of Nénette, please, once you and Liline were married and the child you had given her had been born?'

It had been a good attempt, he'd have to give the Sûreté that. 'Nénette would continue to live with us and inherit everything when she came of age. If she married, her husband would then take over and administer the estate. That's the law.'

Kohler found he couldn't sit still. A fidgeter always, he got up to move around, took out his cigarettes and lighted one. 'But Mademoiselle Chambert was not so certain Nénette would inherit a thing, eh? She feared you would put the child on a train to nowhere.'

One must remain unruffled by such insolence. 'I beg to differ, Inspector. I thought of doing no such thing.'

Ah *mon Dieu, mon Dieu*, he was tough. 'Then why, please, in her desperation did Mademoiselle Chambert turn to the one person she could trust the least?' asked Louis.

'Your wife,' sighed Kohler, flicking ash. 'The girl panicked. She knew *exactly* what you'd do to your niece.'

'When confronted by Madame, Mademoiselle Chambert told her the truth and begged for help,' said Louis.

'Help she got!' swore Kohler, crossing to the candelabrum to rattle its strands of beads as he snatched up the police photograph.

Thrusting it into Vernet's hands, he said, 'Look at it, you smug son of a bitch, and start talking or we'll see you in hell.'

'You will never be able to prove a thing.'

'Monsieur, we will prove everything,' said Louis sadly. 'We have a habit of doing so no matter who is involved or how powerful.'

'You're hated by the SS of the avenue Foch. Even Gestapo Boemelburg, who depends on you to combat common crime, says your days are numbered. I have only to turn to either of them.'

'Then do so and accept the scandal of your wife's affair,' snapped Kohler, trembling a little.

'Tell me what you want.'

'The Sandman,' said Louis so gently it was but a breath. 'Only you can help us. That wife of yours refuses.'

'Then ask her in and I will get her to confess.'

All along the corridor there were panic-thoughts of running, but where could she go? *Where?* wondered Bernadette Vernet. The detectives with Antoine were waiting for her in that room of Liline's, that room where so much had gone on. All the years of bitterness would erupt. She would throw herself at him, would try to tear his eyes out, eyes that had mocked her, defied her, passed over her to another and another. He had done it in this house . . . this house that was rightfully hers, not Nénette's. Things would be shouted. Things no one else must ever hear. Her rage, her pent-up jealousy, the sly and wicked rejoicing of her fornicating with a boy from the gutters just to get back at him, the triumph at last that it had been settled . . . all settled, only to find that a stupid, stupid mistake had been made.

She came to the door and tried to stop herself. Her bare toes dug into the carpet. What are they thinking? she demanded, her heart racing. That she could not see herself cast out on the street in favour of another and one so young? That the Vernet wealth would no longer be hers and that she had had to stop it from happening, that she could not let him *marry* that little bitch!

Antoine would be smugly sitting in one of the armchairs. Would the pleasures of possessing Liline be there in memory, her breasts, her thighs, her beautiful cunt. . . ? Was it beautiful, Antoine?

With a scream no one heard, she roared into the room and there he was standing between the two detectives. Antoine . . . Antoine . . .

He slapped her so hard and so swiftly that she ducked away in shock. '*Bâtard!*' she swore.

'*Putain! Fille de joie! Paillasse!*' he hissed. 'Horning yourself with a stableboy. Hah! did you not think I would discover what you had been up to?'

'*Pardon?*' she shrilled and ripped her nightgown open. '*Roué! Fornicateur!*' She grabbed her breasts and held them out to him. 'Suck . . . go on and suck them for nourishment, eh, or is it that hers were a little bigger, a little softer since we were both with child? *Your* child.'

Ah *merde* . . . 'Madame . . .' began Louis, only to hear Vernet laugh tauntingly at her.

She shrieked, 'It has to be *his*—HIS!' and held her belly, distending it in mockery of him.

Both detectives were taken aback and that was good, yes,

good! thought Vernet viciously. He'd heap scorn on her. 'It's impossible, Bernadette. Please don't make a mockery of yourself. Be dignified. You're a Vernet, isn't that right, eh? Walk to the guillotine with pride.'

She withdrew a little, planting her feet more firmly apart. *'What have you said to them?'* she said gratingly, cocking her head sideways to hear him. *'Well?'* she shrilled and yelled, *'Debaucheur! Maudit salaud!* Liline was not the first, messieurs. Ah no, no. There have been others. Tender little things. Two former maids he had to pay off. Schoolgirls if he could get them—yes, yes, I swear it! He did not use the brothels for fear of disease. He concentrated on the inexperienced because with them they gave him that feeling of immense power a man such as he requires.'

'You always were unsatisfactory, Bernadette. With you there were never the cries of joy.'

'Or despair.'

Ah *nom de Dieu, de Dieu.* 'Monsieur—'

'Piss off! Don't interrupt. Let me finish this bitch once and for all!'

Kohler rolled his eyes up at the ceiling. Sex was the great leveller. High-class, low-class, sophisticated or not, they all went down into the sewers to fight it out. Every time.

Quivering, her face livid, she drew in a breath. Her dark brown eyes flashed hatred, hesitation and then uncertainty. 'Well, what is it then? *What* have I done? Put holes in your condoms? You did that, Antoine. The little rips, the simple tears. What did you tell that shameful slut? That the rubber wasn't so good these days?' she mocked. 'You got the poor thing pregnant. She was so stupid and naïve she didn't realize what you were up to until it was too late. Did you offer her marriage when she discovered she was pregnant, eh? Well?'

His gaze must be like the guillotine before it falls and she must see this. No quarter, only triumph. 'In Rouen I had time to think, my dear. What must she do? I asked myself, and put in a call to my solicitors. They've been with us since the days of my grandfather, Inspectors. Vrillière et fils, Number six, place de Valois and long ago they learned the art of discretion, especially in matters between husband and wife.'

It was coming now, and she could only hate him all the more. He gave her a moment to savour it. He ran his eyes over her forgotten breasts not with pity, ah no, but with utter contempt.

'Last Wednesday, Bernadette, you told Monsieur Charles that the affair between myself and Liline had ended and that I wanted no trouble and wished to settle the sum of two hundred and seventy-five thousand francs on the girl. This sum, which you gave them on condition of silence, they were to hold until Monday at nine a.m., as it would be picked up then by a close friend of your family, a priest who would act as intermediary. A Father Eugène Debauve, who would present them with a sealed envelope for me containing some letters I had written to her. This he has, unfortunately, done. How could you have been so stupid?'

A sum of 275,000 francs in cash . . . 'Madame . . .' began the Sûreté, only to hear her say, 'Nénette can answer all your questions, but I greatly fear she will not be able to. Will it be the Sandman who kills her, Inspectors, or my lover, since both must now know she intends to accuse them? Not me. Never me.'

GREEN, BLUE AND AMBER, RUBY RED, THE LAST light of day glowed among the shattered windows high above them while on the floor at Louis's feet the Star of David, drawn by the child in windblown snow, now bore the careless bruises of bootprints. But these were not hers, nor a man's, but those of a woman.

Uncertain and fearing the worst, they followed them from room to room down a corridor, now dark, now brushed with snow. A study, a school where Hebrew and religious studies had been taught, had been turned over to storage. Clothing, blankets, boots and shoes, all to be sent to the needy via the Jewish relief organization, had been left in sodden heaps as if forgotten.

Kohler shone his torch around. Among the rubbish, books littered the floor, sheet music, too. Chopin, Brahms, Tchaikovsky. All of the bundles had been broken open and searched for money. A partly closed door gave access to yet more rooms and then to the cellars, to a dark and forbidding arched brick entrance that shouted up no welcome, only a warning.

Was the child now dead? wondered St-Cyr. Had they failed

her, and who, please, was the woman? Sister Céline, Violette Belanger, Madame Morelle or Madame Rébé?

Or was it none of these but someone else, someone who also knew who the Sandman was but had no fear of him?

Had the Attack Leader revealed his darkest thoughts to his psychotherapist?

At the foot of the stairs a river of black ice led to heaps of broken crates, smashed picture frames and jackboot-torn canvases . . . Raphael . . . Leonardo . . . ah *mon Dieu*, Fouquet that master of fifteenth-century French painting . . . A Madonna and child . . . A Botticelli, the *Birth of Venus* perhaps . . . Mould on everything, no time to look closer, no time . . . all stored for safety . . . safety . . .

The smell of coal dust and long-cold ashes came to them. The furnace was huge, the boilers even larger, the coal bins empty, the bootprints clear. Those of the child, too. Her explorings, her sitting on an overturned pail to think things through. Droplets of wax, the stub of a candle fixed to an up-ended coffee can. A wad of chewing gum parked behind a water pipe.

The door of the furnace was closed, its cast-iron draught plate open.

Kohler swung the beam of the torch around, letting it pierce the web of grey-white, asbestos-wrapped pipes, thin coverings of soot on each and on the gauge. Here and there the child had boldly printed her name and those of Andrée Noireau and Liline Chambert in the soot. ARE WE ALL TO DIE? she had asked, and had left that question for them.

'Hermann . . .'

Kohler switched off the torch and they listened to the silence, breathed in the smell of the place, the frigid mustiness. 'Block the doorway behind us,' he sighed. 'This is a dead end except for the hand-operated lift they used to bring the coal sacks down and take the ashes out before the war.'

They waited. They stood their ground but had not brought their guns—ah! it was Hermann's responsiblity to take charge of the guns until needed and they'd been in too much of a hurry.

When he found the hoist well, Kohler looked up it into the night. Already the stars were coming out. It would be clear and very cold.

There was no sign of the child's having been taken forceably up the thing, not even her bootprints, only a notice she had written in soot. THIS IS THE WAY OUT AND THE WAY IN.

Whoever had come for her had known of the place but had departed some time ago, having returned the lift platform to the cellars.

It was now 5.27 p.m. Berlin Time, and they had been in the city not quite forty-four hours. Since well before dawn, their only sustenance had been two cups of coffee and a few croissants, courtesy of von Schaumburg, a bowl of the acorn water with Oona and a little of the National bread.

They were hungry and running on Messerschmitt Benzedrine, which could and would fail them if too much was taken and yet . . . yet the child might still be free.

In the Jewish part of the *ancien* Cimetière de Neuilly behind the ramparts of headstones, the few and scattered mausoleums had been broken into during the desecration. Bronze doors when pushed further inward revealed shattered cremation urns or family burial vaults that had felt the sledgehammer blows until their seals had crumbled and their coffins had been dragged out in search of gold wedding rings and other trinkets.

In one such mausoleum the child had placed silk flowers she must have stolen from Gentile graves. In another, behind a cut-stone menorah and opened Talmud, she had bedded down for a night, having swept the floor clean with a broom of straw she had acquired from God knows where.

In the dust she had written: *Andrée, you must forgive me. Liline is also dead. I went to the place where she was and I saw them taking her out.*

'The dogs, Louis. We have to ask von Schaumburg to allow us to use them.'

'She'll be terrified.'

'But safe.'

'Unless held hostage.'

'All right, let's pay Sister Céline a visit and hear what she has to say.'

'Madame Morelle, I think, and Violette Belanger, but first the Vernet solicitors. Let us hope they are not now gone for the day.' Could God not grant them this one small miracle, a conscientious solicitor? wondered St-Cyr and answered tartly, God thinks nothing of solicitors and hasn't the time of day for them.

The envelope was sealed and soft, the eyes of the elderly solicitor concerned.

With care Louis opened the thing the 'priest', Eugène Debauve, had left for Antoine Vernet. Emptily he said, 'The underpants that were taken from the site of the abortion. But not to sell on the black market, simply as proof so that the last touch Monsieur Vernet would have of Liline Chambert would be this one sad memento from his wife.'

'*Merde, merde,* Louis, she must really hate him.'

Like the rest of the city, the house on the rue Chabanais was now in darkness but cigarettes glowed, the line-up was long, boots shuffled, men coughed. And as before, the Feldgendarmen were discernable only because of their size and because they stood in the street, not on the pavement, their breath billowing in the frigid air.

'Madame Morelle doesn't want to see you. She has asked us to keep you away.'

'St-Cyr, Sûreté. Please step aside.'

Oh-oh. 'Louis . . . '

The burly Feldgendarm broke the rules by switching on an unblinkered torch to flood their faces, distracting no one but himself. Louis took a step back. There was a crack, a sigh, a burst of wind. The torch flew up, the lead-weighted baton clattered. A cry of pain was stifled as the knuckles of a left hand were cradled.

The Feldgendarm crumpled to the street. The roar of others descended on them. 'Who's next? *Well,* who is it to be?' hissed the Sûreté in fluent *Deutsch.* A tiger.

'A revolver . . . he's got a revolver,' managed Kohler, a lie. 'He's come to make an arrest.'

Arrest . . . arrest . . . the word fled down the line, pillaring the Feldgendarmen into indecision while the wise among the clientele sought greener pastures.

'What arrest?'

'Please don't be difficult,' winced the Sûreté breathlessly. 'If you want answers, ask the Kommandant von Gross-Paris.'

'We're under his order,' managed Kohler. *'Orders!'* he shouted.

This they could understand, but it was with regret that they let them pass, for one could never predict the future, and the job of policing the Wehrmacht's largest brothel had carried certain privileges.

They hoped it wouldn't be Madame Morelle. They had heard no police vans turn into the street, so knew it was not a raid.

The place was crowded, full of tobacco smoke and ripe with the stench, and through this boozy haze, and seen against the overflowing, bulging pulchritude, the voluminous black lace of Madame Morelle circulated. To her, arrest was the furthest thing from her mind. These two could prove nothing. Ignoring them, she sat down and spoke softly to an SS major, offering pleasures he could not find in one of the two houses the Generalmajor und Höherer-SS Oberg had reserved for his kind.

'Ah!' she said, as the two of them strode into the waiting room where the girls waited, too, until enlivened by this little interlude. The din from the staircase only grew louder.

'Madame Morelle?' began the Sûreté, using the voice of Judgement.

Her pudgy, be-ringed left hand lingered on an SS-trousered thigh to get the feel of it, then patted the knee sharply as if to say, Leave this to me. 'Brigitte, please take the Major up to Violette's room. Ask her to let him watch. It's all been arranged. If he likes what he sees, he is to enjoy himself and we will discuss things further.'

A schoolgirl, was that what the smirking son of a bitch was

after, wondered Kohler, or was he a reminder sent to them from the avenue Foch via the escort service on the Champs-Élysées and an urgent plea for help from Debauve? Ah *merde*, that must be it. 'Just a minute. No one visits Violette.'

'*What's she done?*' hissed Madame Morelle, raking them with kohl-rimmed eyes. She wet her ruby lips. 'Well, eh? Come, come, my fine messieurs,' she shrilled. 'I demand an answer. I have a right to see the magistrate's order, and please do not tell me you haven't one!'

Snap, snap went her fingers.

'Look, we only want to talk to her about a missing child,' sighed Kohler.

'*Talk!*' shrilled the woman. Her hands were tossed, her shoulders shrugged. 'Who has time to talk to such as you in a place like this? Violette was here all day and all last night. She has not left the premises. *Not* for one minute. This I will swear on my father's grave.'

'But not on your mother's,' sighed the Sûreté, forgetting his sore knuckles at last to run his eyes over her. 'Madame Berthe Morelle ... Berthe Lefebvre of the rue Saint-Denis and les Halles. The jet-black hair, it is a wig needed due to recurring bouts of *la syphilis*; the cheeks, they are fleshy and deeply rouged to hide the sugar scars of displeased *maquereaux*. Gone are the days of your youth. Please let me see your licence, madame, so as to remind myself and refresh your memory.'

Ah no ... 'The rue Saint-Denis?' she bleated, still slow to tumble to it.

'And an arrest that was made more than thirty years ago in a house on the corner of the rue des Precheurs [the street of the Preachers]. A prostitute you helped. A friend, you said, and like a sister to you—wasn't that it, eh? An unwanted child she had refused to bear—ah, of course nothing could be proven. You had arrived too late to caution the girl and could not hold the abortionist for the *gendarmes* you yourself had summoned because that one, she had vanished. Others swore to it. There was little we could do, since you willingly slept and did other things with the presiding magistrate, who had a taste for whores that were cheap. You've changed. You've grown older. One would have hoped, wiser.'

St-Cyr . . . St-Cyr . . . ? A blue cape and *képi* then and no moustache but boots and a persistent air that could not be bought off. Ah, why had Madame Rébé not forewarned her of this one at their last reading? 'You've changed yourself,' she said tartly. 'Violette has done nothing. She was here all day and last night, and others will swear to this.'

'Swearing's in your blood,' he snorted lustily. 'We'll ask them, of course, but first, madame, please take us to the room and leave that one here unless he wants trouble. We will question the two of you upstairs where you belong.'

She tossed her head as if wounded. 'There is no need to be offensive. The past is over. The legs, they are closed, and the door to heaven, it is shut. We've both come up in the world.'

'*Good!* I'll bring you down, then, shall I? You're wanted on the charge of abortion and causing the death by it of Liline Chambert. Please save your breath for the stairs.'

He'd make it stick, she knew he would. '*Abortion?*' she snorted. 'I did no such thing. Pah! the years have addled your brain, my fine Sûreté. Why would I indulge in such an illegal practice when I have all this raking in so much more?'

'That is just what we'd like to ask you. Now move.'

'Louis . . . '

'Not now, Hermann. Get her upstairs.'

'But—'

'No buts. Just do as I say.'

'Okay, Chief, you're the boss but that one's SS.'

'*Idiot! did you think I hadn't noticed?*'

They were on the stairs and moving. They were on the first floor and heading up five flights. Big men, little men, some with grins, stood on each step of the way. Whores came down, whores went up. Peignoirs were open, some wore none at all . . . One said, 'Ooh, they are in such a rush, those two, madame. You haven't lost your charm. The older the sweeter, eh, my fine messieurs?'

'And both at once!' hooted another. 'Give her port and

advocaat, the half-and-half, messieurs. By midnight she'll be opening all the doors and you can enter where you please!'

'But not both in the same place!' tossed the other one over her shoulder as Louis tripped and piled into a brunette, grabbing her bony hips for support.

'Have you paid?' she hooted, her face overly made-up, the lipstick smeared, the hair dyed a violent red.

By now the Wehrmacht's finest had got the message and all were shouting, *Get them. Stop them. Throw the bastards out.*

'OUT! OUT! *RAUS! RAUS! RAUS!*'

They stamped their boots each time they said it. They pushed, they shoved, they heaved on the line, and the ripple of their pent-up dislike of the police raced on and up . . . up.

Madame Morelle burst on to a landing, threw out her black, lace-clad arms and went down in a welter of other legs, arms, breasts and bare buttocks. Now everyone was laughing and shouting, 'Grab them. Hoist them. Pick them up and pitch them out.

'OUT! OUT! *RAUS! RAUS!*'

Kohler dragged the woman up and grabbed Louis by the overcoat collar. She gasped and rolled her dark eyes in panic. 'My heart,' she managed, placing the flat of a be-ringed, pudgy hand on her heaving chest.

He shoved, and the ripple on the staircase behind them reversed itself as they raced upwards, pushing the woman ahead of themselves. Couples began to leave their rooms, only to hesitate, some clutching their clothes or a bedsheet, others trying to get dressed until . . .

'Violette, no! *No*, do you hear me?' shrilled Madame Morelle.

They had reached the fifth floor, were right at the top of the stairwell. Wild-eyed and desperate, the schoolgirl, her white shirt-blouse torn open down the front, her breasts hanging out, the dark blue pleated skirt and kneesocks stained and dishevelled, faced them. Arms out, feet out and planted, panic in her deep brown eyes, the shaggy mop of dark brown hair now braided so that she looked not twenty-three years old or seventeen but no more than thirteen or fourteen.

'Violette . . . ' said Madame Morelle, catching a breath and trying to hold the detectives back. Everyone was watching. No one made a sound. 'Violette, *chérie*, come to mother.'

With the back of a hand the girl wiped her mouth and spat furiously to one side before repeating the gesture. 'You're *not* my mother.'

'Don't jump. Please don't. It's too far even for angels.'

'I want my little farm, damn you. I want to leave this place and raise flowers and birds to sell in the market. I want to taste honey, not cloud-custard. I'm sick of men jerking off into my mouth.'

'*Chérie*, please don't do it. Please. I swear I'll take you to Spain with me. From there you can go to Provence, to your little farm if you wish.'

'Father Eugène has the money. He really has it, hasn't he? *Tell* me, damn you! Tell *me* he hasn't stolen it all.'

Ah *nom de Jésus-Christ*, why *did* she have to ask? demanded Madame Morelle of herself. There were only the two of them facing each other in this *impasse*. The child climbed up on to the railing and clutched a support. It was a long way down the spiral of those stairs, and as all looked up at her and craned their necks to watch their little bird fly, Violette looked down at them.

She'll push me, said Violette to herself. She'll have to do it.

'Madame,' breathed St-Cyr, 'please step aside.'

'*Don't be a fool!*' hissed the woman, her bulk stubbornly blocking their way, all lace and flesh, perfume, jet-black beads and dangling jet-black ear-rings. 'Darling,' she crooned to the child, 'be sensible. Take me by the hand and come down from there.'

Perhaps five metres separated them and this was clear, except for the open doorway from which the schoolgirl had come.

'You did it,' she said. 'You killed that girl who was pregnant. You pumped air into her *passage de Vénus* and she died from the shock. How did it feel to have her die so suddenly?'

'Don't be silly, *chérie*. I did no such thing. These men, they speak lies.'

'Where is Father Eugène? Why isn't he here to tell them that you owed him money, *mother*, and that, with one bold stroke, one gamble, all your debts to him would be erased? Is he the Sandman, do you think, messieurs?' she taunted. 'Is he the one who violates little girls like me and then kills them?'

Little girls . . .

Frantically Kohler searched for a way to get at her. Had her clients beat it? he wondered. Was that room of hers now empty, that schoolroom? Was there another way into it?

'She'll see you leave,' confided the Sûreté softly. 'This matter has, unfortunately, to be settled by the two of them.'

The girl looked down, and as she did so, she dragged off one of the elastics from her braids and let it fall.

There was a hush that only got deeper and deeper. 'If I could undress, I would,' she said, 'so as to be that much closer to heaven. I've done nothing that can't be forgiven—my sister tells me this constantly, messieurs. "You *will* be accepted into the Kingdom of Everlasting Love," she says, "but only if you ask for His forgiveness instead of praying He will fuck you." The *grand frisson* of *frissons*, eh? The one a girl would feel all the way up her spine and into her brain if only she could feel anything at all. At all!'

Ah *nom de Dieu, de Dieu* . . .

'She thinks all girls of my age have the devil in their bodies, messieurs, but please, is it not the devil in the minds of men to which she refers? Is it not *they* who want to undress and violate girls like me? Ask her. Ask Céline. See what she says. Tell her that's what the father we shared did to me. To *me!*—at the age of eight. Have her anoint my naked body before she drives the skewer into my heart.'

Plunged into darkness, the house waited a split second, its breath held for the shrill scream that lasted long after the floor below had been solidly struck and the rain of wooden balusters had ceased. Everyone cried out. A great, sad sigh went up. They began to move, to panic in the darkness. Someone shouted, 'The electricity has gone off!'

Arrondissement by *arrondissement*, the Occupier could do such a thing without notice.

'The SS,' breathed Kohler, moving forward with Louis's shoulder under one hand. 'The railing's gone. Ah *merde*, Louis . . . L . . . O . . . U . . . I . . . S!'

Dragged back, they lay there propped against the wall. Candles were lighted. Matches struck. One by one these tiny lights grew into a softly fluttering glow that filled the stairwell.

The property in Spain, the bank accounts, too, would be of little use. Madame Berthe Morelle, blood gathering in a large dark pool about her head, was spread-eagled on the floor. Her wig had flown off. Her head was totally bald. The ripples on the back of her neck were pale and flaccid.

'Louis, the schoolgirl . . . '

'Across the roof-tops, I think.'

'Ah *merde* . . . It's too icy.'

Ice or not, there she was caught momentarily in the beam of Hermann's torch and then fixed more firmly, perched up by the chimney pots, daring them to follow.

Pale, greeny-blue beneath the ice and encrusted snow, the copper sheathing sloped steeply past another flimsy skylight to her feet. Walls separated the houses. Some roofs were higher, others lower. The wind was increasing, the cold was fierce. Above them the stars climbed into the heavens. Smoke from the coal fires of the brothel drifted past.

When they found a torn patch of skin, they knew she had clutched an iron pipe. When they saw her again, she was trapped against a dividing wall, the roof between them sloping away on either side while that behind her rose up a storey higher.

'Father Eugène does things for the SS,' she shouted tearfully. 'He is a spy for them. A *spy*! He hears the confessions of the really sick ones they send him. You should talk to some of those, messieurs. Ask them about schoolgirls. Ask what they've done in the past and still want to do. He doesn't send them to me. He says I'm not suitable, that we must be discreet. They're officers. *Officers*, damn you!'

Blood was frozen to the bare flesh of her left palm. Her skirt clung to her thighs. Louis started forward, balancing. Kohler kept the light on her as best he could. 'Mademoiselle,' began the Sûreté. 'Please, it's over. We desperately need information . . . '

'*Over, is it?*' she cried. 'The SS are using him. He *reports* to them!'

Half-way along the crown of the roof, the ice was thick. Louis slipped. He went down hard and cried out. She screamed and, turning, nimbly climbed the wall, to look back once and then to cry out, 'I SAIL TO HEAVEN!'

And was gone. No sound. No scream.

Louis cautioned his partner. 'Stay away, idiot! You've Giselle and Oona to look after. Me, I am alone but for Gabrielle. Say goodbye for me. My shoes, they aren't up to this. My hands, they are freezing.'

He had pulled off his gloves and had thrown them away.

Madly the torch beam danced over him as he clawed his way back up to the crown of the roof. Then, balancing again, he stubbornly went on.

'She's gone across the next roof,' he shouted, having climbed the wall. 'She's left a skylight open in her haste and is safe.'

Back in the house on the rue Chabanais the lights had come on, and they knew the SS major had been the one to switch them off.

He was standing on the ground floor next the body. He was grinning up at them.

'Hasse, Louis. The escort service,' cursed Kohler. 'Debauve must have found things out about him the SS now know. They must believe the Attack Leader is the Sandman.'

'Perhaps but then . . . ah *mais alors, alors* . . . '

'Save it. We haven't time.'

There were no lights at all in the impasse Maubert where the SS-Attack Leader had his atelier. Come to think of it, there hadn't been any at all on the Left Bank. The houses on either side of that narrow slot crowded closely. The one at the far end showed only the dark silhouette of its roof-top against the night sky of stars.

They paused. They did not like the situation at all. They had to find Nénette Vernet but feared they were too late.

The Daimler wasn't there, the entrance to the house was locked. All window grilles were bolted solidly.

When they rang the bell, they had to wait, and the sound of it, escaping into the *impasse*, was overly loud. 'Ah *merde*, Louis, why does that God of yours have to do this to us?'

God had nothing to do with it, and Hermann knew as much. 'Maybe He's trying to tell us something about the SS.'

'As if we didn't already know enough! *Verdammt*, where the hell is the piss-assed concierge?'

He rang the bell again, yanking so fiercely on its chain the damned thing snapped, and for some reason the bell-stop jammed and the bell rang and rang until its ancient spring finally tired itself out.

At last the thing shut up. Sometime later a bolt was slid back, another and another.

From the darkness, a voice said, 'He's not here. He has gone to his lesson.'

They moved aside. They shone their torches into the concierge's face, causing him to blink and yelp and duck away in fear. Kohler towered over him. St-Cyr simply said, 'Take us up to his rooms. Open the flat and wait in the corridor. We haven't time for magistrate's orders. Not now, so do not bother to ask.'

'The . . . the electricity in this *quartier* has been off for some time, messieurs. There . . . there are no lights.'

The SS again.

'That doesn't matter,' breathed Kohler. 'We're getting used to the dark. Now move.'

'A child of eleven,' hazarded St-Cyr as they went up the stairs. 'Has he been keeping her here?'

'How should I know? I don't live in the front of the house but in the cellars. I *can't* watch everyone.'

'Yet you knew he had gone to his lesson.'

'Because I had heard the car start up and every Tuesday night he takes the life-drawing class at the Grande-Chaumière.'

'And afterwards,' asked Kohler, 'where does he go?'

'To be with the older ones, *les filles de joie* perhaps. One does not ask of such as him. One only tries not to notice.'

'How many schoolgirls has he had visit him up there?'

'Lots. This I do know. He pays them. He tempts them. Most are from the streets and so poor he can do what he wants with them.'

'*Merci*, that is just what we needed to hear,' said the Sûreté grimly. 'Please wait for us. We will close the door but will not be long.'

'You won't touch a thing, will you?'

'Ah, don't be silly. We will only touch what is necessary.'

As before, the place was pungent with turpentine and oil paints and cluttered with canvases, but it was to the storeroom they went, not to the studio.

On canvas after canvas there were schoolgirls, most with their hair in braids but few with smiles, for here most had been captured, here most had been terrified.

'Louis, take a look at this.'

By the tone of voice, Hermann had betrayed his sorrow. The beam of his torch faltered. He shook the thing and it came on a little stronger.

In the paintings, in corpse after corpse, schoolgirls of perhaps eleven to fifteen or sixteen years of age lay about the floor of a gymnasium. All naked, all lying there, just lying there.

Trapped ... they'd been herded in and forced to strip and their screams, their cries rose up from the paintings as one.

They shut their eyes. They switched off their torches. It was Hermann who, breathing in deeply, said, 'Ah, *Gott im Himmel*, Louis, it has to be him.'

How many had been violated only then to be shot down and silenced forever except for this? In painting after painting Hasse had recorded their demise, the triumph of war unleashed on children. All girls.

'Let's go and pick him up.'

'Oberg isn't going to like it,' said the Sûreté.

'That can't be helped.'

The cat was at its saucer of milk. A tin of sardines had been emptied for it into another saucer, enough to feed a child and keep it alive for a week at least.

When the creature left its supper to find a radiator near the front windows, they saw it licking something and then playfully pawing at it and licking its claws.

A black cat with mucus-clotted sea-green eyes. A mangy, torn-eared thing.

'Chewing gum,' breathed Kohler. 'Louis, it hasn't been here long.'

There was a packet of the stuff on the cluttered coffee table among the jars of paintbrushes soaking in turpentine or standing upright and ready. '*Banana*,' he said, reading the ersatz flavour, one of so many that had been concocted and mixed with saccharin to tempt the taste buds of a defeated nation and keep the memory or the hope of better times alive.

In a land of approximate jam, mystery meat and non-alcoholic near-wine, port or Pernod, flavour was seldom totally captured, only reinvented, but kids would chew on this stuff anyway, especially if offered it and they wanted to calm their nerves. Ah yes.

'She sat in this chair, Louis. There are dried oak leaves on the cushions.'

So there were, and some had all but been crumbled to dust while others still held their shape. Had they worked their way out of the coat lining they had stuffed? Had they come from a bouquet Hasse had set near his easel, upon which sat the unfinished sketch of Andrée Noireau and Nénette?

'Hasse has used the leaves as models for those the girls are kicking in their three-legged race,' said Louis. 'They may not be from the child's coat, Hermann. Indeed, I don't think they are, but perhaps he has held a few as he thought about those girls before crumbling them to dust.'

'Then how about this, eh?' demanded Kohler harshly. He held out a child's tooth-brush, its bristles well-worn and all but flattened. The torchlight shone on it.

Louis took the thing from him and read the name the manufacturer had given it. ' "The Little Princess, fabricated in Lodz." The Blitzkrieg in the East, September of thirty-nine. Ah *merde* . . . '

Nénette could have bought it on the black market, but that didn't seem likely even though the whole of Occupied Europe was awash with the debris of war. More likely Hasse had found it for her and she had forgotten to take it with her, or he had simply had it out to remind himself of what had happened in the gymnasium.

'And this?' snapped Kohler, shining his torch on the thing. 'A sketch map of the Jardin d'Acclimatation, Louis. The riding trails they followed, the stables, dressage grounds, pigeon-shoot and cage, ah damn.'

'All with the distances marked off. The puppet theatres, the children's zoo, the restaurant with its *salon de thé*, the Musée en Herbe where he and Liline Chambert taught.'

' "*Sunday 10 January at about 3.20 p.m.*" He's got that written down too. The cemetery, Louis, the convent school. Ah *Gott im Himmel, mon vieux*, what the hell are we to do?'

Sickened by the thought, they had no other choice but to continue. They had to find Julien Rébé, of course. They had not forgotten him. It was only that the SS had inadvertently put Hasse foremost in their minds by trying to shield Debauve and save that bastard from arrest.

They had to find Violette Belanger, they had to find Nénette.

And when all of that was done, or before it, they had to talk to Sister Céline. They had to find the Sandman.

Montparnasse was alive in darkness. At the carrefour Vavin, the intersection of the boulevards Raspail and du Montparnasse, the firefly-glows of hustling cigarettes and probing torch pinpricks were turbulent. The great *brasseries* of the late 1920s and before, the Dôme, the Rotunde, Sélect and Coupole, were all doing a roaring business. Troops eddied and flowed, staff cars emitted tiny, piercing beams from their headlamps, there was much honking among the *vélo-taxis*, the *gazogènes* and ancient, nag-drawn *calèches*. Lorries brought the boys in. Later the Feldgendarmen and the Paris *gendarmes* would either lock them in each establishment at curfew or drag them back to their *Soldatenheime*.

Girls stood on the street corners. Girls sold themselves in the freezing cold. In desperation, for it was against the law for her to make the approaches but okay if the man went to her, one banged on the Citroën's side window. Louis rolled it down a centimetre.

Not realizing to whom she was speaking, she said, 'I will do anything, monsieur. Anything.'

Kohler avoided argument by leaning over Louis to stuff a 100-franc note through the gap and tell her to go home. 'You'll only catch the flu.'

'I already have it!'

The window closed. They nudged on ahead, the acid of 'Must you waste our money?' ringing in the driver's ears. They tried to pass a disgorging lorry. Sailors beat upon the car, hooting, shouting, rocking it until the accelerator was touched.

The boulevard du Montparnasse was pitch-black but through this the white metal studs of a *passage clouté*, a pedestrian crossing, glowed eerily. A whistle was blown.

'Turn here,' said Louis.

'It's one further.'

'Idiot! How long have you lived in this city?'

'Okay, you win! Don't get so uptight.'

The Académie de la Grande Chaumière, where sculpture and painting had been taught since 1904, was at Number 14. It was a street that, in the 1830s and '40s, Louis Philippe had frequented, dining and playing nearby in a dance hall—one could call it no other—which sadly was no more, thought St-Cyr. Well, no matter. If not the boulevard du Montparnasse, then the clubs, the bars and cinemas of the rue de la Gaîté, the rue

Delambre, ah yes, and others. Yet here it was reasonably quiet. Here the steam had not yet been released from a boiler of a different kind.

No one could have been less intelligent or more desperate for money than Julien Rébé. The fortune-teller's son was the mannequin. The drawing studio was huge, antiquated, panelled in darkly stained tongue-and-groove cedar and, because of the electricity outage, lighted by kerosene lamps that smoked. It was crowded and stepped down in tiers, while a balcony above was reserved for those who wished only to think about art as a life's work and could dwell on the subject from rows of wooden benches. Far below them, the budding artists stood or sat and the scratches of their charcoal sticks on drawing paper rose up to fill the hall. Now a cough, of course, for it was the season for them. Now a quiet exchange with the drawing master, now a look, a line, a scratch, a rubbing with the thumb to shade and work the charcoal in.

Kohler heard Louis lightly tap the brass railing that kept them back from the precipice. 'Down there. To the far left. Herr Hasse, but he is not sketching our mannequin. He's working on something of his own.'

Two *flics*, one a giant, were far too conspicuous. They sat down. They took off their fedoras but kept their overcoats on. More than half the students were men of the Occupier and most were in uniform. All were bent on sketching, all were very serious about it. Laced among them there were a few older Frenchmen, many more women, some of the grey mice but most French. Old, young, lots of the not so young, the lonely whose husbands were locked up in prisoner-of-war camps or eternally in the arms of death.

A discus thrower Julien Rébé was not—well, not tonight. Tonight he was the standard bearer who clutched his staff and wore a Roman centurion's expression but nothing else.

He had a good body, was of medium height and well proportioned, lithe and muscular, with lots of dark reddish brown hair on his legs, groin and chest, far less of it on his head, for he'd saved money and had had the haircut of haircuts. It was not the

Fritz-cut of the Occupier. It was far shorter. A bristlework for the ladies to rub.

He had started to grow a beard but it simply made the narrow face, high forehead and deeply sunken eyes look damned scruffy, though somewhat older perhaps than his twenty-six years. Two of the kerosene lamps stood on the dais before him, one on either side. The only heat in the place, of course, was from those lamps and from the students.

The girls, the women with fingerless gloves, were attracted to him and had obviously arrived early, since most of the nearest positions had been taken up by them. Rébé, though he held his pose, was still free to seek and maintain eye contact with some of them. There would be smiles, demurely affected or boldly provocative, given by some of the women but not visible from up here. Unspoken exchanges. Slender hopes perhaps or silently-agreed-upon assignations.

'That clairvoyant mother of his must have looked in her crystal ball and then thrown him out without a sou, Louis.'

'And disowned him. At break-time he will go into the corridor to where his clothes are and will try to use them to get warm.'

'I'll tie them in knots, shall I?'

'Herr Hasse seems not to care about him at all.'

Was the centurion so completely without conscience or so desperate he could ignore the killing of Andrée Noireau, or had he silenced Nénette and now thought he had no further worries? And what, please, then, of the Attack Leader who now spoke quietly to the drawing master?

Rébé heard two of the young women giggle. There was a faint murmur, another giggle, a hand to a mouth, a burst of ribald feminine laughter. One old man threw down his charcoal in disgust and cried out, 'Shut your mouths, you silly bitches! Let those who wish to work do so.'

Rébé had noticed them up in the balcony. Unbidden, the erection he had been thinking about because of some attractive woman had suddenly become a strong reality. In panic, he turned and bolted from the dais, tripped, went down hard, knocked an easel over, and fled. There were hoots of laughter, much thrown charcoal, dismay on the part of some, and a sketch torn to shreds and offered up as a confetti.

He was trying to drag on his trousers when Kohler slammed him against a wall and put the bracelets on him.

Grabbing him by the neck, he pitched him back into the drawing studio, where the students now stood and gaped or sat still, not wanting to believe their centurion had been arrested.

'Hasse,' swore St-Cyr, moving up the tiers, knocking things over. '*Hasse* . . .'

The easel was there, a tin of pencils, one of charcoal sticks . . . little else but a small rag and an eraser.

Out on the street, they heard the Attack Leader's car join the traffic on the boulevard du Montparnasse.

The drawing he had been working on was not of Andrée Noireau but of Nénette Vernet and obviously done from memory. She did not smile. The silent scream she gave leapt from the sketch. Her sealskin hat had fallen off, the overcoat padded with leaves was buttoned up. She looked an urchin, a child caught up in a war zone. The Blitzkrieg in the East and Poland . . . Poland . . .

'Come on, Louis. Let's take this one to where he won't cause trouble any more, then we'll go after Hasse.'

The look in Rébé's greeny-brown eyes was empty of all feeling, of all conscience. Staring straight back at them, he refused to say a thing.

'Good. That is as it should be,' said the Sûreté softly. 'Save it all for when you face Madame Vernet. We'll let her accuse you, then maybe you will accuse her and the child you share can cement the relationship by giving you both away.'

'The heiress is dead. He killed her. The one you chased. The German.'

They could not leave Rébé in the cells of the rue des Saussaies for fear the SS would silence him to protect Hasse, they couldn't call for a salad basket and request a guided tour of the Santé Prison, not just yet.

They would have to leave him somewhere safe.

'The Club Mirage,' breathed Louis. 'The Corsicans can take care of him. It'll be their contribution. It's time they did something useful.'

'Is the kid really dead, Louis?'

'Ah, let us hope this one was lying to save himself.'

'I wasn't. I saw the German in the Jardin d'Acclimatation this afternoon. He was following Nénette. She got into his car.'

Ah no . . .

The lion was tame. He had had his canines and his claws pulled but still could inspire unease, for he was uncaged and nervous when there was too much shouting, and eight hundred servicemen on leave did tend to make noise.

The Club Mirage was on the rue Delambre—just a brief hustle from the Gande-Chaumière and convenient even in the dark, but now there was light, now the thirsty thronged the zinc. Now eighteen all but naked women who should have been ashamed kicked their gams and thrust their bare bottoms at the troops as the band hit everything it had and the clarinetist pinched his reed and blew the highest possible C.

It was deafening, and under normal circumstances Kohler would have grinned and lapped it up from the front-centre table he had appropriated by kicking others out. He fed the lion a titbit, some salty ersatz thing the troops seemed to gorge on with their beer. He said, 'Nice pussy, rest your head in Prisoner Rébé's lap. Yes . . . yes, that's just the way. Uncle Hermann has to find us another beer.'

The lion's handler was wrapped in narrow straps of gold satin that let her skin breathe a little too much on the flimsy bed she and the lion shared on stage among other things, but it was a nice outfit all the same. Blonde and blue-eyed, with extra long lashes, she was about forty-five, had had three kids, and was trying desperately to make enough to feed them and get on with her career as a torch singer.

'Bijou, I won't be a minute,' said Kohler kindly, even though he was really worried. *Ja*, really worried. 'If the son of a bitch farts, slap him for me. If he bolts, tell Hercules here to bring him back. If the lion is too tired, I'll have my shooter out before this one gets to the doors, no matter what the crowd want to do with him. Right, eh, Julien?' The guns had been under the seat of the car.

Now clothed but still handcuffed, Rébé had wet himself. The lion was refusing to rest his head in the stableboy's lap but was curious.

'Naughty, naughty,' said Kohler. 'Champagne, was it, Bijou?' Christ, the champagne in this place was usually owl piss.

The lady nodded. The throng at the zinc parted easily, for by now they were certain, without having been told a thing, that the Sandman had been apprehended, and if Herr Kohler should turn his head, they would tear Rébé to pieces.

Rémi Rivard, the taller of the two Corsicans who owned the club and worked the pumps, was not happy. The face that was all clefts, crags, blackheads and paralysing cliffs was grim. The jet-black greasy hair was that of a gangster, the barrel chest that of the Marseillais stevedore and smuggler he had once been, though both were still vehemently denied under the happy guise of having been 'a fisherman'.

The Corsican had caught the temper of the crowd. 'Okay,' he breathed, leaning over the zinc when he saw Kohler returning for an answer, 'take the bastard out back and wire him to the pipes. Let him freeze to death. That way he won't wear out the bread-slicer.'

'Worried, are you, about your own neck and a nice clean cut, eh?' snorted the opposition. 'I told you what we want. A small favour in return for our magnanimous custom. We need him to sing. So, soften him up with the lion, eh? Let us lock the two of them in a closet.'

'Bijou might not like it.'

She would be a few acts short and would lose money. Ruefully Kohler dragged out the remains of the bankroll he had once had on the Breton coast and found two miserable five-hundred-franc notes. 'There'll be more. Hey, I'll make it five thousand each and another ten for her.' Rivard stank of onions, fish, olive oil, garlic and peppers and the smell was nearly as bad as that of the lion, though different, of course.

'Why should we trust you?' he asked.

'You don't need to. Your *chanteuse* will okay it.'

'You must really want him.'

'We do.'

'Then walk him out of here, my fine detective. Bring him back inside via the courtyard, eh? Use your head. Gabrielle will let you keep him in her dressing room. That way, if the SS and the Gestapo want to keep him silent, she'll be responsible.'

'Now look . . . '

Rivard held up a hand signaling finality. 'That's how it is because that's how it has to be. She has friends we don't have. Generals, people in high places. Others who can take care of things for her if necessary.'

The Resistance . . . Kohler knew that was who Rivard meant and nodded. It would have to do, but Louis wasn't going to like it, especially since the dressing room had been bugged by Gestapo Paris's Listeners, though the Rivard brothers weren't supposed to know this and neither was anyone else.

Nothing had been said yet in the tiny dressing room into which St-Cyr had slipped after first quietly knocking. His nostrils still taking in the scent of Mirage, that exquisitely delicate perfume Gabrielle always wore—it had been made especially for her—he stood hesitantly facing her.

Trouble . . . we've really got trouble this time, his look seemed to say.

She touched her lips again, a reminder of the hidden microphones, and silently formed the words, Things, they are not good here either. The Gestapo still suspect me but of what I do not know.

Ah *merde*. Perhaps they had picked up someone connected to the tiny Resistance cell to which she belonged and that person had said something, perhaps they only thought to

monitor her since she knew so many big shots among the Occupier and the Occupied.

'What is it? What has happened?' she anxiously whispered
into his ear, breaking the rule.

He trembled at her touch. He found a scrap of paper he
would destroy as soon as possible, and wrote: A child is missing.
An heiress. A *voyou* a Nazi has picked up. He may already have
killed her.

'Ah no. The Sandman?' she asked, a whisper.

He gave a nod and wrote: *We've a suspect in another killing
and must keep him some place safe for a little.*

'A *little*? Here? Are you crazy?' she whispered urgently.

A *bargain*, he wrote. *I bring information.*

'That's not fair.'

He shrugged. He wrote: *The SS over on the avenue Foch may
want him. We have no other choice.*

No choice . . .

As *chanteuse*, Gabrielle Arcuri received 10 per cent of the
take of this place, a fortune that would be of no use in her
defence. None at all. Nor would her 'friends'.

Tall and willowy, she was a good head taller than himself. A
White Russian who had, as a girl named Natalya Kulakov-
Myshkin, fled the Revolution in 1917, and arrived in Paris at
the age of fourteen, having lost her family on the way. But she
hadn't done what most girls in such circumstances would have
had to do. She had been a singer right from the start. A widow
now, whose husband, a captain, had been badly wounded at
Sedan during the invasion of 1940 and had died in the late
summer of that year. She had a son, René Yvon-Paul, ten years
of age. How was he? he wondered, and saw her in the stunning
sky-blue sleeveless silk sheath that, with the scent, was her trade-
mark. Thousands of tiny seed pearls in vertical rows from hem
to diamond choker made the thing opalescent, shimmering and
electric every time she strode on stage under the spotlights or
stood, as now, under his scrutiny. Very aristocratic, very finely
moulded, the nose aquiline, the brow and cheeks so smooth,

the lips magnificent, the hair, the soft, soft shade of a very fine brandy and piled up in waves and curls.

She had the voice of a nightingale, was astute, clever and courageous if a trifle bold—had got the drop on him completely with an ancient fowling piece. It had taken place in an abandoned gristmill on a small island in the Loire near Vouvray, not far from the château of her husband's family. She'd been a suspect then, and they had shared the simple meal of a *crottin de chèvre*, a small round of goat's cheese, very strong in flavour, very dry and dusted with chopped dill and chives. A real treasure perhaps four weeks in the aging. That and crusty bread and real coffee. All from her rucksack.

The Resistance had sent her one of the little black coffins they present to collaborators who have been marked for death. He, too, had received one and she had been trying ever since to clear his name.

There were scattered Resistance cells, tiny groups—two or three persons each, perhaps five at the most—he really did not know. Others, too, outside and working in and through Paris, chains of them, he thought. But making all aware of the truth about an individual was far too difficult and dangerous. He was still on several lists, still marked for death by some.

Finding another scrap of paper, he sat down and quickly wrote: *Antoine Vernet, industrialist, accidentally revealed this during questioning. The* Relève *is definitely to become the* Service de Travail Obligatoire *next month. Lists are being drawn up naming those in each factory who are expendable and those who must remain. The selection will perhaps begin with students or simply all remaining young men of the ages 18 to 22, but eventually they will take all able-bodied males up to the ages of 45 to 55.*

'Ah no,' she said and covered her mouth. Tears filled her eyes, which were not blue, as he had first thought, but a lovely shade of violet. Hermann's Giselle had eyes of that same shade. Was it merely coincidence, he wondered sadly, or was God trying to tell them something? A warning perhaps? A last look before the Gestapo descended and swept her away.

Hermann was on very, very dangerous ground with this one.

She tried to kiss Jean-Louis, but he was still far too timid, still feeling the loss of his wife and little son and blaming himself for what had happened to them, though worried also about her. Ah yes. 'We should have spent Christmas and New Year's at the château as you said you would,' she whispered, damning the microphones. 'We may never get another chance.'

You know I wanted to but couldn't. Will you see that the Rivards take care of our suspect? he wrote.

'The cellars,' she whispered, wishing they could be together in peace, if only for a moment. He needed that and so did she.

It was Hermann who brought the prisoner in from the court-yard. She objected to the lion. She refused to sing any more. 'I quit,' she seethed at Rémi Rivard, the mountain. 'That thing stinks too much!'

Rivard pointed to the hidden microphones and shrugged before drawing a forefinger across his swarthy throat.

God knows what Gestapo Paris's Listeners made of the exchange or of the lion's greedy licking of the salty ersatz things Hermann had sprinkled on the floor near one of the microphones.

Rébé kept silent and, once on stage, the *chanteuse* clasped her hands before her with childlike innocence and, giving the crowd the warmth of her smile, said, '*Mes chers amis*, I have a little song for you of love—the love one feels right from the soul, yes? It is such a terrible longing, isn't that correct? So intense, one wishes only to lie down in the soft, sweet clover of home and kiss the earth.'

She sang for them *J'ai deux amours*, 'Two Loves Have I', France and Paris, and followed it with *Paris sera toujours Paris*, 'Paris Will Always Be Paris'.

A foolish, foolish gesture of defiance. Few seemed to notice anything out of place. Stolidly Germanic, they watched the stage, and when she sang *Lili Marlene* for them, there wasn't a sound other than that of her voice. It filled the club and they were spellbound for the sound transcended all carnal thoughts. It took them right out of themselves and made them yearn desperately to pack up and go home.

'Come on, Louis. We've got to find Hasse before he kills that child.'

'Yes, yes, I understand.'

To drive through the city during the blackout was to have its map in mind at all times. One ticked off the major intersections, counted the streets, computed speed, distance and compass bearing, searching the memory always for landmarks, the darkness for their silhouettes. A blue-washed lamp whose bluing needed replenishment, another which had been done too much, the outline of a *métro* entrance, a roof, a sculpture, a mothballed fountain.

On the boulevard Raspail the *vélo-taxis*, those ridiculous bicycle contraptions, were like gulls migrating along a river of black ice and snow. In the faint pinpricks of the headlamps, and those of the *autobus au gazogène* and lorries, they showed up suddenly, their drivers frantically trying to get out of the way and not hit one another. Breath steamed in the fifteen degrees of frost. Their eyes were harried, desperate, their passengers laughing, making a great joke of it all or simply not caring as they kissed their girlfriends and tried to do other things beneath the heaps of throw rugs, old scraps of carpet, or blankets.

Hermann turned on to the boulevard Saint-Germain. They

were making for the quais and the pont de l'Alma. Then it was straight north up the avenue George-V to the Lido, the Champs-Élysées and Number 78.

Hasse had been under psychiatric care for some time. There had been repeated visits to the escort service, weekends with a Mademoiselle Monique Reynard at Saint-Germain-en-Laye. A qualified psychotherapist, or so they had been told. Everything had been laid on by Oberg of the avenue Foch, the Butcher of Poland. 'One has to learn to live again,' Hasse had said, 'that's what they tell people like myself. Personally, I think it's a waste of time.' Of time . . .

No matter how hard St-Cyr tried not to think of it, the sketch of Nénette they had found in the Grande-Chaumière was seen in memory against those of Herr Hasse's storeroom, sketches of naked schoolgirls whose screams the Attack Leader had once heard and still did.

It has to be him, he said to himself, dreading the thought, but then . . . then why *did* that child get into his car today, as Rébé has claimed?

Had she been that desperate? Had she *not* thought him the Sandman? And why, please, had Liline Chambert agreed to let those girls pose for him? Why? Why?

Hasse had told them the girl had found it hard to reconcile him as an artist with his killing of children, but by then he had known Liline was dead and could simply have said it to protect himself.

He had felt it necessary to be forthright. He had admitted the killings in Poland, the clandestine taking of photographs in Paris, the Lycée Fénelon. A soup kitchen in its cellars. Bare knees, bare thighs, skirts flying as they skipped and played hop-scotch and other games. Soup kitchens elsewhere . . .

'The artist seeks only the absolute truth of each moment,' he had said.

In snapshot after snapshot he had captured young schoolgirls of the same age as Nénette and her little friend. 'I want you to find the person responsible for the killings, especially those of Liline and Andrée.'

Had he a death wish, then, a need to be found out? He had paid Liline a total of one thousand francs in return for convincing the girls to pose for him. She had not seen his sketches from Poland, the nightmares. She couldn't have.

But had Nénette found her way to that storeroom unnoticed? Was that not why she had taken the badges, the pencil case, the crumpled empty tube of paint? Then why, please, had she got into his car today? He had drawn a map of the Bois . . . a map!

'Louis, we're here. His car's parked just ahead of us.'

So it was, and when they shone their unblinkered torches in on the front seat, they saw the dust of crumbled oak leaves where the child had sat. Her sealskin hat was on the floor. There were breadcrumbs, even a curled shred of ham. A half-eaten biscuit lay there, too, a forgotten stick of chewing gum. 'Banana,' breathed Hermann sadly. 'Ah *nom de Jésus-Christ*, Louis, I had hoped and even prayed it wouldn't be him.'

'We can't touch him if it is.'

'We're going to have to.'

Hasse was waiting for them. He had run to his psychotherapist and now stood behind Monique Reynard, who sat at the desk in the foyer, all business, all seriousness. A woman of thirty-four, thought St-Cyr, the cinematographer in him recording detail after detail, her manner, her straight back, hands folded on the bulging dossier of her patient, the nails beautifully manicured and clear-lacquered, the eyes so blue, the hair so blonde, a wave of it successfully hid from all but the most careful scrutiny the birthmark on her brow she must have hated as a child and probably still did.

'Messieurs,' she said, and he noted the Alsatian accent. 'Messieurs, what you think is so very wrong. Herr Hasse would not have harmed that child, nor has he killed anyone in Paris, in France even. Indeed, he is most distressed and wants only to assist your endeavours.'

A man of conscience, was that it, eh? snorted Kohler inwardly. Rouge and powder hid the scars on her pleasantly plump cheeks—burns there, he thought. Were they cigarette burns? Ah *merde* . . . Those on her throat were all but hidden by the soft blue scarf that went with the clean-cut, very stylish business suit.

She would choose her words most carefully, she thought. 'If you persist, it can only destroy all we've accomplished. Is this what you wish?'

'He must answer some questions, mademoiselle,' said Louis gruffly.

'It's "Doctor", please. Dr Reynard. You may examine my certificates if you wish, Inspector.'

'It's Chief Inspector,' said Kohler. 'He's the Chief, I'm the Inspector.'

'My degrees are Swiss and from Berlin. Jung and Freud, with extensive research into the theories and the work of von Krafft-Ebing.'

This was not easy ground, and it must have been hard for her to admit to such tainted learning even though the Nazis had found a use for her. 'The child was in his car today, Doctor. Where is she now? What has he done with her?'

Hasse took out a cigarette, but his fingers shook so much he had to say, 'Monique . . .'

She turned. She tossed her hair back a little as she looked up at him and smiled so softly it had an automatic calming effect. 'It's all right, Gerhardt,' she said in German. 'Everything will be fine, you will see.' And taking the cigarette from him, she lit it and blew smoke up at the ceiling before handing the thing back to him. 'Tell them, *Liebling*. You must,' she said earnestly. 'Go on. You've nothing to hide, nothing to fear. Not any more.'

The stork took a nervous drag on the cigarette and then another. 'Nénette complained of her scalp itching. I took her to the convent school—she refused to go to her house and said she mustn't do that. I left her in the care of the Mother Superior. They will have bathed her and put her to sleep in the infirmary.'

'But . . . but did the child not also object to being taken to the sisters?' managed Louis.

'Very much so, but it was for her own good.'

Ah damn, the stork was too wary. 'Then why, please, did you draw that sketch of her at the Grande-Chaumière?'

The woman stiffened. 'What sketch, please?' she asked, alarmed.

'Yes, what sketch?' asked Hasse, forgetting that his cigarette was telegraphing agitation.

'Oh, come now, Herr Hasse,' enthused the Sûreté as if they were old friends, 'a sketch of Nénette Vernet in her leaf-padded overcoat but without the sealskin hat we found in your car.'

'Ah no . . . What hat?' demanded the woman, sickened perhaps by the thought of what might have happened.

'The child was terrified,' breathed Kohler. 'She was screaming her heart out in that sketch.'

'You've killed her, haven't you?' said Louis sadly.

'Easy,' cautioned Kohler.

'Herr Hasse has killed no one. He was only trying to help the child.'

But what had Hasse really done with that child? Disgruntled, St-Cyr tossed his fedora into the empty chair that sat between himself and Hermann. 'Did you take her to your studio first?' he asked, his voice deliberately harsh and accusing.

They had been there, then, thought Hasse. They had found the sketches of the Lodz affair. Somehow he must try to calm himself, somehow Monique must guide the discussion on to more even ground. 'Why yes, I did. She was hungry, but I had little to offer. Some chewing gum. She said she needed a tooth-brush and asked had I an extra one.' He would try to smile now, thought Hasse. He would draw on his cigarette and give them a moment. Yes . . . yes, that would be best. Monique would agree. He was certain she would. 'I . . . I found one for her and apologized for its being so used. You see, I'd come across it in Poland. I'd lost mine then and felt the same as she did. The teeth are so important, aren't they?'

Ah *merde*, he really has killed her. 'The tooth-brush?' hazarded St-Cyr, a reminder the woman noted only too well.

Hasse was bitter, the grin he gave, sardonic. 'She said it didn't matter that it had been used so much, that anything was better than nothing and that by first melting the snow in her mouth, she would then have the water necessary to clean her teeth. She was very grateful.'

'I'll bet she was,' seethed Kohler. 'So grateful she left the thing behind. I have it here.'

He tossed it on to her desk. The woman's eyes flicked anxiously from it to himself and back again. Warily she glanced at Louis. 'Tooth-brushes . . .' she began, only to stop herself and bite her lower lip. Louis let a breath escape.

'The tooth-brush of a raped and murdered Polish schoolgirl, mademoiselle,' he said flatly.

'It's Doctor.'

'*Merci.* Doctor, please ask him how he felt in Poland when he used that same tooth-brush?'

'I didn't mean to upset Nénette,' blurted Hasse. 'She must have realized where it had come from and that's why she left it behind.'

'Gerhardt, please don't distress yourself. Please listen to me,' urged the woman, turning to take him by the hands. 'No, you must look at me, my darling. Forget them. They are nothing. They are mistaken, yes? We both know this. We were in Saint-Germain-en-Laye, isn't that so? My parents, Gerhardt. You visited them. They had moved there in forty-one so as to be close to me.'

'It's not the death of Andrée Noireau they're interested in,' he said sadly. 'It's those of all the others.'

'Did Nénette say anything about the Sandman?' asked Louis. 'DID SHE?'

'Please don't shout. *Please,*' urged the woman, trembling.

Hasse straightened. He became in that one brief instant the Attack Leader he had once been. 'Only that she hoped you would catch the criminal before there was another killing.'

Kohler leaned on the desk and all but shouted, 'Do you fantasize about little girls, Herr Hasse? Schoolgirls, eh?'

'*How dare you,*' swore the woman. 'You cannot ask such things. You will only undo all we have accomplished.'

'Then ask him where he left her body,' sighed Kohler. 'Let's make it plain and simple.'

Hasse tried to object, but she silenced him with a touch. 'He isn't lying. He did deliver the child to the sisters. Please avail yourselves of the telephone. I'm sure the Mother Superior will be only too glad to tell you the child was exhausted and is now soundly asleep.'

'Who watches over her, then?' managed Louis anxiously.

'One of the sisters.'

'Which one?'

'This the Mother Superior did not say.'

'Then tell us where Debauve is. Tell us, damn it!' shouted Kohler.

'Not here,' she said, her gaze unwavering. 'The good Father seldom visits. Our clients are mainly businessmen and officers from the Reich. Many are veterans of the campaigns in the East, yes, and North Africa. The Freikorps Dönitz also, the submarine service—we get quite a few of those—and lots from the Luftwaffe. They are here for either rest and recuperation or simply business. Relaxation is needed, and this we provide.'

She must have a damned cold heart not to care about that child, thought Kohler bitterly. He wanted to take her aside and breathe a few words into the shell of her ear, just to remind her the end was coming, that the war was going to turn sour someday. 'Then why is a psychotherapist needed?' he asked, shoving stuff aside to sit on a corner of the desk.

Was it to be just between the two of them now? she wondered, smiling inwardly. 'A therapist decides what is best for all, but is really only needed for the special cases,' she said, taunting him further.

'There are others like him?' he asked, nodding at the Attack Leader.

How stupid of him. 'Of course. Like Herr Hasse, they require sensitivity, understanding and a willingness to listen, to believe and to guide their steps down the path to healing.'

Verdammt, the bitch! 'How much does Oberg pay you?' he asked, knowing Violette Belanger had told them they were spying for Oberg, sucking up blackmail details for him to use. Those juicy little things that are whispered, confessed to some defrocked priest or simply revealed in a moment of bravado over a meal, a glass of wine or in bed.

Herr Kohler was trembling ever so slightly. The avenue Foch had said he was on Benzedrine and that he was dangerously close to becoming addicted if not already so. The voice of a robot would only further torment him. 'Our rates are set. Consultation is voluntary on the part of the patient. The reports and diagnoses are strictly confidential.'

'*Bananas!* Since when has anything the SS ever had a hand in been confidential if they thought they could use it? Just why, please, *meine gute Frau Doktor,* have you taken this out?'

He thumped the dossier she had in front of her.

'Because Herr Hasse has asked me to allow you to peruse it, since he has nothing to hide. His is not an easy past to reconcile, but with persistence, determination and hard work, a full recovery is quite possible, though I must say he does not believe this. We have constant debates about it. They are healthy, yes, Herr Hauptmann *Detektif Inspektor* Kohler? He's come a long way, believe me.'

'But you've not slept with him yet, have you?'

Hasse put a restraining hand on her shoulder. 'I didn't kill the child, Inspector. Nénette can easily tell you this herself, and as for Andrée and the others, *and* Mademoiselle Chambert, I have already told you I want the person or persons responsible apprehended.'

'Ah yes,' interjected the Sûreté, 'but, please, did you and Nénette discuss the killing of her little friend?'

'She said only that the Sandman could not have done it.'

'And she did not cry? She did not burst into tears at the mention of her friend? You did not enquire further? *Well?*'

There was no need to answer any of their questions, but he would do so. 'Why should I have asked? I was just glad to have her safely with me. I didn't want to upset her any more than she already was.'

He's lying, said St-Cyr to himself. The woman felt it, too, and nervously pressed her hand flat on the dossier as Hasse spoke. 'And where, please, did you pick her up?'

Monique Reynard dreaded the answer that was to come and averted her eyes from Hermann and himself.

'On the allée de Longchamp,' said Hasse with all the dignity he could muster. 'I admit I had been searching for her. That was why the sketch map was in my studio.'

'But you didn't take it with you,' said Kohler sadly.

'I forgot. In . . . in my anxiety to . . . to find her, it completely went . . . went out of my head. Can't you see I was—'

'Gerhardt, *please!* It's all right. Just tell them how it was.'

Ah *Gott im Himmel*, they were a pair, the two of them. How often had she tried to sleep with him and failed? wondered Kohler. Far more times than five lost weekends in the countryside.

'I wanted to help,' confessed Hasse, silently cursing the two of them for doubting him. 'Then there she was, running out of the woods to flag me down and scramble into the car. She . . . she said she was being followed and . . . and had no other choice. "Quickly," she said, "before she sees you've got me." '

'*She?*'

'Yes.'

St-Cyr took the two of them in at a glance before letting his gaze settle on the woman. 'Whom did she mean?' he asked Hasse.

'She didn't say.'

'And you did not ask?' demanded Kohler fiercely.

'I knew she was distressed—I feared for her. She was safe. I thought perhaps it had been one of the sisters. I knew that all things would be revealed in due course.'

All things . . . A solid citizen, then, simply doing his duty, was that it, eh? thought St-Cyr. A *woman* . . . A *woman* . . . 'Exactly where along the allée de Longchamp did you come across the child?'

'Near the Carrefour de Longchamp and the Grande Cascade.'

Kohler heard Louis suck in an impatient breath. 'Almost at the Hippodrome, Hermann, and quite some distance from the Jardin d'Acclimatation. A good two kilometres to the southwest of the stables. From there, a kilometre farther to the children's restaurant and *salon de thé*. Why, please, do you think you found her so far from the Jardin?'

Again Mademoiselle Reynard betrayed how much she dreaded the answer.

'I've already told you,' snapped Hasse. 'She was being followed.'

'By whom? Come, come, monsieur, you know all about who was following her. You'd done so yourself many times before— isn't that correct? Well, isn't it? You had secretly taken photographs of her and Andrée Noireau. You knew she was being followed by others, yet you did nothing about it. *Nothing*. I want to know why!'

'Inspector, *please*! You don't know what you're doing to him. All I've worked so hard for may well be lost. *Lost*, do you understand?'

She was finally in tears, not sitting now but standing in front of Hasse, prepared to keep them from taking him.

Several seconds passed. The detectives wanted to find the Sandman before another young girl was raped—yes, raped— and then killed. 'He's . . . he's incapable,' she said. 'I . . . I've tried. He . . . he simply cannot do it.'

'Do what?' breathed Kohler.

'*Idiot*! Have sex, damn you! Sex in any way, shape or form. There, now are you satisfied? Are you?'

It was Louis who did the sighing. 'Then please inform him that he was seen following the child this afternoon in the Jardin d'Acclimatation and that it was there, not near the Hippodrome, that Nénette Vernet got into his car.'

'*Seen by whom?*' she cried.

'That is not for you to know. For now, it's confidential.'

'Ah, damn you, damn you. *Flics*, that's all you are. Lousy *flics*!'

Louis reached for the telephone. Sadly he watched the two of them. Was he convinced? wondered Kohler. Was he now prepared to call Old Shatter Hand and request that an arrest be made? Sometimes it was so hard to tell with Louis. There'd be a thousand questions in his mind and he'd have to go over every one of them before deciding on the truth, nothing but the truth. He hadn't been wrong yet, well once perhaps and not really. Not in the nearly two and a half years they'd been working together.

'Inspector,' she pleaded, hastily wiping her eyes and cursing her tears. 'We knew of his association with Mademoiselle Chambert and thought it a good thing. We encouraged it, yes. If he could get those two young girls to accept him as he was, we felt it would make such a difference.'

'There were others he paid to go up to that flat of his,' said Kohler harshly.

'Others?' She was sickened by the news and turned quickly away.

St-Cyr got through to the convent instead of the Kommandantur. It took several rings before a harried voice, just awakened, asked who it was and told him Nénette Vernet was asleep. 'I've only just left her, Inspector. The poor child is safe at last.' A yawn was heard. 'You need have no more fears. She had a bowl of warm milk with bread dipped in it. A few drops of laudanum were felt best.'

A tincture of opium ... Ah *merde, merde*! 'Are the doors secured between the convent and the church?' he asked and heard her say, 'Of course.'

'Then please have three sisters watching over the child at all times. Please do not let her out of your sight.'

They ran. They tried to make it to the convent before it was too late. Banging on the heavy oak door did no good. Pulling on the bell chain produced only an utter refusal to answer.

Against the loneliness of distant stars, the frozen sickle of a new moon stood as if grinning in judgment.

'*Debauve and Violette!*' cursed Louis. 'Madame Vernet figured it all out from the trash in that child's coat pockets. She *knew* who the Sandman was.'

'A crucifix and a Number Four knitting needle in the child's desk,' swore Hermann. 'A map of the Sandman's murders. "*This one is next*".'

'A used condom in her change purse.'

'From the coffee can of a whore.'

Kohler gave the door a last kick. They'd have to get the army to batter the thing in. '*Idiot!* You would warn them. Now they're so darned scared they won't let even us in!'

The nuns weren't just scared, they were desperately afraid, and when at last, after much deliberation within, entry was allowed, nearly all were on their knees crowded into the infirmary, gathered around the child's bed. Nearly all were in tears and praying.

The bed was empty, the child was gone.

'She left us, Inspectors,' seethed the Reverend Mother, yanking the pillows away to reveal the soggy stains of milk and mush of uneaten bread. 'She *dumped* the laudanum into the sisters' mugs of tea. *Look* at the two of them. Just *look!*'

Sister Dominique, her mouth wide open, slept the sleep of dreams in a nearby chair; Sister Edith, under whose care the infirmary lay, that of nightmares perhaps.

'And Sister Céline?' he asked hesitating. 'Was she the one I spoke to on the telephone?'

Anxiety, pain and grief—ah, so many things filled the deep blue eyes of the Reverend Mother. 'Céline, Inspector? You see, she, too, has left us.'

'Was she out this afternoon?'

'In the Jardin d'Acclimatation?'

'Searching for that child—Reverend Mother, you know this is what I mean.'

'Céline . . . Céline thinks all girls of that age have the devil in their bodies, Inspector. She doesn't really mean to say such things. It's her past, that father of hers. It's Violette and . . . and the life that one insists on leading. The constant shame of it, the ridicule of our girls, the whispers, the secretly passed notes with filth written on them. Shameful things the girls themselves cannot possibly understand.'

'Let us go into your office, Reverend Mother. Let us take a moment.'

She would have to tell them and beg God's forgiveness for

doing so. 'Céline Belanger has . . . has very bad thoughts, Inspectors. They come and go. There are times when she is quite calm, times when very upset and agitated. She is constantly visiting Violette not only because she feels it is her duty as an older sister but also because she secretly blames herself. I'm certain of it, certain, too, that she knows very well what their father did to Violette because he'd done the same things to her. Oh yes, this, too, I am certain of, but each visit seems only to reinforce the hateful thoughts. They are like the migraines. They come on suddenly and stay for days.'

He must go gently. 'Does the sister think bad thoughts of your girls, Reverend Mother?'

'She sees flames.'

'Flames, but. . . ?'

'Yes. I know the *milieu* are fond of saying that when they see the police but Céline's flames, they are different. They are of girls of Nénette's age letting men do filthy things to them. Wanton things. Things they themselves don't anticipate but have secretly encouraged simply by a smile, a desire to feel wanted, a need to get attention. To Céline their unawareness of the danger is just a lie hiding base desires to know and experience everything about sex even though desperately afraid and ignorant of it. She . . . she has tried many times to suppress all such thoughts. We have prayed constantly for God's help but you see, recently our girls, they only made it worse. They sensed Céline did not just dislike them but felt them guilty of such things. They became convinced she wanted to punish them.'

The age of innocence shattered by a nun. 'Did she try to find Nénette this afternoon? Was she following that child only to have her turn up here?'

'Céline's cloak was torn. Her face was scratched—a branch perhaps, or a briar. Sister Dominique came back early in great distress to tell me Céline had deliberately left her.'

'Where will she go, if she finds Nénette?'

To the Notre-Dame, was that what he was thinking? To Suresnes or Aubervilliers, to some run-down tenement? Or was it to les Halles and empty stalls where no food is brought for sale because there is so little of it getting into the city? 'She will try to find Nénette, Inspector, to save her from what Violette and that . . . that "priest" of hers would do to the child. She will take her to the house on the rue Chabanais because only then can she confront the child *and* Violette with the truth.'

It was now nearly 11.00 p.m. The *métro* would soon stop, as would the city's much diminished bus service. Céline could know nothing of what had happened to Madame Morelle or that Violette had run from the house.

'What was the child wearing?' he asked and she could see how very concerned he was that Nénette might freeze to death.

'The overcoat that is padded with leaves. The sealskin boots and mittens. A tea cosy for a hat. She found her things in the larger of the kitchen stoves, where Sister Céline had placed them to burn but had been distracted by your telephone call.'

'Then the child must have hidden in the kitchens until the sister had left the convent?'

'Yes. Yes, I am afraid that is how it must have been. Céline will be looking for her; Nénette will be trying desperately not to be found, but the sisters, Inspector, they have been searching so much for her, they have come to know well the places in which the child might attempt to hide.'

'The cemetery, the synagogue, the Bois, the Jardin and the Villa Vernet.'

Flames, verdammt! thought Kohler. 'We're going to have to check out that tenement on the quai du Président Paul Doumer, Louis. The concierge can identify Debauve as the one who came to collect Madame Morelle. Our priest will be only too aware of this.'

'Gloves . . . I no longer have a pair of gloves.'

'Mittens,' said one of the sisters. 'We've been knitting mittens and sweaters, Inspector. Take some. Bundle up. Please don't freeze.'

'There are socks, too, warm socks.'

'A thermos, someone. Quickly. Quickly.'

'No laudanum. No laudanum, please.' Ah *merde*, Sister Céline . . . ? Had she drunk her tea? Had that yawn she had given over the telephone been but a sign of things to come?

High above the synagogue, the moon split the clouds that had come to blot out the stars. As the curfew descended on the city, the night threw up the singularity of its sounds. Everything seemed simply to stop running, to be replaced by a silence so penetrating each footfall was heard, each intake of breath. Though both of them instinctively listened for the faint and ominous drone of distant bombers, each knew the weather had interfered to give a night of peace to cities on both sides of this lousy war.

Louis would go inside the synagogue to flush them out, if they were in there; he, himself, would watch the exits, particularly that of the lift from the furnace room. 'Take care, *mon vieux*. Shout if you need me.'

'You also.'

And then he was gone—had vanished inside, into what? wondered Kohler, saying, Ah damn, damn, why does it always have to be us?

When it began to snow quite hard, he knew that God of Louis's wasn't treating them very well.

The cellars would be freezing. They'd be damp—that icy dampness that clings and penetrates even two layers of heavy woollen undergarments, socks and sweaters. The river of ice on the crowded, cluttered floor would be slippery. 'Let's face it,' said Kohler, aloud to himself. 'I hate like hell waiting for things to happen.'

In the furnace room, St-Cyr let the beam of his torch dance uncertainly over the maze of pipes, grey-white beneath their dustings of soot. Now the words NÉNETTE . . . ANDRÉE . . . appeared, now ARE WE ALL TO DIE? and then . . . then LILINE with hardly time for her to finish printing the E.

The firebox door of the furnace had been wired shut. He could swear it hadn't been like that. Closed, yes, but not secured. Whoever had done it had twisted the wire several times. Was the child in there, then? Had she scrawled in to hide, only to find herself trapped?

Again he shone the torch around the room. Again he had to be certain he was alone. Hermann . . . Hermann, he began.

Setting the torch down on the overturned bucket the child had used as a stool, he tried to untwist the wire, saying softly, 'Nénette . . . Nénette, it's me, Jean-Louis St-Cyr of the Sûreté.' Had the Sandman killed her?

The wire had been snipped off with wire cutters. It had been twisted tightly with pliers. Whoever had done this had come prepared.

He cut his fingers. They very nearly froze to the wire. Leaning down, he caught at his sleeve and used it to slide the draught plate open and shone the torch inside.

The firebox was huge, the many-toothed bars of the grate, sturdy. A nest had been built in there of leaves last fall and it would have been big enough for those two girls to have used but had been set afire some hours ago. Now there were only its ashes, grey and light against the deeper, older, more solid ash and clinkers.

There was no sign of the child.

This is the way out and the way in, said Kohler to himself as he stood with his back against the wall in moon-shadow watching the lift, waiting, hoping, remembering the footprints they had found down there, those of a woman. Violette, he wondered, or Céline?

'It's been jammed,' hissed Louis furiously from below. 'Whoever did it knew the child hid out here. That person may have been waiting for her, Hermann. The child may already have been taken.'

Verdammt! Whatever footprints there were looked old and were being rapidly obliterated by the cursed snow. 'The cemetery,' sighed Kohler, not liking it at all.'The vaults, Louis. The crypts, that mausoleum where the kid bedded down.'

And wrote in the fine dust of spilled cremation ashes, *Andrée, you must forgive me. Liline is also dead. I went to the place where she was and I saw them taking her out.*

Steps led up to the mausoleum, but the bronze doors, with their shattered stained-glass panels, had been wired tightly shut. Kohler shone his torch inside only to find that the words the child had written had been rubbed out. 'Debauve,' he said. 'A man's handprint, Louis. I'm certain of it.'

The silk flowers still rested in another mausoleum among the broken coffins and scattered bones, but here, too, the doors had been wired tightly shut.

In every place she could have run, steps had been taken to thwart her escape. The snow hid all tracks. It was impossible to find any. It beat against the face and stung the eyes. It said, Give up. Let it be. There is nothing you can do.

While they had been at the house on the rue Chabanais, Debauve must have been searching for the child, but had he finally caught her? Had he? It was not pleasant hunting for her corpse among the rows of tombstones, some broken, others pushed over. Behind the mausoleums among scattered bushes there were places she could have hidden had she got away, places she could have been caught and killed, but she wasn't there. And as for looking in the rest of the cemetery, there simply wasn't time.

When they got to the tenement house on the quai du Président Paul Doumer, it was to find the door haphazardly repaired after Hermann's splintering of it. Pounding did no good, so he broke it in again, using one good kick and the flat of his shoe.

Yvette Grégoire, the concierge, lay at the foot of the stairs to the cellars. Her false teeth had popped out when her head hit the stone floor. The faded blue eyes were bloodshot and glazed, the hairy lips split.

Hastily St-Cyr crossed himself and said, 'Dead for several hours. Why has no one reported it?'

'Too afraid, probably. Each waiting for someone else to speak up, all thinking that tomorrow would be best. They'll have seen and heard nothing. An accident, eh, but what else could be expected since the stair runners are so old and torn?'

When they got to the Villa Vernet there wasn't a sign of the child. Not in the folly, not in her room or anywhere else.

Madame Vernet paced the floor, smoking cigarette after cigarette under the watchful eyes of a severe, grey-suited young woman with a pistol. Vernet brooded in his study.

There would be time enough for them later.

'The Jardin, Louis. The children's zoo or the puppet theatres.'

'The cage of doves, the stables . . . Ah *merde, merde, mon vieux,* why can God not give us some sign? Has she been taken, or is she still on the run?'

God couldn't see them. Like the bedsheet the sisters used to hide the nakedness of their girls from Him, the sudden blizzard hid virtually everything. It froze the windscreen wipers to the glass. It made the car skid. Somehow they reached the Jardin, somehow they managed to get out of the car, but would they ever be able to return to it in this, would they ever find that child?

'She knows this place too well,' said Louis grimly. A *voyou* Sister Céline had called her, a guttersnipe, a brigand of the forest.

Very quickly, and totally without intention, they became separated. Each felt at once the other wasn't there. Each thought to call out but knew it would be quite useless.

The child, whether by design or mistake, had put things squarely on her own footing. If still free, this wearer of a tea cosy, a leaf-padded overcoat, sealskin boots and mittens would try to hide where no one could find her.

And if not free? asked St-Cyr and knew he must not ask such a question until they had found her.

A shutter banged, a large cage of wire appeared out of the blinding snow. Faltering, his torchlight shone on a signboard and, brushing the snow away, he read: OLD WORLD MONKEYS. Poor creatures. They must be frozen stiff or huddled in their little house wishing they could hibernate.

The Enchanted Garden, the Miniature Autodrome, the statue of the naturalist Daubenton, the aviary, the lions' den—past each of these he forced himself, into the wind that brought snow and freezing cold until he thought he might just as well be in the Yukon with Charlie Chaplin in *The Gold Rush* and saw himself picking nails out of a pair of boiled boots on which he was dining.

'*Nénette,*' he called out at last. '*Nénette Vernet.*'

The wind took her name and threw it away.

The aviary stank of birds, but it was warm if fetid, and, once out of the wind and snow, all Kohler could think to ask himself was who had opened the door, who had broken the lock?

There were parakeets and cockatoos, macaws, parrots, budgerigars, canaries and finches. There were violet-eared waxbills, Java sparrows, golden pheasants, peacocks, guinea fowl and one hell of a racket among the drooping rubber plants, the creepers and coconut palm forests. Aisles and aisles of cages demanded attention now that the light from his torch had passed over them to settle on one of the four or five large cast-iron stoves with pots of water simmering and coal fires banked for the night. A furnace somewhere, too, and real coal! Von Schaumburg must have okayed the supply. Tropical birds above children and old people. A sensitive men, a kind heart. A Prussian!

Violette Belanger sat on the floor beside the stove. There was a small, blue-green parrot in her lap, and this she stroked and fed bits of dried apple. Her knees were bent, her lower legs folded demurely to one side. The woollen kneesocks were pulled up, the pleated skirt of her tunic was pulled down and closely wrapped about her legs. Her shirt-blouse was done up and from somewhere she had acquired a cardigan, much worn and badly in need of mending, an overcoat, too. The shaggy mop of dark brown hair was a tangle though now dry, so she'd been in here for some time; the dark brown eyes were earnest, watchful and very conscious of him as he cautiously approached.

Her cheeks and the tip of her nose were still red from the wind and the cold, the rest of her was pale.

'She's out there,' she said at last. 'She has to punish that child—isn't that correct? Schoolgirls shouldn't think the things Céline thinks they do.'

'Where's Debauve?'

'Where indeed? He has to find her, too, and Céline. I'm supposed to stay here. I'm to wait for him. My priest. My pimp. My lover. We're going to Provence. We're going to buy my little farm.'

'He's the Sandman, isn't he?'

How cruel of him, how harsh. One must be soft and gentle, then. 'The Sandman. The one who puts things into the mouths and other places of schoolgirls before he kills them. Why, please, then would he use a knitting needle, the weapon of a woman?'

'It can't be Céline, it can't be you.'

Was he so lost, this giant from the Kripo, this detective? 'Why do you think Madame Morelle made us collect the used rubbers?'

'To count. To make sure her girls didn't cheat.'

He tried to shake the snow from himself, and she could see that he wanted desperately to warm his fingers at the stove. 'We collect the used rubbers for those reasons, yes, of course. All the girls do, but also so that their madams can then sell them to others, to those who obtain the release of their little burden by simply fingering that of others.'

'Pardon?'

Was it such a revelation? 'To each appetite there is an answer. To all must be given satisfaction, even to those who cannot touch a woman because they are too afraid. Those types, they stand at the door to the courtyard behind the house. Madame, she treats them very badly. She makes them wait for hours and they do. Ah! they're so eager, she makes them pay really high prices. Those types, they are beneath her. Well, not any more, I guess, unless there are the *maisons de tolérance* in hell. But she would often make them kiss her fingers, too, as she stuffed rubbers into the mouths of some of them. They enjoyed it. They loved it. They were humiliated, very ashamed of their strange desires, and she rejoiced in her hold over them as she wiped her hands on their clothes.'

'Céline can't have done that to those girls. The semen in those rubbers would have dried and been no good to her.'

'Oh? And is the weather not cold? Can the cloud custard not be frozen first if . . . if one puts the coffee can out on one's little balcony, or at least keeps it very, very cold by placing it in the crushed ice of the champagne bucket after first adding a handful or two of salt to the ice so as to make the water colder? Can the custard then not warm in my sister's cloak pockets even as she finds the rubbers I have placed there for her? Like snakes; snakes through which she must then run her fingers not just in agitation, yes, but in rage, I think. A demented rage.'

Ah *merde*, *merde*, the days of the soup kitchens, the blood groupings of the semen stains, no pubic hairs . . . It was just not possible.

Kohler dragged off his mittens and then the gloves Louis had pinched for him at Chez Rudi's. He warmed his hands at the stove while still keeping the beam of the torch on her knees. He let her look up at him and met those deep brown, innocent eyes with concern.

She stroked the parrot. She opened her sweater and shirt-blouse and carefully tucked the bird down her front, saying, 'Don't scratch like the men who have pawed me so many times and sucked my nipples. Just keep warm.

'He's going south like me, Inspector. I'm going to name him but have not yet decided. Perhaps you have a suggestion?'

He had no time for dreams, he had only time for Céline and that child, that child. She'd have to tell him. She'd have to keep him here as long as possible. 'You see, Inspector, when my father took me, Céline, she got very jealous, very angry and blamed me. To her I was a little cunt in heat and awakening to it. No longer was she the favourite, no longer papa's little schoolgirl.'

'And now?' he asked.

'Now she hates me for what I do but condemns all girls of that age. To her they have the devil in their bodies just like me. To her they think of doing things they ought not. Can you imagine how it must torture her to have to teach them? It agitates her. It drives her to a frenzy, and the little bitches feed this by making fun of her. She becomes insane. She has to visit me

again and again, sometimes twice in the same day. I have to
listen to her. The least little thing sets her off. A stolen zebra,
was it?'

'A giraffe.'

'An elephant. A baby, but that was taken on a last dare, I
think, and much later, and by then, why then, the identity of
the Sandman, it had been discovered by that child. My sister.
My Céline. A nun.'

'You're lying. You're only trying to protect your priest.'

Even now he could not believe it of a nun. 'Then wait and
see. Find what you can. Please close the door. Henri and me,
we wish to be alone.'

'Henri?'

'Yes. I have decided to name him after my father. It's the least
I can do, but if he scratches me, I will have to kill him.'

The barn of the Norman farm was not warm—no, of course
not, thought St-Cyr. Hay had been forked out for the two milch
cows and the nanny goats, and he could hear them softly
chewing and moving about in their stalls. There was a loft
above, and from this the sound of wayward chickens, disturbed
at their roosting, came to him. Others began to stir down here.
He waited. He pressed his back to the wall and rubbed the
muzzle of the ancient mare the Germans had not thought fit
enough to send to Russia.

The chickens up there didn't want to be disturbed. The
rooster objected. When the child hissed, '*Shush!*' he began in
earnest to seek the ladder that must lead to the loft.

Someone else sought it, too. Unfortunately, the Sûreté did
not have the use of his torch anymore. The batteries hadn't
liked the cold weather. Having taken them out, he was trying to
rejuvenate them with body heat in his trouser pockets.

Ah *merde*, but it was dark! A button or clasp hit a rung of the
ladder. After this there were only the sounds of the chickens,
the cows, the goats and the wind, which found every chance to
enter the building. Paris seldom saw such storms. Hundreds
would freeze to death.

'Nénette ... Nénette Vernet, is that you?' asked the nun. 'Attend to me, child. You are in great danger and should not have left the infirmary. We would not have harmed you.'

Steps sounded above him. Bits of straw filtered down and these were caught by the wind and blown into his eyes ...

'Child, stand up. Don't you dare hide from me. Now, come along. You must be frozen. Here, give me your hand. Why have you taken your mittens off?'

The beam of the sister's torch flitted around up there. He climbed. He tried to reach them unnoticed. He ...

'You did it. You killed them.'

Ah no, go carefully, he cried out inwardly to the child, carefully, please, and grasped another rung.

'I did no such thing. It is despicable of you to think this. Those girls were hungry. I fed them, as did the other sisters. We gave them love. God's love.'

The child must have swallowed or tried to look for a way out, but then he realized she had simply been screwing up her courage. 'Not in the belfries of the Notre-Dame. Not there, Sister,' she shrilled. 'After that girl was killed, I ... I found some things in the pockets of your cloak on the very same day. I did. I really did. After the murder in les Halles also.'

'*What?*'

It was almost a scream.

The smell of the stables came to him strongly, the sound of the wind and something else, something down there at the entrance. Had someone come into the barn?

'Lots of those ... those rubber things, Sister. All sticky. *Really* sticky.'

Ah *nom de Jésus-Christ*! He reached the loft. He saw them against a far corner. Crossbeams separated him from them. The nun had her back to him and seemed to tower over the child, who was scrunched against the walls. Under the light from the sister's torch, the child's big dark blue eyes gazed up warily from a pinched face. A fringe of jet-black hair protruded from beneath the crocheted pink-and-white tea cosy.

The cloak was of coarse black wool. It was webbed with snow. Now it all but hid the child from him. The hood was thrown back. The sister's hair was as if hacked off with scissors. Closer . . . he must get closer. Someone . . . someone else had come into the barn . . .

The chickens moved about up here, complaining. The child had several eggs clutched in both hands.

'Don't lie to me, Nénette.'

Somehow the child found her voice. 'I'm not, Sister,' she quavered. Neither of them realized they were no longer alone or that he was but two metres behind the nun. *You didn't kill Andrée, Sister, but . . . but you killed all the others and I . . . I must tell myself not to cry. I must!*'

Something went out of Céline then. Her voice dropped to a weary sadness. 'Please just trust me, child. There are things you cannot possibly understand, but as God is my witness, I have killed no one. You must believe me. Violette, she . . . she is not well. It's the devil who makes her do what she does. She must have put those . . . those filthy things in my pockets when I was last with her. You had no right to touch them.'

'Then did she put them there also after les Halles?'

'You're lying! Don't lie! It isn't right! It's shameful!'

The outburst passed. Again the child somehow found her voice. 'She gave me the coins the soldiers throw away because they cannot spend them in our country, Sister. She told me all about you. She said you were *E-VIL* and that we were *R-IGHT* about you.'

The beam of the torch wavered but then it came back to shine more fully on the child. 'Please come to me, Nénette. Let's both ask God to help us. That man Violette calls her priest will kill you to protect her.'

'And you?' croaked Nénette all but to herself. 'What, please, will he do to you?'

The child was evil. The child was afraid. She could so easily freeze to death, an accident . . .'He will ask to hear my confession. He will try to be the priest he once was.'

'He'll kill you, too, won't he?'

'Céline . . . Céline, is that you up there?' called out Debauve. She switched off her torch. She whispered. *'Nénette, we must leave here at once!'*

St-Cyr took a step. The child did not throw the eggs. She leapt at the sister and smashed them into Céline's face, smashed them and smashed them. There was a cry, a shriek, another and another. He tried to wrap his arms about the nun and pull her down, down, tried to stop the child . . . the child.

The girl kicked and bit and scratched and smeared broken eggs fiercely into the sister's face, shrieking, *'LET ME GO. LET ME GO. YOU DID IT! YOU DID IT!'*

Ah *merde, merde,* the child had escaped. She ran full tilt into something in the darkness, fell back, scrambled up—dashed across something else, slipped, threw baskets behind her, chickens, anything that came to hand, and when he reached where he thought the ladder had been, it was no longer there.

'Nénette . . .' he began. He coughed. He tried to catch a breath. Something touched his back. It sent shock waves through his spine. It made him cry out, *'H . . . e . . . r . . . mann!'*

He threw out his hands and tried to grab something . . . anything. He twisted, he turned, and as he fell, he was reminded briefly of himself as a boy falling from the roof of his Uncle Alexandre's barn. He must never do that again. *Never.*

There was a crash, a splintering of flying boards, the stench and taste of manure, hard and frozen in the straw.

Dazed and in shock, numb all over and then in pain, much pain, he tried to move, and only when he had rolled over on to his good side, his right side, did he see between the canted iron spokes of a barrow's wheel the first flames being sucked up and teased against a far wall.

'Hermann . . .' he managed. *'Hermann, where the hell are you?'*

The bears in the bear pit were not friendly. Captured in 1934 perhaps, and now unaccustomed to the cold but intuitively rejoicing in the blizzard, they had heard him climbing the fence to he had known not what, and when he had slid and rocketed down into the pit they called home, they had come to find him.

But now they sniffed the air. Now they stood on their hind legs and even he smelled the smoke.

Polar bears, ah *Gott im Himmel*!

Cautiously Kohler pulled himself up to a sitting position. The female—was it the female?—moved away to climb out of the pit and up to the fence. The male still sniffed the air. Then he, too, romped up to the fence.

Driven by the wind, the flames soon filled the snowy air with soot and sparks and glowing bits of debris. Now he saw the fence and the bears, now he didn't. He climbed. He dragged himself up the opposite wall of the pit. There was sheet ice under the snow. He slipped, he went right back down again, all the way.

One of the bears had turned to keep an eye on him, but the pit was large. There was ice beneath the snow on the pond at its bottom. There was a den, a roof over its entrance. That den would lead to a cage door that would be padlocked.

Half-way up the slope, he heard a rush of flame, felt the blast of it and scrambled up to the fence, but the damned thing was too high. There was barbed wire at the top, three strands. He'd been able to cross the wire going in but now . . . now as he climbed, the top of the fence protruded above him towards the pit. He dangled in space. He pulled himself along, hand over hand, the mittens catching on the barbs, reminding him of the Great War, the war . . .

When he came to a post, he pulled himself up, bounced uneasily, his boots on the strands, and then was over.

One of his mittens remained behind.

He ran. He tried to reach the farm. He ducked sparks and cried out, 'Louis . . . Louis . . .'

The nun was on the roof, the child was nowhere to be seen and neither was Louis.

✳   ✳   ✳

'*Burn . . . let her burn. She did it. I know she did!*'

Hot . . . it was so hot. Torn by the wind, flames poured from under the eaves at both ends of the barn. The mare tried to free herself. Her screams were mingled with the constant bawling of the cattle and goats. Why had he not taken the time to see to them?

Aching all over, St-Cyr knelt in the driving snow behind the barn, still clutching the child he had caught and dragged down.

'She did it. She really did.'

'*Sister,*' he cried out. '*Sister, run down the tiles and jump. It is the only way.*'

Her back was to them. Caught in the blizzard, perched standing astride the crown of the roof well above and to one side of the dormer window she had crawled out of, Céline clutched something in the crook of each arm. The heavy black woollen cloak blew about, revealing black skirts and black leather boots.

One after the other, she released the chickens she held and they saw the things fly panic-stricken to be singed, torched and taken by the wind.

'Sister, don't make me do this.'

'You can't go up there,' swore Nénette.

'I must. Don't argue. Behave yourself.'

'I won't.'

'You had better. The Petite Roquette, the prison for women, it is not very nice and is at present terribly crowded.'

'You're cruel.'

'One has to be.'

'There are some barrels. If we put them on the wagon, you can climb up there.'

'Thanks.'

The tiles were cracking with the heat. They popped. They shattered. Smoke seeped from under them. The snow melted instantly. The roof sloped up and up, and *what the hell was he doing this for*?

Caught in the chimney funnels of the loft's dormers, flames roared out at him only to be taken by the wind, torn upwards and then pushed away. Sparks, glowing bits of rubbish and dense smoke filled the air. His eyes watered. His nostrils burned. Swallowing tightly, he clung to the tiles and cried out, *'Sister, give me your hand.'*

She must have heard him, for she turned, and when he reached her, Céline said bitterly, 'You fool. Why have you come? I wanted those girls to die.'

'We can discuss it later.'

She backed away, held out her hands to fend him off. Tears streamed from her. That defiance, that fierceness of prominent cheekbones and wide-set dark eyes said, Ah, no, monsieur. *No!* I am finished.

'Please, Sister. Later, yes?'

'I did it! I fed them first and then I took them to the stair-wells. Dirty . . . they all have dirty little minds. *Filthy*, do you understand?'

He would have to distract her. He would have to rush her, grab her and fall. Together they would roll down the roof. Bones would be broken . . .

He saw the knitting needle gripped fiercely in her right hand. It had been hidden in the sleeve of her cloak.

'Now do you believe me?' A tile popped near her left foot. 'I could not kill my girls, but I could kill others, those we fed.'

'You did not feed them all.'

'I *hunted* others. That little bitch I killed in les Halles had eaten at the soup kitchen of the Germans. Her underwear was dirty. When I turned her over on to her stomach, she screamed and tried to get away, but I gave her what she so desired. I made her feel the shame of it!'

Ah no . . .

'The one in the Notre-Dame had lost a part of an ear-ring and was in tears. I helped her look for it and I killed her in a corner of the south belfry.'

She waited. He did not say a thing, this detective who had risked his life to come after her. 'I opened her blouse. I tried to feed things to her, things she would not let me stuff into her mouth. Things that sister of mine had crammed into my pockets. Filthy things. Rubber things. I squeezed and turned their contents out. *Out!* do you understand? Then . . . then I wiped my hands on her seat, her mons, her breasts and face and I . . . I left her.'

Dear Jesus, save him. The needle was gripped like a stiletto of the streets and all around them the tiles were popping and sloughing, but he could not hear them sliding down the roof and wondered at this. The noise was too great. It was far too hot . . . too hot. Light danced over her face, sharpening the hatred in her eyes. Shadows . . . there were shadows.

He wet his lips in fear. He really did not know what to do.

'*Louis . . . Louis, catch hold of the ladder.*'

'Hermann . . . Hermann . . . *Sister, please, if you love God, drop that thing and come with me!*'

She lunged. He leapt back, slipped, went down hard on to his knees, looked up in pain and defeat, tried to see her through his tears. Smoke was billowing. Glowing bits of ash were funnelling between them. He ducked. He tried to shield himself, but the wind was blowing too hard, the snow was blinding. Meltwater and sweat stung his eyes and clung to his face.

Out of the blizzard she came at him. He grabbed the hand that held the knitting needle. He tried to stop it but seemed to have no strength. Ah, *nom de Jésus-Christ!* her wrist . . . he *must* grab her by the wrist and bend it back . . . back.

There was a snap, a shriek as the needle fell. Then he heard her voice, heard the strangeness of it as she cried out in anguish, '*Please, God, forgive my Violette!*'

Kohler caught her by an ankle. For a moment he had a glimpse of her hatred, haunted by tragedy, gaunt and raw, streetwise and ever-watchful. Then she bent down, took him by the hair and put her lips close to his ear. 'Violette is innocent. Please allow her to go to Provence, to her little farm, but not with her priest. Never with that one.'

Ah *merde* . . .'Louis . . .' he managed. '*L . . . o . . . u . . . i . . . s!*'

'*Don't let go of her!*'

The wind came. It blew the flames up over the roof in billowing smoke and sparks. Tiles fell. Tiles slipped and popped and cracked. A hand gripped him by the wrist. An arm was swiftly wrapped around his own. A last glimpse revealed her perched up there, making her way steadfastly towards the conflagration at one end of the roof. For a moment she was engulfed, a dervish. Her screams, her cries were lost.

Somehow they made it to the ground, somehow they got clear before the roof finally collapsed in a rush of fire. Bathed in that terrible light, they searched but saw only the flames.

'Louis . . .'

'Yes, what is it?'

'The child. She's been taken—dragged away. Look, I'm sorry. I . . . I had no choice but to go after you.'

The birds were everywhere in the aviary and the smells of their feathers and their dung were heavy in the warm air. Madly the things flew about in the darkness, shrieking, chirping, giving their raucous jungle-cries or singing.

Softly Kohler eased the door shut behind him. Violette Belanger had been sitting on the floor near one of the stoves. There were aisles and aisles of cages, and she must have opened every one of them.

Taking out his torch, he shook it and tried to bring it to life. 'Louis, where's yours?' he breathed, a whisper.

'Incapacitated.'

'*Verdammt!*'

'No guns, Hermann. He'll have the child. Nénette will be his ticket to freedom.'

'Or the end of him.'

They began to feel their way forward. Cages to the left and to the right. Birds perched up there or swooping down. Birds screaming in fright, colliding in bursts of feathers and broken wings.

One flopped desperately on the floor. St-Cyr felt for it. Poor thing, he said silently. A finch, he thought.

Knowing he could not let it suffer, he twisted its neck, then gently tucked it away in a pocket. Are we to find that the child has also been killed? he asked himself. Is it to be from a cage of doves to this?

Aisles branched. Touching him on a shoulder, Kohler indicated Louis should take the left one, himself the right, and when he neared the stove, the smell of burning human hair came through the bird-stench and he said, Not her . . . not her. Please don't let it be her.

The child . . .

The parrot was dead and, in the soft light seeping from around the firebox door, he could see it lying between Violette's breasts, the soft mounds on either side of it, her hand still clutching it.

Blood trickled from the right corner of her lips. Scratches marred her breasts.

The hole in the middle of her forehead was clean and round, a nine millimetre, he thought. She had been crying, had killed the little parrot, and had looked up into the eyes of her priest a last time.

Vomit rose into his throat. He couldn't stand the sight of her. He . . .

Gently Louis took hold of him. 'Turn away. Leave this to me.' And opening the firebox door for a little light, he cast his eyes swiftly over her, the cinematographer within him willing himself to record what he could before he closed her eyes and pulled her away from the stove.

He covered her bare knees by tidying her pleated skirt. He laid her other hand over the parrot. It would have to do for now. Raw . . . the skin had been pulled from the palm of that hand. Was it years since the death of Madame Morelle and this one's flight across the roofs?

'Open the firebox door a little more,' breathed Kohler.

'Fire,' came the whispered warning.

'*Do it!* Stay here. Let me find him.'

'No guns.'

'He's got one, idiot!'

'Then I will close the door.'

They moved away. They knew Debauve must be in the aviary with the child. Had he killed her, too?

Did he now realize it was too late for him?

The SS of the avenue Foch had allowed Debauve a pistol. Were they hoping he'd put an end to this partnership and wipe the slate clean? wondered St-Cyr.

Kohler went down another aisle. The place was like a maze. Cages upon cages. Birds everywhere . . .

One flew into his face. He pulled it away, cried out, '*Louis! Verdammt!* Ah *merde*, the thing has claws.'

He wiped his face, felt blood and torn skin. He tried to calm the creature but it was frantic.

'That's far enough.'

Ah *Gott im Himmel*, the bastard had the muzzle of a Luger — was it a Luger? — jammed against the right side of his head.

'Don't move,' said Debauve.

'Of course not.'

'Tell the other one to call out to you.'

'Where's the child?'

'*Do it!*'

The bird didn't like being held. 'Louis . . . Louis, if you're still here, he's got me.'

'*Louder!*'

'LOUIS, THE SON OF A BITCH HAS ME!'

Swiftly Kohler pivoted, ducked and thrust the thing into the bastard's face. There was a flash of fire, a bang so loud his ears rang. Debauve fell back. He fired again and again, screamed once, twice, and fired once more. Ah no . . .

The birds flew madly about. Their sounds filled the air. On the rush of their wings there was a sigh, a '*Pater noster qui es in caelis . . .*'

'*Sanctificetur nomen tuum, adveniat regnum tuum: fiat voluntas tua, sicut in caelo, et in terra,*' breathed Louis, releasing Debauve's gun hand, the priest's accidental *coup de grâce*. 'Are you all right, *mon vieux?*'

'*Ja . . . Ja*, I'm okay. Ah *nom de Jésus-Christ*, Louis, tell me the kid is alive.'

They opened every firebox door, and in the soft, soft light, the birds of colour flew about, casting their shadows and emitting their noises.

She was lying between cages, lying just as her little friend had. The padded overcoat had been torn open. Her arms had been flung back. One white woollen kneesock had lost its elastic and was badly in need of mending and a wash. Her seal-skin boots were turned in a little at the toes. Her legs were slackly spread.

Debauve had made the killing look as if Céline had done it.

'Louis . . .'

'Leave this. Go outside if you have to.'

'No!'

It was a cry. Hermann tried to get past him.

She stirred. Her eyelids fluttered.

'Alive, I think,' said Louis. And then . . .

'Is it over? He . . . he smothered me. I . . . . I couldn't breath.'

'It is not quite over. There are still one or two small details best kept for another time.'

'The lion, Louis.'

'Yes, yes, the lion.'

The Tarot cards were down, the Ace of Swords was last. The hand that laid it on the gilded Louis XIV table paused to smooth it out and touch the upraised sword whose point was encircled by a golden crown.

'A tragedy,' sighed St-Cyr. 'A toy giraffe . . .'

He put it on the table in front of the Ace of Swords. 'A murder so different from the others.'

'I didn't tell Julien to do it. *I didn't!*' swore Madame Vernet, colouring quickly and clenching her fists only to release them when others noticed.

They were gathered in the *grand salon* of the villa. The afternoon's rare sunshine melted yesterday's rare snow. Soon there would be freezing rain. 'You did, madame. You saw in your niece's search for the Sandman a way of getting rid of her. But the girls used those same bits and pieces to trap you.'

'Bernadette, admit you're guilty. Be brave. Distinguish yourself.'

'Antoine, don't be a fool. I'm pregnant, yes? There isn't a court in the country that will send me to the guillotine until the child cries and the cord is cut. You have months of me yet. Please think of the scandal.'

Vernet was not happy. General von Schaumburg sat bolt upright on the edge of his chair, a monocle clamped fiercely to his right eye.

Kohler pitied them. For all his visits of inspection to the Wehrmacht's brothels, Old Shatter Hand was a prude. Infidelity ranked very high among his most despised sins.

'You said to Monsieur Julien that he must kill me, madame. I heard you,' said the child earnestly. 'You were in the folly together. I . . . I was up on the balcony making plans to escape and live the life of a brigand. You . . . you were standing right below me in the dark. Pompom was peeing against a table leg.'

'When?'

Startled, the child flinched. 'In the third week of December. On a Sunday night. Uncle . . . Uncle, he was away on business in Clermont-Ferrand, I think.' She pointed at Vernet. 'Your . . . your lover Julien didn't want to kill me, but you . . . you made him say he would. You slapped his face. You said—'

'I did no such thing! This is—'

'Bernadette, let the child finish. Is it not enough to have killed her little friend and Liline? What more do you want?'

'Tears. . . ? You who are so cruel, are shedding tears, Antoine? Hah! Drink them, then. You will get nothing from me.'

The child could not look up. 'You . . . you said his name would appear on the lists of those to be sent to Germany to work, madame,' she whispered. 'You said he probably wouldn't come back and that . . . that only you could see that this did not happen.'

At a nod from Louis, Rébé was brought in to stand in leg irons and handcuffs, ashamed, afraid and in tears himself. 'A former bicycle thief, a gigolo, General,' said Kohler softly.

'Boy, state the truth, then take your choice of the bullet or the rope.'

Rébé's knees buckled under him. Dragged up, held up, he wept and managed to blurt, '*She made me do it. She made sure the other one got it, too!*'

'Take him out. Let him make his choice. He may have a priest if he wishes,' grunted von Schaumburg. 'Just don't waste time with him. The Santé will do.'

Old Shatter Hand was grim. St-Cyr studied the quartz crystal the child had had in her coat pockets. It was one of those 'diamonds' of the curious stone and mineral trade, a dipyramidal crystal perhaps two centimetres by one and a half, six-sided and pointed at both ends but grown awkwardly and full of internal fractures that caught the light and sparkled. 'General, what madame says of our courts is only too true. There is always a penchant to excuse a betrayed wife or husband on the grounds of insanity due to jealousy. In such cases—'

'There is only one solution. She waits her time. One cannot blame the child within her.'

'Then let it be born in the Reich, General,' urged Vernet. 'Attend to her there after its birth.'

The bastard . . .

'Ah no . . . NO!' shouted the woman. 'You cannot do that to me. You can't! This house is rightfully mine, do you hear? *Mine!*'

Again the crystal was searched. 'Madame,' said Louis sadly, 'you knew your niece had discovered who the Sandman was, yet you did not speak out. Instead, you plotted her death and used that information to blackmail Violette Belanger and her pimp into helping you with Liline. The sum of two hundred and seventy-five thousand francs changed hands. I have it here.'

One by one the bundles of notes were arranged on the table. Then he took out the envelope that had been left at the solicitor's for Vernet. 'Mademoiselle Chambert's underpants, General. A last touch Madame Vernet could not resist presenting to her husband.'

When she spat in Vernet's face and stamped a foot, she was led away. 'She'll be on the evening train to Berlin. That is all I can promise,' said von Schaumburg gruffly. 'These things are never easy, and once out of my jurisdiction, her fate falls into the hands of others.'

She could well become the toast of Berlin, thought Kohler ruefully, and, taking the little roulette wheel, pushed in the plunger and let the ball bounce and land where it would.

At another nod from Louis, the General found a letter and, handing it to Vernet, said simply, 'Sign it. Refuse to do so and you will join your wife on that train.'

All it said was that should any harm come to Nénette Micheline Vernet, her uncle and guardian would forfeit all interest in the family holdings.

He signed without a murmur. It would have to do, but could the child remain in the same house with him?

'You will move to your club on the Champs-Élysées,' said von Schaumburg. 'You will bear the ridicule your associates will heap on you. You will have no further contact with your niece, who will remain here in her home. That is an order.'

They met in secret in the Bois near the Carrefour des Cascades overlooking the Lac Supérieur. Three days had passed, three days of rest, reports and healing of bruises that still caused St-Cyr to limp.

'Jean-Louis, it's good to see you.'

'You also.'

He took her arm in his and it felt good to be here with her. Gabrielle Arcuri tossed her head to indicate the coming rain. He said, 'It does not matter.'

'Then walk with me to my place. I'm cold.'

'Don't prolong things, please.'

'Very well. The message from London was received on the fifteenth at oh-one-fifty hours. When decoded it read, "No news of Henri-Claude Vernet and wife other than official view. Sorry. Better luck next time." '

'Then the child's parents were really killed in the bombing. I had hoped . . . An industrialist like that, a brilliant designer, a maker of weapons at a time when they are needed.'

'Ah, stop worrying. If it helps, I don't think so. The official view is simply what they had to give us. The "better luck" tells me her parents are alive and well but that you cannot give her such information.'

'Even though she needs it?'

'A suggestion perhaps.'

'Will you come with me?'

'It's a long walk. Let's take a *vélo-taxi*.'

'Those things are too easily followed. Besides, the Gestapo's Watchers are often lazy. We can talk on the way and cut through the woods. The child will give us tea.'

'And cakes?'

'Yes, cakes.'

The child presented them with the crystal of clear quartz. 'It is magic,' she said seriously. 'You will need it, I'm afraid, for the cards, they are not good. A visitor is to come into your lives— both of you. This person will pit you against each other with terrible consequences. Please do not forget this. Remember to be true to each other.'

It was von Schaumburg's chauffeur who caught up with them on the way back to hand St-Cyr a telex Heinrich Himmler had sent to Mueller, Head of the Gestapo in Berlin, who had then sent it on to Walter Boemelburg, Head of the same in France, and it was really for Hermann, who wouldn't want it at all and was probably asleep in some freezing cinema while his Giselle and his Oona watched with rapt attention some tired rerun from the thirties.

MOST URGENT. REPEAT URGENT. IKPK HQ BERLIN REPORTS INTERNATIONAL SAFE-CRACKER GYPSY REPEAT GYPSY HAS REPORTEDLY SURFACED. LAST SEEN TOURS 1030 HOURS 14 JANUARY HEADING FOR PARIS. APPREHEND AT ONCE.

HEIL HITLER.

The IKPK ... the International Criminal Police Commission thought to have ceased to exist at the outset of the war ...

'Gypsy. . . ?' blurted Gabrielle, sickened by the message. Jean-Louis, he could not know the Resistance had received a wireless message tacked on to that about the child's parents. GYPSY ... REPEAT GYPSY DROPPED TOURS NIGHT OF 13 JANUARY. PROVIDE EVERY ASSISTANCE. MOST URGENT. REPEAT URGENT. WILL HAVE EXPLOSIVES. GIVE FULL PRIORITY. CODE NAME ZEBRA.

'Hold my hand,' she said.

'Of course.'

'Please remove your mitten.'

'It's too cold. Here, put your hand in my coat pocket with mine. I've emptied it.'

Emptied it of all but the child's crystal.